T0355055

TICONDEROGA PROJECT

TICONDEROGA PROJECT

CAPTAIN ALLISON MACKENZIE

Eric McMurtrey

Archway Publishing books may be ordered through booksellers or by contacting:

Archway Publishing
1663 Liberty Drive
Bloomington, IN 47403
www.archwaypublishing.com
844-669-3957

ISBN: 978-1-6657-6755-2 (sc)
ISBN: 978-1-6657-6757-6 (hc)
ISBN: 978-1-6657-6756-9 (e)

Library of Congress Control Number: 2024922172

Print information available on the last page.

Archway Publishing rev. date: 12/10/2024

PART ONE

CHAPTER 1

16 MAY 2126

Captaining Earth's first interplanetary explorer was relatively simple, but keeping my hair under control while doing it was another skill entirely. Regardless of what I tried, one tendril always escaped and got in my eyes before the day was over. I leaned back from my terminal, tucking my haphazard bun again into its restraints and enjoying a long stretch.

Three displays filled most of my vision when I leaned forward. The left showed me the ship's status, the center held a three-dimensional representation of our position relative to *Everest*, and the third was my in-progress daily status report back to my commanding officer on Earth, Admiral Vergé Kegar. My fingers rested on the keyboard for a few more minutes, but when nothing else came to mind, I transmitted the report.

An alert flickered across the left screen as soon as the report was away, followed by an unfamiliar klaxon.

Internal structural integrity alert?

Walter Brinn, my engineering chief, appeared on the right screen. He scratched his gray beard, which was usually not a good sign. Sweat glistened through his close-shaven hair. "Captain Mackenzie, the alert's on deck two, section B, frame 120. I'm on my way there."

"Are we all right?"

"No idea, Captain."

"I'll meet you there," I snapped as I pushed away from my station. "Commander Hayes, please mind the store."

"Yes, ma'am."

I strode out of command. The frame Brinn had specified was near the back of the ship, right along the midline. The ship's most critical systems ran through that area—that's why they were inboard. Less chance of taking damage if something bad happened externally.

It wasn't a particularly good place to have a problem.

When I arrived, Brinn's engineering mate, Mirvai Pitka, stood next to a hole in the corridor floor where a deck plate had been removed. I peered through the opening into a shallow crawl space running parallel to and beneath the corridor.

Pitka's Russian heritage was obvious whenever he spoke. "He's down there, Captain. Go in headfirst. Is easiest."

I nodded and half slid, half fell on my hands and knees into the crevice. As soon as I landed, I shimmied forward on my stomach, ignoring the choking claustrophobia.

The crawl space soon opened up into a tiny compartment—a little too small to stand in or for two people to occupy comfortably.

"What's going on?" I asked as I tumbled out of the narrow tunnel.

Brinn wiped perspiration from his forehead. The heat radiating off the power distribution conduit next to us didn't have anywhere to go, so it circled around and struck us in repetitive, brutal waves. The older man traced the highlights on his engineering scanner display, trying to concentrate while the emergency klaxon blared around us. "This conduit is the source of the structural integrity alert."

"Cause?"

His bristly brow furrowed. "I don't know yet. But firing the mains increases power flow more than all the other systems on the ship put together, so the computer is giving a 98 percent chance the conduit will breach if we surge power through it to fire the brakes."

"Can't you reroute the power?" We were both shouting, but I could barely hear him over the roar in the alcove.

"The main distribution system on this side of the node has no redundancy, Captain. The power loss isn't the main problem. When this conduit breaches, coolant will be drawn into the environmental recirculation system and redistributed throughout the ship. It's toxic. We'll all be dead before we can make it to the escape trunk."

"Can you replace the conduit?"

"We have a spare section onboard, but I'll have to shut down the distribution system to swap it—the main engines will be offline completely."

"We're almost to the asteroid belt, Brinn. Are you sure we can't stop first?"

"I don't suggest it if you want to live."

"What about the atmospheric engines? Don't they use chemical fuel?"

"The atmospherics require oxygen for combustion, Captain. If nothing is available externally, they have to be fed from an internal source. We can do that, but I don't think it's a good idea—the odds of making oxygen out here are pretty low. The delta-V is also relatively low at this velocity. We might end up taking an asteroid in the side."

A 98 percent chance of death by power distribution coolant or a 100 percent chance of death by hypoxia.

Options flooded through my brain, but only one stuck.

"Brinn, tell me the Tomcat deck and the concussors will still have power."

"Yes, ma'am. They may not have given *Ticonderoga* redundant brakes, but they made sure she'd go down fighting. Defensive systems will be the last thing to go down, right before life support."

"Start your repairs, Chief. I'll be back when I can."

Brinn keyed his handheld com as I turned back to the crawl space. "Pitka, drop the mains offline and get both of the DC teams and anyone else that can turn a wrench to junction 2B-12. We're replacing the main conduit."

"On our way, Chief!" came the harried reply.

Pulling myself back into the crawl space was no easy task. The distribution node where we'd met was underneath the floor on deck two, and this almost person-sized tunnel was the only way to get to it without removing several deck plates. Like food climbing back up your esophagus from your stomach, it could certainly be done, but it was painful.

After I banged my head on the third low brace, I stopped crawling long enough to wonder how in the hell Brinn had even fit in here. Rubbing the sore spot didn't help any—in fact, my fingers came away with a slick smear of blood.

Hurry, Mackenzie. The orders I had to give couldn't be lost in translation over a com channel.

Less than three minutes later, I rushed into the command information center.

"Set condition red and bring all hands to combat stations. Energize all defensive systems," I snapped at Major Trulani, the tactical operations officer, on my way to the big black situation display console, the SDC, at the center of the command deck. I stood across the flat-topped console from Tom Hayes, my first officer. "Status?"

The alert klaxon sounded as the lights shifted to red.

"We're at cruise speed on an intercept course to *Everest*, Captain. Next course correction is in . . . one hour, thirteen minutes, forty-five seconds . . . mark."

I raised my voice and looked over Tom's shoulder toward the helm. "The mains should be coming offline any second. Under *no* circumstances should you fire the main engines without confirmation from Chief Engineer Brinn or myself. Is that clear, helm?"

"Clear, Captain," Lieutenant Marlin Salinski confirmed.

Tom stepped closer. He and I had worked together since I took command of *Ticonderoga*, and he knew well enough to close the space between us so I could fill him in. The acoustics in the command area were impressive, designed so any order could be heard effortlessly. Exchanging information covertly in the space was difficult.

"There's a problem with the engines' main distribution conduit," I whispered. "Brinn says the casing is going to crack if we fire the main braking thrusters, and when it does, system coolant will escape into the ship and kill us all."

To his credit, Tom didn't even raise an eyebrow. "Can he fix it?"

"He can. We just can't fire the mains until he does."

Tom glanced back at the situation display. The green icon marking our position was entirely too close to the red icons denoting the main asteroid belt between Mars and Jupiter.

The distance was closing rapidly.

Doing anything in space without maneuvering capability was a bad idea. Entering a field comprised of millions of unpredictably moving rocks was insanity. Unaided, calculating the odds of survival was pointless. *Tico* was tough, but she'd never survive contact at speed with anything much bigger than a marble.

"Any help in the neighborhood?"

I shook my head. "We're going to use the Tomcats to clear the way a bit. I'll brief the crews—we'll launch them in an hour if Brinn doesn't have us back online beforehand." I raised my voice and turned back to the helm station. "Project our course over the next three hours, please. Send the data to the SDC." The data appeared promptly. "Thank you, Salinski."

"Aye, Captain."

"At least we're going to stay out of the heavy stuff," Tom said. "Tactical, grab that trajectory, add in a 1 percent margin for error, and package the data for the Tomcats, please. Start crunching on a program to auto-fire the concussors to open it up as well."

"Aye, sir." Major Trulani tapped her console.

"Tom, I'm going out with the Tomcats. I'm more help out there than in here."

Tom grinned a little. "With all due respect, Captain, you're needed aboard to direct the repair efforts. Let's send Daniels instead. I'll brief the concussor teams while you deal with the throttle jockeys."

I nodded, disgruntled but unable to argue against his logic. "I'll check on Brinn after the briefing. See you back here in an hour, and we'll figure out where we are then."

"Roger that, Cap."

~

Ticonderoga's corridors were excessively wide to guarantee the crew could move about in an emergency without getting in each other's way. Like everything else about the ship, they were overdesigned with the worst-case scenario always at the forefront. No crew member would wait for personnel or machinery to pass by—today, no one would stop even to snap a hand salute. The lighting had shifted to red, reminding everyone of the emergency, and all unnecessary pomposity went out the nearest air lock. Despite the feverish activity, my people would have heard and followed even a whispered order. The crew knew their duties and always completed them with efficiency and excellence.

We had drilled endlessly, and today was the real thing.

I purposely avoided the main corridor's aft junction for much the same reason I didn't demand salutes in an emergency. Brinn was setting up for the repair, and his teams needed to focus on solving the problem. Even with my detour through the forward landing bay and past the pilots' locker and ready rooms, the Tomcat launch bay wasn't a long walk from anywhere on the ship. I was heartened to find it bristling with activity when I arrived.

Ticonderoga carried twenty Northrop Grumman Tomcat II fighters. Even resting in their launch gantries, they looked every bit as formidable as their twentieth-century atmospheric predecessors. Primarily intended for the vacuum of space, they were coated with multispectral-EM-absorptive paint everywhere except on the ventral surfaces, which were instead covered in heat-shielding tiles. As such, the fighters sucked in the light around them like black holes. I took a second to survey the two rows of spacecraft, all pointed nose-outward and ready for battle against deadly interplanetary rocks.

"Status, Lieutenant?"

Charlie Benson, the deck officer, answered me confidently. "All the birds are fueled and combat armed, Captain. The pilots are waiting for you in the ready room."

"Rig the shuttles for evacuation. I want the first three launched with noncritical crew within the hour."

"Yes, ma'am," Benson said before he turned away, shouting orders.

I moved on to the pilots' ready room without a backward glance.

"Captain on the deck!" snapped Major Jim Daniels, the commander of the air group.

"As you were," I said as I stepped to the podium in the center of the room. I dimmed the lights and brought up the flight data that tactical had prepared for the Tomcats on the central viewer. "I'm not going to lie—we're a little off the map here. If you have a suggestion, speak freely."

The room quieted appropriately.

"Engineering has discovered a potentially fatal failure in the primary engines' power distribution system. We can't fire the engines until repairs are made, and we'll arrive at the asteroid belt before the repair is complete. Our estimated course track is on the viewer and will be sent directly to your birds as well. Your job will be to help clear a path for *Ticonderoga* until we can get her turned around and out of trouble."

Lieutenant Matthew Rogers, my problem child, smirked widely. "Captain?"

"Was I unclear, Rogers?" I let his eyes roll once before I continued, "I'm not asking you to endanger yourselves outside the norm. *Ticonderoga* will still do most of the work. Her computers will supply you with targets through the tracking system—things she can't take out with her own concussors. You fly to whatever she aims you at, knock it out, and head to the next objective. It's little more than target practice."

He continued to glare.

"Or . . . if you're not up to it, Rogers, I can take your bird and handle it myself."

That roused substantial commotion. I waited for it to subside, and then widened my focus and continued, "Listen, everyone, the escape trunk's estimated survivability in the asteroid belt is not ideal. This isn't a perfect plan, but it's all we've got. It's up to my throttle jockeys to save the day. Have you got this?"

"Atten-hut!" Major Daniels ordered.

The men stood and shouted in unison. "*Tico*! On the go!"

I nodded approvingly. "You have the room, Daniels. Please have your crews at their launch stations in thirty minutes."

"Yes, Captain." Major Daniels was all business as he slid behind the podium to take over the more technical aspects of the briefing. I spared a second to look the room over for trouble spots, and once I found Rogers was attentive to the cause, I strode out with a mental note to be back in half an hour.

Activity in the launch area had intensified appropriately as I walked through on my way to the aft stairwell. Plane crews swarmed over the Tomcats, pulling arming pins, double-checking systems, and even giving the canopies a final cleaning. No doubt remained—it was game time. A sense of longing tugged at my heart with the knowledge I'd still be standing on *Tico*'s deck plates when the fighters launched.

I knew I could make a difference out there. I wasn't so sure about what I could contribute from the command deck. I didn't need to watch them launch—I needed to feel useful.

"Down ladder!" a tech shouted from the top of the stairwell. I stepped aside. Unlike in the corridors, two people would usually brush elbows when they passed each other on the stairs between decks. Getting out of the way was safer if someone had to get by in a hurry. Seconds later, an engineer carrying an equipment case chased an ordinance technician onto the deck. They dashed toward a Tomcat with several panels removed below the cockpit.

The relative order of the flight deck fell away as I took the steps two at a time and emerged into complete bedlam on the habitation deck's corridor B. Twenty meters of deck plates down the length of the central corridor and a few wall panels had already been removed. The junction ahead was a jumble of exposed conduits, pipes, and cables, every bit as alarming to see as any exposed artery. Flashing warning lights preceded a tracked yellow lift that crawled through the corridor with a replacement section of conduit suspended on the end of its boom. The machine inched closer to the opening in the deck plates, handling the heavy lifting as the furiously working engineers uncovered the damaged conduit.

Too slow.

I surveyed the chaos. Pitka flitted by, so I asked, "What can I do to help?"

He looked up from the data interface he was disconnecting. "Bolts hold primary conduit to bulkhead, Captain. We need someone to start removing them."

I liked Pitka. He didn't bat an eyelash at asking the captain to do scut work—he saw a job and someone to do it.

"Got a wrench?"

His heavy Russian accent bled through again as he called to a young blonde woman on the other side of the junction. "Powell, find Captain Mackenzie a power driver with number twenty adapter and get her started removing conduit retainers."

She nodded and turned toward a big metal toolbox on wheels.

I grabbed the mic from a nearby com unit and toggled a few switches. "Mackenzie to ExO."

Tom answered after one click. "Hayes. What do you have, Captain?"

"The Tomcat pilots will be ready to launch on your order. I'm going to monitor the conduit problem—I can help here. What's our status?"

"We're about twenty minutes from the field boundary."

"Move all noncritical personnel to the evacuation points and launch the shuttles."

"Yes, Captain."

"You know the plan, Tom. You're in command. Mackenzie out."

I turned back to Powell, who was waiting at a discreet distance with two matching power tools in her hands. "Ready?"

Her nod was hesitant as she handed me one of the drivers. She had none of Pitka's ease in a crisis, but in her defense, she seemed awfully young. I noticed the yellow band on her left sleeve indicating she was new onboard.

I put on my best reassuring voice. "It's game time, Technician. Show me what to do."

Following her around—under and sometimes through the tangle of exposed cables, conduits, and furiously working engineers—was challenging. We stopped underneath an exposed floor support near the conduit junction Powell identified. She demonstrated our task, removing a couple of fasteners from the bracket cradling the conduit above the lower bulkhead.

"Looks simple enough," I said. "Do you want me to start on the other side?"

Powell nodded. "Can you squirm between the brackets and get over there?"

"No problem."

Even though I felt alone in the far corner of the work area, I still managed to get stepped on and kicked more than once. I didn't expect or want apologies for the minor inconveniences. Getting ourselves out of this meant getting the job done. My driver kept pace with Powell's, clicking as it engaged on a bolt and whirring noisily as it did its job. I let the tool pause long enough to remove the bolt and pile it with others on the bulkhead before cycling again.

"Doing all right, Captain?" Powell called.

"Five to go!"

"Get clear as soon as you're done. They're ready to lift the conduit out."

Tom's voice boomed over the One-MC speakers. "All stations brace for Tomcat launch."

Subtle vibrations rattled the bulkhead below me as the launch gantries transported the Tomcats into their air locks.

I hooked the driver into my belt after the last bolt was out and slipped between two pipes above me. Bracing against them, I pulled myself out of the crawl space. "I'm clear!"

"All right, people!" Brinn snapped. "The conduit comes up far enough to clear the brackets and shifts to port. Let the forward end down, and then move it aft and out. Any questions?"

A pause stretched, then two short beeps echoed as the lift unit took the slack out of the line.

"Station check," Brinn said. "Aft?"

"All good."

"Mid, check."

I waited to hear about the forward end before I realized I was by myself on that side of the conduit.

"Fore is clear!" I shouted back.

"I have the load," Brinn said.

Another two beeps sounded. Then the deceptively small lift cable groaned under the strain as the conduit's weight transferred completely from the mounting brackets. The conduit made it about two inches out of the brackets before it swung slightly and caught against a floor support above it. Scraping sounds intensified, and the conduit stopped moving.

"Hold!" I shouted. "It's bound up back here!"

I lowered myself between the pipes and back into the crawl space. Bracing against a bulkhead in the tiny fissure, I pushed against the conduit with my legs. It screeched free of the support, jerked upward, and then spun violently, crushing me against the wall. The pain in my chest was incredible. Screaming was out of the question—I couldn't even breathe.

"Powell, take the lift! Pitka, Benjamin, get in there!" Brinn boomed. He was by my side in a flash. "Hang tight, Cap."

"Aft end, push to port," Brinn snarled as he strained against the conduit himself. "Up on the lift! Get the goddamned thing out of here!"

The pain eased as the conduit raised, but moving as much as an eyelid brought it screaming back.

I could breathe, but only barely.

Reverberations from the concussors echoed through the corridor in the confusion, reminding me how completely screwed we were going to be if I didn't drag myself off the floor.

"Can you move?" Brinn's look of worry was genuine, but his involuntary flinches at the dull explosions of asteroids rattling the hull made it clear I wasn't his only concern.

"Yes." I winced at my first attempt to prove it. The pain was staggering.

I made it to my knees and then back onto my stomach to wiggle under the remaining floor braces and cabling. The pain was easing, replaced by adrenaline washing through me like the vibrations now rattling the deck plates. There wasn't room for anyone to help me, but a moment later, I struggled out of the crawl space with far less grace than either Brinn or the damaged conduit.

One of the damage control teams had the replacement conduit rigged in a lifting sling before I was back on my feet. It rose into the air and was soon wedged into the crawl space, effortlessly settling into the brackets two minutes later. I cringed as a particularly loud tremor echoed along the corridor. The crew's chatter reduced to single words and occasional hand motions. The clatters and booms around us reminded everyone of the urgency. Once Brinn's crews had confirmed the alignment, they sprang to connect one end to the existing power conduit and the other to the distribution node.

"Aft splice complete!"

"Forward splice complete!" another crewman shouted.

"Everyone out of the pool! We'll bolt it down later!" Brinn snapped. He pulled a handheld com from a coverall pocket and keyed it. "Reinitialize the transfer conduit for the main engines."

"Yes, sir." A hissing noise accompanied the response over the com, and a visible tremble went through the length of the conduit. The pressure inside the tube was enormous, and although it was connected, it wasn't bolted down yet. After the commotion subsided, the voice added, "Coolant integrity is positive, Chief."

"Power it up," Brinn said. An alarmingly loud crack made me wince before the observation ports in the side of the conduit glowed to life. "We're good, Captain."

He tossed me the com unit, and I keyed it again. "Mackenzie to command. Repairs are complete. Maximum power to the midline bow engines. Repeat—repairs are complete."

"All hands, brace yourselves for maximum delta-V," Tom called over the One-MC. The glow of the conduit observation ports changed from bright red to fierce white as the energy transfer rate multiplied exponentially. Even the bulkheads groaned in protest as small parts and people slid forward on the deck plates.

Tom's voice hummed over my com unit. "Helm now answering. All stop."

"Back us out of here nice and easy, Tom." My crisis-driven infusion of adrenaline was suddenly spent as I dropped the com unit and sank to the floor.

Pain.

Someone was impaling me with a broken baseball bat in the right side of my torso every time I took a breath.

"Cap, you all right?" Brinn asked.

"A little banged up." My breaths were ragged.

"Powell! Get over here!" Brinn shouted. "Escort the captain to the medbay. Don't leave her until she has treatment."

"I'm fine, Brinn. I need . . ."

Brinn prodded my side until I squirmed and backed off. I panted.

"Let's get her up," Brinn said as he took my left elbow. Powell supported my other side, and with cringes all around, I stumbled back to my feet. "Got her?"

Powell nodded with the same lack of confidence I'd seen earlier.

We'll need to talk about that.

"On your way, then."

~

The relative youth and the level of knowledge my crew possessed never ceased to surprise me. Service in the UPE represented an opportunity for education unsurpassed on Earth, but it simply felt like another sign I was getting older.

A slight blonde medical tech hurried toward us as we limped into the medbay. She looked like she could have been Powell's twin sister and also seemed too young to be out of basic training. "What happened?"

"She got pinched between a power conduit and the bulkhead. I think it's the ribs on her right side."

"We will take care of her, Ms. Powell," Dr. Hawshmore said in his booming Caribbean accent as he relieved her at my side. "The pain is bad?"

"A little tender," I admitted through gritted teeth.

"I would think so," he said, stopping at the closest examination bed. "Getting up here is going to hurt even worse. Ready?"

I nodded and regretted it instantly. Screaming wasn't an option, but it wasn't for the lack of desire. Tendrils of pain far worse than the original injury lashed across my abdomen as they awkwardly helped me onto the table.

"We would have done this differently had you called for a trauma team, Captain."

"What can I say, Doc? It would have taken longer for a team to arrive, and I couldn't wait to come see you. I miss you when I'm not around."

Irritation sparked to life between his eyebrows. Not a little, either.

"We'll run a test, but I think it is safe to say you have broken a rib or two, Captain. Hopefully you have not exacerbated the damage with your separation anxiety issues." He pulled a privacy curtain closed and stepped closer to me. "Do you think you can handle pulling the uniform off?"

I raised my arms and reached the first clasp. The motion felt like someone drove a dinner fork into my ribs.

"I'll get it," I wheezed.

Geez . . . how can it hurt that bad?

"Hold still." Dr. Hawshmore finished freeing the clasp at my neck and then unzipped my duty tunic. "Unfortunately, the pain of jagged bone rubbing against nerves has no equal. Hang in there. We'll diagnose the damage, and then we'll control the pain. Try to remain as still as possible."

He wasn't particularly gentle as he slid my tunic over my shoulders and off my arms. He might be my doctor, but I was still glad I had a regulation bra on. Even banged up, I felt so exposed.

Trained to guard his patients from unintentional expressions, a professional like Dr. Hawshmore should have had the ultimate poker face. But I still saw it—even if only for a flash.

A cringe from a physician is never a good sign.

"That bad, Doc?"

To the technician standing inside the curtain, Hawshmore said, "Bring the tomographic scanner." He turned to me. "Bending down to look will only cause unnecessary pain and concern at this point. We're going to scan the bruised area on your abdomen and see what shuffled around in there."

"Am—"

"Johns Hopkins has nothing on me. I have you covered," Hawshmore interrupted.

The tech returned pushing a cart overflowing with interconnected cables, peripherals, and perhaps medieval torture equipment. Hawshmore reached into the jumble and pulled out what looked like a landing signaler's wand connected to the system by a heavy black hose.

Like the stuff I used to build when I played with Dad's Erector Set as a kid.

I smiled. "Build that yourself, Doc?"

"Relax, please." He plugged a sequence into the old-fashioned keyboard, and the wand glowed bright orange in his huge brown hand. "This is going to tickle a little."

I shied away from the instrument involuntarily as it emitted a low-pitched hum. "Tickle? Interesting euphemism."

"It is no euphemism. The sound waves from the scan bar hyperstimulate the nerves in your epidermal layers. Try not to move, because it will muck up the scan clarity. Giggling is going to hurt with those ribs."

"Let's do it." I sank my fingers into the cushion of the exam bed. He moved the scanner closer to the underwire of my bra, and a holographic image appeared over the cart. I instantly fought a snicker. "You weren't kidding about the tickle."

"The sound waves do what they need to." He worked the bar back and forth in a repetitive grid pattern. The more he moved, the more defined the image grew. "Combine them with some magnetic imaging, and we get a picture of what is going on. Like an X-ray, a sonogram, and an MRI in one."

He worked for about five minutes and then tapped some controls on the main part of the machine. "Nothing unexpected, but I need to analyze the computer data. I will be back in a few minutes." With that, the big man disappeared.

"Captain?" a familiar voice asked from the other side of the curtain.

"It's all right, Tom. I'm decent." He'd seen me exercising dressed in less every day.

Hayes pulled the privacy curtain open and appeared in my field of vision a second later. I didn't try to sit up. It didn't seem like a good idea.

"What's our status?"

Tom smiled. "Thanks to you and Brinn, good. We're easing back out of the belt and should be on course to rendezvous with *Everest* shortly. I ordered a wing of Tomcats to ride shotgun until we're clear of the asteroids, but they're pretty much just for show. The shuttles are stationary at the edge of the belt. We should have everyone back onboard in about an hour."

Everyone pulled together to hold us together. "Casualties?"

"Rumor has it we have one extraordinarily banged-up CO. It looks like it hurts."

"I haven't looked yet," I said. "You're right, though. Brinn's damage control teams did good. Tom, please express my commendations to everyone. It's important. Make the rounds and shake some hands. The crew deserves it."

"I'll take care of it, Cap. Anything else I can do for you?"

"I've got this." I grinned fractionally. "Hawshmore hates me. He'll patch me up just to get rid of me."

"I was going to try and horse him into keeping you here. Command is nice and quiet for a change."

"Not for long. You did good, Tom."

He nodded. "You too."

"If I had done better, I wouldn't be here."

"If you'd done worse, none of us would."

I struggled to prop myself up, lowering my voice. "This conduit incident smells bad, Tom. Everything associated with the reactors was designed to last 150 percent of the lifetime of the ship. She's just shy of fifty."

"It was just an equipment failure."

"I don't think so. You know we have to report this, and I want you to handle the investigation. Include a full forensic analysis of the conduit in your report as well as all of engineering's inspection and maintenance records. If we missed something, I want to know what and why. Off the record, I want a list of anyone with access to that conduit since we left home. It's responsible to have a look, but I don't want to start a witch hunt without a good reason. Keep this as quiet as possible. Talk of sabotage won't benefit crew morale."

"Roger that, Cap."

Dr. Hawshmore reappeared through the privacy curtain. "Let's get you wrapped up and out of here, Captain. You never know when I might have an actual sick person to care for."

CHAPTER 2

17 MAY 2126

I had every reason to believe we were in fine hands with Tom in command. The time was late, or early, depending on how you looked at it. Nonetheless, getting back up front was still my priority after the doc had done what he could. His gadget stimulated a rudimentary support matrix around the fractures—not that I could feel any difference. He promised that even if the bone was fused, I'd deal with the bruising and abdominal trauma for a month or so.

In the end, he sent me on my way with a bottle of ibuprofen and an immobilizing wrap that bit right below my bra every time I took a breath. Getting off the bed was nearly as unpleasant as getting onto it, but I figured out how to walk without making my eyes water before I'd gotten to the midline corridor junction.

I mocked Dr. Hawshmore's rattling baritone as I made my way to command. "I don't want to give you anything too powerful to mask the pain. Pain is the body's warning it is being pushed too hard."

Whatever . . .

Navigating the steps down to the SDC was agonizing, but with the crew watching, I tried to make it look effortless.

"Mr. Pierre, please try to raise *Everest*."

"Yes, Captain."

I let out a triumphant breath when I reached the console.

"You all right, Captain?" Tom asked from across the display.

"Fair to middling, as my dad used to say, Commander." I looked over the data in front of me approvingly. The green icon representing

Ticonderoga was heading away from all the round red icons representing asteroids in the belt. Our other concerns were definitely secondary to the ship-crushing rocks now in our wake.

"I have Captain Connors on the com."

My heart throbbed once and then fluttered, so I swallowed around the lump in my throat. Must have been a reaction to the painkiller.

"Speakers, please, Lieutenant." I waited for Pierre's nod and turned to the audio pickup. "Captain Connors, what's your status?"

"We're waiting for a ride, Legs. Are you still coming?"

Tom's attempt to stifle a grin failed miserably. He mouthed, *Legs?*

I turned my back on him as the heat of a blush rushed to my ears. "We had a little engine trouble ourselves, Captain. We'll be there as soon as possible. Can you hold out a little longer?"

"Sure," Jake said. "*Everest* is standing by. See ya soon, Legs."

"This should be interesting." My head was starting to ache along with everything else.

"Have a history with Connors, Captain?" Hayes's grin hadn't left his face.

I'm not in the mood for this.

I snorted. "Jake Connors suffers from a . . . unique personality."

"It seems like you're the only one suffering from Connors's personality, Captain."

"That feels like a problem for the morning. I'm going to bed, and I invite you all to do the same."

Discussion was minimal as people locked down their stations. Major Trulani crossed to take my seat. As always, I had no doubt she would look after things through the night, short though it may be.

Besides, I'd be just a few steps down the corridor if anything happened.

~

I didn't want to get out of bed.

I didn't want to stay in bed, either. Even pulling the covers up hurt. I'd always heard busted ribs were miserable, and now I had proof.

I felt like I'd been run over by a Transport Division freighter.

UPE regulations required everyone to log an hour of daily physical training. Even injured, I was expected to participate within my ability. The dress standard for exercise was flexible as long as people stayed covered in public areas. Like most women, I generally wore a sports bra and loose running shorts. Usually, all I had to do was pull on shorts, shoes, and a baseball cap to restrain my hair and I was ready to go. But after checking myself in the mirror and noting how deeply the bruise had set on my midriff, a T-shirt seemed like a better idea.

I was cringing through tying my shoes when the door chimed.

"Come in."

"You ready?" Mindy asked brightly once the door slid open.

Straightening was as agonizing as bending over had been. "As much as I'm going to be, I guess. How do you always look so much better than me in the morning?"

"I don't get hit by things as often." Her smile felt like a competitive warning. Mindy Stykes was *Ticonderoga*'s chief of sciences and my morning jogging partner. "Let's go."

She went relatively easy on me as we set out through the corridor at what was little more than a brisk walk. It only took a couple of steps before the pain in my abdomen settled to nagging discomfort.

"You doing okay?" Mindy asked.

"I'll be all right," I said. "Let's head for cargo pod three. It's empty."

While the corridors served as the primary makeshift running track before the morning shift, going to an empty cargo pod meant we wouldn't slow down the serious runners.

We hadn't gotten far when a younger woman with familiar blonde hair passed us.

"Powell?"

She turned around like she'd been called to attention.

"I didn't mean to startle you. Would you like to run with us?"

"Uh . . . sure." She looked about as willing as she sounded.

"Mindy, this is, um, Powell. I'm afraid I didn't catch your first name yesterday."

"Jennifer."

"You're working with Brinn, aren't you?" Mindy asked.

Powell nodded.

"Welcome aboard," Mindy said as they shook hands. "Let's go."

We ran single file until we got to the bay. The doors were already retracted. A few other runners had the same idea. We spread out as soon as we were inside and jogged side by side, with Powell in the middle.

"Have you settled in?"

It took Powell a beat to understand Mindy was talking to her. "How could you ever settle in to this?"

"You have to have confidence in your ability to handle the unexpected," I said. "You've been through a lot of testing and training to do this. Put stock in that."

"Can I ask why you picked this life?" Powell asked.

"I love science," Mindy said. "It all fascinates me, but nothing as much as physics. What we do is physics gone mad in every way—this is the height of the field, and I wanted to be on top of it."

A few puffing breaths allowed me to frame my answer. "I grew up on a farm in Idaho listening to my dad's stories of service to the old United States and then in Myanmar and Nepal for the West's Diplomatic Corps. The only window from my tiny world was hearing stories of how my dad had interacted with the wide world. I wanted to live the same life."

"I enlisted for school." Powell sounded like she was admitting to a crime.

"What's wrong with that?" I asked. "Knowledge brings us power to effect positive change. You don't need to command a ship or discover a wormhole to contribute, Jennifer. Sometimes you just need to teach someone how to use a power driver when it really matters."

I guessed her reddening face was from embarrassment, not physical exertion. I ran beside her for a while, hoping I'd get more out of her. When it didn't come, I added, "Setbacks and successes. You'll have both in your life. Learn from the one and cherish the other. A lot of people threw in yesterday to keep us alive—you included. It's okay to take pride in that."

"I was so scared," Powell answered like it was a revelation.

"We were all scared, Jennifer." Mindy was smiling. "Standing at your station while you're terrified shows you're up for this."

"I do like it here."

"We like having you here, Jennifer. Don't ever question that," I said gently.

✣

Showered and dressed in a fresh duty coverall, I made my way into command far closer to the start of my watch than I would have preferred. A quick look at the status displays told me I needed to start making decisions.

"Mr. Pierre, signal *Everest* and let them know we're on the final approach to their location for rendezvous."

"Yes, ma'am."

I jabbed the com pickup. "Chief Brinn, please report to the docking latch and prepare for mag-grapple assisted capture. We're about thirty minutes out from *Everest*."

"I'm on station now." Brinn's reply came. "We'll be ready."

Various yellow system malfunction warning lights winked throughout command as I closed the com. A low warning tone sounded as well, indicating the alert hadn't been immediately acknowledged.

Lieutenant Salinski spoke from his station at the helm. "Captain, the autonav has slipped us off course. The variance is half a meter and widening."

"Recalibrate the system."

"I've tried, Captain. It's not taking. I need to do a hard reset."

"We don't have time. *Everest* is short on power," I said. "If we can't trust the computer, we need to see what we're doing. Deploy a flight of remotes."

"Sensor drones away in three . . . two . . . one . . . mark," Trulani reported.

Tom entered a series of controls on the console between us to cancel the alarm and then reconfigured the display. A three-dimensional representation of our course, calculated with *Ticonderoga*'s position in relation to *Everest*, appeared in front of us. Secondary visual displays from each of the four drone remotes appeared as well, along with raw numerical data on the side of the screen. A lot to take in, but it gave us plenty of information to get the job done.

We didn't have to bull's-eye the linkup to grab *Everest*. She was a big ship, and *Tico* was far bigger. Trying to align them exactly was a virtual impossibility. But once we got within range of the magnetic grappling system on the bottom of the hull, the system would take over the docking details. Even if that failed, we could still run umbilicals between the ships to provide *Everest* with air and power.

I did some rough math in my head. "Mr. Salinski, give me a three-second burst on the portside bow thrusters and two seconds on all of the dorsals, please." I toggled the com to docking latch alpha. "Chief, what's the grapple status?"

"It'll be charged by the time we're in position, Captain."

"The autonav is acting up, Chief. We're old-school today."

"Roger that, Captain. Get me within 125 meters any which way, and I'll snag it."

"Estimating interception in three minutes," Trulani interrupted.

Tom's focus was locked on the display. "We're coming in too hot."

"Braking thrusters, please, Mr. Salinski. Full burn." I braced myself.

"Full burn, aye." A rumbling vibration followed Salinski's last word as the maneuvering engines strained to slow us down. "Zero delta-V estimated at interception point plus eight hundred meters."

I tapped another com control. "Captain Connors, how is it looking from your end?"

"We're showing two degrees of x-axis rotational deviation for docking clamp alignment, *Ticonderoga*."

"Mr. Salinski?"

"I'm on it, Captain," my helm officer replied. I threw him a glance, but his controls engrossed him, his hands a flurry of movement. In a few seconds, the correction washed across the ship like we'd hit a wave on the ocean.

Tom fiddled with more controls, and the view from the remote sensor craft maximized to dominate the situation display. He keyed another sequence into the system that superimposed a target icon over the grapple receiver mounted on top of *Everest*'s hull.

"Range to target?"

"One thousand meters," Trulani said.

"More brakes, Salinski," I whispered to myself. I knew the kid was doing everything he could.

"Firing main bow engines, two-second burst," Salinski said.

Instinctively, I grabbed the side of the SDC as the entire ship shuddered to a stop in space. The displays showed *Everest*'s docking port closely aligned to our own.

"Chief Brinn," Tom said into the com. "Expedite docking procedures."

"I'll need a word with the helmsman after this is done, Commander," Brinn said sharply. "A bit of forethought would have alleviated the need for emergency maneuvering and stress on my ship."

My arms stiffened on the console. *His* ship? Threatening my helmsman for doing exemplary work? *What in hell has gotten into Brinn?*

"You'll have any words you want with me, Chief," I interrupted over the com. "A large portion of them will comprise your explanation for why our ship seems to be falling apart."

"Aye, Captain," Brinn said with notably less fire behind his words. "I've engaged the grapple. Contact in three . . . two . . ."

A dull thud echoed throughout the ship as the hulls of *Everest* and *Ticonderoga* settled together.

After Tom closed the com channel, I turned my attention back to the young helmsman. Salinski was my newest crew member, having come to *Ticonderoga* less than a month ago. While I assumed he was probably here for the educational benefits a career in the UPE provided, his presence reminded me that interplanetary travel was generally considered a pursuit for the young.

The poor kid seemed to be having something of a nervous breakdown at his console. I didn't try to hide my concern as I stepped to his station and quietly asked, "Mr. Salinski?"

His eyes opened. A sheen of sweat had darkened the fabric of his uniform's tunic.

"You okay?"

His eyes were empty as he nodded.

"That was a crude but effective bit of helmsmanship. Please see to the recalibration of the autonav system."

He nodded slowly. "Yes, ma'am."

"You did good work, Salinski." I smiled.

He only nodded and curled over his panel.

I turned to Tom. "Get us on our way to Alpha Station as soon as possible. You have command."

"Want me to deal with Brinn?"

"In all fairness, yes," I said tiredly. "But it's my job. I'll see to it."

✣

Running through the corridors would have been improper and, given my injury, impossible. That fact did nothing to quench the desire.

Jake had emerged from the lift when I made it down to the Tomcat deck. I ignored Lieutenant Benson's prattle, deliberately sidestepping him so I could see down the platform all the way to the docking latch. My grin tugged painfully at my mouth, embodying the excitement I knew Jake would have. The sight of his face was a balm that wiped my stress and pain away.

Jake's joy evaporated seconds after he saw me. He left Brinn behind and strode toward me with a worried look on his face.

"I heard about the accident. Are you okay?"

I nodded, but even that made my ribs flare.

"Just a scratch or two. I'll meet you in the galley in a bit, Captain Connors."

Jake seemed confused by my formality, but I'd take care of that in private. Right now, I needed him to leave so I could deal with Brinn. It would have been less uncomfortable had he picked up on it faster, but he finally nodded and headed down the corridor.

I was careful to make sure Jake was out of earshot before I began. "Chief . . . I know things got a little out of hand today, but I need to ask you to keep yourself in check when you address fellow crew members."

"I'll not apologize for pointing out incompetence, Captain."

I fought the urge to snap. Taking a step closer, I lowered my voice to a whisper. "Let me rephrase, Chief. When addressing an officer, be it me or a person straight out of the academy, you will demonstrate military respect and decorum. In addition, you will refrain from publicly critiquing the performance of anyone outside your chain of command. You will bring your concerns to me, and we will discuss them in private. Am I understood?"

I watched his eyes as his own internal battle raged. I had to stand firm—this would go badly if I let him think I would brook any argument.

His eyes closed and he took a steadying breath. "Yes, Captain. If you give me the opportunity, I will apologize to . . ."

"Mr. Salinski." I crossed my arms. "An apology is not necessary, Chief. Salinski was too scared to notice. Just don't be so abrupt with the kids."

"Fair enough." Brinn nodded.

"Chief, I know you don't have your crystal ball with you, but what's happening to our ship? Did we bring a gremlin aboard?"

Brinn's eyebrows raised—his body language made it clear the recent events puzzled him as much as they did me. *Ticonderoga* always needed maintenance, and infrequent mechanical incidents could be expected, but nothing like this had happened before. The navigation system that had gone down had many fail-safes to prevent emergencies, but either its malfunction or the conduit failure could have led to the destruction of the ship.

Or the loss of *Everest.*

"I wish I had an answer for you, Captain. I assume an investigation will begin—hopefully it will turn something up."

I nodded. I would have Tom widen the investigation to include the autonav failure. *Once is an occurrence; twice is a coincidence.* We couldn't afford to wait for enemy action.

"Anyway, I also came to thank you, Chief. You and your staff performed exceptionally yesterday. We wouldn't be alive without your guidance—that fact is not lost on me. Please pass my compliments on to your teams."

"I'll do that, Captain. I appreciate your . . ."

The compliment had made him uncomfortable like a dressing-down never could. I smiled and gave him a friendly pat on the shoulder. "Thank you, Chief. Carry on."

"That we will, ma'am. We always do."

My ribs froze as I turned to walk away. I sucked in a gust of air reflexively, which made it even worse.

"You all right, Cap?" Brinn asked.

"I'm still standing, Brinn."

"Carry on, then."

"We always do."

"Aye, Captain."

✣

I almost never used the cargo lift to travel between decks, but my journey down the stairwell to find Brinn had been torture on my ribs. The empty compartment looked irresistible. I stepped in and, once the doors closed, found myself with a few heaven-sent seconds to myself. For two of them, I allowed myself to fall completely apart. Then I spent ten or so wiping the tears out of my eyes and putting myself back together before the lift reached the habitation deck. Pizza's heavenly scent and murmurs of the crew's merriment met me before the lift doors opened and revealed an impromptu and well-deserved party. You couldn't order a crew to celebrate a victory, but many military types were workaholics and needed some encouragement. They had pulled together and, against formidable odds, saved the ship and kept us all alive.

Jake wasn't hard to spot—he held court at a table with Mindy Stykes. Several members of Mindy's staff and what had to be the entire female portion of Jake's crew were listening intently as he spun a yarn about his time in the academy. We had enough contact with *Everest* that our crews had made some friends—it didn't surprise me to see the other members of Jake's crew scattered around the galley interacting with my people.

As much as I wanted to see Jake, I was relieved no seats were available in the entire room. With a little luck, I might be able to make this short and hit the rack.

My ribs hurt like hell.

"Hello, Captain," Mindy said as soon as she noticed me. "I was keeping Captain Connors entertained while you were tied up. I needed to . . . oh, Sam! Excuse me Captain, Jake."

Mindy sashayed into the crowd.

Even I had to admit she was a truly beautiful woman. Perhaps 120 pounds holding a hair dryer, she could still easily pass for the bikini model of her graduate school days. Her appearance matched her intelligence, which was definitely formidable. Despite her average conversation, Mindy held a doctorate in theoretical physics, a master's in biology, and a bachelor's in aerospace engineering.

She played the ditzy blonde well.

The rest of the table emptied. Partially because the party always followed Mindy, and mostly because I had a pronounced lack of social acceptance aboard my ship. It was only one of the costs of command.

Nobody likes to sit with the captain.

Jake grinned and patted the seat Mindy had vacated beside him. I grimaced as I settled into one across the table instead.

His eyes narrowed with concern that matched his tone. "You okay?"

"Doc Hawshmore says I'll be all right." I regretted the deep breath I pulled in. "Things got a little exciting yesterday."

"So I heard. Any idea what happened?"

"Plenty, but none of them are good, and none are fact. The investigation hasn't even started. It might take a bit, but we'll figure it out."

"I can't say much about your problems. We've had issues of our own."

"Yours are unexplained, too?"

"Well, no." He examined me, as if trying to gauge whether it was sage to change the subject. Finally, he ventured, "How's your father?"

"Mom paints a rosy picture, and I haven't been home to find out otherwise."

"But?"

"How can everything be okay, Jake? He had a stroke."

"He still gets around, doesn't he?"

"She says he hasn't spoken a word since it happened."

Jake smiled. "Some women would call that a blessing."

A wave of fire flashed through me and settled behind my eyes. I winced as my broken ribs ground uncomfortably against each other.

"Allie, I'm sorry. I shouldn't have said that." Jake looked contrite. "Are you okay?"

"I told you I'm fine."

"Look, I might as well—"

"Stay and visit a little more, please?" I flashed him puppy-dog eyes.

Don't leave me.

He nodded, reached across the table, and laid his hand on top of mine. The gesture forced my heart into my throat—I couldn't remember the last time I'd touched another person.

Then he withdrew. It took me a minute to force words out. "So . . . have you taken any leave lately?"

"We rotate off during unloads. Even a few hours wandering around the receiving port in Bilbao helps."

"When you work in Spain, do you need vacation?"

"I work in space. I just deliver ore to Spain."

I made a show of rolling my eyes. "You're not Captain Kirk."

"I'm not?" His smile was boyish and charming, and I felt it in my belly button. "I take it you haven't been planetside in a while?"

"No, but we're scheduled for an overwatch op when we get back. I'm thinking I'll go down and get some air."

"Where?"

"I can't say. We were heading that way when we got the call your ship was in trouble. We'll be back at it once we get you taken care of."

"Sorry to hold you up."

"I'm not." I smiled, wanting him to feel I was trying to ease the tension in the conversation. "You know I'm always glad for the opportunity to see you."

His expression didn't soften.

"Jake, my feelings for you aren't going to change."

What am I doing wrong?

His gaze intensified. "How did we do this to ourselves? Aren't opposites supposed to attract?"

"I'm a woman and you're a man. How much more opposite do you want?"

"More opposite than we have it." His laugh was hearty. "I guess we'll find out when one of us retires or gets busted clean out of the service."

I suddenly found myself as serious as Jake had been. "Yes. Yes, we will."

CHAPTER 3

18 MAY 2126

My eyes opened before the vibrations stopped pounding against the hull. The lights in my quarters snapped on automatically and turned red. I regretted my own lack of foresight as soon as I sprang out of bed. It took me a few seconds to corner the stabs of pain in my ribs before I managed to grit my teeth and race for command.

Anything capable of rattling *Ticonderoga*'s hull was a definite threat.

"Status?"

"No idea, Captain. The scans are showing clear," Major Trulani reported.

More vibrations hammered the side of the ship.

"Deploy the remotes. Let's get a look at what's going on," I said. "Charge the concussors. Tell the weapons crews to fire on anything actively attacking."

Hayes pounded into command. "Micro asteroids?"

"Too repetitive," I said. "It has to be mechanical."

Louder than before, rhythmic battering sounded against the bulkheads above.

Tom opened the One-MC. "We are under attack. This is not a drill. All hands to combat stations."

"Captain, Major Daniels is requesting launch clearance," Trulani reported.

"Put the Ready Five 'cats in the air locks, but do not deploy until we know what we're up against."

"Concussor battery three activated," Tom reported.

"Get me the targeting info from that battery. I want to see what's out there."

"The remotes have been destroyed," Trulani reported from the operations station.

"Command to Lieutenant Benson," I said into the open com pickup.

"Benson here."

"I want the entire wing in ready position. Do not further load the air locks without command authorization."

"Roger that, Captain."

"Batteries five and two are firing."

"Where's that targeting video?"

"Sending it to the SDC now," Trulani said.

The image of a blurry round metal pod bristling with gun ports appeared on the display between Tom and me. "What is it?"

"We use to call them battleballs," I said. "They're unmanned drones—completely autonomous. We always thought they were sent by the Oriental Ore Consortium to discourage our mining operations but could never prove it."

"I thought the OOC had worked out a trade agreement with the UPE? So much for *United* Planet Earth." Tom gripped the console as another barrage shook the ship. "How powerful are those things?"

"They're too light to be an immediate threat to *Tico*, but they'll peck away until they hit something critical."

"How do you shut them down?" Tom asked.

"The best strategy is always to run, but we don't have the speed for that." I turned toward operations. "Trulani, do you have the scanners tightened down so we can see them coming?"

"Generally, yes. The runs have a definite pattern. Close lateral passes."

"Captain, Major Daniels is insisting on launch clearance," Lieutenant Benson broke in over the com.

"Cut him off!" I snapped. I keyed my own com controls and said, "Chief Brinn? You in one piece up there?"

"A little busy, Captain. What do you want?"

"Override the safeties on the lateral thrusters and shut down the x-axis inertial compensators."

"Thirty seconds, Captain."

"Thanks, Chief."

"All hands, brace for some chop," Hayes said into the One-MC, already seeing my plan coming together.

"Helm, set the computer to autocorrect the portside lateral spin you're about to induce. Take your cue from operations."

"Aye, Captain."

"Hang on, everybody. Count it down, Trulani."

"They're coming around," she said from her station. "Spin in three, two, one . . ."

Somewhere in the chaos of the unexpected maneuver, I'd heard the battleballs swatted into oblivion by contact with the ship's hull. In the end, I was glad Tom and I were the only ones to get knocked off our feet, but bouncing my ribs into the SDC made me groan on the way down.

Tom tried to help me get to my feet, which hurt even worse.

"Trulani, status?" he asked.

"Several impacts along the lateral axis," Trulani confirmed, shaking her head.

Holding my side was all I could do to stem the pain. "Launch the Tomcats. Tell them to have a look around and do what they can to inspect for damage. I want their throttles maxed until they know the area is clear."

"Yes, ma'am," Trulani said. "Launching now."

I stabbed the engineering com again. "You all right, Brinn?"

"We're picking up the pieces, Captain."

"Damage report?"

"Overstress alarms in bulkhead forty-seven port and sixty-three starboard from the impacts. Teams are on their way to assess."

"I know you're busy, Chief, but we're now short a set of remote sensor drones."

"It will take a few days for fabrications to uncrate the parts and produce another set. We'll get started—"

"In the morning, Chief," I interrupted. "Thank you for your work. Get some sleep as soon as you can."

"Yes, Captain. Brinn out."

I turned back to my first officer. "Hit the rack, Tom. I'll handle the recovery."

He cast a skeptical glance over me. While he was in a hastily applied but crisp uniform, I was dressed in a form-fitting issued black athletic bra and underwear, framing the massive bruise set in my bare midriff. I wiggled my bare feet against the deck plate.

"I'll be fine," I said reassuringly. "On your way, ExO."

I wasn't about to apologize for my condition when I responded to an emergency, and I certainly didn't want my crew to believe uniform regs should matter when our lives were on the line.

Tom hadn't even made it to the corridor when the com officer announced, "I have Admiral Kegar for you, Captain."

"At my station, please, Pierre." I carefully settled into my duty station chair and accepted the com. Admiral Vergé Kegar's dark eyes pierced the screen, framed by close-cropped graying hair and an otherwise clean-shaven face. He was my commanding officer, head of the Ticonderoga program, my mentor and, I believed, my friend. And this was one of the few times I'd seen him look visibly shocked over the video feed.

"Interesting uniform choice, Captain." Since he was in dress blacks, including a chest full of campaign ribbons featuring more than a few earned during his time in the pre-UPE United States military, I assumed he was referring to the fact that I was addressing the most senior admiral in my chain of command in my underwear.

"We had an encounter with what I believe were Oriental Ore Consortium sentry drones. I was asleep when the alert sounded."

"I understand, but I was talking about the bruise."

"We also had a primary power conduit fail yesterday. I was helping with the replacement and got a little sloppy."

"Captain, forget about the status report for a second. Are you okay?"

"Two broken ribs and a little bruise. The doc has done what he can to put me back together. I'll live."

His smile was grim. "As usual, your predilection for understatement is intact. That's no little bruise."

"But it is, in the end, just a bruise, sir."

He looked concerned but pushed it aside and continued, "I was notified when the telemetry reports came in indicating you had been in combat."

"We're getting the pieces together. We'll recover the Tomcats shortly.

The damage control teams have some work on the hull, and we lost our remote sensor drones, but it could have been worse."

"Can you confirm OOC involvement?"

I shook my head. "Even the targeting video from the concussors isn't conclusive."

"The Outer Space Treaty of 1967 is still in effect. The Consortium weapons are purely offensive. If we could ever capture evidence of one, maybe we could pursue this legally."

"The Consortium member countries aren't signatories of the treaty, sir."

"That's true." I never got used to him scratching his head. He did it whenever he was frustrated—the gesture seemed uncharacteristically normal. "I can understand terrestrial squabbles, but there's plenty of room in space for all of us. This all seems unnecessary."

A useless shrug was all I could offer.

"I'd like a full incident report. The Senate will undoubtedly have questions." He stopped scratching when a flash of a grin parted his lips. "I suppose we should leave the interpretation of extraplanetary treaty stipulations to the bureaucrats as well."

"You'll have it. I wanted to clean things up and collect all the information I could."

He nodded. "Is your schedule holding?"

"We're a little behind. The incident with the conduit put us a little over minus six hours when all was said and done."

"Make that up if you can. The Slovenian Operation has a hard deadline, and the mighty UPE Senate wants *Ticonderoga* to help out with operational security." He paused, and his expression softened. "I didn't mean that to sound sarcastic. I'm a little groggy yet."

I nodded. "I'll confirm with Chief Brinn, but we should be able to figure it out. The conduit repair brought us back to full engine capacity. We'll make up some time once we drop *Everest* at Alpha Station."

"Give me a Polaroid of this conduit incident."

I smiled. "A Polaroid? I ran out of film 130 years ago."

His only response was a look I privately referred to as *the Keglare*. No surprise—he seldom appreciated my attempts at humor.

"One of the structural integrity sensors on the primary distribution conduit alerted. We haven't really started the investigation, but my belief at this point is de-crystallization of the casing's compositional matrix was induced. Complete failure appeared imminent. We replaced the conduit, eliminating the risk of a breach."

"Induced?"

"Heat is the only thing that makes sense. Something like a plasma torch could induce the heat if it was set correctly. Any external marking could then be removed or recovered mechanically. I'm no expert, but exotic alloys like the casing aren't receptive to heat and some forms of radiation. The heat rearranges the crystalline structure of the alloy, creating structural weaknesses that allow for potential failure. That casing is a pressure vessel—it's meant to hold in coolant, not survive uneven heating."

"You're suggesting sabotage."

I lowered my voice. "I don't see another explanation at this time, but as I indicated, we haven't gotten wheels under the investigation."

"Your telemetry shows you chose to risk uncontrolled entry into the asteroid belt instead of firing a braking thrust?"

"It wasn't an *instead*—it was a risk either way, sir. Had the conduit breached, the ship would have been rendered environmentally nonviable. Trying to stop increased the probability of failure almost a hundredfold. I took the more viable option. I saw no third choice."

"I'm not saying you should have, Captain. However, you know eyes are on this project. The vote for *Ticonderoga*'s operational refit isn't far off, and the UPE Senate will ask why they should spend $1.2 trillion to keep you doing what you do."

"We might not be funded?"

"You must have been hit harder than you thought, Allison. The Ticonderoga Project always has a chance to lose funding."

"We can go on without the refit, if we have to."

Kegar grinned. "Don't say that on an open channel."

"Yes, sir."

"I ask some hard questions, but that's because these people ask me hard questions. I never doubt you're doing good things out there. I look forward to your report."

"You'll have it, sir. *Ticonderoga* out."

I stared at the dark screen. Kegar wasn't a metallurgist either, but he hadn't shied away from my assessment of the conduit incident. Talk of sabotage seemed crazy, but I saw no other explanation. The battleball was happenstance.

Wasn't it?

I finally realized how fuzzy I'd gotten. In fairness, I'd only had a little over an hour's sleep. I wasn't going to solve all my recent problems sitting there. I stood, knowing I needed coffee and clothes.

Clothes first.

Once I was out in the corridor, my quarters were a few steps ahead on the right. I could have easily disappeared behind the door, but I waited when Jake rounded the far end of the nearly empty corridor.

"Now that's an appealing uniform, Legs," he said as he came to stand in front of me.

My exhaustion disappeared with the warmth of his smile. I wondered if he could see my insides squirming under his gaze as I punched open the door to my quarters. "They're the finest in UPE-approved undergarments. Come on in for a minute. I just came to grab some clothes."

He shrugged and followed me inside.

"Jake, what has you up this late?"

"It's technically early, isn't it? Chief Brinn has crews working on my ship around the clock. We'd still be there if it wasn't for—" He fell suddenly silent.

"What?" I asked once the door was closed.

"All these years we've known each other, and I've never seen your quarters before."

"It's a room," I said, moving toward the closet. Pulling on a uniform was the last thing I wanted to do.

"You have a shower."

I smiled. "*Tico* was designed a long time ago. Artificial gravity was new, and sonics weren't standard yet. It was considered a little treat from home that was worth the trouble."

"I don't suppose you'd let me . . ."

I smiled as I zipped up my uniform coverall. "It's all yours."

"Cool."

I nodded. "I'll hang around and make sure you get started okay."

"I can probably handle it."

My voice purred. "So can I."

I stepped back into the corridor a few minutes later, pleased with the sound my slap had made on his bare backside.

~

I was well past ready for a second cup of coffee by the time I sent my official written report to Admiral Kegar.

"Captain?"

"Mr. Pitka." I turned in my seat to face the haggard engineer's mate. "You look tired."

He handed me a sky blue bundle of clothing. "*Everest*'s quartermaster asked me to bring this to you for Captain Connors, ma'am."

"What's the repair status?"

"We're all done, Captain. She's ready to go."

"Thank you for this, Mr. Pitka," I said, acknowledging the bundle. "I know you've been instrumental the past day or so, as always. You've done stellar work helping to resolve our recent issues."

"No . . . it . . . thank you, Captain."

"Get some chow and hit the rack, Mr. Pitka."

"Yes, ma'am."

My heart swelled with pride as I watched him disappear. A lot of good people ran *Ticonderoga*, but the engineers were her backbone.

"Sleep well, kid," I whispered under my breath. Commander Hayes took Pitka's place at my side. "Good morning, Tom. You're just in time—I'm making a coffee run. And probably a detour for a shower. Mind the store, would you, please?"

Tom looked concerned. "No sleep?"

"Not another wink. The admiral wanted a report."

"Take your time, Captain."

"We're about three hours out of Alpha Station."

He nodded. "I'll take care of the pre-approach procedures."

"Thanks. Back in a bit."

The yawn came from the balls of my feet as I neared my quarters. Lack of sleep was catching up to me, and I had a long day ahead.

My hunch was right.

I found Jake sprawled across my rack when I stepped into my quarters. He looked like he'd only made the two steps between the shower and the bed before he collapsed. I set the clean uniform from his ship on my desk and stripped my coverall and undies off. He never stirred, and I took the opportunity to read the story the bruises, scars, and tangles of muscle his body told in the dim light.

God, he's beautiful.

I stepped into the shower myself. I was relatively sure the noise would wake him. I wanted it to—I wanted him to come and scrub my back and whatever else might get in the way. The cool water woke a little more of me than I'd intended, but I was okay with that.

All fantasy aside, I was okay with the fact that my military shower was done before he woke. I hated it, but I knew we were better off not to give in to desire.

The towel was still damp from his use, but I didn't mind as I pulled some of the water from my hair. I'd finished drying myself but wasn't quite done feeling frisky when I woke him.

I tried to act natural but made sure the towel didn't cover sufficiently when I took a step closer to my rack and whispered, "Jake, rise and shine."

"Hey." His smile was sunshine.

I turned back slowly and reached onto my tiptoes to deposit the towel over the shower wall, opening the drawer in my closet and pulling out fresh underwear. "We're about three hours out."

He nodded, rolled over, yawned, and stretched.

My heart pounded in my ears. *He's definitely beautiful.* "Pitka says they're done patching *Everest* up."

I couldn't tell if he was looking at or past me. He might have been groggy, but I hoped he was enjoying seeing me as much as I enjoyed seeing him. Officially, a relationship wasn't possible. These stolen moments were all we could ever have.

It doesn't matter. I can't stay away from him.

Crossing back to the bunk as I adjusted my bra, I leaned over and brushed a hand through his sleepy hair. If I touched him anywhere else, I wouldn't be able to stop.

"I brought you a clean uniform."

"I was pretty tired, and then the shower . . ." He yawned again. "I'm sorry if I made you uncomfortable."

"Not at all." I smiled, hesitating—maybe too long or not long enough?—and kissed him lightly on the lips.

"That will have to do until next time."

~

Alpha Station was an interesting page in Earth's space history. Originally funded, designed, and built by the now defunct Wood Space Enterprises, it had been intended to refine shipbuilding ores. The premise was that it would, in the end, be more cost-effective and environmentally friendly to place all aspects of the deep-space shipbuilding process in a high-Earth or lunar orbit than to repeatedly suffer the expense of lifting components out of Earth's gravity well. The idea came before its time. The Wood family exhausted their resources before realizing their dream, and the station was abandoned for some time before the United Planet Earth coalition eventually took over the derelict, unsure of what to do with it even then.

They eventually decided to move the station to the asteroid belt beyond Mars. Although it came at extraordinary expense, the increased availability of materials and the presence of higher-value ores in the belt more than justified the cost of the present-day infrastructure.

The station had, over time, "eaten" its way far enough into the ever-shifting field to make the approach interesting. Navigating the corridor in wasn't a problem for its purpose-built transport ships—*Kilimanjaro*, *Fuji*, and Jake Connors's *Everest*.

For *Ticonderoga*, the approach was another matter. She was built for exploration. Big, fast, and strong, she handled like a wounded water buffalo compared to Transport Division's vessels. And that was before factoring in *Everest*'s additional mass, which was still mag-grappled to the hull. It was a job for an experienced officer, but this was my new helmsman's first time in the barrel.

"Easy as she goes, Mr. Salinski." The poor kid had sweat through his uniform.

"It's a little tight in here, ma'am."

"Just like life, Lieutenant. Take it one twist and turn at a time." I had the SDC programmed to show a variety of navigational and engineering displays, which Salinski undoubtedly also had in front of him. "Five-second pulse on the ventral bow thrusters on my mark, Mr. Salinski."

"Five-second ventral bow thrust, aye."

"Mark."

The deck plates shuddered under my feet as the thrum of the mighty engines rattled even the air inside the ship.

"Portside bow thrusters."

"Firing," Salinski said.

"Z-axis plus fifteen hundred meters."

"Ventral thrusters all firing. Nose is fifteen degrees positive, Captain."

I watched the displays as the ship swung around on two axes, still traveling forward on the third. "Z-axis neutral, Mr. Salinski. Autocorrect the spin in three, two, one . . . mark."

"Course shows a straight bearing into the station void, Captain."

"Nice work, Mr. Salinski. Best speed, please."

"Aye, Captain."

"Captain," Pierre said from the main com station. "I have an urgent message from Admiral Kegar. It's marked your eyes only."

"Excuse me for a second please, Tom," I said. Once he had moved away from the console, I added, "Up here, please, Mr. Pierre."

"*Oui*, Captain."

The console performed a biometric scan before it displayed the text. Once the display filled, the header showed a bunch of routing information. The body of the text was notably short:

> Allison,
>
> A news report was sent to my desk. A fire has destroyed your parent's home. There is one confirmed fatality—identity unknown. I have dispatched an agent to get more information.
>
> Admiral Vergé Kegar

Setting my jaw, I cleared the message from the display and deleted the file before I waved Tom back down. Pulling into a holding orbit at the station wasn't a big deal, but it still didn't hurt to have another set of eyes watching the procedures.

"Is everything all right?" Tom asked.

"Captain Connors is on the line," Pierre said.

"Put him through to the SDC please, Mr. Pierre."

Jake appeared on the screen in front of me, all business. "We're ready, Captain Mackenzie."

"Major Trulani, disengage the mag-grapple, please. Z-axis positive point-oh-one, please, Mr. Salinski."

"*Everest* is navigating freely," Jake confirmed.

My smile became genuine. "Come again when you can stay longer."

"See you on the station?"

"Not this time. We're late for another op back home. They've already positioned a cargo pod outside for us. They'll swap it, and we're out."

"Well, may the wind be at your back, Captain."

"Best wishes to you as well, Captain. *Ticonderoga* out."

~

I could still smell Jake's scent on my pillow when I snuggled under the covers. I didn't want Jake sleeping on my bed. I wanted him in it with me, every night.

But that wasn't the order of things in the military.

Nonetheless, that little reminder of him was with me as I drifted off to sleep and dreams . . .

✣

"The meat loaf has been here since yesterday," a tall, handsome cadet said from behind me in line.

"And the lasagna has been here since last week," I said as the server flopped a large chunk of the meat loaf onto my tray.

"My name's Jake. I'm in Transport Division." The lasagna thudded as it fell onto his plate. He acknowledged it with a smile. "It's packed with vitamins."

"I'm Allison Mackenzie. Space Command Defensive Forces."

"Impressive."

"Time will tell," I said as I motioned toward the tables.

He nodded and led the way.

The requisite awkward silence ensued as soon as we sat down. The cafeteria was next to empty—one of those moments. No other audible conversations hummed nearby to eavesdrop on.

"Is this your first year?" he asked finally.

I nodded and tried to swallow a large lump of compressed meat. "I came in a week ago. How about you?"

"Senior year. I'm almost done."

"That must be exciting."

"It is, but . . . I'll miss life on the ground, too."

"I can understand that." Another lump of meat loaf struggled down. Why had I forgotten how to chew my food? "I grew up on a farm in Idaho. I never understood how special the place was until I left."

His smile was instant. "From horses to space."

"Well, I've never ridden a horse. You're thinking of a ranch, where they have cows and pigs and chickens. Where I grew up, we raised wheat and barley and had a pickup truck."

"I didn't know there was a difference."

"It's not a clear-cut line." I forced myself to slow down and stop inhaling my food. "How about you?"

"I guess you'd call me a city boy. I grew up outside of Miami."

"You came from a big family."

"How did you know?" he asked.

I shrugged. "People with small families don't have much to leave behind, and those from big families move on to find some breathing room."

"You're from the other side."

"An only child," I confirmed.

His smile was heartwarming. "You can borrow some of my family. They'd love you."

My cheeks flushed with warmth. "I'm not good in situations like that."

"Why not?" he asked, sounding serious.

"Not enough practice, I suppose." I watched him watching me, waiting for me to elaborate. "I never feel like I belong. Just like an intruder."

"Or a pity case?"

I shrugged, trying to brush off feelings that never, ever left.

"We'd never let that happen." His voice was so firm, so solid, I found it hard not to believe him, even though I had only just met him.

"Maybe we'll find out some day."

"They say women don't like overconfident guys, so I'm going to let that hang in the air." He reached across the table and brushed a fingertip over my hand, smiled, and then pulled it back.

CHAPTER 4

19 MAY 2126

I dressed in shorts and a T-shirt, stretched in my quarters a bit, then stepped out into the corridor and ran. My mind concentrated on the simple act of putting one foot in front of another, eyes scanning obstacles in front of me and reflexes dodging those obstacles to keep me moving. Things behind me cleared from my vision as I ran. The world passed by.

Then, slowly, the image in my mind sharpened. Experience taught me everything happened for a reason. Even if it wasn't readily apparent, the reason existed and was worth chasing after.

Everest getting stuck, the broken conduit, an attack from an Oriental Ore Consortium border sentry, and the fire in my parent's home—too many things had happened at the same time. I couldn't find as much as a thread to bind the events together.

"Good morning, Captain," Mindy said as she fell into effortless step beside me. She wore a sports bra, spandex shorts, bright eyes, and a cheerful smile. Annoyance flashed through me—how could anyone be so happy at such an early hour?—but I was glad to see her at the same time. The cautious friendship we'd built aboard *Tico* had become my lifeline, probably because I'd found her heart was bigger than her formidable brain.

"Good morning, Mindy."

"Captain Mackenzie, please report to command," Hayes's voice said over the One-MC. "Urgent com waiting. Captain to command."

My last few steps thundered as I stopped to turn and head for the command deck.

"Have fun in the principal's office!" Mindy shouted from the end of the corridor.

"Righto," I muttered as I took off again, passing crew members like they were slalom flags on a downhill ski racecourse.

I tore into command like a grizzly was chasing me.

"It's available at your station," Pierre said nonchalantly.

"Thank you, Mr. Pierre." I wiped the sweat out of my eyes and keyed in my identification sequence. Admiral Kegar appeared after the scan confirmed my biometrics.

"Good morning, Captain," he said stiffly. "Sorry to disturb your morning exercise cycle."

I glanced down self-consciously, and for the first time noticed my T-shirt had soaked through with sweat. "I got in a footrace with my chief of sciences."

"How did you do?"

"As usual, I lost." I wiped sweat from my eyes again. "Your call sounded important. What can we do for you, sir?"

"I'm sending *Ticonderoga* back to pick up *Everest* again. Evidently, its engine problem went deeper than your engineer assumed, and Alpha Station isn't equipped to handle it. They're not terribly far behind you—it shouldn't represent a substantial delay."

"No problem, sir. We'll take care of it."

"No, Captain, you won't. I need you back here on Earth as soon as possible. The UPE appropriations subcommittee has some questions for you regarding funding for the Ticonderoga Project. Commander Hayes will look after the ship while you're away."

"Sir?"

"It's the conduit breach, Captain. *Tico* has a few years on her, but that conduit was designed to exceed the operational lifespan of the ship. The committee is worried about the program's viability, even with the proposed upgrades."

"Where do I need to be and when?"

"I'm sending an itinerary straight to flight operations for upload to your Tomcat. Leave as soon as possible."

"Yes, sir."

"Kegar out." The screen went blank.

"Mr. Salinski, reverse course, please," I said easily. "Reacquire *Everest*'s beacon and lock it into the navigational system. Execute at best possible speed."

"Aye, Captain."

I turned to Tom, who was across the aisle at his own station. "It looks like I'm taking a trip, Mr. Hayes. The ship is yours."

"So it sounded. Say hello to terra firma for us," Tom said. "I'll mind the store."

With a nod, I stepped back into the corridor, where I fell into a run. In one of the military's little ironies, I still had to finish my exercise cycle before I could stop at my quarters for a quick shower. Almost an hour to the minute later, I was clean and pressed in a crisp flight suit in front of my chief of the deck, Lieutenant Charlie Benson, and Lieutenant Alexander Simkins, the second senior pilot on the ship.

"Gentlemen, I appreciate the sentiment, but I have this under control. I'm fully rated for spaceflight and fully rated and up-to-date on my quals with this airframe. I'll be fine, I promise."

"Captain, regulations specifically state—"

I stepped closer to Benson, purposely lowering my voice as I closed the distance. "Interpreting regulations for a command-level officer hasn't historically proven to be a career booster, Lieutenant."

"Sir—" Simkins said.

"Don't get involved, Simkins!" I lowered my tone and, focusing on Benson, raised my intensity. "Unless I missed a staff meeting, I am the captain of this ship. As such, I am responsible for everything aboard—every single rivet. Once I have made a decision, that decision will not be questioned. I have orders to follow like everyone else, and I do not intend to let you stop me from carrying them out, Lieutenant."

"With all due respect, Captain Mackenzie—" Simkins interjected before Benson could spit out a response. I rounded on him, but he continued hesitantly. "If you would reconsider, I would personally appreciate it. My daughter had an accident. She's in pretty bad shape. Maybe if I got back home, even for a minute—"

"Alex, if you're lying about this—"

"No, Captain. I haven't told anyone, but a car hit her on the way home from school yesterday," he said sincerely.

I glanced at Benson and found his face full of confusion, so I turned back to Simkins. "Why didn't you say something? I could've caught you a ride home."

"Before Lieutenant Benson came looking for someone to take you back to Earth, I thought we were heading home anyway, Cap. I was going to request emergency leave tomorrow morning if the situation hadn't stabilized."

"You should have told me."

"I know you care, Cap. That's why I didn't tell you. Couldn't take that look in your eyes."

"Got your gear?"

"It's already in the bird."

"Let's ride."

✣

"Canopy status?"

"Locks verified."

"Locks verified," I repeated after checking my own set. "Ejection switch ready."

"Ejection switch ready," Simkins said.

"Primary thruster status?" I asked.

"Nominal."

Simkins and I fired off a quick succession of familiar preflight checks, and the tension eased from my shoulders as anticipation built in my chest.

"I show us as go for departure," Simkins said.

"I concur. Retracting umbilical and requesting pushback into the air lock."

"Are you sure you don't want me to drive?"

"And lose the hours I need to stay qualified?" I smiled. "Not a chance."

"You can't blame a pilot for trying." Behind us the heavy metallic thud of the air lock boomed as it closed. "Air lock sealed and depressurization sequence initiated."

"*Ticonderoga* flight control," I said over the com, "this is Tomcat Zero Niner requesting permission to depart."

Tom Hayes's reply came quickly. "Initiating final launch sequence now. Have a safe trip, Captain."

"Mind the store, Commander. We'll see you soon."

"Confirmed, Zero Niner. *Ticonderoga* out."

Stars peered in as soon as the outer air lock doors parted, turning into a real-life planetarium show as the launch gantry extended us beyond the protection of the ship. I gazed around, taking it all in.

The sight was amazing every time.

"Best office in the world," Simkins said from behind me.

"Or out of it, for that matter." I smiled. I fired the Tomcat's maneuvering thrusters, brought us off the gantry, and swung us around to our earthbound heading in one gentle motion. "Firing main engines in three, two, one . . . mark."

"ETA to Earth is fourteen hours and twenty-three minutes," Simkins said. "So what are we going to talk about? Music? Poetry? Jake Connors?"

"We could just enjoy the view."

"What fun is that?" Simkins asked earnestly.

"You'd be surprised," I said while flipping the switch that commanded the computer's autopilot to take over the primary flying duties.

"He never shuts up about you," Alex baited.

I swallowed it. A little banter would pass the time, and what happened in-flight stayed in-flight. "Really? And what does Jake say about me?"

He laughed. "He said you'd kill him if he ever said a word about Fiji, and then you'd come after me to make sure word didn't get out."

"It wasn't that big of a deal. Why are you guys always so fascinated with a girl in a bikini, anyway?"

"Are you kidding me? Listen, Cap, I've got the wife, kids, the whole nine yards, and . . . Jake's my friend, so I think I can get away with saying this. Have you looked in the mirror? Ever?"

My face warmed as blood rushed to my cheeks.

"Why are you and Jake so sure your careers will end if you admit to yourselves what the rest of the world already knows?"

"We know how we feel, Alex. We know our crews have it figured out too—even command. We need to keep out the rest of the world."

"So the reason for all of the coy behavior is . . . ?"

"Circumstances beyond our control. We can more or less predict what's going to happen in our own organizations, but it's a big universe out there. Let's say someone nefarious found out about our relationship and decided to grab Jake. He could be used against me to take over the most powerful weapon in the history of mankind."

His response was instant. "You'd never make that trade."

"Of course I wouldn't, but therein lies the problem. Because of it, I'd more than likely end up letting the man I love die through my own inaction."

"I never thought about it that way."

"Sometimes I feel like I've spent too much time thinking about it. Tell me about your family, Alex."

"I love my wife, two kids, and dog almost as much as this job."

"You're kidding about that, right?"

"Nope. My wife is Sarah. Mikala is seven, Nikki is ten, and the dog is a basset hound called Soup."

"I meant the other part."

He was quiet for a long time before he answered. "Don't get me wrong. My family has been part of my life for thirteen years, but I've worked my entire life to earn this spot. While other kids were playing video games, I was studying physics flash cards. I put everything I had into getting here."

"And it was worth it."

"Is that a question or a statement?"

"Do you really have to ask?"

Try as he might, even Alex couldn't talk forever. I was all right with him starting, but I was also okay with him falling asleep—it gave me a chance to decompress for a bit.

Dad is dead.

His death—for certainly it had to be him and not my mom—wasn't quite the bomb it might have been. In a way, I'd lost him eight months ago when he had the stroke.

When someone never calls and never writes, aren't they gone?

My dad was my buddy—I had no other way to put it. He'd always helped me get myself into trouble, gotten me out of that trouble, and generally made it clear he loved me. Even when I left home, he always did some little thing to remind me he still cared.

And then it stopped. The silence had been deafening.

Mom and Dad lived in the house I'd grown up in. Dad had been raised in the same house, and his dad before that. I had no idea how old it was, but I could still see the ancient multicolored glass globes hanging from the attic rafters. I'd once researched them and found they'd been invented in the latter part of the nineteenth century—an early incarnation of fire suppression. The house was past its prime, no doubt, even somewhat historic.

It wasn't unreasonable to believe a fire in the place had been an accident or that a sixty-eight-year-old stroke victim hadn't made it out.

The timing was suspicious, not the circumstances.

I had to be missing something. So much had happened in the past two days, and I wasn't a big believer in coincidence. It all had to be connected.

But how?

~

"UPE Defense Command to *Ticonderoga* Tomcat Zero Niner."

"Zero Niner," Simkins answered over the radio.

"We show you sixty seconds out from deorbit trajectory burn."

"Roger that, command. Requesting clearance to Joint Base Lewis–McChord."

"Clearance granted, Zero Niner," the controller said.

"Everything green up there, Cap?" Simkins asked.

I checked my display. "Thirty seconds from entry burn . . . mark. Can you project the entry vector graphics onto my HUD, please?"

"Oops, sorry, Cap." A series of computer-generated windows with a multitude of numerical data appeared on my helmet's face shield. "I got used to the front seat."

"You've done fine, Simkins." I activated the appropriate thruster control. "I'm glad you came with me."

"I appreciate the ride."

"My pleasure. For what it's worth, your leave will be indefinite and active as soon as we land. Just stay in touch with me, and we'll figure out how to get you home once things are under control."

"Thank you, Captain."

"Deorbit in three, two, one . . ." The pulse of the maneuvering thrusters roared in the cockpit and pushed us back in our seats, covering the front of the canopy in an orange glow.

"Reentry trajectory confirmed. Keep her between the lines, Cap."

"Roger that. Stand by for com dropout."

Technology had made most aspects of atmospheric reentry mundane. As long as the spacecraft kept the prescribed angle of attack and velocity, entering Earth's atmosphere wasn't much more exciting than crossing the street. Nevertheless, the frictional energy created by the Tomcat's contact with even the thin atmosphere played havoc with communications for a few minutes. The problem would clear on its own once our relative speed slowed and we properly entered the atmosphere.

"We're drifting, Captain. Trim it up."

I nudged the stick a little farther to the right, aiming for the box drawn on my helmet display. I caught the box, but I wasn't aligned like I should have been. In aeronautical terms, our velocity vector was no longer centered.

"Response on the stick is sluggish." Vibration rattled the Tomcat as the next box drawn on my helmet display drifted even further to the top right. "Switch to the backups, Alex. We're losing her."

"Backup circuits are unresponsive, Captain."

The window drawn on my display rotated slowly counterclockwise. "We've lost lateral stability."

"That's not good. Fire the mains and get us out of the atmosphere before we burn up," Alex said.

The throttles made it all the way to the maximum power stop with no reaction. "Negative ignition of primary thrusters."

"That's not good, either," Alex said, a tinge of panic in his voice.

A view of the Asian continent replaced the stars overhead.

Struggling against the straps of my seat, I fought the controls and a wave of nausea. "I can't correct the roll."

"The gauge shows 25 percent, but diagnostics say we're out of fuel, Cap."

Really not good.

"We're going down. Want me to call in the AMF?"

"*Ticonderoga* Tomcat Zero Niner, correct your entry vector," the Defense Command controller's voice broke in.

Unhelpful!

I responded, "Defense Command, Mayday. All control systems are inoperative."

"Backup response, Zero Niner?"

"Also negative, control," I said. My stomach churned as the canopy view accelerated its counterclockwise spin and added an orange glow. "We've developed an uncontrolled multiaxial spin."

"Bail out, Zero Niner. We'll dispatch a rescue shuttle."

I cringed and worked the dead stick pointlessly.

"We're pretty high, command," Alex said, echoing my thoughts.

"Telemetry already has your hull at fifty C above max temperature threshold. Your bird is going to come apart."

The rattle in the cockpit grew.

"Alex?"

"He's right, Cap. We gotta go. Brace for ejection in five, four, three—"

I looked out at the wildly gyrating panorama in front of me and pulled the cinches on my seat straps once more.

"Good luck, Simkins," I said.

Any response was drowned out by the sound of the canopy blowing loose and the Martin-Baker ejection seats doing their job.

~

I knew I was dreaming as soon as I took a deep breath.

Home at harvest time was the only place where dust, wheat straw, and heat mixed together and still managed to smell wonderful. I recognized it instantly. The dirt was so fine—I could feel it caked inside my nose. The combine idled next to the grain truck, and Dad stood on the platform outside the cab.

"I'll get the tarp, Dad. You go back to work!" I shouted, darting forward.

He started down the black steel ladder on the side of the combine. He was still young—he moved fast and precisely. "You're a little short in the beam for that! I'll get it."

Hurrying to the back tire, I grabbed a bar welded into the side of the old red truck bed and pulled myself up onto the side rail—less than an inch was exposed, just wide enough for me to get my toes on. Moving one hand and one foot at a time, I worked my way to the front of the truck where the gray tarp was secured. As I hurried along, my fingernails screeched eerily whenever they slid across the dust-covered metal. Reaching for the rope that held the tarp in place was literally my downfall.

On the way to the ground, I had time to think about how bad it was going to hurt.

I couldn't have asked to strike earth any better, landing flat on my back and shattering wheat stubble beneath. The sound it made as it collapsed could have been breaking bone. Agony shot to my ribs and the back of my head.

Dry ground didn't have a lot of give.

Dad's footsteps weren't rushed at all.

I tried to inhale, but only more pain came.

"Get up," he said as he appeared over me with an outstretched hand.

"Can't," I managed to squeak.

"Yes, you can, and you have to, Allison. You wanted to climb up there and do the job, so take a deep breath, get up, and get it done."

My next breath brought some oxygen and pushed away the panic.

"Now get up," Dad repeated as he reached down farther. "Get up and finish what you were going to do."

I winced when I got to my feet, but that was the last time I let Dad see I was hurting. I knew he wouldn't help me now, but he watched every move I made until I finished. My movements were the same as before, only a little slower and much more judicious. Soon, I was standing back in front of him.

His words had as much praise as I expected. "Don't ever let a fall get in the way when you have work to do."

✣

"Captain Mackenzie? Are you ready to come back to us?"

My thoughts swarmed. I was aware of enough to know I was well out of it. The image of Jake Connors walking away from *Ticonderoga* parked in front of my parent's farmhouse didn't make any sense, and I knew it.

"Allison, wake up," the voice said more firmly.

I struggled against the swirling images in my mind. When I saw the talking raven in the UPE uniform, I knew it was time to leave my dreams behind and rejoin reality.

"Captain Allison Jane Mackenzie reporting for duty." My eyelids struggled open. "Where am I?"

"You're at UPE Medical, Captain. You're suffering the aftereffects of a suborbital ejection from an uncontrolled reentry." My vision focused on a tall, good-looking man. He had spiky black hair and gold-rimmed eyeglasses. "We're lucky we got you back."

"Why?" I asked, trying to straighten.

"Your craft was in a multiaxial spin when you punched out. I'm told you were inverted when the sequence activated and your Tomcat disintegrated above you. Conditions were far from ideal."

"Simkins . . . my copilot. He got out, right?"

The doctor's expression betrayed him. "His—"

"Leave me alone for a minute," I interrupted. I sank back against the pillows.

"Captain, I have to—"

"Am I going to die in the next half hour?"

"No."

"Then please excuse me for a moment, Doctor."

I watched as the man collected his data tablet and reluctantly stepped out the door. Losing Simkins didn't shock me. He was my fifth command loss, but I'd seen many more people die in service. Sometimes accidentally and sometimes through enemy action. None had been particularly meaningful—which wasn't what I'd hoped for when I signed on.

It was unfortunate but inevitable in this line of work.

His wife and family would find it far more difficult to accept.

I needed to gather my thoughts about the accident itself. Simkins and his family would have to wait for me to express my grief. Right now, I had work to do.

Once is happenstance, twice is coincidence, and three times is enemy action.

The old saying nagged its way to the front of my mind. I'd been through the incidents constantly since things started going wrong, and enemy action—sabotage—was the only possible tie to bind the incidents together.

I tried to sit up to look for a com access terminal and almost screamed.

Forgot about the ribs. Fuck.

At least they didn't count in the whole enemy action equation.

Not directly, anyway.

I needed to talk to my ship.

The doctor returned. "Forgive me, Captain, but I really need to check a few things now that you're awake."

I nodded my permission and mustered a weak smile. "Have at it, Doc."

"I've gone from *doctor* to *doc* in a few minutes. You must have quite the ability to adjust. I'm glad to see that."

"I hope it doesn't count against me. I still don't want to be here any longer than I have to."

"You won't," he said after adjusting my IV. "Those ribs are my biggest concern. Mind if I have a look?"

I nodded, and he exposed the skin on my side and carefully palpated the area. His brow remained furrowed in concentration.

"You talk like a shrink."

"I have a double specialty. Psychiatry is the second."

"And the first is?"

"Internal medicine," he said as he squeezed my side a little too hard. Noticing my cringe, he backed off. "Sorry."

"So what's the plan, Doc?" I asked. "I need to get out of here."

"What's the rush?"

"I have no chance of answering that in a way that will get me out of a complete psych eval."

He smiled as he pulled my gown back down. "Try me."

I thought for a moment before I answered. "Sometimes I think if failure were personified and showed up in this room to choke the life out of me, I'd spend my last breath trying to gouge its eyes out."

His smile was warm. "That seems reasonable. You said *sometimes.* What about the other times?"

"Sometimes I just want to go home."

"I can help with that," Admiral Kegar's accented voice said from the doorway. "Doctor, will you excuse us for a moment? I need a word with Miss Mackenzie."

"Of course, sir." The doctor disappeared into the hallway, sensing the need to close the door behind him and hurry to do so.

"Please don't sit up, Allison." Kegar stepped near the head of my bed, close enough to reach out and touch. "How are you doing?"

"Honestly, I haven't been having a good week, sir."

"We'll get to that." He scratched his head while he took an extra deep breath. "Are you okay?"

"Bad headache and sore ribs. I'll be all right."

"I'm glad to hear that. Have you had any contact with your family?" He reached forward, and I thought he was going to take my hand in his. The scene decelerated to slow motion, but then he caught himself and pulled back.

I took a deep breath, pushed that pain back into the closet, and blocked the door. "I haven't had time to work on that, sir."

"Allison, perhaps it's best that you take some time to deal with this. You're completely within your rights to take leave for bereavement. No one will think any less of you for it."

"I have a strong feeling my dad was the one who died, sir. I loved him, but I lost him when he had his stroke, really. I've come to terms with that." I took a deep breath, not sure I was feeling the commitment of my words. "I have work to do. He'd respect me standing to it."

His response was quick. "Are you sure I can't convince you to take some time?"

I nodded.

Firmness filled his eyes and then his voice in equal measure. "I confirmed the design spec of the power conduit in your report. While it's deep-scanned during the repair or complex overhaul cycle, the conduit is visually inspected during every dockside incremental availability. The last was six years ago, and there were no indications of any kind that a failure was even a possibility. As such, your assessment that the most likely cause was sabotage seems correct, as far as I can see. The fact that you've allowed a saboteur aboard *Ticonderoga* seems to be self-evident."

"Allowed? That sounds like an accusation, sir."

"Section seventeen of the UPE Code of Defensive Forces Justice indicates the commanding officer is ultimately responsible for the acts of any below them in their chain of command."

I choked on the intake of breath that pushed my lungs too far. "I would have been killed myself. It doesn't make any sense to accuse me of letting it happen."

Kegar shrugged. "Who do you hold responsible for the condition of a Tomcat once it's airborne?"

"The pilot's responsibility is to make sure their craft is safe and ready to fly, insofar as the inspection criteria are feasible."

"The maximum range of a Tomcat should have been 125 percent of the distance yours traveled today, Allison. Again, I've done some checking—access to the fuel level display calibration is four security levels deep. The system also has a redundant backup. Someone would have had to hack through eight levels of security to recalibrate the gauges causing a false reading to display. Isn't it easier to believe you didn't check the fuel level before you took off?"

Grasping to fit the pieces of my enemy together, I retorted, "The Consortium formed over a hundred years ago. We've been scuffling with them over borders since before then, if you count pre-UPE times. You don't think it's possible they might have finally decided to try something new?"

He shook his head. "Not really, no. Are you familiar with Occam's razor?"

"Paraphrased, it says the most likely explanation is the best one."

"Under that basis, is it more likely that the Oriental Ore Consortium staged an elaborate accident to kill you or that you've overlooked a simple task requirement and caused the death of a crew member under your command?"

"And the battleball incident?"

He shrugged again. "While it's tempting to believe it's connected, our trajectories to and from Alpha Station are relatively predictable. I admit, that incident does not stand out of the ordinary on the surface."

Anger swelled next to my ribs. "So you're saying I'm not completely incompetent?"

"Can you assure me no member of your crew fed your location to the OOC to facilitate the attack?"

"That's a foolish question."

"Is it? Is it so far outside of the realm of possibility that someone is working as an agent for an enemy power aboard *Ticonderoga*? Removing *Ticonderoga* from the global playing field would undoubtedly shift the power dynamic on a planetary scale. While it might be one person's goal, I won't allow that eventuality to be realized."

"What does this mean? I'm to face disciplinary action?" I asked, heart hammering.

"I have no confidence that discipline would be beneficial under these circumstances."

My first meeting with Kegar was when I was floated as a candidate to replace Captain Torres as *Ticonderoga*'s CO. I was a scared kid, and he was as supportive then as he had been every step of the way since my confirmation.

Until now.

"You're pulling my ticket?"

He nodded. "One day, you'll understand this was the right thing to do, Allison. You might even approve, once you have the chance to take it all in."

"But who has the Senate appointed in my place?"

He no longer met my gaze. "Effective immediately, I'm replacing you as captain of *Ticonderoga*. I'll clean up your mess."

"You can't."

"Given the present state of affairs, I not only can, but I am." He turned to leave and made it two steps before he paused and said over his shoulder, "Go home, Allison. Leave this all behind you."

When my doctor returned, I only had a few words to say, and I repeated them until he complied.

Get me out of here.

~

The military's personnel onboarding efficiency was only surpassed by their ability to egress an officer. They took my rank insignia and military identification when I requested release from the hospital. A set of MPs escorted me to the front gate and left me on my own as soon as I stepped through.

Getting back to, and then into, my apartment was interesting. The actions themselves weren't notable—it wasn't even a hard walk from the base's gate to my home. But I was literally walking away from everything I'd come to know in the past nineteen years. I had come to identify as a member of Space Command Defensive Forces. For the first moment in a long time, I was just Allison Mackenzie.

The cantankerous old building manager made it abundantly clear he couldn't have cared less who I was. As far as he was concerned, I was nothing more than an inconvenience around dinnertime and wasn't afraid to treat me as such. After a flurry of questions and a forceful admonition that I should be more careful not to get myself locked out in the future, he decided that, given the circumstances, he could justify opening the door for me this one time.

Once I finally got through my otherwise nondescript front door, I took a deep breath and felt a little better. I had always known my career could end badly, but once I was appointed to command *Ticonderoga*, I knew making the wrong enemy would be even easier—and riskier. Few people on Earth didn't know of *Ticonderoga* or her captain.

In the entryway, I hesitated, unable to decide whether to start with my com terminal or my bedroom closet. I wanted to find out about my mother and father, but I needed to get off the radar and assess the situation. Recent events indicated that whoever was coming after me wasn't afraid to go through my family to get to me. As such, I probably needed to distance myself from the career I had dedicated my life to building and worry about myself for a while.

But why would anyone come after me? What had I done?

The lack of an answer reaffirmed my conclusion that I needed to hide so I could safely stop and think.

Time to disappear.

I didn't dally on my way to the bedroom closet. Hidden behind the half-filled shoe rack, the black canvas backpack was as far out of the way as I could make it without being completely inaccessible. As soon as I had my hand around the straps, I felt a little better. Straining against my wounds to lift it from its hiding place, I breathed a sigh of relief.

The bag held two civilian IDs that weren't entirely legal. One picture showed my hair as its natural blonde color while the other showed me with artificially colored raven black hair and glasses. The necessary hair dye and glasses were present, as well as a sizable amount of currency, pre-funded and disposable credit cards, toiletries, several sets of clothes, and an as-of-yet unused personal com unit. An off-the-books nine-millimeter semiautomatic pistol with two extra clips was hidden at the bottom of the bag.

I snatched the bottle of dye and hurried to the bathroom. Stopping for only a moment to say goodbye to my hair, which I dearly loved, I altered my appearance. It took a while, but after I pinned and capped my much shorter and darker hair, I stepped into the warmth of a steamy shower.

The whole breaking down and crying thing wasn't my speed, but propping myself against the wall in the hot spray allowed me to clear my mind. I stayed there for a long time, unmoving.

Unexplained damage to *Ticonderoga*.

An OOC sentry attack.

Fire at my parents' farm.

Sabotage to my Tomcat.

The only person who had the kind of access necessary to orchestrate all those things was Admiral Kegar. But he was my friend and mentor. I couldn't believe . . .

And now he had my ship.

But I was powerless to do anything about it since he had pulled my commission. So then what?

If my dad was the one killed in the fire at home, which made the most sense, then finding my mother and protecting her was my priority. Anything else could wait.

Well, everything can wait for a bit.

The warmth of the water made the bruise on my ribs feel better. My headache had eased—it all allowed my mind to focus.

It was about me.

Kegar had attacked me personally and professionally to get me out of the way so he could fill the void. The position as captain of *Ticonderoga* required unanimous appointment by the UPE Congress, which wasn't a particularly easy feat to achieve.

My relative inexperience helped in that regard. I had good academic references and hadn't been active in the military long enough to make any notable enemies. Kegar, on the other side, had worked his way up through the ranks and was never afraid to step on people along the way. His list of enemies was long. It didn't take a genius to figure out he'd never be appointed to command *Ticonderoga* because he was too controversial.

But whoever controlled *Ticonderoga* had the ability to control global politics.

Now that was him.

And I couldn't do a thing about it.

So . . . I cried.

I didn't mean for it to happen, and I didn't know why it did, specifically. But it wouldn't stop once it started. I sank to the floor and hoped the water's heat would wash it away. My mind wandered through it all, around and around, back and forth. Somewhere in the midst, an image formed of me lying naked on the floor of the shower, crying and getting water up my nose.

It made me laugh. Well, snort. Whatever it was, it certainly wasn't ladylike. Or authoritative. But I couldn't take it back. My captain's voice rang in my head.

Get the fuck off the floor.

Determination replaced the laughter. Naively, perhaps, I assumed I'd experienced the last stop on a rollercoaster of emotions. I stood up and started soaping and lathering, cleaning and inspecting. A little battered and bruised, I was still in one piece.

CHAPTER 5

20 MAY 2126

After drying off, I worked lotion into the multiple damaged spots on my skin. The lotion had a topical repair accelerant. Small cuts and bruises would heal a little quicker with its use, and I felt a bit better as I dug in my dresser until I found underwear that wasn't UPE issue.

Passing by anything black, I finally chose a set of dusty-pink barely there panties and bra, far from the confining black underwear I was used to. What fabric there was felt fresh and new against my skin, and I spun once in front of the mirror, inspecting the changes.

A strange civilian looked back at me. I added the glasses to assess the change.

Except for the bruise, I looked good.

I was about to step into the kitchen and find some food when three hard knocks thundered from the front door. "Allison Mackenzie! By order of UPE Security, open the door! Now!"

The voice was familiar.

"I'm coming!" I shouted back, lunging for the gun in my go bag and throwing on a cap to contain my dyed hair. My personal experiences had taught me that keeping security division personnel waiting for too long wasn't a good idea. "Don't break it down!"

Peering through the peephole, I saw two security officers standing in front of Admiral Coleman West, a CO I had served under when I was just out of the academy. He had been a great influence early in my career. He couldn't possibly be wrapped up in Admiral Kegar's grab for power, could he?

Only one way to find out.

Stashing my gun in a drawer within easy reach, I opened the door and did the best I could to try to own my appearance. "Admiral Kegar suspended my commission, boys. I'm not in the service anymore."

Unlike the expressionless guards, West looked a little shocked as he stepped between the burly men. "I know we haven't worked together for a while, Captain, but I'm here to bring you back. We have a problem."

"With all due respect, Admiral, *you* have a problem. I have a life to get on with."

"Cap . . . Allison, could we please talk for a minute? I know I can't force you, but I think you'll want to hear what I have to say."

I looked straight through him while my past and imagined future flashed by. I didn't like how the latter played out. Grudgingly, I said, "Come on in, sir."

The security guys stepped forward, but West said, "I think it's safe to say she's not packing a weapon, gentlemen. I'll be fine."

I tucked a lock of black hair back into my cap, grateful that the security guys were professional enough to pretend to be undistracted by my underpants. They turned their backs to my door and stood at attention as the admiral stepped inside.

"Let me grab a shirt, sir," I said once the door was closed. "Have a seat."

His boots scuffed the kitchen floor as I ducked into my bedroom. He raised his voice a bit. "I feel bad I didn't keep in touch with you better, Allison. I hate to say hello this way."

I laughed as I pulled a long, gray knit sweater dress over my head. "I hate to say hello this way too, sir. Talk about getting caught with your pants down."

"You'd look even better in a uniform."

I crossed my arms behind my back as I returned to stand next to him, looking at the framed family pictures on the wall of the short hallway. "It's not appropriate anymore. I've heard this is how civilians dress around bedtime."

"I can make it appropriate again. Kegar exceeded his authority when he pulled your ticket."

"I think he had my dad killed." It was the first time I had said the words, and somehow, I knew them to be true. "I don't know if my mother is even still alive. Maybe he gave me an out. I have business to see to."

"I have no doubt he's done you some wrongs, but I'm not sure he's after your family, Allison. *Ticonderoga* broke orbit and headed toward Alpha Station. They're not communicating. I think he intends to hurt more people."

"Oh no."

"It gets worse," West said. "Can I continue?"

I gestured to the couch and then, once he was seated, sat in the chair across from him with my bare legs folded beneath me. "Of course, sir."

"What's gone on wasn't completely unforeseen. I've just left an intelligence briefing where it was made clear to me that Admiral Kegar has been acting erratically for some time now. They're still trying to crack fully into his messages, but it appears he's been communicating with the Oriental Ore Consortium regularly and on an unauthorized basis."

"Why would he do that?"

West took a deep breath. "Allison, this is need-to-know information. Before I say anything else, I need your personal word that what I'm about to say will go no further than you."

"You have it, sir. Always."

"The Consortium applied for UPE membership. They did so with two caveats from the beginning. Military sovereignty was to be allowed and continued planetside mining of precious metals."

"That's against most everything the UPE is about. Why would they even bother?"

"Presumably, they wanted access to the UPE's humanitarian arm. Famine has been an issue for a long time, but the OOC hasn't placed the necessary emphasis on agricultural production to compensate. They knew we could help but were unwilling to give up their perceived security to get it. Admiral Kegar reacted badly when he found out. He believed we should consider their application in the name of planetary unity."

"I don't get it. The income from their portion of the off-world mining operation would have offset anything they could have accomplished on their own with a fraction of the environmental damage. Military issues were much the same. Why wouldn't they accept that?"

"Pride," West said definitively. "We haven't evolved to the point where it's stopped getting us in trouble as a species."

Suddenly glad I was no longer required to muddle through such convolutions, I simply shrugged. "I've only reported to him for a little over a year, but I'm told he has always walked the edge."

"We think he's fallen off it." West's features deepened with concern.

"We?"

He nodded. "I've been tasked with bringing him in."

"Sir . . ."

"At the very least, he's committed piracy by taking your ship, Allison. Conspiracy to commit that crime is almost a given, and murder is a strong possibility. He's a senior command officer. This must be addressed without mercy for the sake of the UPE organization. This can't—in any way, shape, or form—be seen as acceptable."

"How was this allowed to happen, sir? You know where I got buffaloed, but how was the entire system fooled into letting him take *Ticonderoga*?"

"Enough rank brings fewer questions. Marines generally take that to an even higher level for a trusted commander. We believe he leveraged his relationships within the Marines hierarchy to provide the logistical backing he needed to pull it off."

I didn't need to be reminded that *Ticonderoga*'s jarheads were a pack of wolves on a thin rope.

West jumped back to the point of his visit. "If patriotism won't convince you to come back, how about good old-fashioned revenge?"

"That doesn't sound like you, sir."

"I didn't teach you all my tricks. If pure hatred is all you have, you use it until something better comes along." When I didn't answer, he added, "We'll find your mother, and uncover what happened to your dad, Allison. More appropriate resources can be dedicated to that investigation, but I need you out there."

My own personal feelings aside, I knew he was right about my family issues. Once I'd worked through his words, I was down to understanding the intent. "You want me to kill him?"

"Officially, he needs to be stopped. Unofficially, at best, a court-martial would be . . . inconvenient."

"But how will we get to *Tico*, sir? It seems I left the keys to my interplanetary cruiser in my other pants, sir."

"I accept that." He smiled. "I have an idea. It's far from conventional. In fact, I'm not sure anyone in their right mind would try what I'm intending, but I think we might be able to get out of this."

I raised an eyebrow. Unconventional? I liked the sound of that. I liked it a lot.

CHAPTER 6

21 MAY 2126

I wore a dark blue dress to the briefing, the only thing I had that was professional but not military—a lot like me right now. I glanced down at the shiny security badge clipped precariously to the navy fabric and expected to see my own picture, not *consultant* printed in big red letters.

Fifteen minutes early, the briefing room was already packed. I had hoped to disappear into a corner and sink into the relative camouflage my lack of uniform, changed hair color, and nondescript ID should have provided, but even in the crowded room, I was immediately recognized—and welcomed. I had a feeling they'd been there for hours, discussing my fitness to carry out their proposed mission.

I knew little of most of these people. Nonetheless, they asked after my family and expressed concern about my health and hope that I'd choose to accept reinstatement.

It felt okay.

Admiral West was the only person who seemed to avoid me. It made me a little uncomfortable since he was the only person I truly knew and wanted to speak to, but I realized he was more than likely getting his thoughts together. Perhaps he was trying to appear impartial. Whatever the case, I found a seat near the back of the room as the lights dimmed. The main projection screen flashed on, leaving me with the impression I was about to watch a movie instead of a mission briefing.

"Allison," the man next to me whispered in my ear, "my name is William Moore. I trained with your father after we enlisted. I'm sorry for what you've gone through. He was a great person."

"Thank you, sir," I whispered back. Two gold stars sparkled on his shoulders, and moisture glistened in his eyes. I reached for his hand and patted it. He wrapped his gnarled fingers over mine for a brief moment—his grip told me there was more to the story.

Admiral West acknowledged the display behind him as he spoke. "We received a communication from *Ticonderoga* at 0400 hours before she broke orbit under the command of former Admiral Vergé Kegar. Put succinctly, he has claimed all extraplanetary assets for the Oriental Ore Consortium. Obviously, this places us on a wartime alert status."

Rumblings of surprise. I might have been shocked too if Admiral West hadn't visited me last night. Looking at the situation now, it was a logical turn of events.

"We have nothing to fight your war with, admiral." A hidden voice spoke from the crowd.

West pressed a remote and the display changed to show the moon. The perspective rotated to the backside of the planetoid, focused on a particular crater, and zoomed in until the image became a computer-enhanced representation of a ship.

"Pre-UPE, the United States built and designated this *CSX-01*, which inadvertently served as a test article for the Ticonderoga Project. She is complete and spaceworthy, but due to issues found in the early test phase, as well as UPE treaty stipulations, she was never activated. We believe Kegar is busy enough consolidating Alpha Station and the related transport vehicles that he hasn't gotten around to CSX-01 yet. He might not even be aware of her existence, as the ship was designed in a black program using research reappropriated from the original Ticonderoga Project design team. We can retrieve the ship and mount a resistance if we move quickly enough."

Another voice from the crowd laughed heartily. "You can't be serious. You want to pull that out of mothballs and put it up against *Ticonderoga*? The most powerful ship ever designed?"

I leaned forward in my seat involuntarily.

"Our research indicates that *Ticonderoga* isn't the more powerful of the two. This vessel was designed as a straight-up warship. There were no concessions made in the name of science." Admiral West continued unfazed, "From the information we have, the ship is operable. The instability in the drive system should be manageable, providing system output is kept below 73 percent. It was equipped with weapons and a large supply of emergency rations when it was placed into operationally ready storage. A wing of Thunderstrike attack fighters is also aboard, as they were retired at the same time. If we can get a capable crew to man it while *Ticonderoga* is otherwise occupied, we have a chance."

"And if we can't?"

"General Morse, isn't it?" West asked.

"Yes, Admiral. I believe you knew that."

"I also knew you were a strong supporter of Admiral Kegar. Further, I know you were passed over for my command of Lunar Station One, General. Your conventional forces will be the next to confront *Ticonderoga* if she can't be stopped or reclaimed. These facts on the table, I ask you—impartially, of course—if you have a better idea."

Morse didn't answer.

"People, *Ticonderoga* enforced the peace. She did it because of UPE control—not because that's all she was capable of. We don't have control anymore. So who will go to stop *Ticonderoga*?"

"I'll go," I said spontaneously.

Morse stood as well, and after a glance to both sides, he left the room.

"Maybe we're not saving the world, but I guarantee you we're saving *our* world, people. Anyone else want to walk out?" West asked.

✣

The group had thinned to a semblance of a command team over the past several hours. A few might have left due to apathy but most had set about tasks to get the operation underway.

One young man had been acting as liaison between our team and Defensive Forces Operations all day long. He'd been in and out of our meeting room constantly, but I hadn't managed to catch his name. "Airframe Maintenance and Regeneration Group reports they can have the last two Thunderstrikes available by morning, sir. They're being pulled out of storage right now."

"Send orders to transport *Starliner* to Davis-Monthan as well. It only makes sense to stage there if that's where the fighter screen will originate," Admiral West said. "Crew status?"

"Except a few key positions, we haven't had a problem acquiring a crew for the ship," a woman with commander's bars said. "What are we going to call it, anyway?"

"Call what?" West asked.

"It's bad luck to send a ship out without a name, sir. CSX-01 is a designation, not a name."

West looked frustrated at the distraction. "Do you have a suggestion, Commander—?"

"Boone, sir. UPE Logistics."

Admiral West waited impatiently.

"How about *Lexington*?"

"We'll have to christen her another day, but that sounds fine," West said with a wistful smile. "What were you saying about crew issues?"

"We're short on pilots for the fighter wing. Most of the qualified pilots are still aboard *Ticonderoga*."

"How many are you short?"

"At least two, sir."

"I'll fly," I said. "I have more experience in the Thunderstrike airframe than I do with Tomcats anyway."

"Allison, you can't fly in the air wing and command the mission," West said.

"So come with us," I said. "You command the mission, and I'll take care of the fighter wing."

"You don't want an old dog like me in charge."

"Kegar doesn't know you, sir. It will be an advantage."

West laughed. "Oh, he knows me, Captain."

The silence was long enough to become uncomfortable. "Help me kick his ass, sir. I can't take him on alone again."

"Fair enough, Captain. But we still need another pilot."

I thought for a moment before I said anything. Edgar Stratford had saved my life once. He was a jack-of-all-trades, doubling in special forces as well as being one hell of a pilot. "I know a guy, but you'll have to help me get him out of the clink."

"What's he in for?"

"He accidentally killed a guy that was beating his wife. He's good, sir. Better than me."

"It looks like we have a plan," West said, thumping his hands down on the podium. "The last bus leaves Davis–Monthan tomorrow morning at 0500 hours. Make it happen, people."

~

Since I was only able to see the back of a man's head and an orange jumpsuit on the cot in the cell, I used the nickname that was sure to confirm I had the right guy. "Stratford-upon-Avon."

"Lieutenant Allison Jane Mackenzie." Not even his English lilt smiled as he slowly turned to face me through the bars of his cell.

"It's *captain* now."

"Captains have ships. Rumor has it yours got grabbed while your back was turned."

"True," I said. "Rumor has it the same guy that grabbed my ship offered you up to satisfy some nonsense political bullshit when you defended the poor girl in the apartment next door from her overprivileged, useless asshole husband."

He shrugged. "I did commit murder."

"True, but the guy deserved it."

"How do you know?"

"Because I know you," I said firmly. "Listen, Edgar. It's always fun to spar with you, but I don't have the time. I need you to ExO a mission."

"Okay." He nodded.

"You—"

"Don't care what it is," he interrupted.

"Good enough." I turned to the guard. "Lose the shackles. We're short on time."

The guard immediately opened the cell and did as he was told. He then extended his hand to Stratford. "I always knew this day would come, Strat. Best wishes."

Stratford smiled and clasped the hand. "You're a good bloke, Willy."

"Well, c'mon then," Willy said.

Swiftly and efficiently, the guard led us through the maze of passageways, locked doors, and security checkpoints that eventually spat us into cool night air. A UPE atmospheric shuttle's droning engine was all that broke the stillness. It struck me how easily such a moment came to Stratford, who once again thanked Willy for his friendship and casually stepped into the shuttle.

We were halfway to Arizona before he spoke again. "You never asked, Allie."

"I never needed to, Strat. I knew you did the right thing. What needed to be done."

"So?"

"Do you really need to ask, Strat? I may have a few more stripes, but I haven't changed that much."

"That's true." Stratford laughed.

I was tired, and my ribs weren't the only thing that still stung since Kegar's betrayal. I wasn't in the mood for games, so it made me more than a little defensive. "What do you mean by that?"

"I'll never forget the look on your face the night I came to get you in Atlanta. You looked like you'd lost all hope and would do anything to get a little back."

I stared down at my knotted fingers and the shuttle's deck plate, remembering things I would have preferred to forget.

"The fire in your eyes was pretty weak when you came to see me in the hoosegow now and again. But the old look was back today—the one that said you'd do what needed doing to get the job done, as long as someone would stand beside you. So yeah, I'm taking your wing."

"He beat me, Strat."

"Not yet he hasn't," Stratford said. "Maybe the first round went to the bad guys, but we're just getting started."

"He stole my goddamn ship. He killed my family. How can I beat him?"

"First off, you can't, but you know that," Stratford said. "*We*, however, can. And you know how. We just have to do what we always do."

"Only one choice."

Stratford nodded. "Give everything."

~

Visiting officer's quarters at AMARG resembled a small hotel room like what would be found on any other United Planet Earth military facility. When I stepped back into the sleeping area wrapped in a towel, I found myself staring at my dress, which hung next to the crisp captain's uniform I'd drawn from the quartermaster.

I was scared.

Civilian life was alluring. Seeing my apartment, wearing actual clothes, and accepting even for a second that I had a personality of my own and the freedom to express it . . . how silly and shallow was it to miss wearing pretty underwear and going where I wanted when I wanted? Regardless of what I chose, I was leaving something great behind.

Of course, I'd felt the same after Admiral Kegar stripped my commission.

I lost track of how long I stood there before I let the towel drop and slipped between the scratchy sheets of the bed. So different from the pillow-top king-size bed in my apartment, but it felt more familiar.

Odd.

My wet hair was going to be unruly in the morning, but I didn't care. I fell straight into a deep sleep and dreamed.

✣

"I'm not the terrorist you believe me to be, Allison," Admiral Kegar explained calmly. He sat behind the ornate desk with the confidence of a bad guy from an ancient spy movie. A jade frog about the size of my fist stared at me from its place on the left corner of the dark wood surface, unblinking like Kegar himself.

"How do you figure?" I scoffed.

He straightened the model of *Ticonderoga* on the front right corner of his desk, orienting it so it was pointed exactly at the frog. "What would you say if I told you the Oriental Ore Consortium applied for acceptance to the United Planet Earth but was turned down?"

"I'd say you're lying. Global peace is the entire mandate of the organization. If it did happen, there had to be a reason."

"Of course there was," Kegar said flatly. "Every great force for good needs an enemy."

"That doesn't make any sense. To be accepted, they'd turn their entire military over to UPE Command. The Consortium wouldn't be an enemy anymore."

"And that's why they weren't accepted, Allison. Think about it for a second. You'll stumble over it."

"Admiral, with all due respect, this isn't some political thriller written for the big screen. This is reality. It's a day-to-day grind where we do our part to help the world become a more peaceful place—the place it wants to be."

"And you don't think some people want to stop that?"

"Of course they do, but that's why we're here."

"You're not seeing my point, Captain."

"Why would anyone drag this out? Why would anyone derail global peace?"

"Let me put it in simple terms, Allison. Where would you go if the Ticonderoga Project ended? What would you do?"

"I'd go home, sir. My family needs my help."

"Most of the other officers in the Defensive Forces Command don't have families, Allison. Eighty-seven percent of the personnel ranked colonel or higher are not in any sort of a relationship—familial or romantic. Their life is the job—literally. And the job requires an enemy."

I shook my head in disbelief. "The implications of this . . . my God, sir . . . if what you're saying is true, you'll completely undercut the UPE's foundations."

"I'm not undercutting anything, Allison. They—the parties that pick a fight where there is only peace to be found—are the ones who undercut our United Planet Earth."

"I won't . . . I can't take this at your word, sir."

"You disappoint me, Allison."

"I made a vow to support the UPE's doctrine, sir. I won't betray that on one man's word, even yours."

"But you'll consider them."

"Now you're disappointing me, sir. You know I consider everything."

"I'd expect no less, Allison."

CHAPTER 7

22 MAY 2126

I hadn't seen daybreak through the canopy of a fighter in a long time. And through a Thunderstrike's canopy? Even longer.

"Do you even remember where the throttle is in that thing?" Stratford asked over the com.

"It's the red lever here by my right hip, isn't it?" I asked, feigning innocence.

"That'd be the eject lever, ma'am."

I smiled despite myself. "You take the lead, Thunder One. I have *Starliner*'s six."

"Roger that, Two." The whine was like music as the high-mounted engines of Stratford's awkward little fighter spun up. "Thunder One rolling."

"*Starliner* rolling," a nervous voice said over the com as the fighter's opposite pulled onto the runway. With her elongated body, engines integrated into swept-back wings, and tall stance on fragile landing gear, *Starliner* looked like flight personified in a mixture of carbon fiber and titanium. She lifted into the air and climbed in the blink of an eye.

My turn.

"Thunder Two is zone four," I said as I pushed my own throttle forward and felt it lock into the maximum power stop. My own departure didn't look nearly as smooth as the others. From my perspective, it vibrated viciously under screaming engines.

It felt awesome.

"You all right back there?" Stratford asked.

"Two is airborne," I said into the pickup. I retracted the landing gear before I added, "It's been a while since I've done a rolling takeoff."

"Those fancy Tomcats have spoiled you, haven't they?"

"I wouldn't say *spoiled*," I said. "I just got used to vertical departure."

"Horsepower shouldn't be wasted like that."

"Maybe not, but it looks cool." I beamed, enjoying moments both present and remembered. "Do you have the hydrazine station navs locked in?"

"Roger."

"We need to be in and out lickety-split. The clock's running."

"You talk too much when you're nervous."

"Roger that." I tried to get comfortable in the Thunderstrike's marginal excuse for a pilot's seat. The last time I'd sat in one, it had saved my life, but I pushed that particular flashback into memory for a better time.

We had to assume Admiral Kegar had other eyes within the UPE. With those eyes, he would figure out what we were up to and move to stop us. Stratford and I could hold off a battleball or two, or perhaps even a Tomcat, but we wouldn't have a chance against *Tico* if she came down on us before we got *Lexington* up and moving.

Even then, it would be a push at best.

"Strat, take the boom first. I'll fly cover."

"Roger."

Ticonderoga was headed out to the asteroid belt, or so we believed, so anything the Consortium threw at us in the short term would launch from the planet. I slid my fighter into position a good distance below the fuel station, maneuvered the nose toward the planet, then watched and waited.

Unfortunately, it didn't take long.

I snapped the throttle forward as soon as I spotted the glimmer of thruster exhaust in the corner of my eye. The Thunderstrike's threat sensors alerted as I thumped the com. "Thunder Two is engaging."

"How many?" Stratford asked.

"One on the scanner. I have it."

"Hang tight. I'll back you up," Stratford said.

"Negative. Stay with *Starliner*. Get out of here as soon as she's fueled."

"If there's a second—"

"Dammit, Strat—I've got it. Stay on mission."

"Roger that."

The balance of power had inverted since the last time I'd operated with Strat. Having rank over him was new, and it threw us off. Even *Starliner* didn't have the speed to run from a drone directly. I needed him to make as much room as possible between our people and the threat.

I lost my visual during the short argument, so I only had the bogey on my scanner and targeting displays. Whatever was out there, we'd be closing at unthinkable speed. I didn't have time to be wrong. I toggled the concussor weapons control to auto-range and confirmed the system was armed. I'd hit the little bastard on the first pass with a little luck, but . . .

Luck hadn't exactly been falling my way lately.

I pulled the trigger just before the indicator changed to green on the targeting display. Concussor rounds exploded into a cloud of debris. If the primary impact failed, closer proximity to the target would make secondary damage more likely.

I felt a trickle of satisfaction after the threat indication disappeared from my scanner, only to lose it a heartbeat later as my Thunderstrike shook from the battleball's weapons fire.

Instinct took over, and I heaved back on the stick with the trigger pulled again.

Ideally, the sentry wouldn't have been quite so close when it exploded, but I wasn't in a position to be picky.

The shock wave knocked my Thunderstrike into an intestine-wrenching head-over-teacup roll.

Stratford's shouting voice over the com replaced the ringing in my ears. "Allison? Thunder Two, respond!"

"I would if you'd let me get a word in sideways," I mumbled into the radio pickup. I fought a tsunami of vertigo and the stick as I brought my bird back under control.

"You all right, Two?" Stratford snapped again.

I gulped back a foul taste in my mouth.

That was close.

"Fine."

"I'm coming back for you."

"Stop arguing, One. Target eliminated, and I'll catch up," I said. A half dozen different alarms started blaring, drowning me out as I added, "I hope."

"Allison, you can't take anyone on in your condition."

"*Starliner* can't defend itself either, Commander," I said, then forced myself to soften. "I'll be all right, Strat. Keep those people safe. I'll see you when I get there."

Somehow, the com channel's silence was all the more glaring with the cacophony of alarms blaring.

The autopilot wouldn't engage due to the flight instability caused by the damage, so I kept one hand on the stick, guiding my bird manually back to the hydrazine station for fuel. I waded into the computer input with my free hand, trying to clear what alarms I could. Things didn't look too bad, but I needed to hit the hydrazine boom on the first try.

I was way low on gas.

With my mind on my problems, I was caught completely off guard when the com crackled back to life and Admiral Kegar appeared on the primary display.

Inside job, indeed. How the hell had he gotten this short-range com frequency?

"Say it, Vergé. I'm a little busy here."

"So I've been told. I knew it would be you out there, Allie."

My insides flashed into a blaze of hatred. "Spit it out or shut it off." As if to emphasize the criticality of my situation, a fresh and distinctly ominous fuel warning started hollering.

"Do a one-four-alpha override."

"I know the drill, Admiral." *Shit.* I didn't mean to call him that. I executed the sequence on the primary system interface and was rewarded. Fuel transferred from the landing reserve and silence fell in the cockpit.

"The recent stream of events has more behind it than you know, Allison. I'd like you to understand. I'd like you to join us."

"How many?"

"How many what, Allison?"

"How many bloodstains on *Ticonderoga*'s deck plates?"

I finally managed to slide my Thunderstrike into the refueling terminal. The fuel arm swung into place after I tapped in a sequence on the system interface. Umbilicals followed to refurbish the atmospherics and power.

"Not as many as you may think."

"Because you made sure you put people loyal to your cause in my command."

"Yes, I did. I thought you were one of them."

"I'm loyal to the UPE's ideals, Vergé."

"So am I! You can't believe I wanted this. This wouldn't have been necessary if the UPE was the organization it pretended to be."

"That's ridiculous."

"It is also true."

"Nice. You conveniently omitted that you tried to have me killed."

"That decision hurt, Allison. I thought, in the end, it would be the best way to achieve the outcome we needed. We had to protect the many, even if it came at the expense of a few like you."

"The fact you would combine that principle with that course of action proves you've lost your damned mind."

"Perhaps," Kegar said as he motioned to someone offscreen. Bound and gagged, Tom Hayes appeared in the frame a moment later. Whoever pushed him into the camera's view also handed Kegar a simple black handgun. "The good commander is one of the people now aboard *Ticonderoga* who doesn't see things the way I do. You can save him, and many more, if you join me."

"I will never join you."

Kegar shot Tom in the head. He didn't even watch the body crumple to the deck.

I gaped.

"Allison, because of your decision today, his blood now stains the deck plates. I'll call you again tomorrow, and we'll see if you're ready to look at the situation objectively. I'd hate to have to take another ship from you."

Blackness fell across the screen and my heart.

With full tanks and shaking hands, I backed away from the fueling port and entered a course to the moon. Pushing the throttles forward was the biggest challenge. The otherwise simple act of moving the control lever into the thrust detent was a small representation of the decision I faced.

Who was I loyal to? My people on *Ticonderoga*? Or everyone else in the UPE and in the known world?

I pointed my Thunderstrike's nose toward *Lexington*.

Once I was underway at top speed, I engaged the autopilot. As soon as I took my hands off the controls, I lost my composure. But crying in a helmet and pressure suit could be deadly, as there was no way to clean debris off or out once it started floating around between your eyes and the faceplate. So I wouldn't allow it to happen.

Reflexively, I tensed, physically fighting against the hurricane of emotions as my mind replayed Kegar's trigger pull and Tom's fall. What little rational self I still had eventually managed to shout around the maelstrom in my heart, and I grabbed hold of it like a lifeline once I finally realized its truth.

Kegar had first tried to remove me, and now he wanted me to join him. If that was true, what was he doing heading all the way out to Alpha Station? Whatever his reasons, and whatever more he had planned, I knew that was an opportunity to work the problem.

Sometimes opportunities were scant, but there was always a way out. I gave a silent word of thanks to my dad for one of his favorite lessons.

Inhale. Exhale. Get up and finish the job.

I felt no thirst for revenge—no need for blood. Only determination to see one more day, and to make sure no more people died on the altar of Kegar's arrogance.

There is always hope.

As strange as it sounded, the moon felt familiar. I'd spent a good portion of my career there in one capacity or another, and being back in a Thunderstrike, reporting to Admiral West, even feeling uncertainty and a little fear . . . I'd survived it all once before, so I drew strength from it. Déjà vu pulsed in my mind as I topped the rim of the last crater and found *Lexington* at her storage dock.

What I could see of her looked strong.

"*Lexington* control to Thunder Two. How do you read?"

"Lima Charlie, *Lexington*."

"Stand by for docking instructions, Two."

"*Lexington* control, request you advise CO hostiles are inbound," I said into the pickup.

They're going to think I've lost my mind.

Admiral West's voice replaced the unfamiliar com officer's. "How do you know, Two?"

"I destroyed a battleball and got a call before I broke high orbit. Kegar knows we're up to something. It won't be hard for him to figure out where I've gone."

If he hasn't already.

"Our intel indicated *Ticonderoga* is heading to Alpha Station," West said.

"Trust me, he's coming."

"Clear the umbilicals!" West snapped at someone. "It's time to ride out. Send the navs for landing to Thunder Two."

The proximity warning on my console's threat display sounded. It was too large to be another battleball—oh no. *Tico.* "Inbound confirmed, *Lexington.*"

"Go slow them down, Allison. We need more time."

I heeled the stick over and flung my bird around in a stomach-churning lateral spin. "Roger that. Can you send me some help?"

"Negative. The flight deck lifts aren't online. We're working on the problem, but we can't get anything into the launch air locks now. You're on your own."

"Roger that. Thunder Two has a go. Out."

Far from sure about what I was going to do, I centered the threat on my targeting display and pushed the throttle to zone four.

Ninety-three seconds to figure out my next move.

My best option was attacking head-on, straight over the dorsal midline. The primary landing bay, plasma cannon, braking engines, and sensor suite were all mounted along the midline of the ship, so concussor coverage was relatively scarce. *Tico* had one battery just above command I particularly needed to watch out for.

She will get me if I don't get her on my first pass.

Kegar appeared on my com screen again. "What do you hope to accomplish by sacrificing yourself, Allison?"

I hope to accomplish not *sacrificing myself.*

"You wanted me to join you," I said as I pulled the throttles back. "I'm requesting landing clearance."

Maybe he'd drop his guard.

"Eject where you are. We'll pick you up."

So much for that.

"The sentry I took Earthside damaged my control systems. I can't blow the canopy, Admiral."

"Last warning, Captain. Ditch your aircraft."

Close enough . . .

I jammed the throttles back to zone four, simultaneously releasing a set of missiles centered on the concussor on top of *Ticonderoga*'s bow.

I flew through the remnant of the explosion. Debris clattered against my bird as I cut loose my remaining ordnance over the primary sensor suite.

The second round of explosions was impressive—too impressive. I was way too close when my projectiles struck, but I didn't have any choice. The concussor would have cut me to pieces if I'd come in any higher. My Thunderstrike's computer sensed its own impending destruction and ejected me before I went up in the explosion that consumed the little fighter.

Any of my regrets were swallowed with me by the embrace of space while *Ticonderoga* was hopefully wrapped in turmoil below me. Maybe the result of my attack was what I was after, but I wouldn't get any extra points for delivery style. I couldn't do anything other than hope I'd done enough. *Ticonderoga* was now blind.

That should be enough to get her to run and lick her wounds.

✣

My loneliness in the Thunderstrike on the way out here was nothing compared to my experience when I opened my eyes. The ejection seat had blasted me to the minimum safe distance and then counterthrusted so I didn't keep going.

The bumpy ride left me hanging. Literally.

I was pointed away from the moon's surface, so not even the warmth of its face was in my field of vision.

Who will be the first to arrive to pick me up?

The moon base didn't know we were even here, so it would either be rescue from *Lexington* or capture by *Ticonderoga*. That is, if I didn't find the bottom of my dwindling oxygen supply first.

Death was a valid concern.

In that moment, I thought about Tom more than my dad. Maybe the wound was fresher, or maybe I felt like I'd killed him myself. Whatever the case, it hurt worse.

Lexington's presence swelled behind me before I saw her. A humming sensation enveloped my suit, confirmed by a simple flash of light on my outstretched arm shortly after. Scratchy com static followed, and finally, an arm clamped around me as a crewman in an old-style MMU turned me toward the unfamiliar vessel.

I'd only glimpsed *Lexington* on the aborted landing approach. My first real impression of the ship that now held all our hopes was not at all favorable.

Bearing a striking resemblance to a flying shoebox, she was ugly.

We weren't far off the dorsal hull when I realized a series of large, roughly square doors were set in the plating. We were within fifteen feet or so when two of the huge plates parted, sliding outward and creating an opening big enough to hold a Thunderstrike or perhaps even a shuttle. We approached and settled on one. Before the doors closed above us, temporarily swallowing us in complete darkness, the telltale click of my rescuer's magnetic boots engaging comforted me. The floor below us bucked violently before it started slowly dropping.

It's a lift.

Like an old aircraft carrier, the ship raised fighters all the way up to the flight deck to launch them instead of ejecting them out the sides like *Ticonderoga*.

Getting inside was notably slow. My rescuer was the first to remove his helmet. I followed suit and breathed in my first lungful of stale, musty air. Tired though it might have been, that air was more wonderful in every way than any provided by my survival suit. I glanced at the monitor built into my left sleeve and found it blinking red—less than 1 percent survival capability remained.

A grin stretched across Stratford's face. "The nick of time."

"Indeed," I said as the weight of the close call fell on me. I tried to shrug it off as I extended a gloved hand. "Thanks for the save."

"No worries, Allie." As he shook my hand, he sounded as if he'd built his career around plucking women from death in the sky.

Our elevator had dropped to the hangar deck, giving me my first view of the chamber filled with people, crates, aged combat spacecraft, mayhem, and one more thing—hope. Emptiness fled my heart.

A whistle sounded throughout the cavernous space, followed by a voice announcing, "All hands, brace for acceleration."

We were still fifteen or so feet above the hangar deck and dropping slowly on the elevator. Without asking, Strat wrapped his arm around my midsection and again activated the magnetics on his boots.

I was about to take him to task for the unwelcome contact when the ship lurched underneath us. The feeling wasn't unlike riding in my dad's pickup when he popped the clutch. Caught unaware, I would have fallen without the support. Strat pulled his arm away hastily, but the sensation took me a bit to shake off.

Once the elevator was nestled into the hangar deck floor, we stepped forward together to be greeted by a young woman wearing a quartermaster's insignia. "I need to get you to the bridge, Captain."

"Lead the way," I said.

✣

"Permission to come aboard, sir?" I asked, snapping to attention.

"Granted. Welcome to *Lexington*," Admiral West said. He didn't seem to care for the formality as he stopped to wipe the sweat out of his eyes. "You all right?"

"Fine, sir. What's our status?"

"Near as we can tell, we're going after the son of a bitch."

"Do we have anything to work with if we catch him?" I asked.

"Elevators that won't move, rail guns that won't charge, targeting systems that aren't calibrated . . . we may have to open a window and throw rocks at him."

"Shouldn't we lie back and get ready before we take him on again?" I asked. "I know I popped him in the eye, but I got lucky."

"*Ticonderoga* has turned for home, Allison."

"Can we catch him?"

"It's not impossible. Get cleaned up, and then see what you can do to get the squadrons in order."

"Yes, sir," I said, then saluted.

I needed a shower. Even wrapped in my flight suit, I couldn't have been particularly pleasant to smell. It was a simple matter of human physiology—what went in came out, eventually. The MAG, maximum absorbency garment, took care of what it could, but plenty was left for the shower. The same quartermaster was waiting for me in the corridor, this time with a tote bag over her shoulder. She explained along the way that she was leading me to the only working shower on the ship, and, as such, it was coed.

I had no choice, but moreover, I didn't care. I had to get cleaned up. Besides, I didn't mind the idea of someone appreciating my body. We were professionals. More or less, anyway.

Most of my liberal beliefs flew out the air lock when I walked around the corner of the shower wearing nothing but my own dried-on filth and found six-plus feet of Stratford dressed in nothing but his freshly showered, chiseled muscle and a disarming smile.

"I'm glad you're safe, Cap," he said, not missing a step on the way to the locker room.

"Me too." My voice echoed in the empty shower.

"I've an idea to slow down *Tico*."

"What's that?" I looked toward the doorway and found him slipping on a pair of gray briefs.

His look felt appraising. "We leapfrog a Thunderstrike. Launch two and mag-grapple them together. One pushes the load until it's empty, disconnects, and the solo takes a full-burn ride to target. Put a missile in *Tico*'s engine core and let *Lexington* show up to finish the job."

I turned on the shower and went to work soaping and scrubbing. "Kegar doesn't want to attack Earth. He's a patriot—at least he thinks he is."

"He's got a bloody cack-handed way of carrying the flag."

"He is a man of principles, Strat."

"Buggered if I know what they are," he said as he zipped up his uniform coverall.

I shut off the water and grabbed my towel, drying my hair with it as I strode into the locker room. "I promise you, he has something up his sleeve."

"Obviously," Stratford said. "He wants to kill us all."

"If he did, we'd already be dead." I turned to the bench where I'd left my bag. We were both quiet while I dried myself off. I glanced at him when I bent over to slip my underwear on. Not that I blamed him, but he had definitely been watching. "Strat, we run into OOC interference with asteroid mining, right? It's always when we head to Alpha Station or when one of the ore transports pick up a sentry. Sideways of that, they leave us alone."

"Sure," Stratford said. "I guess."

I couldn't resist. I stepped closer to him as I pulled on my bra. "Are you even paying attention?"

Stratford's eyes turned to fire while his voice turned to gravel. "I guarantee you, Allison, you have my undivided attention."

I bit my lower lip. "Good."

I let my mind wander through a few possibilities while I spoke. "Like I said—*Ticonderoga* could have cut us in half if they'd wanted, so it's not about that. He thinks he controls the solar system because he controls *Ticonderoga*, so he thinks he's taken the ore trade. It's worth uncounted billions. If we even threaten it, we'll get his attention."

"I'm lost."

I pulled my damp hair back and into a ponytail before hurrying into my uniform coverall. "We're chasing him. It's a bad tactical position. He's in front, making the rules. We need him to chase us. Then we can make the rules."

"And how do we do that?"

I stood with my boots on and headed for the door. "We head for Alpha Station, and we make it clear we intend to destroy it."

"Allison, do you know how many people he'll kill on Earth if you're wrong?"

"None, because he doesn't want to. It's not about killing people, Strat. *Ticonderoga* was in planetary orbit when this started. If he wanted to randomly attack anything, it would have already happened."

"So what is his motivation?" Stratford asked.

"He wants to cripple the UPE. The fact that he hasn't already done it militarily says he's going to break our back. He's got to be going after the off-world production of precious ores—and the money, industry, and advancement that comes with it. We've gotten too technological for our own good—if you control the flow of metals, you control everything in an industrialized society." I shook my head. "I think he's working for the Consortium. Or with them."

✣

Admiral West was an easy sale.

He'd always told me even a bad plan was better than no plan.

Barking orders in between curses at himself for not seeing the bigger picture, he made it clear he believed Admiral Kegar didn't want to attack Earth but our resistance might have forced his hand.

"Communications, open up a wideband channel," West snapped.

"Channel open," the com officer acknowledged.

West picked up a handheld receiver and spoke into it without preamble. "This is Coleman West, captain of UPE *Lexington.* This message is being broadcast in the clear as a warning. Evacuate the facility known as Alpha Station. My ship is en route, and we will destroy the station on arrival to stop it from falling into enemy hands. Message ends now."

West didn't even have the receiver back in the cradle before another indicator sounded. "Incoming communication," the com officer said.

"I'll take it here," West said as he put the receiver back to his ear. He listened patiently, taking a deep, steadying breath before he responded. "Vergé, I didn't think my previous message was confusing. It was, however, incomplete. Frankly, I would have thought it was obvious. After we destroy the station, we're coming for you."

He thrust the receiver back into the cradle without another word.

I looked at West with raised eyebrows.

"Too much?"

I shrugged. "The stakes are too high for subtlety, sir."

"Well, that should buy us a couple of days to figure out how not to get our ass kicked," he said with a grin.

"We'd better get to work then, sir," I said, acknowledging Stratford with a wave. "If you'll excuse us?"

"Dismissed."

~

"All right, Strat, catch me up with what you know," I said as we walked.

"Most of our pilots have only seen a Thunderstrike in a museum. The birds are in good shape, but no one except you, me, and our crew chief has ever laid hands on one. The other problem is, as it stands, we can only off-load one at a time. We only have one operational launch elevator."

"Out of?" I asked.

"Twenty."

"How about the ship?"

"It has a big engine. Flat out, we think she'll outrun *Ticonderoga*. Weapons are operational, but targeting isn't locked down. She's got old-school rail guns around the sides and an accelerated particle cannon pointing forward. It'll stick one on if we can hit anything, but it also looks like the power draw from the main cannon will shut half of the ship down every time we fire it."

"What about sensors?"

"We haven't had time to calibrate anything, but they look like they'll be decent out front and degrade to rubbish in back."

"We have a blind spot," I said.

"A big blind spot," Stratford corrected.

"What do the flight crews look like?"

Stratford shook his head in disbelief. "West broke an old friend of his called Hutch Drummond out of retirement to be crew chief. He knows Thunderstrikes inside, outside, and backward, but—he's a little eccentric."

"No, goddamn it!" a gritty voice boomed through the corridor. We were still ten meters from the hangar. "You're going to blow yourself to oblivion and take me with you. I might be old, but I'm not ready to die yet!"

The shouting ebbed to the tone of a teacher lecturing a student as we stepped into the bright hangar. We followed the voices to where a young technician stood beside a Thunderstrike. Above his head, another man's legs stuck out of the atmospheric access hatch behind the canopy.

The technician snapped to attention and announced, "Flight Technician Perry Chase!"

"Who in the blooming hell are you talking to, Chase?" the voice that owned the legs asked.

"It's a captain and a commander, sir," Chase said.

"Well, what do they want?" the legs shouted.

"At ease, Technician. Can you point us to the ordnance shop?" I asked Chase.

He pointed to the far end of the hangar. "In there, ma'am."

Quirking my lips, I silently urged Strat to follow me out of earshot. "Who's the chief ordie?"

"A bloke called Glen Deschamps," Stratford said.

The shop itself was merely a series of cranes, fixtures, and workbenches where various missiles and bombs could be armed, disarmed, or otherwise maintained. Several more elevators were set into the floor. The weapons magazine was evidently another floor below us.

"Chief Deschamps?" I asked a middle-aged, dark-haired man with a goatee that appeared to be in charge.

His red-shirted crew members scattered to attend to various tasks.

"I take it you're Captain Mackenzie," he said as he shook my hand. He turned and did the same with Stratford. "Pleased to meet you, Commander."

"How does it look down here, Chief?" I asked.

"We're still pulling inventory, but it's all pretty straightforward, conventional weaponry. The magazine looks full, and what we've seen is in good shape," he said. "We have what we need to fight a war against a good-sized country."

"What about *Ticonderoga*?"

"Captain?" he asked, confused.

"I understand the magazine is full. It's the conventional nature of the weaponry that worries me," I said.

"We have a small complement of nuclear weaponry, Captain."

"That's not what I mean," I said, suddenly exhausted. The words took me longer to find than I would have preferred. "We're in this mess for several different reasons, Chief. One of them is because the guy that pulled this off came at me sideways. He didn't take me on head-to-head. It's in our best interest to take a page out of his book."

"You want to fight dirty," Deschamps said.

"Call it what you want, but if we take him on straight-up, we're going to lose," I said. "I've had my share of beatings lately. I'm not up for any more, Chief. So what can you do for me?"

"I can make you any kind of boom you can dream up, Cap," he said with a smile.

"I'd like you to work on three of them, Chief. Make sure we have what we need for an assault, emphasizing our Thunderstrikes against *Tico*'s Tomcats."

"Antiaircraft," he mumbled. "We need to tweak the autonomous scan range and the fuel cell so we can open up from farther away and still take it to target."

I nodded. "I need mines with proximity detonation. Here again, remember we must deliver them with a Thunderstrike."

"Or throw them out an air lock," Stratford added.

"Agreed," I said. "Last, I need one big boom."

"How big?" Deschamps asked.

"Big enough to make the son of a bitch think he won."

Deschamps's eyebrows rose.

Since Stratford was behind me, I couldn't see his reaction. If I couldn't surprise him, I'd never surprise Kegar.

"I don't have anything onboard to create a sizable EMP," Deschamps said.

I chewed my lip. "Can you turn a Thunderstrike into one?"

Deschamps paused, his eyes focused beyond us, mentally calculating. "Nukes are all we have to work with. What's onboard is relatively small, but they could be daisy-chained together and locked to the Thunderstrike. But how are you going to get home if you blow your bird up?" Deschamps asked.

"I'm not going to need a ride back."

"Are we really down to suicide?" Stratford snapped.

I glared at him. *You know me better.* "I'm not ready to cash it in yet, boys. I mean to get my ship back. It might be easier if we had a way of clogging up her sensors for a bit longer."

"You're going to retake *Ticonderoga* alone?"

"Kegar took her away from me alone."

Deschamps shook his head.

"Leadership by committee isn't my thing," I snapped. "Can you give me a major EMP? Yes or no?"

"Yes," he said stiffly.

"When you're done here, hit the rack. Start in the morning," I said. "Dismissed."

Deschamps didn't look pleased when he left, but so be it. Sometimes, only obedience was required.

"Captain, are you sure you're not looking for revenge?"

"Don't patronize me with the *captain* crap, Strat."

He blinked.

"You're only formal when you disagree with me. So what if I am looking for revenge? If I get *Tico* back, all of this is over."

"Is it, Captain?"

~

"All hands to combat stations. This is a drill—all hands to combat stations." West's voice was clear over the One-MC.

"All right, people, let's move!" I snapped.

Running straight to the lift my Thunderstrike was staged on, I grabbed my helmet and gloves off the canopy rail before strapping into the seat. Rising as soon as I stepped on it, the lift's movement brought a fresh warning klaxon and flashing red lights. I surveyed the rest of the hangar through the canopy window and found similar progress all around.

Until it stopped.

This is why we drill.

"Mackenzie to command. We have a little problem here."

"We show you as go for launch, Zero Niner," West said.

"Negative, Admiral. Something is wrong with the lifts' position indicators."

"How do you figure?" West asked.

"All but one of us are only about a quarter of the way up the hangar wall, sir. The birds are nowhere near the air locks."

"Well, try to get yourselves down. We'll see if we can figure out what's going on."

"Roger that," I said as I unbuckled and opened the canopy. Grace was low on my priority list as I rolled out of my Thunderstrike, but after I got to my feet, I did find a ladder set into the wall beyond the edge of the elevator.

Heights. Falling was still a concern, even in the minimal gravity. Looking down, the vague memory of my Tomcat ejection and Simkins' death haunted me. My ribs ached.

After I hit the deck plates, Stratford found me and gently asked, "Cap?"

I ignored him, running through the combinations and variables in my head.

"If we can't even launch, we're going to lose, Strat."

Strat raised an eyebrow. "Quitting so quickly, Allie? *Tico* is top of the line, but *Lexington* is made of sterner stuff. And so are you. Let the technicians do their jobs, and we'll try again."

I grimaced. He was right.

~

I lay in my rack for a long time. My mind wandered in circles. I allowed myself to follow along, deliberately not concentrating on anything in particular. It was effortless to pass over into sleep.

Reality gave way to dream, which in this case was much more pleasant.

✣

The off-white cotton towel was big and soft. It wasn't thick, but it felt good against my skin as I dried off. The coolness I'd felt when I stepped out of the shower disappeared, but I tied the towel around myself anyway.

The extra warmth was reassuring.

After I brushed my hair out, I rubbed lotion with sunscreen from head to foot, scrutinizing my nails and skin far more intently than I would have for any drill inspection. Artificial tan had darkened me enough so I didn't look like a ghost, which was a definite bonus, given what I had in mind.

Two swimsuits were still in my bag—a black racerback one-piece and a blue tankini with lots of fabric. I felt comfortable in both, but neither quite did for me what the three scraps of red fabric and strings hanging on the end of the towel rack did.

That was *if* I could get the bikini back on again. The memory of my initial attempts brought a mixture of amusement and horror.

I'd bought it on a dare made to myself, knowing I wanted to make an impression today. One last fog of uncertainty clouded whether I was brave enough to do it. Then nervous anticipation chased it away. I'd made up my mind.

The bottoms were fairly easy to sort. The fabric covered everything important and most of what backside I had. The ties on the sides made my breath quicken. Getting the knots even was simple enough, but they didn't seem secure, since the strings barely settled above my hips.

I definitely won't be swimming.

I inspected myself carefully to make sure nothing had escaped my razor and then stretched each leg out in turn, testing that none of the fabric bunched or gathered where it shouldn't.

The top was another matter entirely. Support wasn't an issue with my boobs, but the bikini didn't have a lot of coverage either. Just two small triangles of fine fabric and several strings. Tying the string across my back was the hardest part. It kept falling off to one side or looking wonky.

I should have thought to practice this sooner.

I finally decided to tie the strap in front where I could see what I was doing and then shimmy it around to my back. The strap around my neck was much easier. Once I had the fabric positioned in the front, I tied a pretty knot at the base of my neck.

Plenty of definition in my legs, a hint of abs . . .

I decided everything was as good as it was going to get after that last glance in the mirror. Feeling more confident, I stepped into the main room and put on my baseball cap and sunglasses. With my blue-and-white striped beach towel, a water bottle under one arm, and a book in hand, I walked through the doorway of my villa and onto the warm beach sand.

My senses were hypercharged by my scanty clothing. Sunlight warmed my skin, mingling with a tingling breeze. Impossibly blue water was rivaled only by the radiant beauty of the cloudless azure sky. Not many people were out yet, so I walked past the last couple reclining in their lounge chairs and laid my towel out on the white sand. Settling on the fabric sunny-side up, I read exactly one paragraph of *One Step Forward* before I put it aside, closed my eyes, and tried to absorb as much of the sun's energy as I could.

"Allison? What are you doing here?"

I tried to feign surprise, but I was too relaxed to be convincing. I did smile—I couldn't help it. Pride in my workmanship, I supposed.

I stretched contentedly in the delightful warmth. "I'm soaking up some rays, Jake Connors, and they are excellent."

Jake laughed. "Soaking up some rays? You sound like a real girl, not a starship captain."

"If this is how real girls live, I could get used to it. What brings you to the South Pacific?"

"The Material Transport Division is having their annual policy update here. Pretty sweet venue, huh?"

I opened my eyes reluctantly. The sight of him standing over me made my smile widen. "Indeed."

"It's quite the coincidence, running into each other."

"Not really." I shook my head. "I'm giving the briefing on the OOC extraplanetary status and the threat matrix. As little vacation as we get, though, it was nice of the brass to arrange for this to happen in paradise."

"I'm still surprised to see you here."

I stretched my legs out, wiggled my toes, and propped myself up with my arms behind me. "I have a big towel."

Jake smiled. "Yes, you do."

"I can make room. Care to join me for a bit?"

"I would love to join you." He was obviously looking at my exposed skin. "But my next session starts in a few minutes. Can we meet for dinner?"

I leapt up and planted a kiss on his cheek. "Absolutely."

CHAPTER 8

23 MAY 2126

"Good morning, Captain," Kegar said.

Disorientation from sleep brought confusion. I was in my quarters aboard *Lexington.*

How the hell is he talking to me?

I leapt up and met his gaze in the com screen.

"You are a beautiful woman, Allison."

"I'm sure that's relevant. What do you want?"

"I want you to join me. I told you I would call you today to see if you had reconsidered," he said easily, leaning back in what had been my chair. "My preference is to avoid more bloodshed."

"Then stand down."

"That is not an option. Join me, Allison. Help this all to matter."

"I don't want to see anyone else hurt."

"You can only make that happen one way," Kegar said.

"Where are you?" I asked. The gears in my head finally threaded together. "I need to know where I'm going."

Kegar's expression hardened. "No games, Allison. Too much is at stake. If you're toying with me, I'll kill your crews—both of them."

"I'm not playing a game."

"Very well. We're behind you. Head for home."

"See you in a bit."

"Don't be too long. Captain Connors can't live through much more suspense," Kegar said.

I closed the com channel.

The right side of my torso still bloomed in a huge, nasty bruise. In that second, vulnerability overwhelmed me. I could be hurt, badly, but I could also survive.

I had to kill Kegar, and I finally knew how to do it.

But am I up to it? Physically?

I padded to the bathroom in bare feet. The ship was still quiet—near the change of watch. Realizing that fact could save me some hassles, I hurried to Admiral West's quarters and banged on the door.

"Don't you ever wear clothes?" he asked when the door slid open. Dressed in a well-wrinkled uniform, he looked tired but awake.

The issued briefs and bra were all the nightwear I had, but again, I tried to own it. "I packed light, sir."

"It looks more comfortable than that pink number from the other night." He grinned. "How're the ribs?"

"A little tender but mending, sir. I got another call from Kegar."

"What did he say?"

"He wants me to join him soon, or he's going to keep killing people."

"So what's new?"

"I'm going to go."

"Allison, I can't trade—"

"We're off the map, sir," I snapped. "We put all our eggs in one god-damned basket, and now he's carrying it around. I can stop him. I have to stop him before he kills anyone else. He killed Tom. He's threatening to kill Jake."

"And if you go to *Tico*, he'll kill you," West growled.

"No, he won't."

West stared into me, trying to understand how I could be so sure.

Even I hadn't understood it before Kegar called and looked at me that way on the com.

"Allison—"

"It's a small price to pay, sir. The juice is worth the squeeze." The fact that I was willing to put myself up for the job meant I wasn't entirely against the idea of sleeping with Kegar. Sometimes you had to endure unsavory things to get the job done. I could work through the moral ramifications once people were safe and Kegar was in a bag.

"What about the crew? He undoubtedly has people on his side."

"He can't have them all. It's unlikely everyone under my command on *Tico* would accept this without question. Even if he did gain their loyalty somehow, I'll have a chance to chop the head off."

"You think you can do this?"

"I have to, Admiral."

West nodded, accepting the situation. "I'll have flight prep you a bird."

"I'll go get ready, sir."

I was halfway out the door when West asked, "How do you ever get ready for something like this?"

"I think about Tom and my dad, sir."

✣

Strat moved from where he'd been leaning against the bulkhead outside the hangar to block the door entirely.

"Well, this is a cliché."

"I suppose it is, but what else am I supposed to do, Allie?"

"Tell me you love me, Strat. Tell me you're proud of me for doing what needs to be done, and then let me go."

"I will never let you go."

I reached up and cradled his cheek in my hand. I had never touched him before.

"I love you too, Edgar."

~

"*Ticonderoga* control," I said over the com, "this is *Lexington* Thunderstrike Zero Niner. How do you read?"

"It's good to hear from you, Allison," Kegar responded. "Open your transponder frequency to us, and we'll facilitate our rendezvous."

"Zero Niner is squawking open telemetry on transponder frequency one-one-zero," I said after keying the appropriate codes into the computer.

He might be a traitor, but he wasn't stupid. He wanted to make sure I was not up to something again. It would take him a bit to interpret the transponder data.

I pulled the primary thruster control back to zero and waited impatiently. Given all I planned to do, some pangs of anticipation were understandable. Plain and simple, I had no idea what I was getting into. Returning to *Tico* no longer felt like going home.

Odd.

The threat warning light illuminated and the alarm sounded as *Ticonderoga*'s com reopened. "Captain Mackenzie, can you hear me?"

"Yes, Lieutenant Benson. Lima Charlie."

"Captain, you are authorized to make a standard approach into the primary landing bay. If you deviate in any way from the standard approach vector, you will be destroyed without warning. Do you understand my instructions?"

My instructions? That's an interesting choice of words.

"I understand, Lieutenant."

"Begin your approach now."

"Confirmed." I moved the throttles to zone one.

Ticonderoga grew in front of me. The normality of day-to-day life onboard had made her smaller, even cramped, on the inside. Here, staring down the wrong end of her concussor ports, she was intimidatingly large.

I brought the throttle control back to zero and keyed the sequence into my computer that handed control of my Thunderstrike over to *Ticonderoga*'s docking system. The portside landing bay door slid open in front of me, allowing my bird to enter the huge chamber and then settle gently to the deck. Once atmospheric equalization was complete, the interior air lock opened, revealing Lieutenant Benson. With his hand on the weapon holstered on his right hip, he strode to the middle of the deck.

I detached my suit's life support connections and took off my gloves and helmet while the canopy opened.

"Think through your movements, Allison," Benson shouted. "I need you to strip before you come down the ladder."

The confines of the cockpit made it a challenge, but my pressure suit was soon lying in a heap on the deck, and I stood in front of my former officer in nothing but a form-fitting, one-piece bodysuit.

"What now, Charlie?"

"I can't take you to see the admiral until I know you're not hiding anything."

"What could I possibly be hiding?" I asked.

"I don't trust you, so I won't get close enough to frisk you. You'll need to strip further."

Pervert.

I pulled the first strap off my shoulder. "You're holding the gun, Charlie."

"Yes." He smiled. "Yes, I am."

✣

The ship was notably emptier than it had been as Benson paraded me through the corridors in a duty coverall. The significance of the bright yellow *new transfer* band on my left forearm wasn't lost on me.

We passed only heavily armed marines on the way to command. It seemed West's briefing was correct that Kegar, a former marine himself, had used the jarheads to gain and maintain control of *Ticonderoga*. They were both an idealistic and tightly knit group, bound tighter than a pack of wolves.

At least a few engineers had to be minding the reactors and propulsion systems, but besides that, *Tico* could easily function with one or two people in command.

Crew loyal to the UPE and me would be held together—probably in a cargo pod.

Ticonderoga had looked and felt a specific way when I was in command, so I immediately noticed the faint ammonia scent in the air as we approached command. They had obviously tried to wash it away, but the grim reminder of Tom's death still hung in the air and stabbed at my heart.

"Welcome aboard, Allison," Kegar offered cautiously as I stepped into the otherwise empty command deck.

"Thank you, sir."

"Leave us, please, Charlie," Kegar said.

"Yes, sir." Benson's attempt at deference seemed to fall on deaf ears. He turned and disappeared.

"He was a means to an end," Kegar said, confirming the conclusion I hadn't quite drawn.

"Or a beginning, it appears," I said as I stepped forward. Closing the space between us, I took his face in my hands by way of warning and then, when he didn't resist, I kissed him.

He wasn't cautious for long. His tongue and hands were soon exploring me in an unexpected embrace. I was a little breathless as I eased away from him.

His smile warmed. "I've always wondered what that beginning would feel like."

"So have I," I responded, not completely untruthfully. At times, I'd certainly seen him as more than a friend and mentor. I just never acted on them before.

"Welcome aboard," he said with a smile.

My spine prickled. He obviously meant that in more than one way.

"Thank you, sir." The silence between us became awkward. "What happens now?"

"A test."

I steeled myself. I knew where this was going. *A test of loyalty to you and your cause, I assume?*

"Captain Connors has been uncooperative, to say the least. His defiance is rallying what is left of the UPE-loyal crew. Ending his influence serves more than one purpose."

"What of the rest of the crew?"

"I have every hope that seeing your shift in allegiance will facilitate a shift in theirs. If not, they'll be dealt with one way or another."

"How many are there?"

"All but the marines and one or two officers," Kegar admitted.

"Too many to"—I let the words slide off my tongue with deliberate, military ease—"dispose of."

"We'll see. Come. Let's get this out of the way."

I shrugged and followed him into the corridor.

The sight of Jake tore out what was left of my soul. He wouldn't have wanted it, but the pity I felt threatened to knock me to the floor like an artificial gravity malfunction.

One eye was swollen shut and the other was little more than a slit. He had a broken nose, missing teeth, and his right arm hung at an obscene angle. Blood stained the front of his uniform—he had to have vomited it.

Looking past Jake to my loyal crew—beaten, scraped, obviously bullied, but still alive—gave me the strength I needed to manage what was ahead. I took careful stock of the marines standing over Jake and memorized their faces for future reference.

I would make them pay for what they had done.

Jake grunted, bringing my attention back to him. Great pain but no regret was in his simple nod. It was an affirmation, all for me. An assurance that he knew what was going to happen and was at peace with it. Juxtaposed against that bit of comfort, he valiantly raised the middle finger on his good hand and smiled upward at his captors, looking each man squarely in the eye and refusing to lower his head again.

As soon as the bay door had opened, I knew what Kegar had planned for this little test. He'd hinted at it over the com this morning. Kegar had clearly either ordered or allowed what had happened to Jake, but their level of brutality sickened me.

This was not the UPE. He wanted to see how I'd deal with it.

My resolve strengthened instead of breaking.

In the end, Kegar was only after proof that would position me in his corner. I wouldn't stand by and see Jake or anyone else further brutalized. I paid the freight on my choice, and it would be the best for Jake, even if it destroyed my heart.

"Give me your sidearm, soldier," I said to the biggest marine as I stepped forward.

Kegar grabbed my shoulder. "Use mine, Allison."

I took the offered weapon. The weight told me it was preloaded with only one round.

He still was thinking of everything.

I spun and delivered the round right between Jake's eyes. Blood and brain matter spattered the deck and the men around him. The crew's screams and cries filled the air.

Behind Jake's crumpled body, cuffed at the wrists and ankles, stood Mindy. I met her stricken gaze. She pressed her lips together and wiped a smear of blood from her cheek, a flicker of understanding passing through the horror in her eyes.

You did what you had to.

Setting my jaw, I turned back to Kegar and held out his weapon. His gaze was filled with the same shock as the rest of my crew as he took the gun and holstered it. He hadn't truly believed I'd stand to his test.

Throwing him off couldn't do anything but help me.

"What's next?" I asked nonchalantly.

My heart thudding in my ears brought me cold comfort as I followed Kegar out of the bay. I never would have guessed it would still beat after being broken.

✣

I spent most of the day actively assessing *Ticonderoga*'s status and passively avoiding Kegar's crew. Neither task was particularly difficult. I exchanged only four sentences with Chief Brinn and garnered one fact and one supposition from them.

First, the dorsal surface near the front of the ship was still pretty much torn to hell from my impromptu kamikaze run with the Thunderstrike. Everything else was fully operational. Even a half-competent commander could compensate for the deficiency. In other words, *Ticonderoga* would still be more than a match for *Lexington.*

Second, I was left with the distinct impression that Brinn approved of what I did for Jake. That simple understanding helped more than anything.

I mulled my options over while I ate an emergency ration in the empty galley. Without the crew, the smells of warm food, and the chatter of camaraderie . . . the quiet was depressing.

The cold pasta Alfredo wasn't helping, but at least the preserved noodles were filling.

A part of me was glad to see Kegar when he stepped into the galley, collected a ration pack of his own, and sat down beside me. He and I had been so far together during my career, it was difficult not to find some comfort in his presence.

I just had to remember why I was here.

"What did you find on your operational assessment?" he asked after taking a bite of his ration meat loaf.

"About what I thought," I said. "My damage notwithstanding, she's at full strength."

"The ship won't stay that way long without a crew," Kegar said.

"She has a crew."

"Not one loyal to me."

"They're loyal to me, and I'm loyal to you."

"Are you, Allison?"

I quirked an eyebrow. "I killed Jake to prove it."

"I've been thinking about that. The only thing you proved when you put Captain Connors down is that you're capable of choosing mercy above your own feelings. You ended his suffering, Allison, killing two birds with one stone. Now that I realize your motivation, I'm not sure you proved any loyalty to me at all."

I looked into his unflinching eyes. Clenching my jaw, I barely resisted shuddering against a sudden chill as I measured him. All this time, I had operated on the assumption that Kegar was evil.

Now I was afraid he wasn't. And that meant I had to pull out the big guns.

"I think I've loved you for a long time, sir. Recent events have forced me to come to terms with those feelings."

His breath caught while I again considered the truth in my words. Sure, I had loved him like a father—a platonic love. But the difference between platonic and romantic love was largely the physicality. Sex at least should be a higher expression of existing feelings.

He said nothing, but his eyes never left me. Fire shimmered in them, but I couldn't tell if it burned for me as the woman he'd known or the one trying to seduce him.

He had to know we weren't the same person.

Though he hadn't seemed convinced by my earlier actions, I'd found that men generally were less intellectual where sex was involved. For the hundredth time, I repeated the mantra to myself.

I have a job to do. This is my chance to get it done.

The notion was enough to turn my nerves into resolve.

I kept my appraising eyes on his as I stood and took hold of my coverall zipper. His expression didn't waver, so I continued until I'd opened the fabric down to my belly button. Benson hadn't allowed me to put any underwear back on after our encounter in the landing bay.

I felt so exposed.

Surprising me, he reached out and gently took my hand. In the years I'd known him, this was only the second time he'd ever touched me. Electricity intense enough to make me wonder if the feelings were real tingled against the back of my fingers as he guided my hand back from the fabric.

He shook his head. "Not here."

My voice was unintentionally breathy. "Where then?"

"Your quarters."

No uncertainty flickered in his voice or eyes.

I stepped forward, closing the space between us, hoping to project certainty I didn't feel. Another jolt of electricity shot through me when I took his head in my hands and leaned in for our first truly passionate kiss. It was slow and gentle. Everything I thought it might be.

He parted. We were both breathless.

His was arousal.

Mine was fear.

When he leaned in to kiss me again, I snapped my forehead forward as fiercely as I could. Blood shot from his crushed nose as he reared back from my assault in pain and surprise. I used the opportunity to knee him in the groin and then jam whatever was left of his nose further into his head with the heel of my hand in a sharp upward right-handed spike.

It landed perfectly. If everything was as it should be, the bones and cartilage of his nose had punctured his brain—exactly what that strike was intended to achieve. He might well have been dead when he hit the deck, but I threw myself on top of him and punched him in vital areas as hard as I could. Repeatedly.

Making damn sure I was the last living thing he ever saw felt like the least I could do for Tom and Jake. And me.

West was right. When nothing else remained, revenge was a great motivator.

I was crying before I was done swinging. He had a lot to pay for.

✣

"Heads up!" I shouted once I spotted Brinn. I'd seen a compact Asian man dressed in UPE marine BDUs shadowing him earlier in the day and knew he had to be a guard.

Brinn's hands sprang up while the guard drew his weapon. With Kegar's reloaded sidearm already leveled, I shot the marine in the chest before he could react.

I stormed forward. "Jettison cargo pod three!"

Shock held my engineer motionless. Even his extensive experience wasn't serving him this minute. I'd never known anything to hold him to inaction before.

"Snap out of it, Brinn! This is your jailbreak! Jettison the damn pod!"

Maddeningly slowly, Brinn worked his console. His languid compliance wasn't deliberate—multiple safeties guarded the release procedure. Still, I would have appreciated alacrity.

"Glad to see you, Cap. What happened?"

"Too much." I pressed my back to him, keeping both the aft stairwell and the corridors in view, as someone would surely come to investigate my earlier gunshot. "Did the pod release?"

An unfamiliar alarm rang through the hallways, followed by a ship-shuddering boom.

"Pod's away." He stooped to search for the fallen man's weapon.

"We're going to count on our people to deal with whoever's in the pod," I said. "*Lexington* shouldn't be long. They'll pick it up."

"*Lexington*?" Brinn asked, obviously confused.

"Where have you been, Chief?"

"Minding this console ever since Kegar's people took over."

"Well, you're sprung now."

"He said he'd kill my granddaughter if I didn't follow along. Did he really get to your family?"

"Yeah. Someone did." My mind took a second to wonder if Kegar had admitted his guilt or simply used circumstances to his purpose. "We need to move it along. Do what you can to lock the ship down."

Noise echoed from the stairwell at the aft end of the control room.

"Chief?"

"Couple of minutes, Cap."

"Watch your back, Brinn," I said before darting into the stairwell.

A marine poked his head around the opening into the deck two corridor and got a couple of close shots off before I hit him. When he crumpled, I caught a glimpse of a taller man in a business suit vanishing into the frame eighty corridor.

Chase the suit or secure command?

My hesitation allowed someone to get behind me and jam the barrel of a sidearm into my broken ribs.

"Killing Kegar doesn't change the plan," Charlie Benson said. "Drop the gun."

I did as I was told. "Who said I killed him?"

Benson laughed. "Anyone else would have shot him or at least drawn a line before beating him to death."

Well . . .

"You can never tell, Charlie."

"Maybe I'll take some of what he wanted."

"Do I get to kill you while you're in the saddle, Charlie?" I asked genuinely.

It'd be worth it.

Benson was silent as he considered this for an instant. I thrust an elbow into his shoulder and knocked his gun far enough away that the shot he fired struck my side rather than my heart.

Ferocity exploded from its cage down where I kept my guts. This time, I didn't cry as I killed.

Benson wasn't ambiguous. He was an asshole.

Our weapons training instructor once told my class gunshot wounds were funny things. Some people howled in pain and some barely flinched. Sometimes they fell over and never got up, and sometimes they never quit fighting. It seemed I was the fighting kind.

I retrieved the gun I'd taken from Kegar and started toward command.

I ran into another of the interlopers along the way and shot him on sight. Time was running out. The loyal crew was safe, Kegar was dead, and *Ticonderoga* would soon be back in UPE hands. My imminent death didn't have any bearing on the situation.

The chair at my former station was a welcome respite as I opened up a wideband com channel.

"*Lexington*, this is *Ticonderoga*. How do you read?"

"Loud and clear. What's your status?" West asked.

"We jettisoned the UPE-loyal crew in the cargo pod, Admiral. It's set up as an emergency lifeboat."

"We've got it on scanners now. We'll take care of it. I assume you were otherwise successful?"

"It's just me and Engineering Chief Brinn. We don't have sufficient manpower to sweep the ship, but if some of them were with the crew, we should have Kegar's party neutralized."

"You have them in custody?" West asked.

"I was unable to secure their surrender, sir."

"Roger that," West said.

"How far out are you, Admiral?"

"Allowing some time to secure the pod, we should be there in about an hour."

I keyed command sequences into my terminal as I spoke. "I'm going to extend docking latch A and set the computer to automatically accept the linkup, sir. I might not be here for you when you arrive."

"Allison?" West's concern sounded genuine.

"I took a hit. I'm getting pretty woozy."

"Get to medical and patch yourself up as best you can." I could tell he turned away from the microphone. "Alter course for *Tico*'s beacon. The pod will keep. Max thrust—open her up."

The last sequence I entered into my console was a primary systems lockout. Engines, weapons—all of the good stuff would stay offline until someone with proper authority unlocked the system with an authorized code. It would slow down any of Kegar's people that might be left.

"I'm sorry, sir. Kegar, Benson, Hayes, Jake . . . I let it get messy."

I pressed my hand to the wound on my side, and the pain woke me to my situation. I stood shakily and moved toward the corridor entrance.

My vision blackened.

"You did good, Allison," West's voice said from miles behind me. "Do you hear me, Captain? You did good. Hang on—we're coming."

As night wrapped me in its embrace, I didn't feel the certainty he seemed to.

And I didn't care anymore.

CHAPTER 9

24 MAY 2126

"Captain?"

Dr. Hawshmore's booming baritone floated toward me in the black, but I couldn't respond.

"Captain Mackenzie?"

I worked my jaw. Maybe I could respond, but I didn't care enough to try.

"Allison, open your eyes now," the voice commanded.

"Can't," I croaked, but it came out as a hiss.

"Atten-hut, Mackenzie!" Admiral West shouted. "Front and center!"

I pried my eyes open and twitched my arm to salute.

"Not yet, Captain," Dr. Hawshmore said as he gently held my arm in place. "Eyes and mouth only, please. Do not rush."

I'm sleeping. I'm waking. I'm lying here. More sleep . . .

"Wha' ha'ened?" I mumbled.

I had made a sound that time.

"Your abdominal gunshot wound had complications from blood loss and trauma. We were afraid we were going to lose you, Captain," Hawshmore said.

Sure you were.

"Crew?"

That actually sounded like a word. I could do this.

"The cargo pod is back in place," West said. "All of your people are back on duty. Most of Kegar's are in the morgue, but a few are in *Lexington*'s brig."

"Ship?"

"We're getting her put back together, Captain. It'd go better if we could unlock her. Can you help us with the code?" West asked.

I nodded, and West produced a personal data interface. I swallowed a painful, hard lump. "Did . . . call home?"

West looked visibly concerned. "We haven't gotten any response yet."

I coughed. "Plan?"

"Repairs are going to take a few days. I want both ships operational before we move. We'll see what's going on then."

On the data interface pad, I clumsily made my way through the security procedures and unlocked all of *Ticonderoga*'s systems.

I meant to ask first, to say something else, but it slipped away before I could.

While I slept, this time I dreamed.

"Ms. Mackenzie, can you tell me anything about your relationship with Edgar Stratford?"

I nodded. Under other circumstances, the prosecutor, a formidable-looking man with admiral's bars, would have been kind of cute. "I've served with Lieutenant Stratford for the past two years. We are assigned TDY to the UPE Space Command Defensive Forces, specifically ground command."

"What are your responsibilities?"

"We are peacekeepers."

"Would you say you enforce the peace mandated by UPE's political arm?"

"You place more emphasis on enforcement than it deserves, sir," I said.

"Have you ever killed someone in the line of duty?"

"Objection!" Stratford's lawyer snapped. "Relevance?"

"Goes to the character of the witness," the prosecutor said.

"I'll allow it," the judge said. "Don't wander any farther off the road, counselor."

"Yes," I said to the prosecutor.

"Has Mr. Stratford?"

Stratford's lawyer was infuriated, but he didn't waste time objecting. The judge would have overruled it.

"Yes."

"How often?"

"Objection!" Stratford's lawyer shouted. "This is unnecessarily prejudicial against my client. Ms. Mackenzie has no way of defining *often*. Mr. Stratford's military record is clean—that is the important fact here."

"Sustained," the judge said.

"Damn right," Stratford's lawyer mumbled as he sat down.

"Defense counselor, one more outburst and you will be held in contempt. Do you understand me?"

"Yes, sir," Stratford's counselor said.

"Ms. Mackenzie, is Mr. Stratford capable of using lethal force in hand-to-hand combat?" the prosecutor asked.

Stratford's lawyer shot to his feet. "Objection! Of course he's capable of defending himself. Bringing up the obvious capabilities of a special forces soldier goes to unnecessarily prejudice the jury against my client."

"Or to illustrate the capabilities of a member of a classified organization to a jury who might not completely understand Mr. Stratford's skills and training," the prosecutor said.

"Objection overruled," the judge said. "Prosecution, you are out of road. Get to the point."

"Hand-to-hand training is basic," I said. "I possess similar knowledge. I would be surprised if he didn't use that training to stop a man from beating his wife. I understand Mrs. Johansen was nearly killed."

"That is indeed unfortunate," the prosecutor said. "However, Edgar Stratford killed Mr. Johansen during the altercation. Somehow, I feel like that was even more unfortunate."

✣

I didn't like that particular dream, so I told my subconscious to move along to something else. I couldn't always do it, but it was nice when it worked out.

✣

The sky was so clear it tasted dry. The absence of rain carried past me on the warm breeze mixed with the aromas of bleaching wheat straw and fertile soil.

The scents of early fall on a farm.

Home.

Out of sight, Dad's antique tractor's engine was straining, struggling to climb the backside of the hill closest to the house. The rhythmic clattering of its tracks slowed but never stopped. I had spent more time listening to the sounds and feeling the subtle vibrations of the old yellow tractor than I had spent sleeping in my own bed.

The memory was imprinted on my soul.

A wave of dust preceded Dad's arrival near the top of the incline, and he hollered encouragement to the tractor. "Come on, big girl! You can do it!"

She wasn't quite equal to the task, but then again, the old crawler never had been. As Dad stopped the big tractor to shift gears, the cloud of dust rising behind completely overtook him. His eyes were closed, as always, against the grit as he momentarily disappeared. By memory, his experienced hands manipulated the clutch and transmission shifter. He popped over the hill shortly after the clutch was released, and the tractor gently gained speed as it meandered down the steep lee side.

The quickening, excited thrum of its engine matched the beat of my heart.

I'd waited at the edge of the field at least a hundred times for Dad to stop and let me climb aboard for a ride. The anticipation made me dance—*antsy*, as my mom called it—while I waited for the tractor to bring my dad to me.

Dad stopped the tractor when he got close, but he didn't walk straight over when he climbed off. Always the consummate farmer, he inspected his machine first and checked for anything awry. Once he was certain everything was in order, he started toward me.

Large clods of earth had been ripped up by the tractor and magnified by the lack of rain. It was rough to walk through. He didn't rush, and he didn't smile.

I waved excitedly, ignoring his never-changing expression. Once he was a few feet in front of me, he stopped and asked, “Why are you here? You’ve got work to do.”

“I . . .” I was caught completely off guard. This wasn’t my dad. This wasn’t the pleasant, comforting dream I had told my subconscious to conjure.

Even in my own dreams, even in death, my dad knew exactly what I needed.

CHAPTER 10

27 MAY 2126

"I hear you're doing much better," Admiral West offered as he stepped into my medbay alcove.

"I was suffering from a gunshot wound. Now I'm suffering from Dr. Hawshmore's bedside manner." I smiled as the doctor himself appeared to check my chart.

With a cavernous snort, the big doctor boomed, "Now, if I could repair your sense of humor, we'd be back in business."

"No hope for that," West said dryly. "Can I have a minute with her, Doc?"

"Of course, Admiral. She's finished here. Captain, I will see you this evening for a dressing change. We must be sure to prevent infection. Am I understood?" Hawshmore queried.

"Absolutely. Anything to get me out of here."

"I couldn't have put it better myself, Captain." He disappeared wearing just a hint less than a smile.

West jumped straight to business once we were alone. "We've received Maydays from both *Everest* and Alpha Station. I'd prefer not to split up, but we haven't gotten a com through to Earth, either. I'm going to take *Lexington* out to the belt. I'd like you to head home with *Ticonderoga*."

"We should stay together, sir. Earth isn't going anywhere."

"Earth is a powder keg, Captain. The UPE had a growing consensus that Kegar's move was only part of the Consortium's play to dominate Earth when we left. In case that idea is correct, we need you to get back and do what *Ticonderoga* always has—keep the peace."

"How is the crew?" I asked.

"Solid. They know what you did for us, and they're proud of you, Captain."

"Thank you, sir," I said. I hoped my voice held more conviction than I felt. "I'll take care of it, sir."

"I'm going to leave Commander Stratford with you. I might have half of the crew you do, but I have a quarter of the problems. You're going to have your hands full."

"Are you sure you're not trying to get rid of him?"

"You say *tomato*." West smiled. He acknowledged a stack of clothes on the table next to him. "I'll leave you to get dressed, Captain. I'd like to walk you to command before I head out."

"Yes, sir," I said.

The bandages and bruises made getting dressed a struggle, but I refused to let a nurse help me. I didn't want to over-rotate, but someone I trusted had hurt me, and I didn't feel like trusting anyone anymore.

I knew what I was doing, and I knew it wasn't healthy. I didn't care.

I'd never cared for the optional regulation ball cap before, but once I tucked my last strand of hair under it and looked in the mirror, I straightened my shoulders.

Time to get back in the fight.

I couldn't resist pulling out my favorite greeting when I found Strat leaning against the wall outside the medbay. "Stratford-upon-Avon? Admiral West said he was going to walk with me."

He fell into step with me, not mentioning the fact that the strides were half as long as he was used to. "His duties called. It's good to see you up and about, Captain."

"It's good to be up and about. I understand you've transferred?"

"I'm told I'm still your ExO, reassigned to *Ticonderoga*."

"I'm glad to have you, Strat. What's our status?"

"We're still mag-grappled to *Lexington*. We can break off whenever you are ready. The damage control teams have everything put back together. Environmental has all of the . . . biological residue . . . cleaned up, so we're ready to go."

"The calls from Alpha Station and *Everest* are par for the course. One of them has a problem on a good day. What do you think about the radio silence from home?"

"Nothing positive," Strat admitted.

"It's not over yet." I'd meant for it to come out as a question, but a statement was more appropriate.

"No," Stratford agreed. "I don't think so, either."

Command erupted in disorganized applause when we stepped out of the corridor and into the cavernous control center. I tried to give my assembled staff their moment, but it made me uncomfortable. I knew they wouldn't stop until I said something.

"Once this is over, I'll party with you all." I lost the battle against the smile that tugged at my lips. "Hell, I'll buy the beer."

The laughter was polite.

"It's not over, guys. We are going home, but they're not answering the phone. I need information. Major Trulani, do what you can to hack into a satellite—weather, coms, television—whatever you get will be more information than we have. Mr. Pierre, I need you monitoring everything. I want to listen to anyone talking, whether they're on our side or not. Sensors and tactical will be running drills—combat, anti-intrusion, the works. We need to sharpen up fast."

"Captain," Pierre interrupted. "I have Admiral West on the com."

I stepped to my duty station and picked up the hand receiver. "Put the conversation through on the One-MC, Mr. Pierre."

"I'm glad to see you're back to work, Captain," West said cheerily.

I clicked the transmit button on the handset. "With much thanks to you and both of our crews, I am, sir."

"*Tico* is ready to roll?" he asked.

"Always, sir."

"All right then. We'll shove off. Stay in touch, Captain," West said.

"We'll see you when we see you, sir," I said and released the transmit button. "Cut them loose, Major."

Trulani nodded and drummed her controls. "*Lexington* is free and clear."

"Give us a two second Z-axis positive burst, Mr. Salinski. Push us off." My display showed the view from the docking latch camera. Watching the hulls separate and the star field open up was impressive. *Lexington*'s bulk slid off into the night.

I clicked the transmit button once more. "God go with you, *Lexington*."

"And with you, *Ticonderoga*."

~

"See you in the morning, Doctor," I said as I eased off the exam table. "I know how you miss me when I'm not around."

Hawshmore helped me work my uniform coverall into place as he spoke. "You need to be resting, Captain."

"I wish that was an option, Doc. Thanks for the fresh dressing."

I decided to wander through engineering and see if I could find Chief Brinn. I'd only spoken to him twice since I'd been back onboard, and both conversations had taken place under rather strained circumstances.

Brinn had never been overtly mean to me. He was, however, uncharacteristically kind when I found him in the fabrications shop supervising the assembly of a replacement sensor drone. To Brinn, supervising meant being knee-deep inside of the unit while teaching Pitka everything he could fit into his "little bird brain." He caught sight of me when he shimmied out to retrieve a data storage module. Stopping work, he motioned me toward a nearby computer workstation where we could both sit on the tall stools at the worktable. Then he helped me get situated.

"How are you doing, Captain?" he asked. Pitka and his helpers noisily picked up where Brinn had left off, creating a hum that gave us a semblance of privacy.

"We're not having a good week, are we?" I asked.

Brinn nodded.

"I don't think it's over yet."

"It never is," Brinn said. "Why do I think you're anticipating more trouble?"

"Earth has been a lot of things from time to time, but never quiet. Not like this. I'm sending a recon mission once we get closer if we haven't heard anything, but I don't like sending them into the unknown at long range."

"Leaving us defenseless isn't a bonus, either."

"Our reach is in serious danger of exceeding our grasp."

"Captain, what you did . . ."

I lowered my eyes to the deck plates.

"No, don't look so contrite." I looked up, and he continued, "You saved the ship. You saved us all."

Tears welled, but I choked them down, thinking of Jake. "Not everyone."

"Kegar made us watch what he did to Connors. He'd have done worse to turn you. You ended the man's terrible suffering." Brinn propped his head up with his left arm. The gesture made him look young, and light like I'd never seen flashed in his eyes. "I'm sorry I haven't always been nice to you."

I laughed through my tears. "I didn't think you were nice to anyone."

"I'm not. At least to people who don't deserve it. Coming here . . ." He trailed off as I counted rivets in the deck plates and slowed my breaths. He didn't continue until I firmly returned his gaze. "Coming here meant saving not only us but so many other people on the other ships, bases, and Earth itself. Your action was the most courageous thing I've ever seen."

"I didn't do it because I was courageous. I did it because I was angry."

"Anger and courage are seldom mutually exclusive."

"I thought you were an engineer. Isn't Dr. Hawshmore supposed to handle the psych duties around here?"

"Engineer and barkeep aren't mutually exclusive, either." Brinn laughed. "I've always been behind you, Captain. I hope now you know I always will be."

~

I was finishing my status report to Admiral West when the door to my quarters chimed. I fingered my bandaged midriff, visible between my bra and athletic shorts, rolled my eyes, and decided getting dressed properly was too much work.

"Come in."

Dressed identically but looking far more put together, Mindy Stykes flounced through the door. She deposited two bottles of juice on my table before she slumped into the chair across from me.

"Cranberry?" I picked up one of the bottles and unscrewed the top, avoiding her eye.

"I didn't get a chance to replenish the wine stash since we never made it home. This is the best I could do." Mindy retrieved a bottle before she deposited herself on my bunk in a pose reminiscent of the model she'd once been.

Her effortless beauty briefly reminded me of how awkward I felt as I took a sip from my own bottle. "This stuff is great," I said. "I drank it by the gallon when I was a kid."

Sneaking a glance at her, I found a playful smile and not pity on Mindy's face. "I'm sure you've had enough of the 'I'm sorry you went through it' thing, so I'll spare you that."

"What's done is done," I said, taking another swig. "And we have to finish our mission."

Mindy nodded thoughtfully. "Any guesses as to what that'll look like?"

"I can't get all of the pieces to fit together. It's like watching three different people play chess, and one of them doesn't even know they're in the game."

"You're implying that killing Kegar hasn't finished this."

"He raised his fair share of Cain with *Tico*, but whatever happened back home has happened without him. When we get back, we're going to have our hands full figuring it out." The bottom of my juice bottle came too soon. "Do you have family back home, Mindy?"

"Parents. They're anthropologists living on an island in Micronesia. Have you heard anything about yours?"

"Nothing for certain, but I'm pretty sure I lost my dad." Changing the subject was suddenly a moral imperative. "What about a boyfriend?"

"Stratford's the cutest guy I've met since I joined up, and we both know he's yours."

"You're giving me too much credit. I'm not sure anyone will ever hold on to Strat."

Mindy didn't look convinced, but thankfully, she changed the subject before I spent more time thinking about the men I'd had and lost. "You going to stay in when this is over?"

I shook my head. "I lost my ship, Mindy. They won't look past that.

One way or another, my clock's about to run out. I might get promoted if the UPE appreciates what I did, but I'll be dismissed for sure if they don't. My time as *Tico*'s commander will be over soon."

"You wouldn't stay if you joined the admiralty?"

"No. It was hard enough to quit flying when I got this command. I wouldn't want to do it at all if I can't be out here with you all."

"Maybe it won't come to that, Allie."

"It will," I said with certainty. "You'll be all right, but I won't."

"I understand what you're saying, but it doesn't seem fair."

"Right or wrong, that's life in the UPE Defensive Forces."

✣

My mind swam as I slid under the covers on my rack. Emotions warred—mourning Jake, loyalty to West, betrayal from Kegar—all while we investigated the loss of communication with Earth and reported constantly to *Lexington*. Every point had a counterpoint.

The United Planet Earth and the Oriental Ore Consortium . . . it all combined to make things confusing.

Stratford wandered back into the mix, too. I couldn't ignore him, even though the truth revealed in my conversation with Mindy was undeniable.

Stratford is in amazing shape.

Replaying the memory of the showers aboard *Lexington* allowed me a thorough review. I even pressed pause and rewind a time or two.

Get your priorities in line, Mackenzie.

I packaged my desires, stuck them in a filing cabinet, closed the drawer, and turned off the lights for a few hours. Maybe the first wise thing I'd done in a while, at least where a man was concerned. Or at least I tried to.

Stupid dreams.

✣

I'd been staring straight ahead for so long, I couldn't have told you if Stratford was still by my side. My eyes were focused on a spot one inch above the coffin draped with the UPE flag. Storm clouds delivered a deluge of unending rain, confining the sorrow of the funeral in gray, unending gloom.

"Stand by!" The rifle party snapped their antique weapons to attention.

"Ready!" As one, they shifted the actions on the rifles forward.

"Aim!" Weapons lifted to shoulders.

"Fire!" My tears were lost in the rainwater pouring over my cap.

"Lower!" *Surely it's done.*

"Ready!" *No . . . I can't lose him again.*

"Aim!" *Not again.*

"Fire!" *So many tears.*

"Lower!" *I love you, Jake!*

"Ready!" *No.*

"Aim!" *Jake.*

"Fire!" *I'm so sorry.*

"Lower!"

CHAPTER 11

28 MAY 2126

I pounded the com handheld. "Major Daniels, how do you read?"
"Lima Charlie, *Ticonderoga*. Request level Q com protocol."

The top secret, protected com channel for a mission update?

"Wait, One." I shook my head and started keying in the necessary protocols. The channel would be shunted around Pierre's control, the computers, redundancies, and even the signal boosters. No one could possibly overhear. As far as an onlooker was concerned, once the call terminated, it would be as if it never happened.

"Zero One, we are Q com. Status?" I said once the protocol was confirmed.

"All zero-flight units accounted for. ETD orbital hydrazine station one-three minutes. ETA *Ticonderoga* twenty-three hundred hours, shipboard. Request tightbeam download of OBSREC pod to cryptography for level one analysis."

"Roger. Wait, One," I said into the com. "Mr. Salinski, all stop, please. Major Trulani, please activate the OBSREC dish."

Our braking thrusters fired with a gentle surge.

"Reading all stop," Salinski confirmed.

"Set thrusters to station keeping," I said before I turned back to the handheld. "Send the packet, Zero One."

The tightbeam system was pretty cool. It used the standard com dish to orient Daniels' Tomcat with *Ticonderoga*'s OBSREC receiving dish. The Tomcat would then download all the information from the observation recording intelligence pod, encode it into a narrow-beam laser, and transmit it to *Ticonderoga* for analysis.

This great system was seldom used because we rarely ran into a situation where information like this couldn't wait until the recon flight came home.

"Zero One, did you pick up any coms from Earth at all?" I asked.

"Negative, Captain. Lots of clouds, colder weather than I would have thought, and at least a few impact craters, but not a peep of EM transmissions of any kind."

The imaginary click of the puzzle piece falling into place in my mind brought satisfaction to the deductive process but didn't drown the curtain of dread the confirmation created. My stomach roiled at the mental picture forming with increasing clarity. "Get home safe, Zero One. We'll see you in ten hours."

"Roger that, *Ticonderoga*. Zero One out."

I cradled the handheld.

Apocalyptic visions of a planet laid to waste had to be pushed aside. Channeling my worry into action was the only worthwhile application I had for the otherwise useless emotion.

"Major Trulani, can you get us underway once Zero One's packet signals complete?"

"It just came through. Resuming course now."

"Roger that. I need to have a word with Commander Stratford and grab some lunch. Mind the store please, Major."

She seamlessly replaced me at my duty station as I stepped away.

Daniels's report weighed me down as I walked the corridors. The OBSREC pod onboard a Tomcat was designed to intake, process, and record almost everything—visual information, radio frequencies, even laser-packeted communications it might happen to intercept. While the pilot didn't have access to all of the information, Daniels's OBSREC had recorded no com activity at all, which was troubling. Cell phone calls, weather broadcasts, television shows . . .

There should have been something.

An EMP—electromagnetic pulse, which was a commonly known but not completely predictable side effect of a nuclear exchange—was one possible cause of the radio silence that fit with the available data, and it explained why Daniels was keeping things quiet. He wasn't new to the job—the puzzle pieces would have taken him there as well, and he knew better than to spread a rumor that Earth had fallen into nuclear war.

It would be a long wait for crypto to confirm.

I was already asking myself troubling questions. Who started the conflict? Why did it escalate to a nuclear exchange? Were there governments left? Civilians?

Did I do this by losing *Ticonderoga* to Kegar?

Even temporarily removing the global peacekeeper from the political chessboard covering the planet would have changed the dynamics of conflict completely. Kegar's actions had meant the OOC captured our queen. Had we repatriated her in time to watch our king kill them for their temerity?

"Hi, Captain."

"Mindy." I smiled. "How goes it?"

She fell into step on my right, her presence reinforcing the fact that my plan to return to my old-school, solitary, and aloof captain act had completely failed. Mindy's efforts had helped keep me from slipping into the pit of depression I had been skirting from the moment I stepped out of the medbay.

"It's amazing how much equipment needs calibration after what, a week?" Mindy shook her head. "Everything from the scanning electron microscope to the gravitational observatory lost alignment. We get to a place where we feel like everything is automatic, but it takes far more to keep *Tico* running."

"Your team does a little bit every day. Catching up on everything at once is the change. You won't need to get used to it."

"Continuity in command and operation? I could get used to that."

"Subtle, Ms. Stykes, but yes, I think we're back to normal."

"Glad to hear it. So, that being said, how's Edgar?"

"It's Edgar now? Not Commander Stratford?"

"According to him, it is." Mindy's laugh was sheepish.

"You haven't seen him, have you? I was hoping to find him in the galley for lunch."

"I was heading that way myself. Do you want some privacy?"

My first inclination was at war with the lessons I had learned so painfully lately.

You are stronger with a team.

"Absolutely not. I'd appreciate the company."

Mindy didn't say anything, but her ever-present smile widened at the inclusion.

Did she notice mine did, too?

Stratford's tray was empty when we sat down at his table. Mindy sat beside him. Sliding in across from them, I'd be able to gauge their reactions as we spoke. Still something of an Englishman, Stratford sipped his tea while Mindy and I had a few bites.

"I take it the news from the recon flight was not good," he began quietly.

"On first glance, it's definitely not promising. As far as Daniels could tell, he encountered no discernible communications activity. Crypto is working on confirmation of the OBSREC data."

Mindy focused on her salad.

"How widespread was the conflict?" Stratford asked.

"We don't even know if there was one!" Mindy snapped.

I glanced behind them to see how much attention her outburst might have drawn before I focused a scalding stare on her. When I spoke again, my voice was lowered. "That is true, Mindy. This situation, however it arose, is unusual. We'll have to rely on sciences to figure out what happened and exactly how."

Stratford nodded thoughtfully. "The crew will get wise to what's going down."

I checked my watch. "Let's assemble the crew in the cargo pod—no, the Tomcat bay—at 2330 hours. We'll bang through the available data then and move forward together."

"Are you sure you want to start this? We can't command by committee," Stratford said.

"That's true," I admitted. "However, we have to admit a nuclear exchange might have precipitated the conditions we are now seeing on Earth—"

"What conditions?" Mindy's tone was still clipped, but not quite enough to draw more attention.

"Daniels indicated colder weather, excessive cloud cover, and what appeared to be impact craters on the Asian continent in his radio message," I said.

"He's trying to paint the picture of a nuclear conflict without saying the words," Stratford said. "Leaving it to you to put the name on it."

I stopped my hands from rising into the universal "whatever" gesture. No matter what we called it, I had to get on with dealing with it since I'd already worked through the implications. "I'm not going to take the chance some of the crew will hold it against us for keeping that kind of information under wraps. This is too big. We're going to walk into some serious shit, so we're going to do it together from the start."

Mindy was zoned out, staring at the wall like a video display was playing her favorite movie. I had an inkling as to what was going on. The same thing had happened to me not long ago.

"We need medical in the loop," Stratford said. "Hawshmore needs a chance to review his procedures. People will undoubtedly ask questions at the briefing he needs to be prepared for."

"Agreed. I'll take care of it. Mindy has recalibration underway in sciences, so by the time we're home, hopefully everything will be in order. Have we overlooked anything?"

"We need to develop an overall plan for humanitarian intervention. I'm assuming we'll stay orbital."

I nodded. "Landing exposes too many of our vulnerabilities. We'll also need a contingency to allow for Consortium involvement."

"We await the dawn," Stratford said, slapping a hand down on the table hard enough to startle Mindy's attention back to the conversation.

She stood abruptly. "I'll see you at the briefing."

I grabbed her arm, slowing her departure. "I was hoping you'd digest the crypto data and deliver the briefing."

"Crypto. Sure. Yes, Captain. I'll take care of it," Mindy monotoned. Then she scurried away.

I briefly considered chasing after Mindy but decided she needed the same processing time I'd already had. Instant regret screamed through my torso when I leaned forward, having intended to rest my arms on the table and eat my chocolate chip cookie in a moment of quiet.

"All right, Allie?" Stratford asked.

I wrapped an arm around my midsection. "No, but I will get by."

His eyes searched mine, and for a minute, I was afraid he wanted to talk about Mindy, or Daniels, or Earth, or . . .

"We'll never get you back into a bikini, what with that."

Hmm. Playful Stratford?

My gaze darkened. "I'll heal."

The mischievousness vanished from his face. "You need to use me, Captain. You've been holding me at arm's length since I came aboard. You can't do this by yourself, especially not with broken ribs and a gunshot wound."

"Strat, I told you everything I know."

"Did you? Have you? Ever?"

"Strat, I'm the captain. It's my job to carry the weight. I've talked to you—"

A glint of fire strained to escape through his wide eyes. "Only because you don't have any choice in the matter at this point. Captain, I'll follow you into hell. I'll even lead the way for you if you'll let me. You've been betrayed. Now you're overcompensating by not letting anyone in. Particularly not me."

Definitely not playful Stratford.

I smiled in embarrassment as the blood rose to my cheeks. "That's not it, Strat. Maybe it's the effect, but it isn't the cause."

"Really?" Stratford said skeptically. "Haven't we moved past the professional coolness, Allison? We're a team, or at least supposed to be."

I looked around again and found the galley otherwise empty.

"I've always liked you, Strat. We work well together. I loved Jake, and now he's dead. I should be sad, and I am. When I got to *Lexington* and bumped into you in the shower, I . . ."

Stratford stared at me.

I knew he wouldn't help me through this. He would pull the truth out of me and offer nothing in return. So I mustered the courage to look him in those steel-gray eyes anyway. "I realized I wanted you, Strat. Right then, right there, and ever since. That's pretty overwhelming, given the givens."

Your turn, Stratford. My stomach twisted violently.

"Jake was a good bloke," Strat said easily. "I won't take a thing away from him. You should be dead three times over, and I should be in jail. Well, I shouldn't, but . . . you know what I mean. You and I have an opportunity here, Allison. You'll heal while we take care of business, but as soon as we get the train back on the tracks, I'll take you to bed."

I blinked, and a flicker of something like relief warmed my chest. Instinctively, I squashed it. "Regulations, Commander. You just got out of the clink as it is."

He didn't bat an eyelash. "I'll take my chances."

✣

"Dr. Hawshmore, do you have a minute?"

"Of course, Captain," he rumbled. "Would an examination bay be more appropriate?"

"No. Mind if I lock the door?"

He shook his head as he stood and moved to a cabinet behind him. "Mind if I pour the rum?"

"A double." I sat in the consultation chair at the side of his desk and watched as he produced two glasses and filled them with a notable portion of the dark liquor.

"Anti-anxiety medication takes many forms, Captain," he said as he returned to his seat. "I prefer simpler treatments when possible. What can I do for you this afternoon?"

"Tell me you have great knowledge and hands-on skill in mitigating the effects of radiation on the human body."

"I have proficiency in any potential off-world issues we might encounter, Captain."

My eyes watered, and I managed not to cough after I swallowed my first slug of rum. "How about on Earth?"

"The principles are the same. Scale becomes the issue." Hawshmore smiled at my reaction in spite of the gravity of the conversation. "Perhaps you could be more specific?"

I belted back the rest of the rum.

I can't breathe.

"I really can't, Doc, and that's part of the problem—I only have supposition."

"Share the supposition," Hawshmore suggested as he refilled our glasses.

I barely survived the first round.

"I have no facts."

"We have already established that much, Captain."

I downed the liquid in one shot.

Vision is overrated anyway. What's one more drink?

"Our recon flight encountered the aftereffects of an EMP, most likely brought on by a nuclear exchange."

Hawshmore emptied his glass with much more grace than I had. "Scale of the conflict?"

"Fairly limited, based on our data so far. I think mutually assured destruction was a story created to scare people out of pushing the button. No rational government would destroy the world to spite an enemy. Only one side launched."

"How will you respond?"

"Our mandate is humanitarian."

"Of course. I'll be honest, Captain. I haven't kept mass-casualty radiation protocols at the forefront of my knowledge base. I'll need some time to review the procedures before I'm up to speed."

"Fair enough. I need you in the Tomcat bay at 2330 hours. The recon data will be compiled, and we're going to brief the crew. I'm sure there will be questions."

"I will be prepared, Captain."

~

Waiting had never looked good on me. Getting through my watch wasn't a problem, as I had enough paperwork to keep me at my station until about 2200 hours.

The world as we knew it had probably ended, but paperwork still had to be completed.

I hit the deck plates when I was done and couldn't stand the sight of my station anymore. The only active repairs were on the forward-dorsal area of the ship, and even they were winding down as I made my way through the section. The crew seemed focused but generally relaxed, which was what I'd hoped.

When I was alone in my quarters, the enormity of the mission ahead washed over me.

We're in deep shit.

I still heard from and reported to Admiral West a couple of times each day, but he was more than a day out if things went wrong. If we fell, *Lexington* would find itself in the same position we were now in—trying to piece together the evidence leftover from a conflict already fought.

And lost.

I thought killing Kegar would have returned relative order to the universe.

Except it hadn't happened that way at all.

I had not only killed a former friend and mentor, I'd failed to stop—and potentially caused—the conflict on Earth. My insides twisted violently.

What-if thinking isn't going to get you anywhere, Allison.

The long game was now the priority. *Ticonderoga* was almost one hundred percent operational with a nearly full crew complement, and *Lexington* was available as backup, even if she was a bit distant. Both ships had provisions to last a long time, but they would need replenishment and repair eventually.

I made a mental note to send an engineering team to assess the status of the orbital dockyard once we were home. The infrequent maintenance requirements of service spacecraft commonly left the station abandoned, but some consumable inventory would still be stored for our ships—environmental gasses, reactants for the generators, repair parts, and even plain water. The facility would also presumably be out of reach of anything planetside, making it an excellent choice as an emergency reserve.

Daniels had confirmed the orbital hydrazine facility was operational. Its proximity to the dockyard made it another logical stop for *Tico*'s engineering team to assess. The facility would automatically process whatever it could find into fuel for smaller ships. The solar winds would still blow and micro asteroids would still wander close enough to the intakes to be captured and broken down into components for fuel. As such, the materials at the orbital hydrazine facility wouldn't need to be controlled as tightly as those at the dockyard—assuming, of course, that its orbit was also high enough to insulate it from the wildcard EMP.

Completing a thorough planetary survey was the priority, and Tomcats were the only tools for the job. Shuttles could approach if needed once an area had been properly cleared to offer humanitarian assistance. Any which way, all Tomcats would need to carry full weapon loads for the foreseeable future.

Friend or foe assignments would be defined once we figured out why the conflict had occurred in the first place. Assumptions had gotten me in enough trouble—we'd be starting from scratch.

To consider siding against the UPE was either brash mutiny or treason, but I could not take their side if they'd started a nuclear war. Hopefully that wouldn't be the problem.

Either way, organizing humanitarian relief would be *Tico*'s overreaching objective. We could figure out where it was going later, but pulling the disaster pods out of storage, inventorying them, and staging them for the shuttles would take time.

I glanced at my chronometer and then once more at the mirror.

Time to go, I told my reflection.

"As with any dissemination of information, we must first discuss how the data were gathered," Mindy began mechanically. "This is not intended to question the integrity of any particular datum but to complete the picture we have assembled from all the data in context. As a matter of orbital mechanics, the ten type-two, beta OBSREC spacecraft had to insert over the equatorial Pacific Ocean near Guam and split off into equidistant circumnavigatory flight paths at a low stratospheric level." She struggled with the informally assembled projector, which was aimed at a white sheet suspended on the forward bulkhead. "As I hope you can see from the graphic, we received reasonable telemetry of the Oriental Ore Consortium basin, given the operation's limitations. The data are certainly complete enough to be considered conclusive."

Enough crawfishing already, Mindy . . . spit it out.

"We interpret the data as indicative of damage from a type-two thermonuclear conflict."

"What does that mean?" a crewman shouted from the middle of the gathered crowd.

"It was a one-sided fight," Mindy answered. She seemed determined to remain professional in front of the rest of the crew. I wasn't sure whether her renewed battle with the projection was out of necessity or a need to collect herself. Eventually, it cycled through various images of the southeastern Asian continent. "These impact areas were definitely targeted. Each location corresponds to a known military installation or industrial center. Hong Kong has also suffered massive damage."

"There must be radiation," another voice interrupted.

"The data are also indicative of massive rainfall. Weather modification was likely used to induce intense precipitation, effectively washing most of the radioactive fallout back to earth. Unfortunately, the magnitude of the rainfall caused intense flooding and mudslides throughout the basin, which has likely contributed to the humanitarian crisis."

Silence stretched for several heartbeats.

"What about UPE?" Pitka asked.

Mindy took a deep breath. "Some evidence of launch activity has been retrieved from known, if remote, UPE defensive missile launch sites. Other than greatly reduced electromagnetic transmission planetwide, we have seen no evidence of damage outside Consortium borders."

Defensive nuclear missiles . . . there's an oxymoron.

I shifted forward off the bulkhead I had been leaning against, uncrossing my arms and pulling my sleeves up to my elbows as I moved through the gathered crowd toward Mindy. Understanding her job was done, she met me midway. I saluted and thanked her for her work before I took her place and began my practiced speech.

"Given what we've heard, it would be easy to believe we failed. With that comes questions—who are we supposed to fight against? Should we even fight? Are we better off turning around and heading out into the solar system? Do we deserve to continue our mission? What will we do? How will we live?" I took a deep breath and smiled in frustration. "I may be your captain, but I don't have the answers to these questions. I'm certainly not immune to pointless worry."

I acknowledged every face. They looked back—some through downcast eyes and some through tears—but they were all looking to me.

"Focus on the faith you have. Focus on this crew. Both will see you through."

"It's not that easy," another voice said.

"Victory never comes easily," I said. "Sometimes, survival doesn't either. I didn't return to the service because Admiral West asked me to. I came back because it was the right thing to do. So we'll do the right thing here. Recent events have made us question who we can trust, but we will walk out of this on the other side knowing we did what needed to be done."

"Damn right we will, Cap!" Rogers shouted. "*Tico*! On the go!"

"*Tico*! On the go!" two or three more shouted in unison.

"*Tico*! On the go! *Tico*! On the go! *Tico*! On the go!"

When the ruckus finally calmed, I asked, "Does anyone remember the other part?"

"You only have one choice," Mindy said. "Give everything."

"Getting through this is going to take every single thing we have," I said. "Whether you fly a Tomcat or run a mop, you're going to do it longer and harder than you ever have. If you give up, the cost to our whole world will be bigger than ever. Today, Earth needs all you have. Will you give it to them?"

Another even more heartfelt cacophony of agreement filled the bay.

"We are rolling into this hot," I said once a semblance of order had fallen over the crew. "Our emphasis is humanitarian. We're starting over the Consortium. Tomcats will clear the area, and then aid teams will move in."

"The UPE might object if we help their sworn enemy," Brinn said.

"We're going to stop this conflict," I said. "If that means going up against the UPE, I don't have a problem with that. Do any of you?"

"Fuck no," Pierre said with an uncharacteristically thick North American accent.

"Fair enough," I said with a dry smile. "Salinski, how long until orbital entry?"

"Nine hours and change," he said.

"All right—I want pilots, marines, and medical staff in your racks now. Dismissed."

I tried to gauge people's reactions as they departed. One or two looked pretty glum, but for the most part, the staff seemed upbeat as they made their way up the stairs or into the lifts.

No, *upbeat* wasn't the right word. *Determined.*

To the remaining assembled crew, I continued, "The assets in the ship's ventral midline disaster pods need to come inside, get inventoried, and then be loaded into either of the two op shuttles." Some of the assets in those pods dated back to *Tico*'s commissioning. Though under normal circumstances they could be hot-loaded directly into the shuttles, no one had checked them since the last refit, and I wouldn't risk sending useless supplies on a mission this critical. "Priority will go to medical supplies, food, and water. Shelter is a secondary initiative at this point." I looked around, hopefully inviting questions. When none came, I added, "Handlers are dismissed to your duty stations. Be safe."

Everyone left was in some way responsible for preparation, maintenance, or operation of some piece of equipment. These were my engineers, plane crews, sensor operators, and gunners.

"You all have the big job. You're going to get us through this with little sleep and no help. The pilots fly and the marines shoot, but none of that is going to happen without you. I'd send half of you to bed, but I know how hardworking you are, and I can't spare the brig space for a bunch of insubordinate crew."

A smatter of laughter met the exchanging of wry smiles.

"I need ten more good hard hours out of all of you, and then we'll start cycling through to get you some sleep. Charge the defensives on the shuttles. Lock and load the concussor batteries, calibrate the sensors, and—"

"Make ready for war," Brinn interrupted. "You heard the captain, people. Snap to!"

"Atten-hut!" Pitka shouted.

The deck plate thundered in one synchronized boom as they snapped to attention.

"Go get 'em!" I snarled with the requisite dismissive wave.

As the crowd dispersed, Stratford fought the tide and made his way to my side.

"How did I do?" I asked, genuinely concerned.

"You've made short work of the easy part."

CHAPTER 12

29 MAY 2126

Mindy didn't say anything when she showed up at my door for our exercise period. I wasn't always quick on the uptake, but even I knew not much could or should be said. I hoped she was as glad as I was to hold onto the little bit of normalcy this part of our routine represented.

She ran me harder than I needed, but I wasn't going to let her get away since she'd given me the chance to be by her side, even if I did have to work for it.

"You all right?" Sweat shone on her hairline at the end of the hour. She'd found a smile along the way. "I needed that."

"Glad I could help." My sarcasm and my banged-up middle were both on display. I matched her smile. "I know you're having a tough time with this."

"How are you not?"

I took a deep breath. "I had a little more going on before this shoe dropped. That's why it was blue on black for me."

She looked like she wanted to say more but nodded and glanced at her chronometer. "I need to go get ready. Lunch today?"

"Absolutely."

✣

Before all of this happened, I would have used the few minutes before my watch to communicate with Mom back home. Since that was off the table, I decided to capitalize on the lull between shifts and go visit some of my favorite members of the crew.

I'd thought the Tomcat bay was deserted when I first stepped onto the catwalk grating, but it wasn't long before the telltale clank of tools told me otherwise. Curious, I wandered around until I found Powell and a plane chief I didn't recognize working in an access bay below the canopy on One Four.

"What's up?" I asked, trying to sound conversational. Both tried to snap to their feet. "As you were."

"Chet here has been checking targeting scanner alignments, Captain," Powell answered. "The feedback on this one worried him, so he asked me to audit the diagnostic results."

"Problems?"

She shook her head. "No, ma'am. Everything's well within spec."

So much of our crew was so young. "Chet, when's your next sleep rotation?"

He shrugged. "I've lost track, ma'am."

"That's a good indication it's time to go find out. Try to button it up as soon as you can and hit the rack."

"Yes, ma'am." He turned back to the diagnostic display between him and Powell.

"I'm proud of the work you both have done. Take care of yourselves, all right?"

"Yes, ma'am," they chorused. I left them to their work.

Wandering through the bay, I'd hoped to connect with the aircraft somehow—bask in their strength, their titanium-clad resolve to get the job done. Like Mindy had needed a hard run, I needed to be surrounded, for a moment, by our dogs of war.

Like everything else, the solemn walk didn't work out quite like I'd hoped. I was drawn to Zero Nine's now-empty launch gantry. What sounded like my dad's no-nonsense guidance floated into my head as soon as I allowed myself to stop walking.

You can either focus on the one you lost or on protecting the ones you still have. It's your choice, but I know which way I'd go.

✣

Tico's preparations would progress more efficiently if I stayed out of the way, and I knew that. My people were good.

The best.

They knew what needed to be done and would stand to it if I let them. So I stayed at my duty station, trying to pretend it was a normal watch. It worked for a while. I even got a much-needed status report composed and sent off to Admiral West. Somehow, that otherwise mundane act brought back the growing, unshakable, all-around bad feeling that I had killed the wrong man.

Vergé Kegar, my friend and mentor, must have foreseen the circumstances forming that caused the disaster on Earth. Desperate to stop it, he'd wrested control of the only thing powerful enough to keep the peace and protect innocent lives, and I killed him for it.

The Consortium has innocent people . . .

Our politicians had argued with theirs for more than a century. We'd had our share of conflicts with their technological gatekeepers. A lot of machinery had been banged up along the way, and things had likely edged closer to full-scale war more often than even I knew, but we had scraped by without a single fatality on either side.

Until now.

"Captain, I'm receiving some low-grade radio frequency," Pierre said from the com station.

"What?" Shaken from my reverie, I swiveled around in my chair.

"Confirmed. It is a low-grade frequency modulated signal, ma'am. It is faint, but it sounds like modern American music."

"On speaker, please."

"I've lost it, Captain. I can dig the recording out of the computer."

"Don't bother. Let me know if you get anything else."

I leaned back and thought for a moment. We needed to get back to Earth, but I was floundering trying to put the pieces together to form an understanding of what happened. *Where am I going with this investigation, anyway?*

"Where's the planet sitting rotationally?" Stratford asked. "Is there any chance we're line of sight with the capital?"

"Checking," Trulani said. After a minute, she added, "It should cross the terminator in ten minutes and change."

"Spin up OBSREC. Let's see if we can get anything through," I said. "If it connects, switch the system to receive only."

"We'll have to stop, Captain," Trulani said.

"Mr. Salinski?"

Salinski's voice echoed over the One-MC. "All stations, stand by for braking thrust in three, two, one . . . mark."

The big engines set into the bow countered *Tico*'s inertia. The surge was notable but not violent. This time, hearing her stop through the void of space felt eerie.

"May I offer a suggestion, Captain?" Stratford asked. He was at Tom Hayes's—no, *his* duty station. *Right where he belongs.*

"Absolutely, Commander."

"Let's send one shuttle to the lunar base. It might be handy to have an asset on a different part of the game board. Hopefully they can nose around and uncover some intel."

"We're going to need all four shuttles when we get home," I said. "Send a couple of Tomcats instead, Strat. I want them fully armed with an electronic warfare officer on each bird. Sidearms and full combat dress—we don't know what they're walking into, either."

"I don't like the idea of reducing our fighter strength."

"Me neither, but the people we're trying to save might appreciate a medevac more than a missile. Handle it, please, Edgar."

He nodded sharply, then turned and left command.

"Major Trulani?"

"OBSREC online. Connection in eighty-three seconds, Captain."

I launched the data from cryptography on my station's right monitor. The selector allowed me to refocus the display on Victoria Island, the primary base of operations for UPE Defensive Forces. The image was pristine. The numerical display on the side of the screen showed nominal radiation, airborne particulate content, and atmospheric gas composition.

Everything was as it should've been, but none of it made any sense. The Consortium only wouldn't have fired back if they either didn't see the attack coming or didn't believe the UPE would allow their weapons to detonate.

Why else wouldn't they defend themselves?

"Captain, OBSREC has locked on. We are receiving a text message, encoded eyes only for you," Pierre said. "Priority level four."

A self-terminating message. There would be no record.

"No response, Mr. Pierre. Send it to my station, please."

> Captain Mackenzie,
>
> I am sad to report Earth has experienced the aftereffects of a sizable interplanetary coronal mass ejection—the biggest yet in our history. Damage has been cataclysmic. Several samples of ejecta have impacted the planet, mostly centered in the eastern Asian continent.
>
> The severity of the electromagnetic disruption associated with the ICME has thus far hampered any humanitarian response. *Ticonderoga* is our best hope for regaining planetary stability. We rely upon you and your crew to bring safety back to our world. Please return with all speed.
>
> Best wishes for a quick return,
> Secretary General Pons Schweizer

I had to admit, it was a great cover story, even if it proved Schweizer was completely full of shit.

"Get us back underway, please, Mr. Salinski."

"The Tomcats are in the air locks," Stratford said as he strode back to his station.

"Push the button, Strat. Mr. Pierre, have Chiefs Brinn and Stykes meet Commander Stratford and me in my quarters in ten minutes, please."

Stratford raised an eyebrow.

"We need to talk. Now." I turned and started for the corridor. "Mind the store, Trulani."

✣

"Speak freely."

Mindy shook her head. "There's no way, Captain. A coronal mass ejection does not launch solid stellar matter anywhere, much less directly on the OOC homeland."

"I don't disagree. However, we are dealing with the fate of the entire planet. Improbable, impossible, or nonexistent, we need proof."

"The moon base should have consistent data," Stratford offered.

"Can you get a hold of the boys and have them do some digging?"

"They're already set to find out what they can and report back, but I'll update them on the specifics."

"Have them work through Mindy," I said.

"We backed the wrong horse, didn't we?" Brinn asked no one in particular.

Seeing someone else climb on my train of thought made me feel a little less crazy.

"That's a dangerous way to think," I said. "It does appear I killed the wrong guy to stop this, but that's on me."

"Kegar killed Commander Hayes and had Jake . . ." Mindy trailed off. "God knows what he would've done to us if you didn't put him in a body bag. To question *that* seems dangerous."

"Kegar's a nonissue," Stratford agreed. "Let's stay focused on Secretary General Schweizer. This conversation alone would be considered mutiny, but nonetheless, we need to face reality."

"We're still getting ahead of ourselves. We have a hypothesis, but we don't have proof."

"I'll run the scans and gather the data, but the likelihood is low that the sun just decided to rain down hell upon the UPE's archenemy while we were otherwise occupied."

"Mindy, I'm confident you'll come up with the proof we need," I said. "Do we say anything to command at this point? If so, what?"

"They will expect two-way contact," Brinn said. "Standard procedure gives them access to condition reports, telemetry, action reports—even our stores levels."

"We can't give them that," Stratford said. "Not if we're preparing for combat against them."

"Can we taint the feed?" Mindy asked. "Maybe we can select what data gets sent?"

"Not feasibly," Brinn said.

"Com stays down, then. They'll know we're up to something, but we can't risk a direct intel leak," I said. All heads nodded. "Let's stop dancing around the elephant in my quarters—are we willing to mix it up with the UPE?"

"Scuttlebutt says if they destroyed the OOC without provocation, we have to," Mindy said.

"What does your butt say?" I asked.

Mindy glared at me as if it were beneath her to articulate an answer. "Our oath mandates we take them on."

"How do you figure that?" Brinn snapped.

"The UPE stands to facilitate peace across the planet," Mindy said calmly. "Even if some facet of our own organization broke the peace, it's still our job to fix it."

"You're against taking direct action, Brinn?" I asked.

"I'm against fighting our own, but I stand with this ship and her crew."

Fair enough.

"Stratford?" I asked.

"I have no love lost with the roots of the organization."

I was quiet for a long time. "I shouldn't have doubted you three."

"I don't think you did, Captain," Brinn said. "You were just giving us the chance to speak our minds."

CHAPTER 13

30 MAY 2126

Ticonderoga had her game face on while Salinski made the initial orbital insertion. Mindy requested a complete equatorial circumnavigation to give her primary scanners the best possible look at the planet. That same trajectory also allowed us to deposit sensor remotes over the Consortium and North America, which should allow intelligence gathering at minimal risk to us. We then transferred to a geostationary orbit directly over the magnetic North Pole at the atmospheric interface.

It was a problematic place to park a ship.

Ideally, the convergence of the Earth's magnetic field and the atmospheric boundary should confuse any weapons or observation technology. But sauce for the goose was sauce for the gander—it would also make our own navigational and observational equipment malfunction. In theory, the remotes we'd deposited during the equatorial passes should provide good intel, as long as the signal wasn't degraded too bad by the electromagnetic interactions I hoped would conceal the ship. All of the operational irregularities meant the navigation system would have to be manned until we moved into a higher orbit or a more conventional one. It wasn't the best from a power utilization standpoint, and it would be worse on my helm officer, but Mr. Salinski's youth was a benefit.

"Post guards at any possible point of ingress from here on out," I said. "Two-man teams."

"Yes, ma'am," Trulani said.

I keyed a series of controls on my console before I spoke into my handset. "Daniels, status?"

"Alpha flight is in the tubes, Captain. Rogers has been briefed to command beta flight. Sams and Jing will ride shotgun for the shuttle trip to the dockyard."

"Confirmed. Are you clear on the rules of engagement?"

"Earth is a military no-fly zone. Warn first when possible, prosecute any aggressive acts when necessary."

Stratford looked to tactical operations. "Trulani, what do the remotes read?"

"All clear, Commander."

I nodded. "Roger that. Switching launch control to alpha flight. Launch when ready."

The displays lit up as the ten alpha Tomcats launched. They weren't visible on the scans for long—they disappeared into the funnel of Earth's gravitational field interference. Adding in their stealth design, they should be invisible to anyone or anything watching on Earth.

"We're getting a priority com from Earth Command, Captain," Pierre said.

"Any idea who it is?"

"He says he's the secretary general, ma'am."

"Strat, take the call." I don't know how or why this idea came to me. "Tell him I'm dead."

Stratford stepped toward Pierre with confidence, indicating he should patch in the speakers and wireless pickup. "Hello, sir. This is Commander Edgar Stratford of *Ticonderoga*. How may I assist you?"

"I'd like to speak to your captain." The voice was scratchy over the speakers, but it sounded amiable enough. I could glean nothing from his tone.

"So would I, but we lost her on the way in."

"I'm sorry to hear that," Schweizer said. His voice was every bit as even as before. "We know you're orbital and hiding over the pole. I'm going to need my ship back now, son."

Stratford came unglued instantly with a ferocity that surprised even me. "Listen to me, you Swiss prick. I know your people are used to giving up without a fight, but you'll have to step over my rotting headless corpse to board this ship."

"So it's treason?"

"Nope. It's a coup, idiot. You can step down or I can kill you with my bare fucking hands right before I bury you in a shallow grave and piss on it. The choice is yours."

"I don't understand where all of this hostility is coming from, Commander."

"Mr. Secretary General, check my file, and you'll see where the hostility comes from. As far as the UPE is concerned, Earth is now a no-fly zone. Test this declaration and you'll find hostility on a level unknown to cowards like you." Stratford motioned to Pierre to cut the channel.

"Captain, the remotes just alerted. We're seeing launches from the UPE carriers deployed closest to the Consortium," Trulani said.

I opened the One-MC com channel. "All hands to combat stations. Launch all Tomcats."

The hull rattled in response as the launch cycles began.

I keyed another series of com controls. "Brinn, we're going into atmospheric combat."

"I figured as much. Atmospheric maneuvering is available at your command, Captain."

"Pierre, get me Secretary General Schweizer," Stratford said.

"No response, sir."

"I guess I shouldn't have told him I was going to kill him," Strat mumbled.

"All hands, brace for chop," I said into the One-MC pickup. I let up on the button. "Take us down, Salinski."

"Activating thrusters," Salinski said.

"Major Trulani, set the concussors for standoff suppression," Strat said. "Take the locks off the gun crews."

"Aye, sir," Trulani said.

"Attention UPE aircraft," Stratford said into his com. "You have entered a no-fly zone. Return to your home ports immediately or you will be engaged. Repeating—return to your home port and land now, or you will be fired upon."

"Alpha flight is engaging," Trulani said. An unfamiliar alarm blared. "Captain, we have an incoming ICBM on an intercept course."

Satellite killer.

"Launch a sensor remote!" I snapped as I stabbed the com control. "Brinn! Shut everything down!"

He stammered over the open line. I didn't have time to clue him in about the inbound missile or the hope I had to confuse it by changing *Tico*'s output signature.

"Now!"

Five seconds took an hour to pass before everything in command went black.

Without power, coms were dead. I didn't think of that.

"I'm going to engineering!" I shouted as I ran out of command.

I sprinted through the corridor with only one goal. Battery powered and weak, the emergency lights were barely enough to see by when moving at a crawl. Adding in the unpredictable lurching of the ship now that she had entered free fall made it amazing that I didn't run over the top of anyone.

I couldn't believe I didn't think about the fucking coms going offline with the power.

"Bring it back up, Brinn!" I ducked around the last crewman and started up the aft stairwell. "Bring it up—"

The lights came up at the same time an incredible crack of thunder rattled *Ticonderoga*, booming throughout the ship. I was jostled about like a palm tree in a hurricane as the shock wave from the satellite killer's explosion hammered against the ship.

Picking myself up off the stairs hurt, but I had to hurry. Whistling air outside the hull replaced the echoing thunder as the ship's fall accelerated.

Brinn looked only slightly calmer once I found him at his alcove beyond the top of the stairs.

"Max out the ventral thrusters if they're not already."

"Ventral thrusters to one hundred and ten percent," Brinn said.

"I gotta go," I said as I turned and shot back down the stairs.

Multiple concussor batteries activated on my return to command, replacing the turbulence from before with an uneven chattering.

The fight was on.

"We're getting buggered down here," Stratford shouted over the rising chaos. "We need to get back up where we can make real use of the main gun."

"Salinski," I said, "I need a show of force over that last carrier." Glancing across the growing red indicators on the SDC, I wasn't sure it was the best move.

We also didn't have any choice—the last carrier had to be removed from the fight without killing its crew.

"Parameters?"

"As low and hard as you can burn, Salinski. Aim for the center line. I don't want them capsized."

"Roger that, Captain. Going to max thrust now."

"Strat, you're not going to like this, but I've got to go to the surface. We can't win anything from up there without diplomacy on the ground. And before you ask—no one else is coming with me. Every crew member is needed here. But since I'm technically dead, nobody will miss me."

"And what the bloody hell are *we* supposed to do?"

"Go back up. Consolidate your resources. Patch up and stick to the plan—do what you can to protect the Consortium from further damage," I said.

The collision alert klaxon sounded. The data on the SDC was alarming.

"Pull up, Salinski!" I shouted.

Even I could tell he didn't have time to react. He kept his hands on the panel, making minor corrections as the Tomcat deck's starboard side ruffled the hair of the carrier's onlookers on vulture's row. He'd passed straight over, less than one hundred feet above the carrier's flight deck.

The kid has balls.

"Jesus Christ," Stratford said blankly.

"No, Marlin Salinski," I corrected. "That'll blind them for a while. I need to take the chance, Strat. I'm taking the last shuttle."

"Captain—"

"Commander, you have your orders. Stop at the dockyard and fix the ship. Send a crew to the hydrazine station and lock it down. Protect the Consortium and wait for orders from me or Admiral West."

"Yes, ma'am."

"Good luck," I said.

I charged out of command, about to bet my life that my dad's respect for the people of the Asian basin wasn't misplaced. He'd said he'd seen their culture evolve past a desire for war. I hoped they hadn't changed their minds.

~

"Daniels, this is Captain Mackenzie," I said into the com pickup.

"Is that you in the shuttle, Cap?"

"Roger that. Daniels, can you make a guess as to command and control for the Consortium?"

"Yes, ma'am," Daniels said. "It looks like they're a hundred clicks north of Neijiang in China's Sichuan province. You want us to form up and take you in?"

"Negative. Guard *Ticonderoga*'s withdrawal and give me some time to do what I need to do."

"And that would be?" Daniels asked.

End this.

"Look after things, Major. Mackenzie out."

I had no more than a feeling and my dad's stories, but I couldn't believe the Consortium picked this fight. Their resistance to UPE operations hadn't ever been much more than a nuisance. Maybe Kegar had acted on his own behalf by grabbing *Ticonderoga*, but someone else had capitalized on it and escalated the conflict to genocide.

The ride into Consortium territory was uneventful, which was great. I didn't have the weaponry to fight or the speed to run. The computer was in charge for the bulk of the flight. Dead reckoning wouldn't have been possible even if I had been familiar with the countryside, as everything was a uniform mat of destruction.

This was beyond the hand of God. Only humankind would choose to wreak this kind of destruction on its own planet.

The two OOC guys that picked me up after I landed were dressed in regular uniforms instead of protective gear. Frisking me thoroughly, they finally decided to lead me to the armored personnel carrier they had rolled up in. They were likely staff from the command and control bunker, but I wouldn't know for sure until they got me to someone higher up the food chain. Either they were unable to communicate because of the language barrier or were unwilling to communicate because of orders. The end result was the same.

They used a Geiger counter to scan me both before and after I was allowed inside the bunker. After passing through the entrance of what resembled a giant vacuum cleaner, we were all checked a final time before I was led to a small room and left alone.

I wasn't foolish enough to believe my lack of shackles meant I was free. Trying the door was out of the question. Appearances were everything in the early stages of a political negotiation. I wasn't about to do anything to cause suspicion or offense, so I steepled my hands on the table in front of me, sat straight in my chair, and waited.

About ten minutes passed before the door opened and two women walked in. The first had a drawn sidearm, a tense expression, and a uniform identical to the one worn by the men that brought me in. The second woman wore an expensive civilian pantsuit.

Clipped Mandarin words flew between the two. The woman in the suit snapped a short sentence after assessing me. When the guard didn't react, she pointed to the door and barked a word with obvious meaning.

With hesitation, the guard holstered her weapon and disappeared outside. I kept my eyes downcast as the civilian looked at me thoughtfully.

Her heavily accented English was flawless when she spoke. "I assume you are some kind of messenger?"

"My name is Allison Mackenzie. I am the captain of the United Planet Earth spacecraft *Ticonderoga*. I'm here to offer my ship's humanitarian resources and to try to stabilize the situation."

"Neither would be necessary were it not for your actions." The woman's face filled with a mixture of sorrow and rage I found completely understandable.

"Those were the actions of a government I once served. We're not even sure what happened, but either way, my crew and I are here to help."

"A government you once served . . . and yet you just identified yourself as the captain of a United Planet Earth space-based battleship?"

"I've only recently dismissed myself from their service after a lifetime career in the UPE. Surely you can understand that the habit of identifying myself as a member of the organization is somewhat ingrained."

"Yes, I can." The woman's tone was frigid. I wasn't sure she took my meaning. "What do you think you can do to help us?"

"Alone, nothing of note. My ship is ready to deliver what supplies we can and administer aid where we can, but we can't have any real impact without your cooperation. Obviously, we won't violate your sovereignty without your consent."

"As if our sovereignty means anything to you." She sniffed. "Why the mighty UPE would enact contingencies after attacking us without provocation—I can only imagine."

"Ma'am, you might possess facts I do not yet have. If what I think happened matches the facts, you and I need to assure it never happens to anyone—especially not your people—ever again. I'm offering you food, medical assistance, shelter—all of the things your people desperately need. What do you have to lose by accepting our help?"

"Everything we have left," she said. The rage in her voice wasn't subsiding.

I sat back in my chair. Whatever happened next needed to be her move.

I've already pushed too hard.

Composing herself, she asked, "I assume you will now tell me you are not responsible for the recent violations of our territorial sovereignty?"

"Those violations were necessary to ascertain what happened. We also surveyed your territory to formulate a relief—"

"None of which would have been necessary if it weren't for your attack!" she snapped.

"Look," I said, leaning forward. "If you're seriously not going to accept that my crew and I had nothing to do with the attack on your country and that I'm here to help, you might as well move on to torture or public execution. You have better things to do than sit here and chase me in some cat-and-mouse game."

She stared into me. I had a hundred things I wanted to say. I wanted to shake some sense into her, but I felt certain this would fall the wrong way if I spoke first. I kept expecting her to leave the room, check a phone, or knock on the window, but she just stared at me.

"How, specifically, would you help us?"

"*Ticonderoga* has a large compliment of relief supplies. We're inventorying them now, but the basics are water, food, medical equipment, and shelter. We would work with you to deploy those supplies while providing border protection. Maintaining your security would be a high priority."

"You would fight your own people?"

"We already have," I said. "My people are aboard *Ticonderoga*. Anyone who would stand by and perpetrate this kind of attack is our enemy."

She looked hesitant. "When could your efforts begin?"

"I left my crew with orders to prepare for missions to start as soon as possible. The first flights will drop as soon as they get a call telling them where to go."

"And how long would you stay?"

"Until the situation is stabilized, from both a humanitarian and a security standpoint. We will, of course, leave when we are asked. That being said, I think it would be counterproductive for us to leave you vulnerable to more attack." I paused, trying to find the words I wanted. "The real question isn't what we'll do—humanitarian work is our mandate. The question is rather simple. Will we be allowed to do our work?"

"Your missions would need to originate from here. Our people will be more open to your efforts if they see us together. We will send our personnel with yours," she said.

"Fair enough. I'd like to have a crew collect the shuttle I brought down. It is a valuable asset to the relief effort."

"We accept your terms," she said, regaining her original air of formality.

✣

The soldier from earlier was waiting at the door with her sidearm drawn as my interrogator led me out of the interview room to the com station. She stalked a few steps behind, making me less than comfortable.

Significant back-and-forth communication between my new friends in OOC command and Stratford aboard *Ticonderoga* was necessary to get everyone on the same page. Along with organizing the logistics, I was informed *Ticonderoga* had been absolutely pounded while repelling additional attacks against the Consortium. They hadn't taken heavier fire after the satellite killer exploded against the sensor remote, but that damage coupled with the smaller weapons fire from the UPE aircraft had still knocked things around.

They were operational, but only just.

We agreed the first relief flight would come down at 0530 tomorrow with crew onboard to retrieve my shuttle and provide liaisons to the OOC personnel in the command center. In return, several OOC personnel would join the shuttle crew to provide oversight and assistance with the first relief run.

The Consortium got me a real-time com channel to *Lexington*, which involved technical constraints my people couldn't overcome, considering the admiral's distance from Earth. My communications with Admiral West had been text only since he set out for Alpha Station. Debriefing and gauging reactions was nice on video.

Especially to this . . .

"I'm glad you reached out to them, Allison. I have to admit, it was a gutsy move. I'm not sure I could have done the same thing," West said.

"Secretary General Schweizer seems to have lost his mind, sir. It's going to take some unconventional thinking to maneuver him out of the situation."

"We're still a few days out. I don't know how much help I can be. I've never been involved in a mutiny. Allison, you do understand that's what you're doing."

I couldn't tell if he was asking a question or making a statement.

"Schweizer either perpetrated this attack or allowed it to happen—"

"Allison, we've heard back from the team you sent to the moon base. They've confirmed solar stability. There was no coronal mass ejection."

My heart started pounding as another puzzle piece fell into place. I could nearly see the picture. I took a deep, steadying breath. "He can't be allowed to do it again."

"What do you have in mind?" West asked.

"The Consortium has arranged a meeting with him under a flag of truce. I intend to be part of the OOC delegation. I'll try to undercut him publicly—if I can get in front of enough of the right people or cameras, I'll get the truth out and wait for public opinion to do the rest."

"You don't think they'll recognize and arrest you right away?"

"It's a possibility. I've altered my appearance as much as I can. Couple that with a fake credential from the Consortium and the fact that Stratford told Schweizer I died on the way in, and I think I have a chance."

"A pretty slim chance," West said.

"I have to try. Enough of our own people have already been hurt—I'd rather not put any more in danger. The truth is, Kegar saw this coming and grabbed *Ticonderoga* to stop it. We got in the way of that, Admiral.

I got in the way when I stopped him. I can't put this right, but I can try to prevent it from getting any more wrong."

"Your plan is nuts, Allison. You're right about one thing—this is too big to go unanswered. I want a contingency in place in case you can't pull it off. If you fail, I need to be able to take up the fight when I get there."

"Give me three days, sir. I should know then if I can raise internal UPE pressure against him within that time."

"We'll call it four, then," West said. "If I haven't heard from you by then, I'm going to find him and kill him."

"Fair enough, sir."

"Godspeed, Captain."

"May the wind be at your back, Admiral."

CHAPTER 14

1 JUNE 2126

"You are not sleeping." The woman in the pantsuit looked drawn as she stepped back into the interview room I'd been housed in.

I still hadn't spotted the surveillance camera, but I knew there had to be one. It didn't bother me. I would have been the first to admit that I'd have watched, too, if the tables were turned.

I sat up straighter on the cot but made no movement otherwise. "I find it difficult to sleep under circumstances such as these."

"You . . ." She visibly pulled herself back from whatever she had intended to say. I had a feeling it was another tirade, which I also wouldn't have blamed her for. She acknowledged the interview table and chairs where we first met. "May I sit?"

"Of course. I will join you at the table, if that's all right?" I took her nod as approval and padded across the concrete in my bare feet to sit in what had become my chair. "I hope I haven't done anything to contribute to your own sleeplessness."

She took a deep breath. "That is difficult to answer honestly."

As before, neutral ground was difficult to identify. Gently, I said, "I will answer any questions I can."

Her eyes closed, and she spoke hesitant words when they opened. "Why do you do this?"

Right or wrong, I gauged her question's scope as focusing beyond my most recent actions. "I believe humanity needs help."

"Most Americans I have met say they live as they do for their God."

I hesitated an instant before I spoke a truth I had always known. "I don't believe in God."

She looked at me for a long time. "You have no beliefs?"

"I have a lot of beliefs, actually, just not one in the nebulous idea of an all-controlling God." I watched her for a moment and decided she wanted to hear a little more but was unwilling to ask. "I can't argue for or against the existence of a higher power in the universe. In my experience, too many people use God as an excuse for bad choices, poor behavior, or weakness. I prefer to believe in the weakness or power of the individual. Humans can choose to be good or bad." I weighed her reaction for a moment before I asked, "Do you believe in God?"

"I did. How long have you been in the military?"

I dismissed the idea of correcting her, as what was once a defensive force had to look like a purely offensive army now. "I graduated from college with a degree in engineering. I joined the UPE after that."

"You were conscripted?"

"No, ma'am. I went by choice. At the time, it seemed like the best way I could do the most good for the most people. That hasn't changed. I didn't foresee the organization I served causing the problems I wanted to fix."

"It is strange to me you do not deny UPE involvement in what happened to the Consortium member countries."

I shrugged. "A great literary detective once said, 'Once you remove the impossible, what remains, however improbable, must be the truth.' We found evidence of launch activity on UPE soil and impact on your own. There is little to deny."

"Why?"

Again, I assumed her question had wider ramifications. "Money, maybe. Extraplanetary mining generates more revenue than any other industry in the history of the world. The contracts are worth uncounted trillions of dollars. Removing the competition your consortium represents meant the established infrastructure would have the entire mining trade. The beneficiaries of that infrastructure undoubtedly put some of those dollars to work buying our leader."

I once again believed the words she spoke were different than what was truly on her mind. "Do you have family?"

"I did," I said. "I believe my dad died recently. I'm not sure what's happened to my mother."

"No spouse?"

The question stabbed where I didn't believe she'd intended to strike. "I cared for someone. He died as a result of these events."

Her response was prompt and seemed genuine. "I am sorry for your loss."

"As I am sorry for your own."

"Do you think your efforts will be successful?"

"I don't honestly know," I admitted. "But if I do not try, I will never improve anything in this world."

"You're gambling with the fate of my country."

"I'm gambling with the fate of my own, too. Descent into hell is easy, but I'll not see anyone fall deeper into that hole for lack of my trying to swerve them off their path. My own life has been and will be in jeopardy as well. The accusations I must level are not going to be well received by the secretary general. If I'm found out before I can bring the truth forward, this isn't likely to end well for me. No part of this is without risk."

"You would truly risk your life for an enemy?"

I clung to my diplomatic cool like my life depended on it. "You are not, and to my knowledge never have been, my enemy."

Dark eyes, unreadable and emotionless, seemed to examine my words, judging their veracity. If I'd had time to guess what was behind them, I'd have assumed pain and exhaustion, but before I could, she wordlessly excused herself. It took me a few minutes to get past the anger her attitude brought out in me. She had come to see me and left before the conversation became less than civil.

Even though it hurt, that felt like progress.

My thoughts returned to *Ticonderoga*'s structural integrity alarm and our near miss with the belt. They rolled forward through one event at a time. Fire flickered in colored glass globes hanging in my parents' attic, confusing me. Sleep finally came somewhere after I rested my head on my folded arms but before I figured out why my dad had to die.

The dream my sleep eventually brought was disturbing enough that I wished I'd managed to stay awake.

My childhood home was in front of me, ablaze, and someone was screaming inside. I fought the smoking, flaming inferno mere inches from my face with only a short length of garden hose with a weak stream of water.

Hopeless.

~

I wasn't sure if I'd managed to pick the right landing zone or if the area my shuttle occupied had become the landing zone, but Shuttle Four's bulk guarded a sizable group of guards, civilian officials, and me from the frigid wind.

I didn't know much about the Consortium's weather, but it felt too cold to be normal for the region. The dense clouds and dirty sky were consistent with what I would have expected following a nuclear event, a picture that sent a chill up my spine.

"I never asked your name," I told my handler.

"I would not have told you."

"They'll never believe we're on the same side if we don't work together." I stared down at her, searching for a change. I needed to see my words sinking in, even if only a little. "Your people will continue to suffer if we fail."

"Your people caused our suffering." She closed her eyes. The agony that crossed her tired features was not fake. "You are, however infuriatingly, correct. I am Yang Chai."

I extended my hand to her, which she shook. "My friends call me Allie. I'm pleased to meet you, Chai."

We stood in awkward silence again for a long time. "Your UPE Command received and responded to our communication. They are sending a shuttle to collect our delegation this morning."

"Will I still be part of that delegation?"

She looked surprised. "Of course. Did you not say it was vital to the plan?"

You have to build trust—we've got a lot of work left to do and no time left to get it done.

Ticonderoga, as formidable as she was, couldn't hope to protect close to a quarter of the planet. Even with all her cards on the table, we also weren't going to put more than a dent in the humanitarian crisis. We needed to solve the issue with Schweizer one way or the other and fold the UPE back into the resolution of the crisis.

There wasn't any time to spare.

"Yes, I did. Our best evidence says Secretary General Schweizer has kept the truth of his actions from the majority of our people. My hope is that once it gets out, the political and popular pressure will cause change. I know the UPE as a whole will not stand for this."

Thrumming distortion waves from a *Ticonderoga* shuttle's engines rattled the morning as the building-shaped craft dropped through the clouds following my shuttle's beacon, bringing an end to our conversation. Trees around the clearing I'd landed in were leveled by the shock wave of a distant explosion, widening the available opening even more. Plenty of room was left on the leaf-littered soil for anything *Tico* might send down. This would become the staging area for our relief efforts.

Watching a human-made structure with absolutely no aerodynamics settle to Earth so gracefully always amazed me. The familiarity of the "flying telephone booth" brought a little comfort after my night in the Consortium. Yang's troops, on the other hand, were nowhere near relaxed when the shuttle's main door opened and Mindy Stykes appeared alone on the ramp. Both hands were visible, as was her hesitation.

"We have no weapons on board," she said. "Our pilots are the only true soldiers with us. May we proceed?"

Yang showed none of the same hesitation as she stepped forward. "Yes, please."

Lieutenant Rogers and three maintenance technicians came down the loading ramp and moved straight to the shuttle I had brought down the previous day. I moved toward the front of the group of OOC personnel, waiting for Mindy to come to me.

She moved deliberately, finally coming to stand in front of me, omitting any sign of a salute. "Status, Lieutenant?"

"*Ticonderoga* is still docked. Chief Brinn has been working around the clock to repair and replenish the ship. We've maintained a combat air patrol over OOC territory since our initial orbital insertion."

"Mindy, as soon as you get aboard the shuttle, call Stratford and tell him to let the next inbound UPE shuttle through the CAP."

She looked confused. "Okay."

"Admiral West is inbound with *Lexington.* He'll be here in under three days. If I haven't secured the situation by then, he's going in guns hot. One way or the other, Schweizer is going to leave office."

Mindy looked shocked.

"On your way, Mindy. That shuttle won't be far out."

She hesitated, then snapped a salute and ran for the shuttle Rogers was preparing. Two preselected squads of OOC personnel stepped forward and into the waiting shuttles.

They were gone minutes later.

"We're next," I told no one in particular.

"Do you really believe this is going to work?" Yang Chai asked me.

I rubbed my eyes, suddenly feeling exhausted. "If they see any trace of uncertainty in our actions, no. If you think anyone on the delegation will hesitate, then you're right, we might as well give up now. But I do not intend to fail."

Chai didn't say another word until the unfamiliar UPE shuttle landed to take us to Schweizer.

~

Watching the UPE shuttle crew for signs of recognition during the flight constituted the first test of my cover ID. One of the grunts seemed to check me out, but his focus was below my neck. Yang had lent me inconspicuous clothes, but the black blouse was a little tight and the pencil skirt was definitely short.

Tactically, Yang put me out in front once the shuttle landed. UPE culture assumed the most important person would lead the entourage, and Yang did nothing to dispel the thought. The idea of a Caucasian in a position of authority in this case wasn't completely out of the question, either. Naturalized UPE expatriates had become increasingly common in the Consortium in the past hundred years or so. UPE intelligence certainly had nothing to prove I wasn't in charge, and to insinuate that the Consortium was up to something was beyond the reach of the midlevel staffer sent to receive us. Yang could observe the situation while committing to nothing.

We were whisked away on a tour of the headquarters facility. The high point was intended to be a visit to the Grand Assembly Chamber. The proportions of the cavernous space defied description—it was much closer to the size of a sports arena than a simple meeting room. Not a single pillar interrupted the view from the podium centered under a giant UPE flag on the far wall.

So this was where the Consortium would surrender? Under a flag representing global partnership?

"An emergency session has been called for later this afternoon," our guide said, as if able to read my thoughts. He wore an immaculate black suit, glasses the same shade of silver as his hair, and the attitude of an established yes-man.

"Will it be the entire body?" I asked, more out of the belief I needed to say something if I were to be perceived as the one in charge.

He nodded. "The word is that Secretary General Schweizer isn't apt to react well to any refusals to this session."

"And a member of our party will be allowed to speak?"

The guide almost looked confused. "I'm told that's the entire reason for the session."

"Excellent," I said. "Our need to be heard is great. You've been reassuring."

His smile looked forced as he stepped toward the same exit we'd used to enter the gigantic hall.

The completely odd ramifications of the situation washed across me as I faltered, gazing at the banner fluttering in the air recirculation system's breeze. I couldn't understand how Schweizer thought this was going to work out. We were only allowed to linger momentarily before the tour continued to its termination point, a secured dormitory that included anything our delegation might require for a comfortable stay.

✣

"What happens now?" Yang asked.

"We can't do a lot except wait for the news conference," I said, glancing at my watch.

"This will help us?"

I wasn't completely sure what the intent was, but I took her words as a question. "He's betting on the idea that anyone left alive won't know exactly what caused the destruction to your countries. He's not completely wrong. Since the electromagnetic pulses did their damage, we both know you don't have complete proof of what happened. That's where my ship and I enter the picture. We hold unbiased but incriminating evidence."

"Aren't you afraid of being imprisoned?" Yang asked.

"I almost certainly will be. The only question is whether I can get the story told before they figure out who I am."

She studied me for a long time. "You're not the person I thought you were, Allison."

My heart swelled at her use of my first name. It represented a measured step toward becoming true allies. That was a big deal.

"I hope to be the person you need me to be, Yang Chai."

~

I presented my credential when the staffer that came to collect our party requested it. Hopefully, as far as he was concerned, he was guiding Tiffany Evans, chairperson of the Consortium Peoples' Health and Wellness Committee, to the Grand Assembly Chamber.

Our route deviated predictably from the earlier tour as we neared the chamber. Activity had increased appropriately in and around the structure as well. Inwardly, I cringed at the possibility that basic biometrics were tied to the scanner in the weapons check inside the door. But I was rewarded with the green light and reassuring ping.

A few more twists and turns in the corridors brought me to a green room filled with couches, chairs, food, and all manner of professionally dressed political appointees. Tall, fair-haired, and polished, it wasn't hard to pick Schweizer out of the crowd. I'd met with him in person occasionally. Not for the first time, I hoped our acquaintance was infrequent enough that coupled with the physical changes I'd made, he wouldn't recognize me.

I'm about to find out.

He crossed in front of me, politically deliberate in his steps. "Ms. Evans, I presume?"

I nodded and smiled. "You must be Secretary General Schweizer."

"On behalf of the UPE, I'd like to express my sorrow for the experience your countries have been through. No one could have expected our own sun would turn against us this way." He offered me his hand, which I shook.

Does he really believe this shit? "We are fortunate the damage wasn't any worse."

"I wish we could do more for your people than merely offer assistance. Any gesture we make pales in comparison to your people's needs."

"Any act of kindness would be deeply appreciated. Our need is great."

"Your credential wasn't rather forthcoming. Your lineage obviously begins outside of the Consortium. You must have an interesting family story."

"No more than anyone else's," I said casually. "My grandfather was in the construction industry. He and his wife decided to stay in China, and the family line carried on. It's a beautiful country."

"It was," Schweizer said without a hint of sadness. He switched gears effortlessly. "So I'll go out and say a few words before I give you the podium. You'll want to graciously accept our assistance, and we'll be in business."

"And what, specifically, is that assistance?"

"Whatever it takes to get you back on your feet so you can contribute to our global community," he said lightly. "We hope you'll finally come to understand we're better off working together than against each other. I trust I have your support."

Assuming he knew the answer, he whispered something in an aide's ear and allowed himself to be spirited out the door toward the assembly hall.

As if on cue, the staffer who had originally gathered our party reappeared at my side. "Ms. Evans, would you follow me, please? We have some people standing by to get you ready for the cameras."

I exchanged a glance with Yang and nodded, following him away from her and the other delegation members. The pomp of such an idea reaffirmed my opinion that I was a participant in a dog and pony show. The image of a makeup chair and artists standing by with rouge, lipstick, and curling irons formed in my mind as we strode through a less crowded corridor. I couldn't imagine being the right kind of desperate to accept what was about to go on here. If I failed, Admiral West would ride in and make sure Yang didn't have to find out what bowing to Schweizer felt like, and that was all that truly mattered.

I wasn't able to avoid the list of potential charges for my court martial. Impersonation, mutiny, humiliation of a political ruler—however justified, I wasn't going to get myself out of this. And my casual acceptance of that fact didn't surprise me anymore.

I'd pay the price when the bill came.

The two plain-clothed guards didn't react as my guide indicated the door between them. Once I'd passed through without him, the door closed, followed by the not-so-subtle click of a heavy lock.

Mistakes generally happen when one acts without first considering the consequences of those actions. I certainly didn't consider mine when a minute or two later, the lock clicked, the door opened, and my mother appeared.

"Mom!"

"Allison?"

Every time I'd imagined reuniting with my mother, she ran to me without hesitation. But I'd evidently been more successful changing my appearance after things went to hell than I'd thought.

I took my heavy-framed glasses off. "It's me, Mom. What are you doing here?"

The crushing hug and tears I'd imagined in the fantasy came late but just as hard.

"I'm sorry, baby. I'm so sorry."

"Mom . . . it's okay."

"I didn't even recognize you. My own daughter, and I didn't even know it was you. They told me you were killed in action!"

I pulled her tighter and made soothing noises until she settled. "Mom, I need to know what you're doing here."

"After the fire, I ran. Or at least, I tried to. I didn't get far before soldiers picked me up and placed me in protective custody."

"Who did they say they were protecting you from?"

"They said the Consortium was after me because of you."

"So why are you *here*, Mom?"

She looked confused.

"Right here, right now. If you were told the Consortium was after you, why are you here?"

"Pons . . . Secretary General Schweizer told me I needed to meet the delegation."

Pons? What's with the first name?

"Why? If they were trying to kill you, why would he send you to do anything for them? Think, Mom!"

"I wanted to ask them why they killed your dad."

"They didn't have anything to do with it, and even if they did, why would they tell you? They're the ones on the short end of this—they didn't do anything to deserve what happened to them."

"Allison?" Mom's face filled with a mixture of shock and panic.

"Mom, the Consortium has been destroyed."

"By a coronal mass—"

"By Schweizer! I saw it from orbit! Seventy-five percent of the Consortium's population is either dead or dying from the effects of nuclear attack. Most of their major cities and ports are laid to waste. They can't even help themselves, and Schweizer ordered this genocide!"

"Allison!"

Rage and stress and lack of sleep fueled my words. "Go back to the secretary general and tell him his term of office is over. We know what he did, and we're coming for him."

The look in her eyes told me more existed between her and the secretary general than I had known. "Tell him now."

"Allison, you're scaring me."

"You haven't seen anything yet." I pointed toward the door. "Go while I'm still willing to let you walk out of here."

She was almost to the door when the realization hit me. "You killed him, didn't you? You killed Dad."

She snapped back to face me. We locked eyes before she answered me. "No. I did not kill your father, Allison."

I met her response with equal fury. "I don't believe you."

Familiar betrayal twisted in my chest. She had a mind of her own and a choice. At best, she was using that mind to play messenger for a war criminal. My thoughts cast about briefly for all the other possibilities of her involvement, but I slammed it shut like my mother slammed the door behind her.

The sob rushed out, and I wasn't able to hold it back. Tears and confusion flowed from me like Snake River during the spring thaw.

What is going on?

✣

Two pairs of boots belonging to UPE enforcement officers on the holding room's tan carpet pulled me back to reality. The owners were familiar—they'd picked me up before, after I was granted command of *Ticonderoga*. The evaluation I'd been subjected to shortly afterward had been . . . unpleasant. I knew they were legit, and I knew the little guy in back was in charge.

Somewhere in the back of my mind, I registered the fact that my mother had been sent to confirm my identity. Schweizer had been suspicious but unsure, so he sent the one person who knew me for sure before he risked a bigger political incident.

Not that the Consortium was in any condition to cause one.

"Come with us, Ms. Mackenzie," the giant in front said.

Where? I found some backbone. "Why would I do anything for a couple of enforcement division lackeys?"

"We're here under orders from the secretary general, ma'am," Little snapped from behind his hulking colleague. He kept one hand on what appeared to be a taser while the big guy reached for a set of restraints. "We won't ask again."

"Are shackles necessary?"

"You're not a captain this time. You get treated like the enemy when you stand with the enemy. You don't get to resist," Giant said as he stepped forward and locked my hands behind my back with one smooth motion.

"Where are we going?"

"You are going to prison, bitch," Little said happily.

~

Clammy weather's wet bite helped me guess I was in one of the northern Baltic states. I figured we'd gone up and over the pole to get here. A solitary building stood away from the landing pad behind an otherwise nondescript barbed wire fence. The building's design didn't tell me much as we entered. Gray-painted cinder block walls and concrete floors didn't exactly require unique building techniques.

With certainty tingling in the back of my neck, I felt this was going to be my home for a while. No one would listen to any of Yang's protestations, and West was still over a day out. Little and Giant had been tight-lipped since they had outlined my immediate fate, reaffirming their lack of knowledge of a longer-term plan.

Physician, heal yourself . . .

There wasn't much to my ingress. No body cavity search. No orange jumpsuit.

I was hurried down a corridor and straight to the block where a solid steel door stood open. The other side of the door revealed a broom-closet-sized cell holding only a stainless-steel toilet and sink and a blue mattress on the floor. I was brusquely shoved inside. The heavy door thumped closed behind me.

I didn't need to check to see if it was locked.

Settled on the blue mat, I pondered the long game. Kegar had wanted me off the board so he could grab *Ticonderoga*, and he failed, more or less, anyway. Schweizer wanted me off the board because I knew what he'd done while I was tangling with Kegar, and he succeeded.

Some comfort came from the fact that Admiral West and Stratford were still active. It wouldn't be clean, but they'd hook up in a few days and deal with Schweizer. *Ticonderoga* and *Lexington* would get the job done—they could remove the secretary general with an orbital assault, if necessary. I came here to force him to see the game was over, which, if I'd been successful, would have avoided a lot of unnecessary deaths. But I hadn't.

After lying down, I eventually found welcome sleep.

My dreams, however, I could have done without.

"Thunderstrike 174 cleared for alert takeoff on runway two alpha."

I struck open the com as I pushed the throttles to the zone four detent. "Lieutenant Mackenzie in 174 beginning takeoff roll."

"Move your ass, 174. *Starliner* is defenseless out there."

I know.

The moon's gravity was about a sixth of Earth's, but there wasn't any atmosphere to help with lift, either. My fighter left the takeoff roll about the same in the end, which wasn't terribly long. Thunderstrikes were spicy little birds.

"Thunderstrike 174 is wheels up. Turning bearing zero-nine-zero relative to engage."

"Roger, 174. We'll get you some help as quickly as we can."

I stayed low and fast. The battleball's radar would lose me in the ground clutter if I was lucky, plus I saved the time and exposure I'd have spent climbing to a safer altitude.

I rapped the com. "*Starliner*, what's your status?"

"Engines three and four are damaged, 174. We're not going to hold up much longer."

"How many bogies?" I asked.

"Two that we know of."

"I'll be there in twenty seconds." I ended the com.

I needed to concentrate. Rocks and boulders flew by below me as my Thunderstrike wound to top speed. My HUD alerted me when I was under *Starliner*, signaling it was time for a high-G turn that sucked the blood from my feet and up to my head, reddening my vision. The sickening maneuver did its job, allowing me to dispatch the first battleball with a single concussor burst.

I'd have to pay dearly to get the second one.

Sucking in gusts of air to constrict my blood vessels and fight off the crushing G-forces, I nudged the stick forward and shot between the battleball and *Starliner*'s portside wing. Impacts from the battleball's particle cannon made it clear that the maneuver worked. I had it chasing me.

That was great for *Starliner* but not quite as favorable for me.

"*Starliner*, your sector is clear," I said into the com. "Proceed to base one."

If I'd been low before, I was positively skimming the lunar surface after I came out of an aileron roll I hoped would throw the battleball's sensors off. My ploy failed, and the little gunport-covered drone punished me for my misjudgment.

Preferring to take my chances with the moon's craggy surface instead of guaranteed death from the battleball's particle cannons, I stood on the left thruster control. Skidding into a turn that threw my stomach against my ribs, I brought the battleball squarely into the weapons reticle. I had enough time to register nothing had happened after I pulled the trigger before the battleball took its opportunity and rammed my Thunderstrike.

Screaming was out of the question—there wasn't time. Bracing was something of a reflex, coming immediately. I tucked my arms inward and down near the stick and brought my head down, which probably saved my life as my Thunderstrike tumbled wing-over-wing into the gray lunar surface. The first roll took the wings, and the next several took the tails, engines, and compressed the remaining fuselage around my body, trapping me effectively facedown.

I couldn't even check my oxygen supply to see how long I had left before I would die.

PART TWO

CHAPTER 15

7 JULY 2126

"Ma'am?"

"Mackenzie, Captain Allison Jane. Nine-seven-three-four-tango-one-five-epsilon."

"We're here to help you, ma'am."

I recoiled. I recognized this guy too. He was the doctor that worked on me after the Tomcat accident. He was with Schweizer's UPE.

"Stay away from me."

He backed off with his hands raised and palms toward me. "How long have you been here, Captain?"

A simple enough question. Why couldn't I answer?

"They never turned the lights off."

"How often did they let you out?"

I shook my head. "Food came through the hole in the door."

"How often?"

I clutched my growling stomach in response.

"Captain, how many people have you seen since you were brought here?"

Simple again. But I shook my head. He inched closer to me. Why wasn't I paying better attention?

"Stay away from me."

"You remember me from before, don't you, Captain?"

I nodded.

"Did I treat you all right?"

I nodded again.

"It doesn't seem like these people treated you so well. Will you let me treat you all right again?"

Another easy question. I nodded. "What are you going to do to me?"

"I'm going to take you home, Captain. Because of what you've been through, I think it would be best if we sedated you. While you're out, we'll run some tests, clean you up, and get you some nutrition. Is that okay?"

At least I won't be here anymore.

"Yes."

"Lie down for me, please."

I did as he asked. He was ready with a syringe.

This time, my dreams were happy.

CHAPTER 16

8 JULY 2126

"Strat?"

He was by my side before I knew I'd called for him or realized where I was. The too-tight pressure of his hand around mine was comforting—it felt good to touch someone I trusted.

"Water?"

I nodded. He disappeared and returned with a cup, accidentally poking me with the straw before I managed a sip.

Resisting the temptation to stroke his beard when he leaned in close was impossible. I curled my fingers in the coarse whiskers. "Is this regulation?"

He set the cup on the bedside table. "I took some leave to sit with you."

I coughed hard. After a bit more water, I managed, "How long was I out?"

"That depends on how you look at it." He pulled a chair closer, sat, and took my hand again. The strength of his grip told me he was still afraid of losing me.

"Who has *Tico*?"

Stratford let out a long breath. "The interim secretary general ordered us to land. The situation was stable. I didn't have a choice."

"Crew okay?"

"Everyone is fine. They're worried about you, though."

"I'm not worth the trouble."

He ran a hand through my hair. "Sure you are."

"Schweizer?"

"He allowed himself to be taken into custody. He claimed the courts should try him and swore he'd be exonerated once the evidence was made public."

"He'll die in custody next to a golf course." I coughed again.

Stratford got me some more water. "Heroes get remembered, but assholes live in luxury."

"What happens to us?"

"We live happily ever after?" Stratford suggested.

"And ride off into the sunset in our spaceship?"

"I don't think so, Allie. The program is on the rocks. They've decided *Tico* is too old to continue funding and too powerful for anyone to control. Rebuilding the Consortium will be the most expensive project ever conceived—they've got to get the money somewhere, I guess."

"*Lexington*?"

"She got sent out after another sick transport ship—*Fuji*, I think. After that, she's to return to her lunar dock for full decommissioning," Strat said.

I was quiet for a long time. "How long was I confined?"

"Fifty-three days, as near as we could tell. A spot in the regs says your CO can make your medical decisions."

"I killed my CO, Strat. His boss is playing golf with an ankle monitor."

His smile was cryptic. "The interim secretary general of the United Planet Earth seems to think otherwise."

"Let me guess. The undersecretary general got a promotion?"

"She's playing golf with Schweizer," Strat said. "Yang Chai of the former Oriental Ore Consortium was voted in under an emergency basis."

"*Former* Consortium?"

"The vote to accept them into the UPE was unanimous once word about the nuclear attack came out."

"He blows them to hell and suddenly we learn to get along?"

"When do you remember a war starting over something that made sense, Allie?"

I yawned wide and hard, letting my eyes stay closed while I thought it all through. The Consortium had wanted into the UPE, but they hadn't been willing to play by the rules. Kegar hadn't approved of their treatment and formed his plan to, in his eyes, put the UPE in its place.

That's where I'd become involved, since he'd also arranged the series of carefully planned accidents to get me out of his way so he could grab *Tico*. Schweizer had seen Kegar's play as a move against the UPE on the Consortium's behalf and decided to nuke them in response. Maybe he'd felt politically threatened, maybe he was trying to put the Consortium out of business, or maybe he was just an asshole. Whatever the case, he'd seen what I was up to and put me on ice as soon as my identity had been confirmed.

Strat was right about one thing—none of it made any real sense.

"I think you've had enough for a bit."

"We've got to get out of here, Strat."

"Don't worry about that now."

"I don't mean the hospital," I managed, then slipped back into unconsciousness.

CHAPTER 17

9 JULY 2126

My lucidity increased the next time I woke. The hospital staff wanted me eating and moving. More than agreeable to their plan, I tried to be in the air before they asked me to jump. Stratford appeared early in the afternoon, pushing a wheelchair through my room's door.

"We've nowhere to go, but it's time to get there."

"You're not driving me anywhere, Edgar."

"Oh, tut. I've been practicing."

"Where do you think you'd take me? This isn't merry old London, you know."

"I'm well aware. A nice park is down the way. The benches are quite comfortable, and they're rather close together. I was able to test one last night after the nurses tossed me out. We'll beat the rush if we hurry."

"I have an apartment here in town. I think it would be warmer."

The smile left Stratford's eyes.

"What's wrong?"

"I know this sounds a bit silly, but I haven't been in someone's flat in a long time, Allie. I sat in that prison cell figuring I was never going to see anything again but four concrete walls."

"Who would have thought I'd actually have more recent experience with incarceration than you, Strat? I'll get you through this. I promise."

✣

My apartment building's manager remembered me, so he thankfully let me in again. His threat to raise my rent if I had another lockout call was the least of my problems.

Stratford dropped his ditty bag next to the door. He seemed drawn to the balcony on the far side of the living room where a glimpse of *Ticonderoga*'s aft section rose above the buildings in the distance. I poured two glasses of wine before joining him.

We toasted in a quiet salute to our ship.

"We've got to get her out of here, Strat."

"I don't see how that's going to happen. Yang didn't want her decision questioned when she ordered us down."

"What is *Tico*'s condition?"

"We'd just left the dock—after completing repairs and reprovisioning from their emergency stores—when Yang's orders dropped. The crew was amazing."

"She's ready to go?"

"Of course she is, Allie. Those were your orders, for all that they matter now. One day soon, she'll make the trip to the lunar storage facility to sit next to *Lexington* for thirty years until this blows over. Or she'll be off to the boneyard to be decommissioned completely. Either way, she's not going far, and more than likely without you or me onboard."

I stared out the window for a long time. "Where is our crew?"

"Enlisted are confined to base. The officers are on a short leash. Most are in the visiting officers' quarters, but a couple got rooms in town."

"Have they been allowed back onboard since you made planetfall?"

"Only to collect their personal items. Except a couple of blokes to mind the reactor, access is restricted to command and above. You and I could probably get back aboard if we wanted, but none of the crew. I'm sure we'd be heavily supervised, too."

I let the ramifications of this roll around in my head. "Want to grab a shower?"

Strat's eyebrows raised.

"I need to make a couple of calls." He looked so deflated, I gave him a peck on the cheek and hoped it would help. "I'll order us some dinner, too."

He nodded and, bag in hand, disappeared down the short hallway leading to my guest room.

I shared his disappointment when I heard the shower start. Fantasizing about his body made my toes wiggle in the carpet while the com connected. The staffer in the secretary general's office required more than a little convincing to squeeze me into Yang's schedule tomorrow. My second call was much easier—I knew the right pizza joint and exactly what to order to satisfy my craving.

My food hadn't been great the past few months.

Pulling my shirt off over my head as I hurried down the hallway, I made one quick run-through of the state of things in my head. I had released the clasp on my bra when Strat emerged dressed in a T-shirt and sweatpants and smelling like shower, shampoo, and man.

"Pizza should be here in a bit," I said, pulling the straps from my shoulders.

"Sounds great," he said with a hint of a smile.

"I'll be out in a jiffy."

Did he look? Was he still looking?

I desperately wanted to turn around and see if he was watching, but that would ruin everything. I left my bedroom door open, tossing clothes aside as I stripped, hoping his eyes were as stuck on me as my desires were on him. Motivated by the thought of pizza piled far too high with cheese and greasy sausage, I made my shower quick, taking the time to clean everything that needed it. Conventional wisdom said I should take it easy with heavy food after my time in prison and the hospital, but sex wasn't the only thing I was starved for.

Maybe learning how to five-S in a hurry from the military wasn't so bad after all.

It probably wasn't right for pizza, but I picked out a long green satin negligee and made sure it hugged, tucked, and pulled where I wanted, even though my toned curves were mostly angles now. I didn't dwell on the mirror, but the delivery guy still beat me—I could smell the food from halfway down the hall.

"Look at you," Stratford said as I stepped into the kitchen.

"The food looks great."

"So do you."

You're not so bad yourself.

"Do you want to eat in front of the TV? We can watch the news and maybe see what the rest of the planet thinks is going on."

He shrugged and handed me a plate. "Sounds like a good idea."

Guiding me toward the living room was an innocent gesture, but the touch of his hand on the bare skin of my back took my breath away. The memory of his fingertips warmed me as I curled my legs beneath me and settled on the couch.

Categorizing it as a good idea turned out to be a matter of perspective. The news centered on the situation in the former Oriental Ore Consortium. The newscaster described the devastation as a "level of destruction never before seen in the history of humankind."

Not an inaccurate assessment.

Ticonderoga and I were both back story. Secretary General Yang Chai was quoted thanking me for the sacrifices I had made to help secure planetary peace. The Ticonderoga Project was acknowledged as a key factor in the planet's unity but also as one whose day had come and gone.

"She'll be in mothballs on the backside of the moon before the year is over," Strat said during a commercial.

"I'm going to get her back, Strat. Yang owes me."

"I don't think she's the type to pay her debts. You'll end up holding the bag on this one."

"No, I won't."

"Look, Allie. I just got you back. Things are getting sorted. Let's not start this. Not now."

"I don't want to, Strat. Circumstances have forced me. I don't have any choice in the matter."

"You always have choices."

"She was supposed to be a ship of exploration. Did you know that, Strat?"

"I did."

"She has never explored. Not on purpose, anyway. Maybe she cast a glance on a slow trip out to Alpha Station, but she's never done her job. Do you know how sad it would be for her to die without spending a single day as a true ship of discovery?"

"The old girl enforced planetary peace for close to fifty years."

"And some will say she caused the worst war in history."

"Allison, that ship didn't cause anything. People did."

"I don't want to be remembered as the captain who let the world fall apart."

"Out to change the past?"

"No, but I'm going to leave them something else to remember her by. She needs another chance to live up to the dream."

"You've been reading too much poetry, Allison."

"You haven't been reading enough of anything."

The look he shot me was pure condescension.

I got up and stomped to my bedroom. I was tired and hurt and wanted to be heard.

And he didn't follow.

CHAPTER 18

18 JULY 2126

Strat was still soundly asleep in the guest bedroom, and I was still pissed at him. I didn't wake him when I left. I knew he didn't have anywhere else to go—it wasn't about him being there. I just felt . . . marginalized.

As big as *Tico* was, she still represented a small world that I'd become very accustomed to. A bright sun burned through a northwest fog, treating throngs of people I didn't recognize to a beautiful morning as they hurried along the sidewalk to and from work. What a reminder of how small I was in the universe.

Stratford's dismissal of my plans for *Ticonderoga* made me feel even smaller. Even I realized the improbability of a successful exchange with the secretary general where the ship was concerned, which added to the helpless feeling. Did what I want matter to anyone? I'd spent the last portion of my career acclimating to a certain amount of control both over my own circumstances and those of people under my command.

I'd said grounding *Tico* would be a loss to the world, but if I were honest with myself, my own loss had me the most worried. Captains lose their ships, eventually. They get old, screw up, die, or just move on—it happens. I didn't feel like simply a captain, though. I was entrusted with *Ticonderoga*'s entire legacy, and I wasn't about to see it end on my watch.

I'd been called in to the SG's office for various reasons since taking command of *Ticonderoga*. The leader of the UPE's sanctum was historical, unchanged in fifty years.

Until now.

"I am glad to see you again, Captain." Asahi Gada, a man I'd interfaced with to facilitate the beginning of *Ticonderoga*'s humanitarian operation in the Consortium, sat behind a spindly, dark wooden desk. He activated a control that opened a matching door covered with intricate carvings inlaid with jade. "The secretary general will see you now."

I nodded in appreciation and smiled warmly. "I like what you've done to the place." Then I stepped through the doorway. I marveled at the changes in the spacious office. "Congratulations, Madame Secretary. I see you've settled in."

"I thought a little piece of my homeland belonged here," she said as she acknowledged the decidedly eastern decor. She got to her feet and met me with a handshake and a gentle hand on my shoulder, guiding me to a padded visitor's chair in front of her expansive desk. These were gestures I wouldn't have expected given her culture and our relative unfamiliarity. "Sit, please."

"Thank you," I said as muscles unaccustomed to this morning's movement got their first chance to relax.

"I have been kept aware of your status, Allison. I'm sorry for what you've gone through on our behalf."

"It needed to be done," I said.

"We've added your mistreatment to the list of charges against Pons Schweizer. I have every belief he will be found guilty of the charges against him, largely due to the evidence brought forward by *Ticonderoga* and her crew."

"Speaking of *Ticonderoga*—"

"All of the crew, as well as the crew of *Lexington*, are in line for commendations for their actions during these events."

"That's reassuring," I said. "I was hoping to talk to you about *Ticonderoga*'s status."

"I am sorry, Allison, but the future of the program is too controversial to be decided at this point. We have an entire geographic region to rebuild with immense need for humanitarian assistance. The allocation of personnel and resources to the Ticonderoga Project isn't justifiable in the present circumstances."

"The resources were allocated when the ship was built, and the personnel aren't trained for mass humanitarian service. Take the locks off the Ticonderoga program. Let me take her out to explore."

"No. I had hoped to allow you more time to heal before we spoke. I have a different job for you."

"I like the one I have," I said.

"Had," she corrected sternly. "In appreciation of your efforts and reflecting the courage you showed in the *Ticonderoga* crisis, you've been promoted to admiral. You will head up the Space Command Transport Division, which I've decided to leave operational due to the need for its revenue. Should you find this unacceptable, you will be asked to retire with the UPE's gratitude for the sacrifices you have made during your career. Either way, I promise you will never be granted command of any spacefaring vessel again. These are your choices."

I ground my teeth. The knowledge that this moment had been brewing since Kegar took *Tico* didn't make it suck any less. Captains that see their ships through major incidents do not stay captains for long. We both knew that was what this was about, and it was life in the military. It had been for a long time.

I swallowed it all. "I accept the promotion."

"Good. Your new rank is effective immediately. Your office will be expecting you by the time you get there. Rank insignia will be on your desk. Please go now and stand to your duties. Your assistant, Paul Trevor, will be waiting to brief you."

I knew I had been dismissed when she turned to her paperwork. I'd almost reached the door when she looked up. "I am happy to see you, Allison, and I am thankful for what you've done for my country as well as the rest of the former consortium. I hope you understand I can't jeopardize this office by making decisions against the best interests of the UPE, regardless of my personal feelings."

A salute would have been inappropriate. She wasn't in my chain of command, and I wasn't sure she would have taken the gesture in context. So I offered a nod and the best smile I could muster. "I understand. Congratulations on your position, Madame Secretary."

I closed the door gently behind me. After all, the meeting had confirmed what I'd known was going to happen. Right then, I supposed there wasn't any more to it than that.

UPE Command was a sprawling structure both horizontally and vertically. I honestly had no idea where to find the Space Command Transport Division office. It turned out it was down two floors on the same wing, but I'd made four mind-clearing laps around the entire structure before I took the advice from an administrative assistant to find my way.

When I finally arrived, it took far longer than I preferred to get my chittering would-be assistant to leave me in the office that was now, theoretically, mine. Two square meters of shiny-black desk held a gleaming admiral's rank insignia in the dead center of the synthetic surface. A standard rolling chair and computer provided the rest of what I needed. I traded my rank insignia out for the bars on the desk without ceremony, simply acknowledging they might come in handy with what I had in mind.

Confirming Brinn was still onboard *Ticonderoga* and then contacting him at his workstation was something of a trick. Proposing what I had in mind over a monitored communication channel wasn't wise, so I needed a workaround. I knew *Tico*'s fire suppression system had a subroutine to scan any compartment using a given workstation's camera. I knew enough code to convince the computer to send my audio and video in lieu of scan results to his display.

Brinn looked a little surprised and then pleased when I popped onto his screen without warning. "I was hoping I'd hear from you. How are you?"

The reality of the situation snuck around the edges of my control. "Honestly, not so good. What's your status?"

"Pitka and I are monitoring the reactors while they figure out this mess. They know we'll have to move eventually."

I lowered my voice. "Do you want to help me steal a spaceship?"

His features deepened with shock.

"They've decommissioned her, Brinn. She's headed for mothballs at best."

"So you're going to take her?"

"When you put it like that, I sound crazy. Before I watch them tear apart a seventy-five-year-old program that was never allowed to fulfill her mandate, yes, I am. I'm going to assemble a crew and explore."

"Explore what?"

"Let's start with the solar system and see what happens."

"You're serious."

"Yes, Chief, I'm serious."

"She's my ship, Captain. I go where she goes."

"Say your goodbyes then, Brinn. We'll leave late tonight."

"Understood."

I had only one bit to handle myself. "Let's meet in the officer's mess about 0200."

"Roger that, Cap. I'll be there."

"Thanks, Chief. Mackenzie out."

Delaying my next call to Admiral West wouldn't gain me anything. I owed it to him to fill him in on recent events, but more importantly, I needed his help and the help of his crew to make this work out. Oddly, contacting a ship several hundred thousand miles away in interplanetary space was much easier than calling one parked up the street on the sly. There wasn't any way to hide what needed to get said this time.

"What's your status, Captain?" West asked. It was obvious he was close—the picture was crystal clear.

"They clipped our wings, sir. The SG ended the Ticonderoga Project."

"You had to know that was coming," West said.

"I thought I'd be able to talk her out of it, but I was wrong."

Again.

I glanced over my shoulder. Paranoia told me I was being watched. "I'm going to take the decision away from her, sir."

West was quiet for a long time. "When?"

"Late tonight."

"What do you intend to do with her, Allison?"

"Explore. She's provisioned for three years with a good margin of safety. She needs a chance to do what she was meant to. They'll never build another one, Admiral."

West was annoyingly quiet again. "What about your crew?"

"It will be difficult to gather them without attracting unfavorable attention, sir. I can get the ship off the ground, but I'll need to procure a crew outside of the usual channels."

Understanding dawned in his tired eyes. "You don't want an old dog like me straggling along. This crew . . . they're misfits, retirees, and second-stringers. We'd all go in a heartbeat, but we're not the right people for the job."

"If you'd go in a heartbeat, you're exactly the right people for the job. Will you ask them?"

"I don't need to, but I will." Anticipation overtook his weariness. "We're about to dock. When will you be here?"

"I'll grab her early in the morning. If I make it at all, transit time should be about eight hours."

"Are you sure you can handle her alone?"

"No, I'm not," I admitted. "Brinn is coming with me, so I'll have an engineer."

"Can't you at least bring Stratford? He's good in a pinch."

The truth stabbed my heart for the first time since last night. "We seem to have come to a philosophical crossroad."

"Give him a chance, Allison. He'd follow you into hell."

"I'm not the problem. It's this . . . mission. He doesn't think it's the right thing to do."

"You took a chance when you sprung him from the clink. Take another and bring him in."

"I'll see you tomorrow, sir."

His disappointment was clear. "We'll be ready, Allison. West out."

The genie was out of the bottle. The wish had been made. By this time tomorrow, I'd know if it was granted.

~

The rest of the day went by in a haze of faces. New staff and would-be colleagues stopped by in a constant stream to wish me luck in my new position. As far as Yang knew, I was settling into the life she had set forth for me. In all honesty, it didn't seem like it would be all that bad, but . . .

My heart was aboard *Ticonderoga*.

Administrative oversight of asset transportation didn't seem fulfilling. I wanted to be out working with people to get the job done. But, as they said in the military, orders were orders.

The building cleared out at about six in the afternoon. I didn't have anything legitimate to do, so I wandered out the door with the crowd and headed for home. It seemed odd to think of my apartment as home, especially since I'd more than likely never see it again.

How many times had I thought that lately?

I pictured Strat staying there alone after I left with *Tico*. Even though I knew he didn't have anywhere else to go, the image wasn't happy.

In a blink, I was in the hallway outside my apartment.

Home smells a lot like breakfast.

The sight of Stratford wearing an apron in the kitchen made me smile. "What's going on here?"

"I had to do something to earn my keep. Besides, I wanted to apologize for how last night ended."

"And how should it have ended?"

"Like tonight is going to."

✣

The end of the second glass of wine brought a smile I couldn't hold back. Licking my lips wasn't only to get the last drop.

I felt self-conscious.

"Allie, I need you to know I respect your views even if I don't agree with them."

"I don't want to fight tonight, Strat."

His stare wasn't giving me anything useful to work with, so I pushed back from the table.

"Where are you going?"

"The short answer is to the shower. As far as the long game goes, I don't know specifically. It's kind of scary, Strat."

"Afraid of the unknown? You?"

"I wouldn't say that. I'm just not into this job."

"Is it really so bad? I know it's not your dream, but commanding the

Transport Division is still an opportunity most people would be quite happy with."

"It's about what I'm leaving behind. It matters."

He managed to be sexy yet condescending with a single word. "Allison—"

Everything I'd been holding in flared. "What does *your* future hold? What do you want to be when you grow up, Edgar?"

"My future is going back to the Special Ops teams, Allison." His eyes closed and he took a deep breath. "But I'd settle for a life spent with you."

"I don't want to be settled for." When no response came, I shook my head and moved toward my bathroom, shedding clothes along the way as I would have if I were alone. It certainly felt as if I was.

The warmth of the water pushed back the chill in my heart but didn't wash it away. The shower was still my special place. Rinsing the suds from my hair, I opened my eyes and jerked around as the shower curtain rustled. A naked Strat slipped in behind me.

"I'm sorry." He touched my face. "I didn't mean to scare you."

I looked into his eyes and decided his words went past startling me in the shower. "What did you mean to do?"

"This."

He pushed me firmly against the wall and kissed me. His questioning eyes met mine when he pulled back for a breath, and I nodded vigorously. He lifted my right leg and pushed forward into me in a smooth motion. His thrusts were hard from the beginning. The water amplified the slapping whenever our bodies connected.

It hurt.

It felt incredible.

He did everything he wanted to me, and that was all I wanted. His arms wrapped around me and his eyes never broke contact with mine. I could see into his soul.

It belonged to me.

Warm water cascaded off his shoulders as he pulled back from a kiss to catch his breath.

His smile was boyish. Charming.

"Allie, haven't I followed you through enough to convince you?"

I was genuinely confused. "Convince me of what?"

"That wherever I am or whatever I do, it's because I want to share my life with you."

His eyes held all the conviction I could hope for. So I kissed him again, deeply, hard, and for a long time.

What else was a girl supposed to do?

I thought we would make love again when we finally made it to my bed, but what happened was better. He kissed my neck and told me he loved me, and he wrapped his arms around me.

And he didn't let go.

Too bad I soon would.

CHAPTER 19

11 JULY 2126

Snoring softly, Strat had disentangled himself from me in his sleep, allowing me to slip out of bed. I struggled into my unused admiral's uniform in the dark, only thinking of him. My apartment's front door was somehow heavier when I closed it and absconded into the night.

Foggy streets felt foreign as I trekked back to the base. Trying to be casual with the rather loquacious guard at the gate was a challenge. I dearly hoped the biometric scanner he activated confirmed my identity but not my intentions with its reassuring ping.

"You're good, ma'am."

"Thank you. Have a nice night, Corporal."

Any differences inside the gate were largely psychological, but the base felt less foreign than Victoria's streets on the other side of the barricade. Low-security portions of the base were along the margins. The officer's mess was sandwiched between the post exchange and a hotel-like building that was the visiting officers' quarters.

My stomach acknowledged the familiar smells with an anticipatory rumble. While it looked far from exceptional, I filled a plate with plenty of protein and took a table near the far corner of the sparsely populated room. About half of the predictably mediocre meal had disappeared by the time Brinn approached my table.

"How're the eggs today, Admiral?"

I hated the sound of that. *I'm a captain.* And that's all I ever wanted to be.

I gestured to the empty seat across from me. "They're certainly not runny, Chief."

"Hard-ass, bounce 'em off the wall?"

"UPE standard."

"All right, then," Brinn said as he settled into the chair with a plate of his own.

I glanced around and lowered my voice. "What's her status?"

His whisper became appropriately conspiratorial. "The reactors are hot and security is minimal. Getting aboard shouldn't be a problem for a division admiral."

I smiled. "I'm an admiral in the wrong division, but thank you. I'm sure I'll find your work most satisfactory."

"We'll need to be ready to get the hell out of here in a hurry once we start."

"Chief, I . . ."

He looked taken aback. "As sure as you're *Ticonderoga*'s captain, I'm her engineer. It's my duty to take care of her, and you, for that matter."

"Brinn, I'm not asking you to commit mutiny."

His smile was uncharacteristic. "No, you're not."

"The secretary general will have us thrown in prison for two lifetimes if we get caught."

"Then we better not get caught."

Fair enough. "Our inspection awaits."

Brinn nodded agreement and stood.

The landing field couldn't have been much farther from the officer's mess. Empty streets had never made me so happy—we didn't see a single security officer during the long walk across the base. More importantly, I took heart from our continued conversation about Earth, our families and friends, what we were leaving behind, and what might be yet to come.

Maybe preparing to commit a capital crime with someone opened the lines of communication?

When the landing field security checkpoint appeared out of the misty night, I'd lost some of the courage of my conviction. Brinn went straight to the desk when we got inside and did all the talking. I straightened my shoulders and leaned on one hip to look comfortable, but my heart was racing. Chiefs pretty much came and went as they pleased.

Since busyness was their default, they never drew a lot of attention. Admirals were another matter—they generally couldn't cross the street without creating a spectacle. This would be over before it started if we didn't get through the door on the other side of the guard shack.

The clock on the wall ticked off seconds that turned into minutes.

Two minutes felt like an hour, then the door finally opened.

I didn't know whether to be relieved or suspicious when the duty officer didn't even ask to see my identification badge. There were plenty of explanations.

Most of them weren't favorable.

Stepping through the doorway onto the field was like waltzing into a dream. The weather was cool and moist with a hint of ocean breeze. The stars overhead comforted me like a cozy blanket on a rainy day. Most importantly, *Ticonderoga* stood without the clutter of buildings, trees, and Earth between us.

Like a vulture crouched at the door, she looked awkward, out of place, and terribly ominous on the ground. Leaving was definitely best for her, at least for now.

"She's gotten dirty," I said. Starlight glinted off the upper portion of the hull.

"We stopped at a car wash on the way in, but she wouldn't fit." Brinn smiled at his own joke. "It's residual carbon deposited during reentry. It's not structural."

"I know, Brinn. She's also our home. Nobody wants to live in a dirty—"

"Can I help you?" A stern voice echoed from the darkness behind us.

"Sure you can," I snapped. "Go on with your inspection, chief. I'll catch up."

I pivoted on my right heel and closed the gap between me and the guard, heedless of the moonlight glinting off the barrel of his shouldered P95. "You can tell me where the other units are."

"Ma'am, who are—"

"I'm Admiral Allison Jane Mackenzie, soldier. I'm the newly appointed head of Space Command Transport Division, here to inspect the actions taken to protect a valuable piece of hardware. So far, I'm not impressed. I've been walking this field since sundown and it took you this long to find me? I'm asking you again—where are the other units?"

"It's a secure base, Admiral. No other units are on the field."

"That's a problem. Where is your supervisor?" I hoped with all of my being that he'd run off to go find his sergeant and then report back. I'd be long gone before he put the pieces together.

He stared at me for a long time. Too long.

"Let's go find him. If you'll come with me, please, Admiral." He gestured toward the little building I'd been so happy to escape a few minutes earlier.

I kept my mouth closed before it got me into even more trouble.

I spent the time waiting for the sergeant in charge hoping for a great many things—most of them related to my sudden need to save my own ass. I practiced it in my head, word by word, until an old gunnery sergeant stomped through the door to the little post.

Glancing at the name tape above his left pocket, I saluted and, once it was returned, surged forward with a smile. "Gunnery Sergeant Reynolds, I'd like to congratulate you on the caliber of marine in your command. Your corporal wasn't about to allow me to get away with anything, regardless of my rank. That's the type of backbone we like to see during an interdepartmental audit like this one. You're running a first-rate detachment, and you and your men deserve to be proud of the work you're doing here."

"Thank you, Admiral. I—"

"Be assured I'll be giving Corporal Kloss high marks for his performance today. By extension, it'll roll your direction. Well done, Gunny." With a final salute, I strode out the door and away from the security post.

Away from *Ticonderoga*.

I wasn't worried about the gunny—men like him didn't escalate anything they didn't have to, and certainly not to the secretary general. Life in the military had always been about knowing when to keep your head down—it went without saying he'd learned that lesson.

It also looked like I'd witnessed the true end of *Ticonderoga*'s mission. Yang was on top of keeping *Ticonderoga* under her own control, and that was a much bigger issue.

I wasn't going anywhere.

There would be no exploration mission, and, it appeared, no tomorrow for the great ship. I'd gone down having tried everything remotely in my grasp to keep her legacy alive, but that did little to ameliorate the impact of my failure.

So I was going to work. Because I sure as hell wasn't going home. I wasn't ready to face Strat. I needed time before I reconnected with him, especially after saying goodbye in the best possible way. Of course, he didn't know what I had intended, which would make it easier.

Wouldn't it?

While walking, I tried hard to compartmentalize this latest turn with everything else and wrap my brain around what might be ahead in the workday. Given no other options that felt less like defeat, I found myself suddenly motivated to be successful as the head of Space Command Transport Division.

~

Transport Division Chief of Operations was the only military posting in the otherwise civilian organization. I had a working understanding of the departmental structure, as all space-going personnel started off in the same academy program before Defensive Forces personnel like Stratford and me broke off into combat, weapons, and flight training. *Ticonderoga* had also spent a good bit of time interacting with Transport Division spacecraft in one way or another.

The Transport Division was primarily comprised of three ore carriers—*Kilimanjaro*, *Everest*, and *Fuji*. Five tugs designed to pull multiple cargo pods, twenty extraplanetary shuttles, and *Starliner* served as supplementary assets. Our mission was defined as support of all extraplanetary activities, including the Ticonderoga Project. All of this was accomplished through the dedication of over five thousand team members.

My assistant, Paul, who I'd thought of as obsequious after meeting him for the first time, conducted an impressive orientation and morning briefing.

"That's a nice piece of work," I said once he'd finished.

He smiled nervously. "Thank you, Admiral."

"I do need *Starliner* to lay in at the lunar CSX dock. *Lexington*'s crew needs a ride home."

His face flashed the question his lips didn't ask. "I'll see to it right now."

"Thank you." As I watched Paul leave to set about his duties, I wondered what Admiral West would think when *Starliner* showed up instead of *Ticonderoga*. Relief would have been my best guess, as he had seemed a little hesitant concerning my ideas for *Ticonderoga*.

Paul's concern was genuine when he returned. "Are you all right, Admiral?"

I jumped. I'd been—somewhere else, to be sure. "Fine. What's up?"

"I just wanted to confirm *Starliner* will be on station in about twelve hours. They're on a personnel transfer to the moon base."

"That's convenient. Our timing was good if they were already headed that way."

"Yes, ma'am." He'd disappeared halfway through the door before I thought to ask, "Paul, what kind of access do we have to planetary security investigations?"

"You should be able to access whatever you need through your terminal."

"Thank you, Paul."

While the layout of the UPE datanet was the same regardless of where you accessed it, I was concerned my access level might have changed now that I was outside of Defensive Forces. If it did, it had increased, which must have been a reflection of my new rank. In the past, had I searched my own name, I would have only found the nonclassified portion of my service record.

I selected my dad's name on the right side of the screen, and chronological entries starting with *17 May 2126* scrolled onto the display—the day his life had ended and all hell had broken loose in my own.

More than a few deep breaths were required before I selected it.

> File A56-7W
> Alan Mackenzie killed in arson of family home. Accelerants found in multiple initiation points around exterior of structure. Mr. Mackenzie is husband of Anna

> Seagull and father of UPE Defensive Forces Captain Allison Jane Mackenzie. Anna Seagull Mackenzie was located after incident on UA Flight 793 to Dulles International Airport and taken into protective custody at order of UPE Secretary General Pons Schweizer. Negative indication of external participation in arson event. Cause believed to be linked to a resident of the home. Investigation closed per executive order AJM-0137, signed by Pons Schweizer, Secretary General, United Planet Earth, 18 May 2126.

I sat back from my terminal as the edges of my vision closed in. Breathing was no longer involuntary as a tingle shot up my spine. My own mother burned my dad alive, and that realization was bringing on a panic attack. I didn't try to fight it, either. Succumbing to it felt like a fine idea.

I have no idea how long I was falling before the chime on my personal com pulled me back from the darkness.

"Got an early start today, didn't you?" Strat asked once the screen activated.

"First day of school jitters, I suppose." I hoped he didn't notice I was trying to catch my breath and get my heart rate back under control.

"Wasn't yesterday your first day?"

I gave him a nervous laugh. "Someone told me I didn't give it a real chance yesterday, so I'm trying to put my back into it today."

He looked at me for a long time before he said, "Are you okay?"

"Fine." I stared right back.

"Have a good day at work, honey." His smile brought light back to my day.

I laughed. "I'll see you tonight, baby."

Once the com clicked off, I took a deep breath and leaned back into my terminal.

"Admiral?" Paul asked tentatively. "Captain Fitzhume of *Fuji* is on the line."

"Got it," I said as I activated my monitor. "Hello, Captain."

"Allison? What are you doing in Transport Division?"

"Exactly what they tell me. What's going on?"

"We've got a flicker in our number two thruster. She's within spec, but our engineer is asking for another set of eyes to look at the problem."

"I'm still learning my way around, but Brinn might be available if I ask nice. What's your schedule?"

"We'll be orbital tonight around 1600."

"Let me make a few calls. We'll hit you back once we know what's going on."

"Thank you, Cap—uh, Admiral."

After a quick call to Yang's office for permission, I made a straight-up call to *Ticonderoga*. As expected, Brinn looked a little weary. The obvious would have to be addressed on another day.

"Chief, the secretary general has confirmed what we already knew—*Tico* isn't going anywhere for a while. *Fuji*'s on her way in with a slight thruster malfunction. Fitzhume's engineer is asking for a second opinion."

"I'd be happy to try to help."

"Can you be at the shuttle pad at 1400 hours?"

"Roger that, Admiral."

I clicked off, got up, and walked into Paul's portion of the office. "Could you schedule a lift for Chief Walter Brinn from the shuttle pad up to *Fuji* tonight?"

Paul nodded. "I'm already on it, Admiral."

"What else is on the morning agenda?"

"Your schedule is clear until the 1300 update with the port in Bilbao."

"Roger that. I'm going to go find some lunch."

And maybe a purpose.

The data spoke for itself.

Transport Division was handling the ore from the mining facility inefficiently. It might have been effective back when the system started, but volume had been increasing consistently, especially since Alpha Station had eaten its way into the rich asteroids of the belt. Couple that with the fact that UPE sciences was interested in developing an outpost on Mars, and the answer was clear. Staging filled containers of ore in Martian orbit would allow Transport Division tugs, which were presently underutilized and faster than the ore carriers, to help offset the transportation backlog. Materials necessary for Martian infrastructure could be utilized planetside while anything extraneous could be sent back to Earth.

It would be an immensely complex proposal to put together. Given the huge amount of revenue from ore mining, it wouldn't be dismissed out of hand, even in the face of the forthcoming relief efforts for the Consortium.

Eyes burning, I leaned back from the readouts, the data, and the future. As I rubbed my eyes, I asked myself if this might be enough for me, and the voice that answered did not scream *no.*

It was a lot to think about. After a glance at my chrono, I admitted I wasn't going to do any more legitimate work today.

Jumping back on the UPE datanet was the best way to kill the remaining time after I'd met my obligations but before it felt like a reasonable time to go home. Letting Paul go early reinforced my belief that busywork was okay for the boss but not necessary for the employees. More importantly, it emptied out the office, leaving me the privacy I preferred to look further into my dad's murder.

Pons Schweizer turned out to be quite the search for the computer, taking several minutes to populate the screen. Every intelligence report, vesting operation, and standard personnel entry in the former secretary general's extensive career was listed. Using the refine function, I added my mother's name, *Anna Seagull Mackenzie*, and redid the search.

Although a surprising number of entries appeared, it was nowhere near what I'd faced with only Schweizer's name. I scanned the list from top to bottom before I selected the first entry.

> File A07-7A
> Pons Schweizer, son of Per Schweizer and Sophia Clapp Schweizer, age seventeen, of Bern, Switzerland, enrolled in International Student Exchange at high school/gymnasium level. Mr. Schweizer was placed in the home of Ernest Seagull and Robin Ackerman Seagull on 12 January 2091. Ernest and Robin Seagull had two children—Anna, age seventeen, and Joseph, age sixteen. Mr.

> Schweizer stayed in the Seagull home until the end of the 2091 academic school year, receiving high passing grades in political science, English composition, and advanced German.

Looking up, I faced the miniature version of this morning's panic attack hovering on the edge of my consciousness. Blackness swirled in my vision before I closed the file and mentally pushed it away with deep calming breaths.

My terminal activated and sounded a tone similar to an incoming message alert onboard *Ticonderoga*. Paul wasn't there to screen the call, and that somehow mattered, pulling me back to the here and now. I selected *receive* and struggled some deep breaths down as Admiral West's face appeared in front of me.

Concern was obvious in his tired eyes. "Allison, are you all right?"

"Fine, sir. How're things going up there?" I had a feeling my smile was unconvincing.

"We've nearly got our bags packed."

"How did your crew take the schedule change?"

"Like everything else on this ride," West said. "We'll be home in about twelve hours."

"Come find me when you get a chance?"

"Absolutely. We work in the same building. I'll see you then, Admiral."

~

The apartment I thought I might see in three years stood in front of me twenty hours after I'd left. I wasn't tired.

I wasn't anything.

Questions about my mother's relationship with Schweizer had been wandering around the back of my mind since I'd last seen her. Knowing where their relationship started was a puzzle piece I needed but never hoped to have fall into place.

The ramifications were messing with my mind.

So much so, in fact, that I'd given no thought whatsoever to the beautiful Brit I found in the kitchen when I stepped inside. His arms chased away the discomfort only I knew the twists in our relationship had caused in the past day.

"How're you?"

"Better than I could have been, I guess. How about you?"

"Hungry for bangers and mash," he said definitively. "You want to get cleaned up while I warm dinner?"

The quick kiss I'd drawn him in for blossomed into a toe-curler. My hips swayed like waves on the ocean as I headed for the bedroom, calling over my shoulder, "There's nothing sexier than a man that cooks."

Cascading water from the rainfall showerhead brought warmth and certainty—I couldn't tell him what I'd gotten caught doing this morning. Tedious in spots, the day hadn't been any more mundane than many aboard *Ticonderoga*, if one forgave the fact that we weren't sailing among the stars. That, and I hadn't been shot, beaten, nearly squeezed in half by a conduit, or almost killed by an out-of-control fighter.

Maybe it wasn't so bad being home.

Scents of dinner made my mouth water as I dried off in the steamy bathroom. T-shirt, soft shorts, and hair in a ponytail later, I padded into the kitchen in bare feet. With the soft clothes, smells of food, and even Strat's presence, I realized I was . . . happy.

"There's a smile I've seldom seen."

I settled onto a stool at the counter. "You look adorable in my apron."

"Oh, so that's what's done it?" His smile was radiant as he poured a glass of orange juice and sat it in front of me. "It wasn't that perhaps, by some chance, your day went better than you thought it might?"

"It might not have been the end of the universe after all. How was your day?"

"Oh no, you'll not get off that easily, Admiral." He placed steaming plates on the counter and settled onto the stool beside me. "I want details. How were things?"

"The busy part of the day was arranging to have Brinn go up and have a look at *Fuji*'s engines. If they do deactivate *Ticonderoga*, maybe they'll put some money into the ore carriers. If we weren't handling a hassle planetside, we were always towing one of them."

"They won't reallocate the funds."

"No, they probably won't."

"What'd you do with the other twelve hours?"

More like eighteen. "I looked up my mother's name in the security section of the UPE datanet."

"Find anything interesting?"

"I don't know if I've ever had bangers. This stuff is good."

"They're just sausages, not proper bangers. Allison, what did you find?"

Now I was baiting him. I didn't have a problem with it, at least for a few minutes. "Bangers, sausages, whatever—this is really good. Who taught you how to cook like this?"

"My gran. Who else would it have bloody been?"

I shrugged. "Mother, sister, cousin twice-removed, perhaps?"

"Mother was rubbish in the kitchen, and my sister followed her ways. I don't have any female cousins I know of."

"A boy cousin could have taught you."

His scowl was an instant reward. "Allison, are you going to tell me what you found in the files?"

"Since you asked so nice." I batted my eyes and waited until a smile cracked his lips before I continued. "I had a few minutes to poke around. I ran a search on my mother and Schweizer and found out he stayed with her family as an exchange student."

"You Yanks call it high school, right?"

"Right in the middle of all the best hormones."

"So the young, passionate lovers are reunited at the change ceremony when you were granted command of *Ticonderoga*? Flames were rekindled and . . . bloody hell."

"Indeed." I finished my orange juice.

"There's more."

"Food? I don't think I could stand it. This was great, though. I was starving."

He shook his head, his frustration now palpable.

I stared at him just long enough to remind him I still had the upper hand before I continued. "The UPE investigator supposedly didn't find any external involvement in the fire that killed my dad."

"Arson."

"That's what it sounds like. There's only one way that pencils out."

"What does that knowledge do for you?"

"Probably nothing happy," I admitted. "I am going to figure out what happened."

"Can I do anything to stop you? Experience has taught me the satisfaction gained from revenge isn't as satisfying as it's cracked up to be."

"Stop me?" I shook my head. "Probably not. You might do something to slow me down a little, though."

✣

His heartbeat was pounding in time with my own when I lay my head on his sweaty chest. If there was to be a benefit to this new life, it was Strat. I finally felt wanted, accepted, and almost at peace with who I was.

"There's no time like the second," Strat said, breaking my reverie.

"Don't accuse us of peaking yet."

"That'll be pretty tough to top."

I pulled my cheek off his chest, moving to kiss him. "A girl can try."

CHAPTER 20

12 JULY 2126

"Uniform?"

"I've been ordered to report to Special Operations Command."

"I guess you warned me that was coming," I said as I turned to the coffee maker. "What's going on?"

"I would imagine they've decided I can't sit about and eat crumpets forever."

"You couldn't tell me this last night?"

"There's nothing to tell, Allison." He leaned in for what turned out to be a quick kiss. "Let me find out what's going on, and then we'll talk."

"Whatever." I slammed doors and scuffed my feet in the kitchen, doctoring my morning cup of coffee and trying to hide the magnitude of my anger. "I've got to go."

"Me too," he said. "I'll walk with you."

So we walked. Last night's passion was today's superficiality. We spoke maybe six words between us—he was defensive and I was pissed. Parting in the lobby of headquarters was beyond uncomfortable.

"You're leaving, aren't you?" I left the *me* out of the sentence, unable to face the possibility of that truth.

His attempt at a smile was sad. "Likely. I'll call you as soon as I know."

"Okay." I shrugged. I'd come to feel like my world was stabilizing, and now the last important thing left might abandon me too. That terrified me.

But I would need to get used to watching him walk away if I let this keep going.

He did turn and look from the escalator. I wished I'd kissed him. I wished I'd told him I loved him. I wished we'd never gotten out of bed. Nothing made the fanciful quality of our dream life clearer than seeing him disappear into the high-security wing of headquarters, knowing I might never see him again.

✣

The morning briefing passed in a haze. My mind was on Strat, special operations, *Ticonderoga*, and even my mother. "Paul, how do I travel?"

"It depends on where you're going. Catching a ride on scheduled transit flights is preferred, followed by commercial transport. We have the ability to send you anywhere you need in thirty minutes if necessary, but the budget office prefers we don't frequently utilize that capability."

"POV?"

"Sure. You can drive where you want, although it would be best for you to keep security in mind. When you're acting in a professional capacity, I recommend drawing a driver and car from the motor pool."

"The duty cycle is nominally Monday through Friday, right?"

Paul nodded. "You can structure things as you see fit, but most of your predecessors have considered themselves on-call permanently. I have requisitioned you an encrypted personal com—tech said it should be ready later this afternoon."

"I'd like to visit the facility in Bilbao sometime soon. I've never seen an offload before—correlating it with a transport arrival would kill two birds with one stone. See what you can set up in the next week or so, would you please?"

"Absolutely."

"How much staff do we have here in the headquarters building, anyway?"

"Right now, it's just you and me. I know that sounds odd, but each of the transit bases and ships have their own command structures. HR and budgetary issues are handled through the UPE. Sometimes the briefing is the most exciting part of the day."

I scoffed involuntarily. "That's why she put me here."

"Admiral?"

"Exactly," I said as if it explained everything. "Could you find me a car for the weekend? Motor pool, rental, whatever. I'd like to go home. I'll be back on Monday. I'll send you my credit account information over the computer. Please make sure whatever you come up with has autodrive."

"Happy to. Delivery to the office this afternoon, retrieval Monday morning?"

"Please," I said as my personal com chimed. It was Stratford.

"I'll leave you to it," Paul said as he stood from my visitor's chair and disappeared into the outer office.

"Where are you off to?" I said once I answered the video com.

"Away. As I thought, I've been activated."

"You're happy to be back." It wasn't a question.

"I was happy with you, too."

I couldn't help a hint of a smile. "So was I."

"This doesn't have to be the end for us, Allison."

Somewhere not deep inside, I heard his words and saw Jake in my mind. "I know. I got used to having you around."

"Part of me got used to being around, but I've gotten a second chance. You gave me a second chance, Allie."

The tear that fell was unbidden. "I didn't think you'd take it and leave me."

"I'll be back when the job's done."

But when?

Only our eyes seemed to connect through the display. "Be safe. Keep in touch when you can."

"You too." I counted fifteen breaths before he ended the com. It took me a long time to realize I was staring at the screen like he was still there, even though he was already gone.

~

I was worried I'd walked into the wrong apartment. Stratford hadn't just left, he hadn't just taken his things—he had erased himself. While little had left materially, my apartment felt stark compared to this morning. His departure was complete to the point that it felt practiced. He'd taken the trash out, laundered the towels in the bathroom, and replaced any food he'd used in the kitchen.

It felt like he wanted to have never existed, so it made it far easier for me to leave too.

The rental Paul arranged for was a hybrid, primarily electric with a supplemental petroleum backup. My parent's farm was eight hundred miles or about twelve hours away, so the comforts the little thing provided were welcome. Although it was perfectly capable of taking off at the push of a few buttons, driving manually was energizing for a while.

After twenty minutes at my first charging station stop, I got back on the road, double-checked the autodrive, racked the seat back, and closed my eyes. It took a little while to get comfortable, but sleep soon brought me a dream to pass the time.

My body wouldn't work quite the way I wanted it to. Arms felt heavier, abs wouldn't contract to help me sit up, and my eyes didn't seem to want to focus. Getting me upright in the well-used bed took a lot more time and energy than normal. I looked into the dresser mirror once I was vertical and noted the gray-haired woman who looked back with little satisfaction.

I was this woman, so there was no use doing anything but getting on with it. I couldn't help but think about all the times I'd pulled on a uniform and all the times I didn't.

My uniform was old.

Two dress standards had come and gone since I'd last worn UPE colors, but wearing the new one they'd offered me would have been disingenuous. After all these years, it felt comfortable on again. It still even fit, even though I certainly wasn't the same shape I'd been.

George Matheson, my dad, Alexander Simkins, Tom Hayes, Jake Connors, Vergé Kegar, Charlie Benson, and the marines I'd killed during the *Ticonderoga* incident were waiting for me when I stepped out into daylight. Dad seemed to have been elected the spokesman, as the others followed at a discreet distance with thin smiles.

My mother and Pons Schweizer joined the group in otherwise empty reviewing stands when we walked up. I struggled up steps I would have taken two at a time when I was younger to the podium with an almost comically oversized antique explosives detonator.

"Honored guests," I began.

Ferocious catcalling boomed from my audience.

"We've gathered together today to bid farewell to the most storied spacecraft in human history."

"How many lives? How much money? How many ruined families?"

"While *Ticonderoga* never had the opportunity to fulfill her highest purpose, she spent her life in service to Earth, protecting humanity as it moved toward a more peaceful society based on cooperation."

"How'd that work out for you?" Kegar yelled.

"No history is without hardship," I said. "No evolution is without pain. Growth brings struggle, and ours have been made easier because of the protections *Ticonderoga* provided the people of Earth."

"The only way those struggles made my life easier was because they killed me," Tom snarled.

"That was all my fault. It wasn't the ship's."

"I was all over the ship by the time it was done," Tom said darkly.

"I didn't mean for that to happen."

"What are you, four?" Tom snapped. "The fact that you didn't mean for it to happen doesn't erase it. It sure as hell doesn't bring me back."

"I couldn't save everyone. I tried, and I couldn't."

"It doesn't seem like you saved anyone," Benson said with his ingratiating smile.

"Blow it up! Blow it up! Blow it up! Blow it up!"

"I don't want to. I never wanted to," I stammered.

"Blow it up! Blow it up! Blow it up! Blow it up!"

"I'll take care of this," said a younger version of my own voice. Full of the life I'd missed for a long time, a more able me from back then appeared at the base of the podium. She climbed the steps with confidence, paying no attention to the cheers and jeers leveled at me, then pushed the T-shaped handle down into the wooden base with almost reckless abandon.

One by one, I watched the people in the stands explode into nothingness like a burning fuse. The younger me was next to last, then the cataclysmic explosion swallowed *Ticonderoga*.

I was utterly alone.

CHAPTER 21

13 JULY 2126

Sunlight blazed over the mountains east of me when I pulled into the farmyard. Even in July, the morning air was crisp enough to make me wish I'd brought a jacket. The place was right along the edge of a desert—it'd melt you like butter in a microwave during the heat of the day and freeze you to death at night.

I spun in a slow semicircle, stretching and purposely avoiding the black pile of rubble that had once been my childhood home. The sight would take it out of my imagination and place it front and center in my reality. Three or four deep breaths was all it took for me to realize how silly I was being. Nothing I saw or found would make anyone more alive, dead, guilty, or innocent than they already were.

Motor sounds and the crunching of rocks on the gravel drive stayed my misery. I knew it was Morton, the next-door neighbor, without looking. He'd been renting the farm since my dad's stroke—I knew him to be a conscientious caretaker.

He was undoubtedly wondering who the interloper was.

"Allison Mackenzie?"

"Hello, Morty. I should have called to let you know I was coming."

"I reckon you own the place," he said with a smile. "I haven't seen you in . . . longer than a while. Except for the obvious, how have you been?"

I shrugged. "Well enough, I guess. Thank you for taking care of things around here. Could you keep at it for a while?"

"Glad to," he said. The silence went on long enough to be

uncomfortable. "I'm going to let you have some privacy, Allison. Keep in touch when you can, okay?"

"Absolutely." I watched as he backed out, leaving a final wave as he disappeared from the yard.

I turned back to the pile with determination, though I wasn't quite sure where it had come from. Burnt chips of stucco delineated the rough margin of the house. Warped sheets of roofing tin covered most of the rubble in the center. The fire had burned hot—there wasn't a lot left.

Dad had been confined pretty much to the living room and the bedroom—the kitchen was always my mother's territory. She would have put anything she didn't want found in a high cabinet, keeping it out of casual reach. Anything interesting should be under the roofing tin and a little ash.

Surprisingly, the toolshed was even more run-down than it had been before I left. I was honestly surprised it hadn't fallen over completely. I reemerged alive, covered in cobwebs, with a metal garden rake in hand.

From there, I went back to the pile and started hunting.

If you knew what you were looking for, the Swiss chocolate branding on the tin now in the passenger seat of my rental car was still visible through the distortion from the fire. I must have been about seven the first time I saw it, because that's about the time I'd learned to read, and *chocolate* was an important word at that age.

Mom told me it was her "little girls don't touch" can, and I knew what that meant, too. Dad had delivered one of the few spankings I'd received after my well-intentioned attempt to make him some muffins by myself with the "little girls don't touch" blender. I doubted he'd ever looked in the tin himself, but I knew he'd remind me of the meaning if I did. That was kind of how growing up in our house worked. Dad made sure important lessons sunk in so Mom wouldn't have to worry about it.

I'd left the tin and the blender alone ever since. Until now.

The tin wasn't technically fireproof. There was no insulation to protect its contents from the heat of a fire, but they had miraculously survived with little if any distortion. I'd had the guts to pull the lid off after

I retrieved it from a pile of rubble just long enough to see that the papers and pictures inside were intact.

I wasn't about to inspect it there. Though I could have figured out the logistics of spreading the contents out and even keeping them clean, I lacked the nerve.

The tin was the whole point of my trip. The house was just a thing. I had a few bits of precious at home that had been Dad's. I'd cherish them all the more for their rarity now. As for my mother's things, I wanted nothing of hers besides what I'd retrieved.

Rental or not, I couldn't wear my shirt in the car—it was too far gone. I balled it up inside out and put it on the passenger side floorboard below the tin I'd found. Washing with water not much above freezing hurt, but the nozzle on the side of the pump house provided only that. It had to happen—I looked like I'd fought a fire alone.

Growling and twisting painfully, my stomach reminded me that a meal was also long overdue. A stop for some chow and fresh clothes was a must. I looked like a college girl sporting the black athletic bra and shorts, but I definitely didn't feel like one.

Pink tendrils filled the western sky, as I'd been at it for the biggest part of the day. It felt like a miracle that my com hadn't interrupted things. Everything done, it was time to head home, but a small part of me said I was already there.

The success of the day fought against the emptiness I cultivated by watching the farm disappear into the rearview, gradually losing the battle. Old wisdom said it was a bad idea to make big decisions when you were under emotional stress. So I concentrated on driving.

A lot of miles of road were left to be traveled.

CHAPTER 22

14 JULY 2126

"I just got home, but come on ahead," I said. "I'm going to jump into the shower real quick. I should be out by the time you get here."

"Pizza or tacos?" Mindy asked over the com.

"That's a tough one. I've got good beer here either way."

"Pizza it is," Mindy said. "I'll see you soon."

My smile faded as soon as I disconnected the com and faced the Swiss chocolate tin. Wrapped in a cheap towel from the same store where I'd gotten my clothes, it was sitting on the edge of the counter.

Something had to happen with it.

If it sat there, Mindy would see it, ask about it, and I'd have explaining to do. A lot of explaining. There wouldn't be any turning back. If I hid it somewhere, it'd be a weight hanging over my head, but its mysteries wouldn't be haunting me in the meantime, either.

Taking one more trip through the possibilities, I grabbed a step stool and slid the tin back onto a cabinet high in the kitchen, not unlike the spot it had held in my parent's house for so long. Once it was safely stowed, I tried to emotionally move on to the business of the evening.

Stratford and Brinn were the only crew members I'd seen since the incident, and . . . they were boys. I valued my fledgling friendship with Mindy, and I had reached out in the hope that we could keep it going.

The thought of having someone to talk to again was appealing.

So was a shower. I still had bits of ash from the fire along with two days' worth of sweat and road grime in places I would have preferred to have nothing. Stripping on the way to the bathroom, I realized my wounds were almost healed. I'd have preferred to see a little less rib sticking out, but I was getting there.

The water was relaxing, but even as tired as I was, excitement still bubbled inside me. My friendship with Mindy had started out a little bumpy in the early days, but I'd grown quite fond of her. The thought of having her around made all the other changes seem a lot easier to swallow. I'd never really had a girlfriend before.

Blonde roots and all, I'd pay for the wet ponytail later. I'd slipped into a soft cotton bra, boy shorts, and sweats just before the door chimed.

Being deafened by Mindy's squeal and enveloped in her around-the-pizza-box hug was wonderful. "I've missed you so much!"

"I've missed you too, Mindy. How've you been?"

"Bored. Haven't you?" My eyes must have been as telling as hers. "Let's eat, and then you have to tell me."

"Fair enough." I gestured inside. "You want a beer?"

"Water would be great," Mindy said with her effervescent smile.

Eating pizza straight out of the box with drinks on the coffee table and legs tucked under us on the couch felt like a ritual we'd been doing forever.

"You were about to tell me about life after *Ticonderoga*, Allie."

"I might have had some trouble accepting it was actually over," I admitted.

"What did you do?"

"Well . . . I might have tried to commandeer the ship."

Mindy coughed. "Seriously?"

"So the rumor has it. It seemed like a good idea at the time."

"What were you going to do?"

"If it was going to happen, I would have made arrangements to hook up with Admiral West. Anyone from *Lexington*'s crew that wanted to could've come along, and we were going to go explore."

"You're unreal." Mindy laughed. "What'd Strat have to say about that?"

"Not what I'd hoped. It obviously didn't work out, anyway."

"Are you two together now?"

"I don't know what we are, to be honest. He's been reactivated. He left Friday morning."

"I hadn't heard that."

"You kept in touch?" I asked.

"Most of the officers did. I saw him a time or two after we landed but before they found you. He checked in on us. I think he was trying to keep us together in case we got to go back up again."

"He wanted to go back?"

"We all wanted to go back up. Morale was pretty low when we got ordered to stand down."

"I can imagine." I emptied my bottle. "Have they attached you anywhere yet?"

"I'm the director of off-world observation here at headquarters," Mindy said. "It's a big title for a little job."

"Not much is going on up there with *Tico* sitting on the ground down the street, is there?"

"It's not exactly what I was hoping for when I signed up." She seemed to be forcing some optimism. "How about you? Is there life after *Ticonderoga*?"

"I didn't think so, at first anyway. I'm trying to give it a chance."

"What are you doing now?"

"Yang has me running Space Command Transport Division."

"You're not flying either, are you?"

I shook my head. "The leash is shorter than you'd think."

"Are you okay?" Mindy's tone conveyed more than her words.

"How much do you know?" I asked with a weak smile.

"I know you've been hurt. A lot."

I wanted to be glib with my answer. Too much was going on for me to sort out on my own—some little part of me decided maybe it was time to accept a little help. "I . . . I found a can in the ashes of my parents' home yesterday. A Swiss chocolate tin. I'd seen it on top of one of the cabinets as long as I was growing up and every time I visited after I left for the academy. It was an old house—a lot of things were always just there, you know?"

"What was in it?"

"I haven't studied it yet, but since I found out my mom has evidently had a lifelong affair with Schweizer, I have the worst feeling it won't be good news."

“Pons Schweizer? The ex-SG? How?”

“He was an exchange student. He stayed in her family’s home and . . .”

“Wow.”

I could feel the tears coming. Once they started falling, Mindy came closer and wrapped her arms around me, and that was it.

CHAPTER 23

15 JULY 2126

Coffee's perfume filled my nostrils as the alarm clock's tone filled my ears. My memory didn't reveal how I'd gotten to bed, but I figured the disturbed covers on the other side were an indicator. Crusted crap in the corners of my eyes stopped them from focusing on my sweats and socks as I swung out of bed and shuffled into the bathroom. Once I was more living than undead, I made my way toward the kitchen.

Get me some of that coffee.

"Good morning," Mindy said from behind a skillet of cheesy eggs.

"Hey," I said sheepishly. "I'm a little in the dark about last night."

"It's nothing to be ashamed of, Allie. You had a lot to unload."

"I had a breakdown?" Even I wasn't sure if it was a question or a statement.

She put a glass of water in front of me on the counter. "Maybe you should start with this. I think you cried until you ran yourself dry."

My chapped fingers wrapped around the room-temperature glass. The liquid stabbed at my throat on the way to a rather tormented stomach.

The dehydration was real.

"Sit down," she said. "This is almost ready."

I did as I was told and wolfed down my portion along with the glass of orange juice she soon poured. She sipped her coffee while I ate and waited patiently, stopping to look at me curiously as I neared the bottom of the plate. The squelching in my stomach built pressure until I couldn't hold it back.

The belch was notable.

"Feel better?" Mindy smiled.

I nodded. "Yes, much."

"I'll help you walk through this, Allie. You've just got to let me in, okay?"

"I appreciate it, but you don't know what you're getting yourself into."

Her look mirrored that of a soldier stepping into combat. "It doesn't matter. You're my friend."

~

I was more or less myself by the time I stepped into headquarters. The place wasn't as busy as I would have anticipated on a Monday morning, but I'd never been here on a Monday morning before. The new experience and unfamiliar circumstances should have meant that a tall guy rounding a corner in a gray suit shouldn't have attracted any particular attention.

But it did.

My skin crawled on a primal level. Worse, the morning briefing with Paul I was about to be late for allowed me an irresistible opportunity for flight. So I ran from whatever the otherwise unassuming sight had triggered.

There was no way on Earth I could have stood and faced him. But I couldn't figure out why, and that unnerved me most of all.

✣

"Are you all right, Admiral?" Paul asked.

"Just a little distracted."

"I noticed. You know, we've covered the priority items in the briefing anyway. There's nothing that won't keep until tomorrow." He watched while I took an unsteady breath. "I've been through three HSTDs. I've learned a lot about helping to settle them in."

"HSTDs?"

"Heads of Space Transport Division," Paul winked. "That's you now."

I smiled in spite of myself. "I sound like a venereal disease instead of a bureaucrat."

"You were lost in thought. Can I help you with something, ma'am? Please don't be afraid to ask."

"I saw a man in a suit downstairs. Just a glance, but I got the worst feeling, and I don't know why."

"Today?"

"Yeah. On my way in."

"Let's see if we can figure out who you saw, and maybe then we'll uncover a clue about why it bothered you."

"You have access to the security feeds?"

"I'm the personal assistant of a major department head. I could charter an expedition to Mars if I put my mind to it." He cracked his knuckles theatrically and leaned into the conference table's built-in terminal. "I'm a trained professional."

"Well, I can get the coffee. How do you take yours?"

"I like a hint of bean juice with my creamer. Three sugars, please."

I wasn't gone long, but he'd already accessed the protocol in the system and found the camera's recording of my own entry into headquarters when I slid the mug of steaming tan-colored liquid in front of him.

"It's a little strong," he winced. He smiled when I made as if to leave. "Sit down, Admiral. Let's do this. If he was there when you walked in, we'll go backward from when you cleared the gate, right?"

"Seems reasonable."

"I'm going to set the filter for male and civilian clothing."

I nodded as my heart started pumping faster.

Paul scrolled through the photos slowly, waiting patiently while I scrutinized each one. Judging by the lighting, we were well into last night when I finally realized the problem. "I've only seen the guy from the back and the side. Can you show me the other angles of some people?"

"Everyone is fully scanned for biometrics. It shouldn't be a problem."

"Can you add filters for male, gray clothing, and six foot or taller?"

"Yeah, I think so." Paul worked through a series of submenus and then nodded with some satisfaction when my photo from this morning was back on the screen. "We'll go five foot six, just to make sure we don't miss him. Which side did you see?"

I tapped the back of my head. "Right rear."

Paul hit a few more keys, and the display panned around my image, proving I wasn't having the best hair day ever.

"Let's see what happens," I said.

Paul tapped a few keys on his console, and the display rolled in reverse from the time I arrived. I watched the time index tick back into last night before I gave up.

"Nothing looks right. No one gets to bypass security, do they?"

Paul shook his head. "I wouldn't think so."

"All right. Let me ruminate on this for a while. Thanks, Paul." I stood and started for my inner office.

I'd settled in behind my desk when Paul chimed. "Admiral, I have Chief Brinn for you."

"Put him through, please." I straightened in my chair as the com activated. "Chief, I thought you'd be home with your feet up by now."

"Honestly, so did I. We think it's an issue with the dispersion matrix on the back side of the engine, but there's only one way to find out. I need to monitor the engine while she's in full operation."

"I feel like it's a big ask, Brinn. Even a short haul is about six weeks, isn't it?"

He smiled ruefully. "Ten, and that's if we don't have any trouble."

"Yang was clear I could have you do anything you were willing to. I'm happy to have you as long as you want."

"There's no news of *Tico*, is there?"

"No, and it doesn't seem advisable for me to ask, given the givens."

"I'm not much of an engineer without a ship, Cap—Admiral. I'll see you in three months."

"Roger that, Chief. Safe journey."

I leaned back in my chair and terminated the com with no small hint of regret. Programs came and went in the military, but seeing *Ticonderoga* lose pieces of what she had felt like losing pieces of my own soul.

~

How do they always catch me half naked?

I rolled my eyes and went to the door wearing a bra and my uniform pants, not at all surprised to find Mindy with an overnight bag. Work had gone fine, but walking home had made me appreciate the idea of some company. "Hi, Mindy."

"You're healing good," she said, completely unfazed by my appearance as she stepped inside. "It smells great in here."

"I had them deliver pasta primavera with the grocery order. It's in the warmer."

"You were on your way to the shower."

I nodded and smiled. "Make yourself comfortable. I'll be out in a few."

Military life had taught me to be quick in the shower, but the smell of dinner wafting through my place provided extra motivation—I hadn't realized how hungry I was. Ensconced in warm jammies, I was in the living room in less than fifteen minutes to find Mindy plating up our dinner.

"Do you want to get the drinks?" she asked.

"Wine?"

She cringed a little. "Water for me."

I nodded and prepared two glasses with ice and water from the dispenser on the fridge.

"How was your day?" Mindy asked once we were seated.

I thought back. "Well, Brinn's going to be off-world for the near future. *Fuji* is having an intermittent engine issue he's not sure they've sorted out."

"He'll have a whole new crew to terrorize."

"I think he's given up on *Ticonderoga* for the short term. He seemed happy to have a reason to go back up."

"How are you handling the end of your era with *Tico*?"

"Better than I'd thought I would." Even as I said it, I knew an element of truth shone there. "I never thought I'd say it, but I kind of like my new gig."

"Good day, then?"

I thought back to the man in the suit. Curiosity churned into fear in my gut. I had made no progress toward identifying him.

"Allison? Allison. Allie!" Mindy was halfway out of her chair before I finally mastered myself. "That's the second time I've watched you freak out in two days. What's going on?"

Mindy refilled her glass and replaced mine with white wine while

I found words. "The truth is I don't know. I saw a guy in a suit walking around a corner at headquarters this morning, and it completely flipped me out."

"You'd seen him before." It may have been a question, but it sounded like a statement.

"That's the frustration—I can't place the guy."

"It's got to be hiding in that brain somewhere. Can we see if we can find it?" Mindy looked genuinely hopeful.

"I've been working on it all day. Nothing is there."

"Allison, I know you don't want to deal with this, but you'll never get past it if you keep running."

I combed my hands through my hair in exasperation. "Okay, Dr. Stykes. Let's psychoanalyze. Where do you want to start?"

"It started with *Ticonderoga*, didn't it?"

I let myself look back long enough to know she was probably right. "*Ticonderoga* was about Kegar."

"We both know that's not completely true. What happened after you killed him?"

"I went to find Brinn. I needed him to jettison the pod to get the bulk of the people off the ship."

"Did you have to eliminate anyone?"

I nodded. "He had a guard."

"Brinn obviously succeeded. I remember the ride. What happened next?"

"I heard noise in the aft stairwell. A marine I ended up tangling with."

"And then?"

"I went down a couple of steps so I could see into the frame eighty corridor."

"Was anyone in it?" Mindy asked gently.

I unconsciously widened my eyes at the ceiling as the memory re-formed in my mind. "A guy in a suit. I decided to secure command rather than go after him."

"A guy in a suit." Mindy smiled.

I nodded.

"Then you went to command?"

"Benson slipped up behind me. Things got a little hazy after that."

"That's when you got shot."

I pressed my lips together apprehensively. "The logs should say, but I don't remember any talk of them finding an Earth-based shuttle. Whatever Kegar took to get there was gone by the time West showed up aboard *Lexington*. I can't believe I never put this all together."

"You can't be hard on yourself about this. Besides, what does knowing about it do to help you?"

"I don't know." I rubbed my eyes with the heels of my hands. "Things have quieted down, but nothing seems . . . solved. I feel like I'm stuck waiting for another shoe to drop."

"Are you sure it's not a little PTSD?"

"Absolutely not." I laughed. "But worrying has kept me alive this long."

"He's a contractor."

"Who?"

"The guy in the suit. It's the only thing that makes sense. Kegar thought he was on his side—that's why he was there in the *Ticonderoga* incident. He was a mole for Schweizer, probably feeding him information about what was going on with *Tico* so he could work his own plan to crush the Consortium."

"And why would Schweizer care about the Consortium?"

"Money," Mindy said easily. "Opportunity is common where there's disorder. He had a plan to cash in on what would follow the destruction he caused. He might still have it."

"And his mole is still running around headquarters." My eyes fluttered shut as I fell into a full-bodied yawn.

"We'll never solve the world's problems tonight," Mindy said. "Do you think you can sleep?"

Another yawn rocked my body.

"Come on. Let's get you down."

CHAPTER 24

16 JULY 2126

I woke four hours before dawn.

Mindy was dreaming away on the other side of my bed, and I was happy with the company. Maybe it was coincidence, but my nightmares had been kept at bay for the second night in a row now. Never before had I had a friend I could count on when the chips were down.

Certainly some of that was on me. Friendship had to be reciprocal, and I hadn't always put in more than I'd hoped to get out of relationships. Yet Mindy had shown up in my world, dragging light in behind her and spreading it around without asking first. It made me want to be the friend she deserved.

Soundlessly dressing in the dark and quiet reminded me how important having her around had become to me. I wanted to return the favor of yesterday's breakfast, but I had to haul ass if I was going to get where I needed to be.

Maybe she'd come back again tonight.

Enough mist floated through the air to obscure any view of the stars when I stepped out onto the street. Another rainstorm would be along this evening to replace the one that had just ended. Warm and pleasant, the walk to headquarters flashed by. I cleared security without conscious thought and found myself standing on the second floor overlooking the headquarters entry lobby long before the sun considered rising over the Cascade Range.

Standing post and concentrating on a perceived nothing is a skill. I'd pulled guard duty at various points throughout my career and always done acceptably, not because I was special but because I was determined. I had the power to solve problems and save lives as long as I paid attention and kept my eyes open.

I'd find the guy I was looking for. I was sure of it.

People came and went in a rhythm. I'd expected a rush of thousands of people as morning shift approached, but the line at the entrance was never completely still. I saw tech guys checking network ports, janitors sweeping floors and watering plants, security guards making rounds, and not a few professionals coming and going.

Three hours brought the early risers and go-getters for the morning crew. I smiled inwardly when I saw Paul come in, waited ten minutes, then called him and told him I'd miss the morning briefing. I waited through rush hour. I waited through the latecomers, and—

Son of a bitch.

There he was. Leaving.

He'd either come before I took my post or spent the night in the building. There was no way I'd missed him at the security checkpoint. Not much else was going on. I knew I'd lose him when I saw him leaving, but I had to try anyway. I couldn't stand here yelling, "Stop that guy!"

They'd haul me off to the loony bin. Or prison, depending.

The whoop of an unfamiliar klaxon filled the air as I started down the stairwell. My heart fell as I forced my way through the throng of panicking people. I could feel it—I'd figured it all out too late, and something bad had happened.

Again.

Guards fanned out in front of the main doors.

"Building lockdown!" one of them shouted. "No one's leaving, so calm down, everybody."

Trying to play it cool was beyond my reach.

If I tackled the guy, now standing in the center of a group of displaced workers, I'd look crazy. Security had no more reason to pay any attention to me than anyone else. Headquarters was a civilian facility outside of my chain of command. Any concern they gave me would have been mere courtesy.

My heart was pounding in my chest as I started toward the man I was now certain I had seen on *Ticonderoga*. Not only did he look right, but he felt right. The people around him acknowledged me first—he had his back turned to me when I walked up.

"Folks, can I have a few minutes with my friend here?" I said once I was a few steps away. Most of the group looked up and responded by backing up. He was slow to turn and make eye contact, wearing a look of confusion. "Hi, there."

"Can I help you, Admiral?"

"Absolutely. You can tell me what you're doing here now that Schweizer has been deposed."

"My job, of course."

"And what would that be?" I could feel the hairs on the back of my neck standing up as I adopted a restrained posture.

"As you've already stated, I'm attached to the secretary general's office."

"Really?" The manufactured confusion in my voice was strained but hopefully believable. "She has surrounded herself with personnel from her homeland. I find it hard to believe she would have left a member of her predecessor's staff in place."

His look told me the conversation was over. The only remaining question was whether he was going to hit me or try for the door.

My flying elbow to his jaw seemed like the best way to avoid finding out. As he slumped to the ground, I realized my next task would be to argue my case with security. Who would they believe?

I wasn't sure it would be me.

✣

The criminal and their accuser always sat across from each other in an overheated interview room. Maybe a cup of coffee sat on the table, and intimidation definitely hung thick in the air. Threats, promises for vengeance, and the criminal getting smacked around a little were always possibilities.

It was so satisfying on TV.

Reality was a mirror image—I'd been hauled into an interview room and grilled by a skeptical shift commander for the largest part of the day. The same questions were asked over and over, different questions were asked the same way, and everything was centered on finding a reason not to believe me.

I agreed with their motivation. That didn't stop me from letting out a huge sigh of relief when the investigator finally indicated he agreed with mine. He promised there would be consequences if I didn't stay out of the issue moving forward.

"What's going on, Paul?" I asked after the short walk to my office.

The struggle not to ask the same of me was evident on his face. "Little of note, Admiral. I received confirmation that *Starliner* is back with *Lexington*'s crew. Admiral West is in his office and wishes to see you when it's convenient."

"Very well, Paul." I stopped myself mid-spin toward the door. "I hope you know I'd have a lot to tell you if I could."

"You're not my first HSTD, Admiral."

I laughed. "I still sound like a venereal disease."

"I'll see you tomorrow."

"Thank you, Paul. Have a good night."

Admiral West wrapped me in a warm hug almost before I realized I'd walked anywhere. "It's good to see you, Allison."

"It's good to see you too, sir."

"Sit down, sit down. Can I get you anything?"

I took a seat in his visitor's chair while he trudged behind the big oak desk. "I'm fine, sir."

"Your assistant tells me you've been out all day."

"I ran into an old—er, friend. I believe he was aboard *Ticonderoga* with Kegar."

"The guy that attacked Yang this morning?"

"Sir?"

"Yang was found strangled in her office this morning, Allison. That's what caused the lockdown."

Shock shot up my spine. "I was here, but I didn't hear anything."

"I'm not surprised you didn't know. Criminal Investigation Detachment locked the scene down to preserve evidence. I was told you brought down the guy that did it."

"The asshole in the suit? I didn't know anything about Yang. I saw him on *Ticonderoga* with Kegar's people."

"Tall, half-bald guy with a goatee, right?" West asked. "He suicided before they could question him."

"And he killed Yang?"

West nodded. "He'd have gotten away with it, too, if you hadn't stopped him. CID found a few strands of her hair on his suit."

"Did they get anything more out of him?" I asked.

West shook his head. "I've never heard of anyone crushing their own windpipe."

"Could someone else have gotten to him?"

"Not a chance. Realistically, we'll probably never figure out exactly what he was."

"What does this mean for us?"

His smile was rueful. "More trouble, undoubtedly."

I laughed first. Once it started, it wouldn't stop. I think Admiral West thought something was wrong with me, and then he gave in to it.

There comes a point where laughing is about all you can do.

A few seconds always come at the end of a meal when you push back from the table with uncertainty about what's coming next. More food? Conversation? Time in front of the TV? Before Mindy and I got further sidetracked by the day's events, I said, "I'd like you to move in. I enjoy having you here. You can pay rent or just stay, but whatever the arrangement, I want you to know you're welcome."

While I thought I'd prepared myself for any sort of an answer, her tears were not on the list. I'd never done anything like it before, but I got up from my chair and went to her side. Gently, I pulled her to my chest and stroked her back while she cried. It was impossible not to wonder what had happened to make her so utterly despondent.

"Will you tell me what's going on?" I asked once the river of tears had subsided to a trickling stream. I stepped away and slid back into my chair but kept her hand in mine.

She struggled to meet my eyes. "I'm pregnant."

I hoped the light that filled my heart made it to my face. "Can I be an aunt? I've always wanted to. I had an aunt—well, she wasn't really my aunt, but she let—are you sure this is something to be sad about?"

"It's embarrassing. I slept with someone I shouldn't have, and we didn't use protection. I was lonely and scared, my parents were killed in the fallout, and you were gone, and . . ."

"The rules are different after an experience like we went through. You have to hold it in while it's happening, but once it's done, you have to let all of the stress and anxiety out somewhere. Sex is probably one of the less self-destructive ways to do that."

"But . . ."

"You're having a baby, Mindy. Is that so bad?"

"Well, no. I just didn't plan for it to happen this way."

"If life has taught me one thing lately, it's that things never happen how we plan. My offer for you to stay is genuine. I would be honored to be a part of a child's life."

"Okay." Mindy nodded.

I wrapped her in another hug.

"So are we going to open the can?" Mindy asked.

Generally, when I'd grown uncomfortable with a conversation, a change in subject like a nine-G turn in a Tomcat was my modus operandi. When delivered correctly, sometimes the recipient never even knew what happened. I certainly didn't see past my thoughts and worries about what might be found to consider Mindy might have been deflecting from her own issues.

My response used forced traces of happiness cobbled together to cover my abject fear. "Let's do it."

"Alcohol?" Mindy asked mischievously.

"Abso—nah." I climbed on the counter to reach the tin in its hiding spot.

Mindy was speechless while I balanced a little precariously to reach the bundle. "It's okay—I don't mind. Want some wine?"

I spread the towel on the table once I was back on the ground and put the tin in the center. "Isn't some rum in there?"

"Where'd you learn to drink rum?"

"Doc Hawshmore administered me a little not long before I left

Ticonderoga." I mocked his grandiloquent rumble, "Anti-anxiety medication takes many forms, Captain. I prefer simpler treatments when possible."

Snickering, Mindy sat down with two glasses, one with a healthy portion of the darker liquid, and the other full of ice water. "It's scary how well you do that."

The liquor still made my eyes water. I picked up the tin and worked the top off. What I wanted to find was a lifetime of love notes from my dad. I feared we'd find a lifetime of love notes from Schweizer. Instead, we found a gold locket, a handful of pictures, a big bundle of handwritten letters, and several pocket-size journals bundled together with an aged-looking rubber band.

We looked through the items one at a time. It took hours. While a lot were present, they weren't enough to completely document an affair lasting decades.

"A lot of their communication must have been electronic." Mindy didn't look surprised. "I guess the age of romance really is dead."

"It's easier to hide and delete emails." *Shit.* "Let me check something."

Mindy misinterpreted my urgency. "You got a hot date?"

Personal com in hand, I sat back at the table and belted down the rum. I had the worst feeling I was going to need it and more as I accessed my message storage. My mother's last message was at the top of my personal inbox. "Schweizer isn't the only one my mother emailed to keep in touch."

Mindy looked interested, and I certainly had nothing to hide at this point. I looked longingly at my empty glass and started to read.

> Dearest Allison,
>
> I hope this finds you well. We are so proud of you and all you have accomplished. We listen for reports from your ship every day. Seeing what you have become is amazing.
>
> The weather here in Pripyat is, honestly, much colder than I would have preferred. It rains pretty much every other day, and that's if it isn't snowing. It's nice not to have to worry about water—I don't miss the droughts

of the West. It would be nice to see the sun. I never feel warm anymore.

The food is surprisingly good. I can't imagine what you're eating onboard your ship, but somehow I think it's probably the same as I envisioned food here would be. I admit, between the borscht and the barabolia, I certainly get my share of vegetables every day. On the upside, I never knew so many kinds of fish existed, and we occasionally see lobster and crab as well.

Pons is happy to be so close to home.

We might be in the shadow of Chernobyl, but I feel like we're on the frontier. It's exciting to be part of this area's recolonization. One hundred and thirty-two years ago, they said it would be three thousand years before anyone could call this place home. Yet here we are, starting an entirely new culture.

I have never liked the word *expatriate*. Nothing about my beliefs (or those of anyone I've met here) is unpatriotic. These men and women believe in the power of the collective; they feel human cooperation can accomplish anything. I'm almost as inspired by them as I am by you.

We'll count the days until we are blessed to see you in person.

All my love,
Mom

Mindy watched as I scrolled down the screen, displaying more than a few emails. All of them were sent after the *Ticonderoga* incident. Mom had become abnormally talkative since she'd "moved on." Like she was trying to justify something to me.

Or to herself.

Mindy looked concerned but forged ahead. "If you needed more proof, I guess you have it."

"I think the only thing I need now is some sleep. Tomorrow's another day, and I've had enough of this one."

"I guess I'll try out my new bed," Mindy said.

I met her hug in the middle. "I'm so glad you've decided to stay."

"So am I."

I wasn't getting anywhere in the dark. Nighttime was like that sometimes—it let everything unhappy inside of you come to the surface. Even snuggling in my favorite jammies didn't help. Yielding to it was the best decision, so I got up and padded down the hallway.

Mindy's light was still on and her door was open. Apparently wide awake, she looked over the top of a paperback with raised eyebrows. She patted the pillow beside her, then put her book on the nightstand and turned off the light.

The bed was smaller than mine.

I think my knee brushed her thigh as we settled—the barest of contact, but a reminder that I wasn't alone. Somehow, that made all the difference in the world.

CHAPTER 25

17 JULY 2126

"Good morning, sir. Thank you for seeing me."

Admiral West looked well-rested and annoyingly chipper. "I needed to talk to you anyway, Allison. What's up?"

Suddenly self-conscious, I figured it was leaking into my smile. "It's nothing, sir. What did you need me for?"

"Allison, we've had quite the ride, you and I. I won't pretend to know you completely, but I can tell when something's bothering you." Authority sufficient to remind me he was in charge sounded through his words. "What was on your mind when you asked to see me?"

My words flung out as the dam was overwhelmed. "My mother met Pons Schweizer in her teens. They fell in love and pursued a relationship she's hidden all my life. I believe she killed my dad and ran off to be with Schweizer during the *Ticonderoga* incident." I let out a deep breath. "I felt like someone else needed to know that."

"I'm not sure if that makes what I'm about to say easier or not. The gentleman you stopped yesterday was, in fact, tied to Schweizer. Given what happened with Yang, the Security Council has decided that Schweizer is still empowered as a shot caller and represents an ongoing threat to the UPE. We're putting together a mission to eliminate him."

A familiar fire rekindled in my stomach. "I want in."

"We can find someone else, Allison."

I shook my head. "I'm good."

The concern on his face was obvious. "We're not in the hospitality business. It's no secret we see and do some dark things, but sending you to possibly eliminate your own mother is beyond the pale."

"Do you remember what you told me about going with revenge when you don't have a better motivation?" I waited until he nodded reluctantly. "It's all I have anymore."

"I'm truly sorry to hear you say that."

I shrugged. "I assume you've assembled a team?"

"Are assembling. We're anticipating a five-person team with three alternates. At least one operator is a person of your acquaintance."

"Stratford."

He nodded. "He was available, capable, and motivated by his own experiences with Schweizer."

"He'll lead the team." It wasn't a question.

"Yes." West's eyes made it clear he was stone-cold serious.

I was still pissed at Strat, but, looking at it rationally, I knew our involvement was my fault. Operators like him weren't suited for long-term relationships. I'd let myself try it anyway, mostly because I'd been lonely and he was sexy as hell.

Stratford had never acted with any pretense. He had been exactly what he was. The responsibility for getting too attached—for being naive—was mine.

"I want in."

"Understood. Cryptography has uncovered increasing communications out of Pripyat. Schweizer's not making much of an attempt to hide what he's up to."

"They're not supposed to have any coms at all to speak of, are they? I thought it was basically a penal colony."

"It is, and they aren't. One direct line straight to UPE Communications is all there should be outside of monitored email access. It may be outdated, but the Russians left behind an incredible amount of equipment when they abandoned the area. We didn't see it as a risk, but it appears Schweizer and the others have been bringing more things back online than we'd anticipated."

"He's not done trying to take over the world, is he?" I asked.

"At the very least, he seems intent on raising Cain to see if he can."

"Yang paid for the decision to let bygones be bygones with her life."

"The Defensive Forces Oversight Committee isn't going to do the same thing. They've expressed a preference for it to be done quietly, but in the end, they want it done."

"What's the timeline?"

"It sounds like you have a capable assistant, from what I see. Work with him the rest of the week to put things on autopilot, or as close as you can. I'll mind the store while you're training—you'll be around for a while if I have any questions. Stratford should be in this weekend—he's taking a look around the target site right now."

I shook my head. "Alone."

West seemed to know it wasn't a question. "Plan for training to start at 0600 Monday morning at the base physical training center. I'll get you details before the weekend."

"Roger that, sir."

✣

"That's about the size of it."

"It's not the first time," Paul said. "I'll try not to let the place burn down while you're gone."

"I have a feeling you won't see much of me for a while after—" Paul moved to get up as the com's message alert sounded, interrupting us. "There's no reason to get up. You can take it here, can't you?"

He started manipulating the controls set into the table in front of him. "It's Chief Brinn."

"Can you hear me, Chief?"

"Loud and clear, Admiral. How's life on terra firma?"

"It's become interesting."

"In the pursuit of scientific knowledge way?"

"More like the ancient Chinese curse way."

"You all right?"

"I've got some work to do. My assistant Paul will be minding the day-to-day stuff. Admiral West will be taking over otherwise," I said.

"Any news of *Ticonderoga*?" Brinn asked.

"She's still here. Not a peep otherwise."

"I guess I'm not missing anything out here, then."

"How is life aboard a freighter?"

"Slower paced, to be sure. We've been monitoring the matrix. I think another round of calibrations to the magnetic field generators will do the job. From then on, it'll be a pleasure cruise."

"Minus the Mai Tais." I closed my eyes and ran my tongue over my teeth, trying to remember something that had seemed important before I forgot to write it down. It took a second, but it did hit. "Hey, come to think of it, I do have a question for you. Can *Ticonderoga* launch Tomcats while she's earthbound?"

"I'd try to avoid it if at all possible. The launch gantries will take the weight, but the heat from the thrusters will likely be too much for them. The atmosphere doesn't dissipate it quickly enough. You can sling-load one off with a big enough crane, the same way they're transferred to the gantries after landing in the main bay."

I didn't quite manage to sound casual. "You never know what will come up."

"Isn't that the truth," he agreed. "I'd best clear the com."

"Take good care, Brinn. Stop by when you get home."

"Roger that. Be careful, Admiral."

"Will do. HSTD out."

~

Mindy and I went for a run around the base after work, my first since I'd been planetside, and honestly, it hurt. She was just starting to show, but she looked as good and ran as hard as she did back onboard *Tico*. The stitch in my side was the least of my problems, but she had another thing coming if she thought I'd stop. She'd woken my competitive spirit, and I needed to get myself back together to face what was ahead.

Endorphins had kicked in by the time we made it back to the apartment. I was hot, sweaty, and on cloud nine, and that was before we came around the corner and found Strat, dressed in camo BDUs, leaning against the wall next to the apartment door. Jumping into his arms felt like the most natural thing in the world.

He smelled like aviation fuel, trees, and sweat as he pulled me into a kiss that curled my toes.

"Hi, there," I said after several breaths. "I didn't expect you for a bit."

"Bloody good hello, for spur of the moment." He turned to Mindy, looked her over, and offered his greeting. I watched his confident grin evaporate into something I'd never seen on him before. Fear. "Hello, Mindy."

"Hello, Edgar." Her gaze fell away, draining every drop of effusive light from her being. I'm not sure Strat caught it, but to me it could only mean one thing—something simple and terribly complex all at the same time.

"Mindy's staying with me now," I said, putting the pieces together. It registered somewhere in my subconscious that she'd disappeared into the apartment behind me. "She just moved in."

"I have to get back to the barracks. I just wanted to let you know I was back."

"So that's it?" I moved closer to him, letting my anger curl my lips into a cruel smile. If only for a moment, I had no idea what I was going to say or do. "The going gets rough, so Special Operations gets going?"

"Allison—"

"I was thinking about it earlier, Strat. You could charm the panties off any woman with a pulse. We were two grown-ups. What we did, we did knowing what could happen, and it was a lot of fun." I stopped and thought for a minute. "What you did with Mindy is different now that there's a baby involved. You need to get your shit together, grow up, and get ready to be a dad. Or at least a man."

He stared at me, shaking his head. I was sure a little part of him wanted to hit me. In all fairness, I kind of wanted to hit him, too.

Instead, he turned and strode down the hallway.

"I'll see you Monday," I called after him as he disappeared.

I was deliberate as I stepped back inside the apartment. It didn't take a genius to figure out Mindy was going to be a mess, and I was trying to figure out how to handle it.

Her back against the wall, she'd slumped to the floor inside the door. Her self-control failed completely seconds after I knelt in front of her. She fought me when I tried to wrap my arms around her, letting some misguided feeling of shame force her away from the comfort she needed.

When she finally regained some modicum of control, she looked up and found me grinning. "Mindy? You know that technically I slept with your man."

Only for an instant, she smiled through a thick layer of tears, snot, and regret, which told me then and there that we were going to be okay. "Hussy."

"Come on," I said as I spread my arms apart. She was hesitant, but I pulled her to her feet and hugged her tight when she finally stepped closer. "You are my best friend, and I want to be yours. Like I said, things like that don't count when you're under our kind of stress. Don't worry about this because of me, okay?"

"I knew you were into him, but I didn't know if you were even alive." The pain in her eyes hurt my heart. "I thought I'd lost you."

"I'm like trying to shake a booger off the end of your finger, Mindy. I'm not easy to get rid of." I wiped her cheeks as best as I could with my hands. "Let's eat some chocolate cake. It'll help."

The table sucked me back in after Mindy went to bed. More specifically, the can filled with ghosts of my mother's romance. While I knew my rationalization was bullshit, I wrote it off as research. I started reading the words, focusing on the outside chance I might pick up something about Schweizer's habits.

Had anyone looked on, I would have insisted that finding the measure of my mother's betrayal wasn't part of my motivation.

Judging by the date, the last letter she'd received had been on 14 January 2126, even though it was the first on the pile.

> Dearest Anna,
>
> As dear as I hold it to my heart, the thought of you holding this in your hands pales against the memory of holding you in my arms so long ago. Knowing what has passed between us and all that is yet to come brings life to me as though a dream is coming to fruition. I'd almost feared it would never be.

I remember the night you told me we'd be together if I could achieve something great. Knowing you were with him as I've made my way through the world was hard. You are right—your baby should have been in my life as well—the ultimate expression of the love we've shared. While I'm glad you've experienced motherhood, knowing I didn't share that life with you is my regret to be carried for all eternity.

I agree with you about Allison. A shame though it may be, she won't understand our need to be together. I'm not sure anyone ever can—I know no one should ever be forced to wait as long as we have to completely experience the love our hearts have carried. It's a shame her stubborn inability to accept the obvious will cost her career, but for her, a life lived in the disgrace of perceived incompetence will be better than no life at all. She won't stand in our way after we've worked to achieve so much together.

The world is soon to be ours, my love. When? Nearly uncountable years have passed too soon—mere breaths in the history of time are all that separate you from my arms.

With Dearest Love in All Things,
Pons

May you find what you are looking for.

I finally understood why it was a curse. I reread the second paragraph repeatedly, not exactly sure what the words meant and not completely sure I wanted to. Taken loosely, it could mean my mother had a second child I'd never known about. While possible, it seemed far more likely Pons Schweizer was implying he should have raised me.

The last time I'd seen my mother, I'd accused her of killing my dad. She had, in return, told me she didn't kill my father. I rarely used that word to refer to the guy that raised me, because he was my *dad*. I didn't know him by any other name.

The brewing panic attack ended as soon as the blood started rushing through my ears. Hearing my own heartbeat brought Dad's words back.

Take a breath, Allison.

My dad had comforted me when I was sick, taught me how to drive a tractor, and warned me about kissing boys. It wasn't my mother and it sure as hell wasn't Pons Schweizer that had led me through life. If Schweizer had knocked my mother up, it meant I had an even better reason to find him and kill him to avenge my dad.

And my mother was in this up to her eyeballs.

Suspecting had been one thing. *Knowing* . . . didn't change much at all when I thought about it.

I went to bed feeling oddly comfortable and slept more soundly than I had in some time. I understood my circumstances and had a purpose that was as clear as glass. I'd see Schweizer dead, and I'd either see my mother to justice for what she did to my dad, kill her myself, or die trying.

What more did a girl need?

CHAPTER 26

22 JULY 2126

Coffee . . .

As I came around the corner from the hall, I wasn't surprised by the scent in the air or the dim lights above the kitchen cabinets. Mindy was positioned at the table, facing the balcony windows. Red and gold morning sunlight glinting off *Tico*'s stern section looked fabulous, but I got the feeling she was looking beyond the view. She was already dressed, leaving me a stitch self-conscious as I pulled my robe tighter against the boy shorts and T-shirt I'd slept in.

I poured coffee for myself and held the mug tight with both hands, enjoying the warmth in my fingers as much as the aroma that wafted up to me. The beverage was borderline military specification—a spoon might have stood on end in the liquid. I wasn't sure I was brave enough to sample it.

"How are you this morning?" Mindy asked softly, as if being too loud would break the spell.

"I've got it under control. How are you?"

Her answer wasn't quick in coming. "It's always about control, isn't it?"

I frowned. Oh how aware I was that asserting control was sometimes construed as a lack of mental stability. The truth was things felt like they were heading my direction for the first time in quite a while. "When we don't have it, we tend to go looking for it. It's human nature, I think."

"I thought we'd come past that."

"You know we're okay, don't you? You and me? About Strat?"

"Yeah, you forming up to go assassinate your mother and my baby daddy issues are on the same level."

"Well, at least I'm taking your baby daddy to go deal with my mother," I said with a crooked smile.

"You're about to be under Stratford's command. How's that going to work out for you?"

"I can follow orders, Mindy."

She digressed into a deep pull from her coffee mug. "I know you can, as far as orders go, but . . ."

The conversation sputtered out after that. While I drank the rest of my coffee, showered, and dressed in a regulation sports bra and spandex shorts, I thought about being in charge. Command had never been in sight for me when I'd joined the UPE, but I'd become a dog with a bone once the idea crossed in front of me. Working with Yang had been difficult for me personally. Like a queen demoted to a pawn, I followed along as we'd made our play against Schweizer, even if I had been a subordinate in name only at times.

Acknowledging the truth meant accepting that I'd stepped into the spotlight and presumed a position of leadership in the delegation at the first opportunity, unintentional though it may have been. And when my mom had appeared, my inability to follow the plan had sent me to a cold, dark cell and sent Yang, eventually, to her death. I had to make reparations.

Glancing at my watch gave me what I needed to push any more concerns into the corner where they belonged. To avoid being late, I pulled my hair into a quick ponytail, zipped a windbreaker over my racerback bra, and stormed toward the front door, where Mindy met me.

She gave me a tight hug goodbye. "Be careful today, okay?"

"I'll be fine," I assured her confidently.

~

Aboard *Tico*, my workout clothes would have been quite comfortable, but in the briefing room, I struggled against the chill of the overactive AC. Admiral West bustled to the podium, though the place was decidedly less crowded than it had been during our organization of the *Lexington* operation.

Stratford and seven of his look-alikes were turned backward and sideways in their seats in the room's left-hand section. They had obviously worked together before. While I couldn't hear exactly what they were saying, I imagined half-complete, classified stories of past battles.

A handful of *Tico*'s former pilots—Daniels, Rogers, Miller, Frederich, and Winter—occupied the other side of the aisle. Behind them sat a few less familiar faces in a secondary group. I recognized them as plane handlers and ordinance personnel.

Both geographically and metaphorically, I held the middle ground, not a member of either side at the time.

"If everyone's amenable, we'll get this show on the road," Admiral West said as he stepped up to the microphone. The room didn't come to attention as much as to focus, mostly as the operators turned in their seats and quieted. "This briefing is classified at level Q. The information dispersed here is not to be shared beyond these walls for any reason whatsoever. No electronic conversations about this information will be conducted on an unsecured communication system. No in-person conversations will be conducted outside of Q controlled areas. Am I clear?"

He waited for an affirmation from each member of the audience before he continued. "Pons Schweizer, former UPE Secretary General and current resident of the UPE Internment facility in Pripyat, Ukraine, is to be eliminated on the belief that he cannot be trusted to stop working against the UPE's ideals."

He clicked a control that brought the screens behind him to life, then turned and acknowledged the displays accordingly with a laser pointer. "The mission will have three distinct phases—infiltration, engagement, and extraction. Stealth will be particularly necessary during the first two phases. Intelligence places the target likely at one of two locations—a reinvigorated apartment complex or the communications facility serving as a headquarters structure."

"Ukraine is a UPE signatory, isn't it?" Rogers asked. "Won't they play ball?"

"UPE leadership has chosen not to ask that question, Lieutenant. Keep in mind the type of mission this is."

"What kind of manpower will go in, sir?" a mountain of a man on Stratford's side of the room asked.

"Good question, Mason. Two teams of two people, plus one on overwatch," West said. "Team placement will be competitive. Commander Stratford will oversee the team selection through the training process. Training will be largely at Commander Stratford's purview, and will include some aspects of Resistance to Interrogation training. The training will be as real as it gets—you can't teach someone how to resist torture without including some aspects of those activities. No one will think less of you if you want to bow out now. Do not come to me if you find the regimen to be too intense. Am I clear?"

Nods of assent came from all of the special forces operators, including me.

"The target is only the former SG?" another of Stratford's group asked, a wiry fellow with a higher pitched voice.

"There is a secondary target, one Anna Seagull, who has been identified as complicit in treason against the UPE government," West said.

I was instantly thankful for the admiral's discretion. The operators mirrored his matter-of-fact manner. No one asked any further questions about targets. The rest of the operation centered on the logistics of getting in and out of Ukraine without being caught.

Admiral West disappeared out a side door once the meeting was over. The pilots walked out in a group, as did Stratford and the special operations personnel. I followed behind, struggling fractionally to keep my head up.

Following wasn't my strength.

Strat milled about in a hubris huddle with the seven other operators. When I strode into the gym, all fourteen eyes locked on me. They looked and talked the same, even had identical haircuts and clothes.

Now free of the strictures of the conference room, their characteristic habits were allowed to surface. Most notably, they referred to each other by their last names. Knowing someone's surname in the civilian world is an intimacy. Generally, military uniforms included a name tape over the left breast announcing the wearer's family name. Special Operators didn't wear conventional uniforms, a habit that had started somewhere in the twentieth century as a security precaution to protect their identities. As such, the customary surname tape was absent.

If you wanted to know an operator's family name, you had to ask. These folks weren't considered highly approachable. If you asked one of them, and if they told you their name beyond "Dave" or "Sam," you knew something about the person most people didn't.

Although small, the surname usage was an intimacy, a ritual step toward joining the brotherhood they were all a part of.

And I wasn't.

I was far from being as impressed with them as they were with themselves. That was the way with operators—they thrived on personal confidence.

"Good morning," I said as I neared. Their circle didn't widen to accept me.

"All right, boys. Let's get after it." Strat was a breath later than he needed to be, ensuring I took the point that I wasn't to be included in their club. "Square off—one fall, full contact. Rotate partners after every fall."

"I'll take the girl," one of the biggest guys said with a slight French accent.

"You would, Claire," another snapped as he and his new opponent faced each other.

Claire crossed in front of me, knocking his shoulder against mine. A warrior's light glimmered in his eyes and a smile stretched across his face when he turned to me.

I took a defensive stance, arms up but close, bracing for his advance. He launched like a coiled spring, intending to catch me in a bear hug. I ducked down and to the left, catching him with an elbow in the back of the knee that didn't send him over. He recovered fast, already charging by the time I spun. My abs tensed before his shoulder caught me in the stomach in a spear that knocked me to the ground.

"Switch!" Strat shouted.

I'd lost, so I had to move. Quite literally, I'd been unable to stand my ground. I rolled to my feet, stepped to my right, and assumed the same stance in front of the guy that had heckled Claire. He was a striker, flying forward with hands up. We weren't sparring—the shot he landed on the right side of my jaw rocked but didn't topple me.

He stepped back and grinned down at me, which was a mistake—it gave me enough time to land an uppercut that put him out cold for a minute.

"Switch!" Strat shouted. Once he saw my opponent wiggle, he added, "You're on the side, Dakota. Go get checked out in the medbay."

"Nice punch," said the wiry guy, an alternate whose surname was Kelly. The others also called him Knockdown, and I was about to find out why. He took a combat stance and squared off with me. Before I even realized what happened, I was flat on my back opening my eyes and trying to breathe. He'd caught me with a clothesline and pretty much run right over the top of me.

"Switch!" Strat shouted as I fought gravity again.

"Ready, Allie?" he said as I took my stance across from him. Having learned my lesson, I sprang before he was ready, landing two rapid-fire punches in the chest before I kicked out and squared him in the balls. When he still didn't fall, I managed to land an elbow in the side of his neck that knocked him to one knee. From there, I had him, using the same clothesline technique the wiry guy had used on me.

"Don't call me *Allie* again." I stepped over him as he struggled to pull air into his lungs.

Strat gave us some time to get our bearings, and for the monster I now knew as Dakota to come back from the medbay. He didn't accept my apology, but he wasn't quite the asshole to me the others were. Strat didn't acknowledge my existence after our match, but given the fact that I'd nutted him to help me win, I figured it was understandable.

That notwithstanding, he was the leader of the club that didn't particularly want me—an admiral and an outsider—to become a member. While I might have hoped for a little more, I wouldn't have expected it in this sort of environment.

Word got around that we were starting our "stroll," so I hurried to the bathroom before I missed anything. I knew I'd be okay with anything having to do with running—period. I weighed 133 pounds. These guys had at least a hundred pounds on me if not more. Leaving aside the fact that running had always been my preferred means of exercise, there was no fighting physics. I carried around half their mass.

I'd match them step for step all day long.

"Ready to go for a walk, little girl?" the one called Claire mumbled as he knocked into my shoulder again. Regardless of his intent, I took his gesture to mean he was ready to bump me out of his way. I felt certain we'd rumble, and soon. I guess he'd find out how easily I was knocked around then . . .

"You big guys are kinda clumsy, aren't you?" I pulled my foot against my backside, stretching my right quad.

"You little things are rubbery, aren't ya?" His teeth cracked in a reluctant smile. "How the hell do you do that, anyway?"

"There's more to working out than lifting obscene amounts of weight and punching stuff. I could show you, if you want to learn."

"Like I taught you what the mat tastes like?"

I grinned. "Don't say I didn't offer."

"Out the door," Strat shouted. "Let's go!"

Strat set an easy pace, right around four miles an hour. There was only one reason to jog that slow—he meant to either do it all day, straight uphill, or both. So I stayed quiet, kept pace at the back of the pack, and made plans to enjoy the trip around whatever I was about to see of Victoria. I'd been in and out of here for my entire career but had never explored it.

Now was as good a time as any.

Listening helped pass the time. Everybody except for Strat seemed to be talking, telling the occasional joke, laughing, and generally wasting air. These were hard men, trained to believe they knew it all and could accomplish anything. Part of me wanted to explain the error in their thinking, but then I would have been the one wasting air.

Mine was better spent staying in the game.

✣

"One fight, one fall. Full contact! Square off!" Strat shouted just before we stopped running.

The clearing was dirt and gravel. Room was at something of a premium—there was the occasional boulder, tree, weed, and who knew what else on the ground. Not a mat to be seen.

Claire knocked into my shoulder when he stepped around me, so I punched him in the kidney.

Fight's on now.

He looked impressed when he took his stance. "Now you're thinking like an operator."

"Let's find out," I said as I dropped my hands to my sides. They weren't defensive, but they gave me balance.

His advance was predictable and weak compared to this morning. I dodged him easily, kicking my leg out and catching his foot as he passed within inches of my right side. He stumbled over my leg, grunting as he caught himself.

His face showed his frustration, and I knew my strategy stood a chance. I had to use my size and mobility to my advantage, because he'd put a solid dent in me if he hit me. I took a low defensive stance for balance and because he was so big he'd have trouble coming down as low as I could.

The roundhouse he threw would have rattled my toenails if he had connected. Ducking below it, I caught him in the midsection with a left elbow and then my right fist before he grabbed me by the back of my top and pulled me upright.

Guessing he was about to headbutt me, I fisted both hands, shooting them straight up to break his hold on me and then bringing them together with the hope of slamming them against his ears. I only caught one, but that gave me enough of an opening to land a knee in his stomach.

What air he had left was blown out in a giant "woof!" Then he doubled over.

I buried one more knee, higher and with everything I had, into the top of his chest and knocked him over backward.

It felt like mere seconds, but our round had gone on long enough that all of the winners and some of the losers from the other bouts were watching as we finished.

"You all right?" I asked as I extended my hand down to him.

He hooted a laugh full of pleasure and, I think, a little surprise. "Jesus Christ—did they teach you that in yoga class too?"

He nearly pulled me over as he got to his feet—he was more than a little shaky.

I shrugged and winked as I steadied him. "It was Pilates."

✣

Since I was the only woman in the training center, it was an easy decision to enjoy the unlimited warm water the women's showers offered after I stripped in the locker room. Water cascading over my shoulders and down my back washed a little of the pain from the day's beatings and a lot of grime down the drain where it belonged.

I didn't have a lot of personal time to look forward to, but I wanted to leave the training center at the training center. Drawing that kind of line between who I was and who I had to be might not be possible, but it didn't mean I wasn't going to try. As much as I loved the thought of seeing Mindy at the apartment, these few minutes of absolute privacy were—

"Happy to scrub your back." Unbidden, Stratford's caress on my shoulders startled and enraptured me in equal measure.

"Men's shower is on the other side of the hall." I felt him brush across my backside as I turned. Toned muscle dripping with water, his crooked smile and bright blue eyes looked down at me with something that set my insides afire.

My imagination got away from me as I looked past him and saw myself pressed against the tiled wall of the shower back in my apartment, warm water pouring over me. I felt him inside of me, almost too full but so good. I felt the soft skin of his lip between my teeth as I bit him before he pulled back from our kiss for a rasping breath.

Maybe all truly great memories were that real.

"Strat, you need to leave."

"Leave?" His head tilted. "Are you sure?"

"No," I admitted. I looked down at his growing erection. He was so close, and it would feel so good. "I'm not sure at all, but you still have to go."

He stepped back. "It's Mindy, isn't it?"

"Yes and no." I went back to soaping myself as if he wasn't there, even though I wished the hands on me were his. I probably washed my boobs longer than I needed to. "I don't think you're unfeeling, Strat. I know you care about me. But I deserve better than someone who's going to fuck the next piece of tail that gets charmed by that smile. We both know there'll be one."

"So now you're puritanical about sex?"

I laughed. "More than you are, I guess."

"There she is. Always needing to be in control all the time."

The feeling in the back of my neck told me belittling him could easily get away from me. Pretending I didn't care what he did, I finished my shower as leisurely as possible and was relieved to find him gone when I grabbed for my towel.

His words bit, mostly because I couldn't dismiss their honesty. His tryst with Mindy didn't bother me so much as the fact that I'd felt so out of control when he left for special ops without considering me at all. That's when the rift had formed between the two of us.

And there the magic word was a second time—*control.*

I'd grown up the only daughter of a farmer. Dad had always said you could do everything right trying to grow crops, but regardless of how hard you worked, it might not come out as well as you'd hoped, or at all, because the weather was in control.

My childhood had been filled with examples of his honesty. As I'd grown, frost at the wrong time, a summer's drought causing a thin harvest, early snows, and late rains had been among the robbers stealing his dreams.

And yet I didn't hate farming.

I hated watching Dad feel like a failure because things beyond his control conspired to wrench success away from him. From the day I'd understood that moving forward, I'd plotted my escape to a world filled with clear orders where success depended only on the righteousness of your cause and your skill in carrying out the tasks you'd been given.

Hysterical laughter took over once I realized my own hypocrisy. Onlookers, if they'd been present, might have assumed I'd had some sort of breakdown. I was still gasping for air while I fumbled with the top button on my shirt.

Apparently, I needed to reconsider a few of the details I'd based my life philosophy on.

Better late than never.

~

"Oh! Hi, Mindy."

She stood up from a bench outside the training center door. "I thought you might like to get some supper."

"Sure." I wrapped my arm around her shoulder in a side hug and left it there. "You okay?"

A firm shake of her head was all the answer I got.

"Nostro's makes a good salad. It's only about a mile."

"That sounds good," she said. "How did your day go?"

I spent the rest of our walk telling her about the fights, lingering appropriately on squaring Strat in the balls. We talked about the run, pacing, and how beautiful some of the nearby mountains had to be to explore, and then guessed about what might be coming. I told her about my rounds with Claire, and the respect I seemed to have gained by the time it was over.

After we'd ordered, I took more than a sip of water before I asked, "Second thoughts, huh?"

She shook her head. "Fifth . . . sixth . . . tenth."

"I can only imagine what's running around in your head. I know I'd be scared."

She scoffed. "You?"

"Are you kidding me? What if I break it? How do I feed it? How do I teach it stuff? What if I'm not good enough? What if it doesn't love me?" I shook my head. "Spaceflight was easier."

A hint of a smile pinched her cheeks.

"You're right, you know? Stratford isn't going to be there for you. One thing I finally realized today was he's not going to be there for me, either. You'll need people to be there for you, Mindy. I want to do that. I want to help you not because I think I have to or that you need me—I want it for me, too."

She was obviously skeptical. "Poopy diapers and midnight screaming? You've thought about that?"

"Hand in hand with everything else. I don't make promises lightly, Mindy. There's too much at stake." I wanted more to be said. I wanted to say more. It didn't matter right then whether she was crew or a friend. I wanted to do enough for her.

Be enough support for her.

In the end, only a glimmer of delight and one simple word emerged. "Okay."

My yawn carried my eyes over the top of one of Schweizer's earliest love letters to my mother. Mindy stood in my doorway looking hesitant. We'd talked some more on the way home from dinner, but I hadn't been convinced she was okay.

I hoped my smile was a warm one. "Need some company?"

She nodded.

"C'mon."

She didn't even look at me as she settled into the unused side of my bed, simply cuddled up with the pillow and pulled the sheets up to her neck. I put the letter I'd been reading on the nightstand, shut off the light, and mirrored her actions.

It was time for bed anyway, and sometimes a girl just needed to know someone who cared about her would still be there when she woke.

CHAPTER 27

23 JULY 2126

The line between caution and paranoia was a knife's edge, and I knew I was in serious danger of losing my balance and being cut in half. I tried to ignore the constant feeling that something bad was about to happen—I would be the first to admit I had a lot of things left in my life to look forward to.

Regardless, that didn't stop me from waiting for another shoe to drop.

What a pity to be walking through the world with apprehension on such a beautiful morning. Mist hung in the crisp air as the sun peeked over the Cascades. The temperature was perfect, and an early morning rain had washed through, leaving the air smelling and feeling the exact opposite of the recycled excuse for atmosphere I'd gotten so used to onboard *Ticonderoga*. Even the best air processors ever invented couldn't make the air smell natural.

A splash of water in the road behind me seemed so commonplace, I overlooked its implications until a bag was pulled over my head and an arm tucked too tight around my neck. I knew on some level that this was a special ops test of my ability to keep my cool in a bad situation, but I had a thing about tight places that the bag played hard against as soon as it was tightened.

As adrenaline took over to help me survive, I remembered Admiral West's warning about the intensity of forthcoming Resistance to Interrogation training. It could have been delirium brought on by asphyxiation, but I'd swear my last thought was, *Really?*

~

Icy water.

I only had time to register my lack of air before I started choking. The cloth of the wet bag pulled into my throat as I sucked in useless breaths. Powerful hands dragged me back from the edge and out of the tank as I'd thought I'd breathed my last.

I was allowed three stabbing breaths of clear air before I was pushed back into the tank. Hands and arms of steel forced me to endure six more punishing rounds before I was allowed to collapse onto the floor.

"Do I have your attention?" a voice asked in broken English.

When I didn't answer immediately, I was yanked to my feet and the cycle was repeated. One extra gasp of air defined my next stay on the floor before the same voice snapped, "Do I have your attention?"

I struggled to a kneeling position. "Mackenzie, Allison Jane. Nine-seven-three-four-tango-one-five-epsilon."

"What are you doing here?"

"Getting wet."

A single pounded footstep signaled my need to start taking deep breaths again in anticipation of the water. The frigid shock was the hardest, but the little prebreathing I'd done helped. That, and I was able to hold my breath completely this time. It was still ice water, though, so I was reflexively gasping as they threw me back on the floor.

"Do I have your attention?" came the voice again.

"Yes," I spat.

"Why are you here?"

"Because someone threw a bag over my head while I was walking to work and dragged me here," I said dryly.

The voice snapped something I figured was the Mandarin equivalent of "do it."

At least two sets of hands started tugging at my uniform. Only then did I realize how my hands were bound behind my back. Uniform catches popped, zippers pulled, and anything that didn't have some give ripped. They pulled and pushed me around until I'd lost everything but my bra and underwear. Concrete slick with water and cold air was all I could feel against bare skin.

I mentally translated the next snapped command as "take her." More hands grabbed me under flailing arms and legs. They were strong—as near as I could tell, they hefted me about three feet off the ground without much trouble. I stopped wiggling and tried to brace myself, assuming I would get dropped on the concrete again. Protecting my body from unnecessary trauma was important if I was going to get through this.

Falling much less than I'd expected, I was tossed on a rough mattress like I'd expect to find in a jail cell.

I lay there for a minute, breathing deeply and trying to collect myself. I listened carefully to the sets of footsteps, the hollow whump of a heavy door closing into its frame, and then nothing else.

As thankful as I would have been to shrug it off, I was stuck with the bag over my head until I dealt with the rope on my hands.

The water had soaked into the rope on my wrists enough to allow some movement. Sliding to the edge of the cot and then off it was far from graceful, but like an action star in an ancient movie, I was soon working my arms up and down in a sawing motion, judging the rope's contact against the rough metal frame of the cot by feel.

My arms were exhausted by the time the rope snapped free.

The bag was easy once my hands were loose. Looking around carefully, I saw nothing other than the bed I'd been deposited on, concrete walls, and a heavy steel door with reinforced window glass.

The door had an old-school lock on it, though. I could work with that.

Thank you, Dad.

Learning how to pick a lock had been one of my earliest lessons. He never told me why he thought it was important, but he made a contest out of practicing. Eventually, I was better at it than he was.

I took my bra off long enough to dig the underwires out of both sides. From there, shaping one into a hook and flattening the end of the other by abrading it against the concrete was a simple matter.

Stratford, Dakota, and Claire stood on the other side of the door when it opened.

I took a defensive stance. "Do we have to fight again?"

Dakota snarled, "There are three of us."

"So grab a few more guys to even it up. I'll wait."

"Stand fast," Stratford said. "The exercise is over."

~

"Tactical gear favors you, Admiral," Stratford said.

"What's next?" I asked, trying to belie the mix of feelings in my stomach. Dressed again, I was less exposed now but felt odd sporting the field gear. It pulled at me differently than a normal uniform. It also provided more protection.

"Admiral West has arranged a final examination. Two atmospheric shuttles are waiting at the airfield. We'll board and be taken on a short hop to simulate insertion on the edge of the base. The rest of you will work with Defensive Forces security to act as our hostiles. The target will be a dummy positioned in the same cell Admiral Mackenzie recently escaped here in the training center."

"Weaponry?" Dakota asked.

Strat passed around rifles that resembled children's toys in appearance. "Don't let the looks fool you—these pack a wallop. These are also the only weapons authorized for this exercise. Am I clear that nothing is to be improvised?"

"Crystal clear, sir," we answered in unison.

"Questions?" Stratford asked, surveying our faces, each in turn.

"It's not a lot of information," I said when he came to me.

"We've done more with less," Claire said with a hint of a smile. "We've got this. You teaming with me, Pilates?"

I glanced at Stratford, who nodded approval.

"Absolutely," I said, fist-bumping the giant.

"I'm with Dakota. Everyone else report to base security. You're on counterinsurgency," Stratford snarled. "Hooah?"

"Hooah!" the rest of us barked in unison.

I pulled the weapon's strap over my shoulder and repositioned the shooting glasses I'd been issued below the bill of my ball cap. "Do you have a plan, Claire?"

He glanced behind us. "I have a strategy."

"I like the sound of that. Hey, by the way, do you have a first name?"

"Sure do."

"What is it?"

"Gunny."

I shook my head to hide my smile. Claire was definitely something else.

~

"You all right, Pilates?" Claire whispered.

Truthfully, I was far from okay, but I wasn't about to tell him that. I'd stopped shivering a while ago, which I didn't take as a particularly good sign. We had to be fifty feet or so underground, and the chill in the air was starting to catch up to me. Surely it wasn't all the temperature, though—I didn't want to think about what was crawling on me or what I'd crawled through, for that matter.

Water was the least of my concerns.

"I'm okay. When do you want to go?"

I felt him shrug and check his watch in one motion. "Another half an hour or so at least. We want 'em good and bored before we move."

Another deep breath did nothing to chase the jitters away.

"Strat and I teamed up to deal with a warlord in this shitty little African hellhole the locals were blood-feuding in. They couldn't bury the dead fast enough. The warlord didn't kill. He espoused terror. I'm not afraid to die, but that dude's murder methods terrified me. The monsters on this planet are real."

Talking to a soldier about their experiences had two rules. You never asked them to tell you their stories, and you never interrupted them once they decided they wanted to tell them.

I scrutinized the darkness and waited, wondering if he'd continue.

"Brutality alone won't carry you to what he'd become. He was smart, and he was in touch with what most of the locals wanted to hear, which made a deadly combination. Operations ordered the hit. Our orders were to cut the head off and hope nature took its course. Intel found him without much trouble. His compound had jungle most of the way around the perimeter and a decent cliff at the back. We judged the cliff as the best way in, so that's what we did."

His hesitation made me shiver again.

"Looking back, we should have guessed, and intel should have told us, but the target took that compound on his way up. The indigenous folks where he set himself up had been peaceful, but they worshiped the wrong god. Every single one of them died because of him. The thing is, you don't waste energy in Africa, and burying your enemies on a rocky mesa is a waste of energy to them. It's easier to toss them off the cliff and let the winds carry the smell downriver. Strat and I had no idea what we were going to crawl through to get to the cliff that night, but I always remember it when I think I might be sitting in the worst place ever."

Something told me one question would be acceptable. "Did you kill him?"

"I did."

Claire gave me the pronounced feeling he was an eye-for-an-eye type of guy. I turned away from the visions I had of him teaching a monster what it was to experience terror and concentrated on the fact that I wasn't sitting in a field of bodies waiting for this operation to commence.

It was suddenly a lot more pleasant.

CHAPTER 28

24 JULY 2126

We waited a lot longer than another half an hour. It was 0313 when I finally wormed my way out of the drainpipe into the fog. The rain had stopped, which didn't make any difference—I couldn't have been any colder or wetter by then if I tried. All things equal, I walked out the cramps in my legs surprisingly swiftly.

I followed Claire on the sidewalk as we plodded across the base. We shouldered our weapons, toys though they might have been.

"People think special ops is all about being covert, but it's about trying to fit in until it's time to not fit in anymore," Claire said conversationally.

"I knew that in my head, but it doesn't make me feel any less vulnerable."

"You're always vulnerable. Once you heft your weapon, you're broadcasting who you are. Look at me. Do I look like someone on a mission right now, or someone returning from one?"

I smiled. "I wouldn't know it was you if I hadn't had to smell you all day."

"Look who's talkin'. When the op orders went out to security to catch us for the exercise, I promise there was a file photo of you and your admiral title. No one's going to see an admiral walking down the road right now when they look at you."

"Is that what all the mud was about?"

"Call it a happy by-product," Claire said. "Hiding in the drain was about staying out of sight. The muck was a cost of doing business."

"Do you have a strategy for getting into the building too?" I asked.

"We'll start looking for a manhole once we're a couple blocks from the training center. If we get lucky, it'll take us all the way into the service basement. If it does, we've got this whipped. If not, we'll go from there."

"You love this, don't you?"

"Nope." He shook his head. "I'm good at it. I think you are too. We're about to find out if the other guys are better. This is the toughest performance evaluation in the world."

✣

"Plan B it is," Claire whispered, staring at the dead-ended drainpipe lit only by reedy streams of moonlight from above. We were still a block south of the training facility. "Conventionally, we should go in the back together."

I swiped the excess sewer muck from my boots in disgust. "I'm not feeling conventional."

"Me neither. We'll expose and separate. You go in the front. I'll go in the back. Winner takes all."

"Hooah."

"Hooah." His smile sobered to focus as he moved to deal with the manhole cover above us. Only a slight grinding of metal on metal and the solid thud of the cover settling back into place broke the stillness of the night before Claire disappeared into the mist like a fleeting dream.

The four sentries in front of the training center weren't paying anything in the way of attention. I thought about trying to split some of them off but decided against it. Taking on four unprepared guys all at once seemed safer than taking on one or two highly trained operators that were prepped and ready for combat.

I'd stand a chance if I engaged them before they got their bearings.

A lot of ground was empty between my sidewalk and the fountain in front of the facility. It was, however, dark, and I figured the fountain would mask the sound of my footsteps.

I lifted my weapon once I was within a few steps of the fountain. The sighting aperture was night-vision enhanced, so seeing wasn't a problem. Slowing my breathing was a little more difficult, but I used the time to visualize my shots. I needed to start with the two guys facing my direction. One of the other two had his gun leaned against the stair rail—he'd be last.

One . . . two . . .

One . . . two . . .

I clicked the weapon's safety to fire and pulled the trigger as I'd practiced in my mind's eye.

Swearing announced my shots' impacts along with visible flinches.

They looked like they hurt.

The third guy got a few wild shots off before I tagged him. The last of them whizzed past my ear. I should have broken off and run then, but reflexes took over and I jumped into the shallow pool of the fountain instead.

It was a pretty defensible position—I'd have an advantage in terms of available field of fire on anyone approaching me head-on. I should have been able to wait anyone out, but I got antsy.

Spewing covering fire as I came up, I focused in the vicinity of my target and jumped back out of the pool. It looked like he'd assumed I would stay covered, because my fourth shot caught him in the chest before he'd realized I was out of the water.

I took a defensive forward crouch and worked toward the door. I knew the guys I'd taken out were watching. They had to be pissed, but no one had called an end to the exercise, and one guard was still unaccounted for.

It wasn't over yet, and I wanted to make it look good.

About ten feet of concrete remained between me and the glass front door when Claire appeared and pushed it open. Admiral West came through the doorway, all business. "This exercise is complete. Everyone hit the racks. Report to headquarters briefing room number two at 1000 hours for the active mission briefing. Dismissed."

I tried to step around him, but West grabbed my elbow and pulled me to a stop. "As mad as they are, you must have gotten dirty."

Dripping water and who knew what else onto the concrete, I acknowledged my condition. "Yes, sir."

"This is your last chance to get out of this. Are you sure you still want to participate in this operation, Allison?"

"Yes, sir."

"Very well. Go get yourself cleaned up and get some rack time."

"Yes, sir," I said with a salute that looked crisper than I felt.

I made it about three steps, loitering behind Claire as he exchanged a fist bump with Stratford. When Claire turned, his face betrayed nothing. "The man with the plan said it's over, Admiral. Let's hit the road."

I *needed* to know. "So did you take out the target?"

He shrugged.

I could only smile at the smug bastard.

I headed off to the locker room, thinking over everything we'd done and trying to see if we'd left any holes big enough to allow us to lose. Had I been less tired, I probably would have realized that was exactly what Claire had wanted me to do.

✣

Showering was a matter of protected self-interest. I didn't want to drag any of whatever I was covered in home and face cleaning it up later. No clean underwear was left in my locker, just a duty coverall I'd brought with me from *Ticonderoga*.

I was way too tired to care by the time I got home, kicked off my shoes, and collapsed on my bed.

Claire was right. That was the toughest performance evaluation I'd ever faced.

I was way too tired to spend any energy dreaming.

~

Coffee in hand, I settled back into my now standard seat in no-man's-land. The conference room was empty, and I was early. With a little luck, the caffeine would have a chance to work its wonders.

I was surprised when Daniels and Claire walked in together, and even more so when one sat on each side of me.

"How're you gentlemen this morning?" I forced as much cheer into my words as I could, even though I still felt like crap.

"Shipshape and Bristol fashion, Admiral," Daniels answered.

"Upright," Claire said with a sly grin.

"Claire, I was kind of out of it by the time the exercise ended. Did we win?"

"Did you learn anything?"

"Yes, but that's not an answer." I smiled in return.

"Sure it is."

Anything else he might have said was superseded when Admiral West entered. We all moved to stand until the admiral commanded us to remain as we were as he took the podium. After a long, appraising look around the room, he said, "It's been a ride getting here, but we're not out of the woods yet. Before we get started, I need affirmations from every one of you that you understand this briefing is classified at Q level and stipulate to the necessary protocols."

We each made the necessary confirmation, recorded by both audio and visual pickups around the room.

As soon as the formality was completed, West continued, "The situation is coming to a head with former Secretary General Pons Schweizer. The operation must move forward now before the situation degrades further."

"Is there a specific concern pertinent to the mission, sir?" Dakota asked.

West's shrug was almost imperceptible. "In and of itself, his rhetoric has remained relatively stable. But intel believes his regime has come into possession of a tactical nuke. It's probably a remnant of the Ukrainian war. While it's likely old nuclear material, we're not in a position to gamble on its viability."

"What's the plan?" Stratford's ears were almost vibrating with anticipation.

West triggered a button, and the display behind him changed to show an overview of the Eastern Bloc, focused on Ukraine. "A set of two-person teams and a sniper for overwatch will insert approximately twenty kilometers north-northwest of Pripyat at point Alpha. The teams will separate and infiltrate point Bravo, which is an apartment building serving as Schweizer's residence, and point Charlie, which is the area's communication center that has been taken for Schweizer's command center."

"HALO insertion?" Mason asked.

"Detection is considered a concern. Our intention is to use a flight of Tomcats from *Ticonderoga*. They should provide the necessary operational flexibility."

"Could the enemy have potential air support?" Daniels asked, waking up his side of the room.

"It can't be ruled out."

"Prep is going to be an issue," I announced. "Chief Brinn indicated a concern about trying to egress fighters while *Ticonderoga* is landed. He's afraid the thrust could cause structural issues in the launch gantries—a question of heat dissipation in the lower atmosphere."

Steel hardened West's response. "We need those fighters, Admiral Mackenzie."

"He said we could sling them off. I can take care of it, sir. Turns out I know some people in the Transport Division."

West returned my smile. "Time and tide stands still for no person, Admiral. On your way."

I nodded and collected my things. "We'll get it done."

~

The shooter's pen was the launch control center elevated at the rear of *Ticonderoga*'s Tomcat deck. Her entire air wing, now nineteen fighters and four shuttles, sat below me in the launch gantries. Ordinarily, an officer of the deck and an operations interface technician would also be there. Today, it was just me. The scene looked like a photo instead of the living, breathing ship she used to be. One other person was onboard as far as I knew, and it felt odd.

I opened the com once I'd settled into the shooter's seat and acclimated myself to the panel arrangement. "What do you think, Pitka?"

"Reactor shows green, Admiral. You should have power to launch gantries."

"Roger that, Pitka." I connected the exterior com. "Paul, we're all set. How are we looking out there?"

"The loadmasters are clear of the air locks but otherwise ready. Let's roll."

Looking at the banks of switches reminded me I'd always been on the other side of this procedure. I pushed a second's worth of regret out of my mind and initiated the transfer sequence that opened the air locks and transferred five pilotless, Tomcat-laden gantries into launch position.

"Structural warnings?" I asked over the com.

"We're good, Admiral," Pitka said. "Don't forget to release landing locks."

I triggered the next line of controls. "Good call. I'm going to go outside."

"Roger that. I'll mind the store."

I emerged from the docking latch a minute later into a sea of lights, cranes, man lifts, and shouted orders. It had taken some time to get them together, but Transport Division's loadmasters were the best in the world. A production of *The Nutcracker* had nothing on what I'd stepped into.

As the first Tomcat lifted into the air suspended from an elaborate sling of thick yellow straps, Paul met me halfway between *Ticonderoga* and the little security building that was now serving as command and control.

"It's not how they're supposed to fly, Paul."

"It does seem like it would have been easier to reactivate *Ticonderoga*."

I shook my head. "It wasn't in the cards."

Paul was watching skyward. "They'll be back in the air before you know it, Admiral. Under their own power."

"Did the ordies comply with our request?"

Paul pointed over his shoulder at a line of heavy trucks idling off in a corner of the field all by themselves. "They couldn't hold minimum safe distance, but it's pretty close. They've confirmed they're ready to equip the flight with the combat weapons load you've specified. We have fuel scheduled in at 0800 to top off the external fuel tanks once they're mounted to the Tomcats."

"It's coming together. You would have made a hell of a deck officer, Paul."

He nodded. "I also have a message for you from Admiral West."

"And that is?"

"I promise not to let the assault team leave without you. Go home and get some sleep, and, yes, it is an order."

I rolled my eyes. "He thinks he knows me pretty well."

"It sounds like he does. Accurate prediction, from what I can see."

"Your work has been exceptional today, Paul."

His smile was genuine. "Thank you, ma'am. And sweet dreams."

"Thanks."

~

Stratford and Mindy were standing in front of my apartment building visiting in the misty light of a streetlamp when I came around the corner. Being unobtrusive on an otherwise empty street just before midnight on a Tuesday was hard. When you knew the conversation they were having would change the life of a person that wasn't even born yet, it was harder.

Mindy wrapped her arms around Stratford and pulled him close enough to kiss his cheek. Her voice was quiet. "Good luck."

"Thank you," Stratford said as he turned my way. He made it a half dozen steps before he stopped in front of me. "Late night, Admiral."

"Indeed. You okay?"

"Fine." The corner of his eye glistened. "I'm told we're to meet at HQ at 1400 hours."

"I haven't checked my messages yet, but that sounds reasonable."

"See you then. Have a nice evening, Allie."

I gave his arm what I hoped was a comforting squeeze. "You too, Strat."

I took another half dozen steps and opened the door for Mindy. She was quiet until we got up the stairs and were in front of our door. She finally spoke while I dug my key out of a pocket. "What's going on, Allison?"

I clicked the lock open and followed her through the door. "With a little luck, we're about to end this."

"End this? Really?"

She was accusing me of being overly optimistic or maybe even disconnected from reality, but that didn't occur to me in the moment. "That's the plan."

"You think killing her will end this?"

"It's not about my mom, Mindy. I can't talk about what's going down."

"It doesn't take a genius to figure out what's about to happen. It's fine you're lying to me about what you're doing, but I hope you're not lying to yourself."

I stripped off my uniform as I turned toward my bedroom. "Did you and Strat get things straightened out?"

Mindy laughed. "I thought I got to ask the awkward questions."

"Captain's prerogative. We can talk about it if you want to."

"You're not my captain anymore, and you might not be coming back either, so . . ."

"Mindy, I'm coming back."

"You can't promise that."

"Yes, I can." I couldn't stop my smile, even though tears fell from my eyes. "I promised my friend I'd be here to help with her baby." Commitment held me in place. I couldn't move.

"Allison . . ."

"Even if I don't make it back, you'll be okay, Mindy. I'll see to that."

"I don't want your money," she said as she stared at me.

I didn't blame her for being unwilling to close the gap between us then. "One way or another, I'll always be there for you, Mindy."

✣

I pulled the comforter a little higher while my eyes swam across the display on my tablet. Blinking a couple of times trying to clear my vision, I hit the "accept" icon a final time with none of the conviction that was probably normal for someone who'd ordered a new home to be built.

Maybe it was the circumstances. Replacing the home you'd grown up in—the one your mother burned down to kill your dad—might take a little fun out of the process for anyone. I was glad to be doing it. I hoped Mindy would make it a home even if I wasn't around to enjoy it.

Once I was done with that, I pulled a large paper notepad and pen out of my nightstand drawer. I had a reasonable idea about what was supposed to go into a last will and testament. A little happiness came from the fact that even an unwitnessed paper document wouldn't be challenged.

No one would be left alive in my family to challenge it. No creditors—it wouldn't be a problem.

Even if someone did find the document objectionable, online materials left in the UPE datanet should take care of my affairs. Regardless, seeing what I was leaving to Mindy and her baby on paper made me feel better before I signed and dated the document. There was no reason to put it back in the drawer.

It needed to be easy to find. Just in case.

I thought about getting back up and putting on some jammies. I never slept nude, but the sheets felt good, the bed was warm and cuddly, and I was finally sleepy. I settled for putting my tablet on the nightstand and shutting off my lamp before I snuggled lower into my bed's embrace.

Exhaustion overtook me in a heartbeat as I fell into a dream.

Dream, memory, and waking nightmare were confused. Sleep had carried me here numerous times, as my subconscious usually brought me here whenever I wondered if I was going to live to see another day. I was near the end of the water war, and unbeknownst to me at the time, very nearly the end of my life and flying career, as well. The dream never ended with the feeling of safety that meeting Strat had brought me in real life—just the uncertainty of being alone and outnumbered in a war zone with no visible way out.

While justified, *unpleasant* wasn't a particularly adequate word to describe what was ahead of me. While it started hopeful enough, I knew how it was going to end.

Pulling on full combat gear instead of a flight suit was enough to make me uneasy. First came boy shorts and an athletic bra top followed by tight black leggings and a long-sleeve, high-collared pullover. One more layer of pants, with ballistic impact resistant plates bonded to the thighs and calves, came next. A dynamic polymer ballistic overlay vest, more commonly known as body armor, nearly forced me to suck in my stomach to get the zipper up. My boots were the only things that weren't particularly beefed up in some way, emphasizing mobility over protection.

Force of habit stopped me in front of the mirror to see a warrior instead of a pilot, perhaps for the last time at that. The West was marching into Atlanta, with intentions of taking by force water that they hadn't been able to secure through negotiation. I was flying cover for what was supposed to be a run-of-the-mill extraction of non-combatants, but I had the worst feeling it would be the last one as I stepped out of the locker room door even though I couldn't put my finger on even half a reason why.

With an FN P90 and a SIG P320 issued from the armory, I thought through what was ahead during the walk to my Thunderstrike waiting on the tarmac. The West wasn't armed with antiaircraft weaponry, and they weren't apt to engage UPE forces under most circumstances.

Admittedly, I'd heard that *piece of cake* was the most poorly used idiom in an intelligence officer's lexicon. Maybe I was still young and idealistic, but it seemed applicable here.

Except for a kamikaze battleball destroying my Thunderstrike and leaving me ensconced in a metal coffin of fuselage with a dwindling air supply, my entire flying career had gone off without a hitch. One incident didn't seem to be worth carrying around forever.

Granted, it wasn't the most pleasant memory, but I'd survived.

I'd also earned a medal for saving *Starliner* that day, and I was a long way from the moon. What could possibly go wrong today to equal that?

CHAPTER 29

25 JULY 2126

The only thing different about the walk this time was a personal weapons update and the Tomcats and the rest of the team waiting for me instead of a single Thunderstrike. The team—and my lack of loneliness—was the most pronounced difference.

"You ready for this, Admiral?" Claire asked.

"I was born ready," I said as I sauntered past Claire, Dakota, Stratford, and the walking, talking oak tree of a man named Mason. Our pilots—Daniels, Rogers, Miller, Frederich, and Winter—were in a circle of their own a stone's throw away.

It took a second, but they widened their ranks a little to let me in.

"Long time no see, Admiral," Daniels said with a hint of a smile.

"You guys remember which handle's the throttle and which handle's the ejection lever?" I asked.

"There's only one way to find out," Rogers said. "Been a long road getting here, hasn't it?"

The rest of the team formed in around us. "One way or another, someone's about to run out of highway, Commander. You ready for this?"

"The birds all check out with full combat loads and have been topped off with fuel. Everything is systematically and visually verified. Arming pins are pulled and the birds are on hot standby. We'll bounce up over the pole," Daniels said.

"Am I with you?"

"Let's ride out." Daniels nodded.

Fanfare was minimal as we boarded the Tomcats. I was glad to see

Mintz, my young plane captain from *Tico*, standing next to the ladder at Zero One's weapons systems operator position. She was young, but she was a familiar face, which was comforting. "Your weapons should fit in the portside cubby, ma'am. If you'll let me have them, I'll secure them and your bag while you get settled."

Reluctantly, I handed my gear over before I started up the ladder. Training took over as I buckled myself in and then started initializing systems under battery power. Mintz reappeared at the top of the ladder with a helmet and cross-checked everything once I had it on and plugged in.

"You good, ma'am?" I gave her a thumbs-up. "All right, then. May the wind be at your backs."

She disappeared as Daniels plugged into the com.

"Watch your fingers." The ladders disappeared as the canopy started down. "You squared away, Admiral?"

"All set."

"Flight status?" Daniels listened as everyone called in. Once he was satisfied, he added, "Go for engine start-up."

Auxiliary power units tied to our planes wound to full intensity, filling the air with a scream that could only be drowned out by the mighty Tomcat's twin engines. Vibrations built in the fuselage around us. "Separate APUs."

Indicator lights changed to green as the umbilicals were cleared from their ports. I checked the power distribution gauges a second time. "We have a green panel."

"Ground crew is cleared," Daniels said.

I swept the ground below us and counted four people well away in front of us. "I concur."

"Zero One is taxiing."

As we moved, I had the oddest sense our Tomcats were the only thing under perfect control.

Once we were airborne, Daniels came over the radio. "I was surprised to see you going on a strike mission."

"Duty called."

"No offense, but you're an admiral in an administrative position. They couldn't find someone better?"

What happens in the cockpit stays in the cockpit.

"I know one of the targets personally."

"How in the world did you manage that?"

"She's my mother."

"I didn't see that one coming," Daniels said. The awkward pause that followed made it obvious he was trying to change the subject. "Say, what are the odds we're going to get to take *Tico* back out?"

"Your chances are better than my own. Just being associated with her at this time is enough to ground me."

"Yang's dead. You're being too fatalistic."

"It's not just Yang. It never was. UPE is a big organization. I guarantee you she's not the only person I failed to impress. A unanimous UPE Senate vote has to approve *Tico*'s skipper. There is no way they'll reinstate me after this mess—it's just not how it works."

"You didn't cause this."

"Yeah, but I didn't stop it, either. That's what they'll remember."

"It's a crock."

"It's politics."

~

The threat com blared out of nowhere, and my gut clenched as I reported it. "Three and Four are on the ground. Five's off the screen. Two's engaged. Schweizer's got sentries in the air."

"Let's go help Two," Daniels said.

"We weren't sure he had any aircraft. Intel doing what intel does, Daniels." Another alert blared. We were being targeted. "Hind mark seven at three-three-seven, flight level two."

Our Tomcat skidded through a seven-G turn without banking. "We'll come at him low. Break into the control system—I need the nose OMS thruster control."

"It's an extraplanetary-only system."

"That's why I said *break in*," Daniels said calmly. "Shut up while I do this."

Pine trees whipped by, alarmingly close, as we dropped into a canyon barely wider than our fighter. Our adversaries' tracking systems couldn't follow us as long as we stayed in here—altitude wasn't your friend when you took on an attack helicopter. Speed and unpredictability were all you had to work with.

"Faint return at two-seven, range two-five clicks," I said as I worked through the submenus in the control algorithm. "Weapons control at pilot release."

"Get low and get fast, Rogers. We're on the way," Daniels said over the com.

"Our number one engine's shot up," came the crackling reply. "We can't do either."

"Allison, any luck?"

I leaned forward into the MFD like determination alone could force the system to comply. It wasn't what I'd call an intuitive design structure, but— "Got it."

"Watch the targeting display. If you get as much as a level-two lock, take it."

I cringed and puffed air out as he rotated us into a left-wing, knife-edge turn through the diminishing excuse for a canyon.

"Now zero-two-zero. Twelve clicks."

"I'm going to unmask. Brace for nose-up OMS burn."

"Roger that," I said. "Targeting sensors to maximum." The attack helicopter appeared outside my sights, and it launched a rocket barrage in Two's direction.

I focused on the weapons display, as the automatic targeting system was having a rough time dealing with Daniels's jinking. A few seconds after we cleared the canyon rim, I selected the target visually, authorized one of the Sidewinder Mark IVs, and fired. Ignoring its own ideas, the weapon ran straight to the target I'd selected, destroying the bogey in the second fireball to light up the evening sky in succession.

We'd been seconds too late. The bogey's rockets had enough time to tear Two, bearing Rogers and Stratford, out of the sky.

"Two is off the screen," Daniels said flatly. "Get ready to deploy. I'm setting you down."

Strat.

The mission was already in shambles, and I hadn't even set foot on enemy soil. I had no idea how we were going to accomplish our objective with two team members already off the board, but I wasn't going to give up without finding out.

This was what could go wrong.

✣

The maelstrom from the portside engine intake I jumped into sucked the air from my lungs and pounded my head with noise beyond anything I'd ever imagined. Daniels had the engines spooled back just far enough to let him stay on the ground, but the vacuum from the engine's intake still felt like it was going to suck me clean off my feet. I hefted my gear in trembling fingers and clawed my way forward on the rigid ground. I wasn't ten steps away before Daniels maxed the throttles and lifted off into the dark of night. I had no question that he'd loiter as long as he could once he was airborne, but even I realized he was nothing but a target on the ground.

I was trying to get my bearings when I heard rustling in the trees. Dakota and Claire looked more than haggard, but my heart swelled at the sight of them. My stomach had only had time to twist with the belief that Stratford was gone when I sensed movement behind me.

He thundered out of the scrub right between us, and my eyes went wide.

How in hell?

He didn't miss a beat. "Dakota, Claire, you're on the com center. Mackenzie, you're with me—we'll take the apartment building."

"Hooah!" the men whispered and disappeared into the woods.

Strat didn't even bother to give me a meaningful look, he simply trekked back into the forest about fifteen degrees north of the bearing Dakota and Claire had taken.

I raised my weapon and followed.

All the UPE's available spy technology plus Strat's HUMINT did little to tell us what we were getting into. Overgrown for more than a century, Pripyat was still largely a mystery. While we had confirmed the city had rudimentary water, power, and even sewers, we didn't know much else.

The things you don't know usually won't get you into trouble—it's the things you know for sure that turn out to be not so. Dad had tried to beat that into me since I was old enough to understand words. As simple as it was, it had taken me a lifetime to understand what that saying was supposed to mean.

So I mentally catalogued the things I didn't know and those I thought I knew for sure.

"We thought you were gone," I whispered. "We must have been down in the canyon when Rogers tossed you out."

"It was a narrow bit," Stratford agreed. "Rogers practically dumped me out on the run. He was on the climb out when he got waxed. Your pilot's a squirrelly bloke. His proclivities saved you the trouble the rest of us had."

"Mason and Winter?"

"We didn't see an explosion—if they went down, they went down hard. They might have turned for home when they got shot up."

"There wouldn't be a point in continuing if they couldn't land," I said. "Either way, losing overwatch is the least of our problems. It's a good bet Schweizer knows we're coming now."

"They don't know *I'm* coming."

Wolves and sheepdogs . . . the line was blurring before my eyes. A sheepdog was a protector and a wolf was a predator. The tone of Strat's voice made me wonder if he wasn't more predator than I'd given him credit for.

The words came out before I could stop them. "You sound excited."

"I don't know that *excited* is the right word, but I am on," Strat said. "The job needs doing."

"How do you know that?"

"Orders are a good indication, Allison."

I was working my way down a dangerous path through more than just the forest. It wasn't a soldier's path, but I couldn't stop one foot from falling in front of the other as we made our way through the trees.

~

Cleared fields waiting to become streets and houses had once buffered the city, but the forest was winning in the game of reverse metropolitan evolution. Sporadic streetlights cut through the gloom in front of us.

"Any idea where we are?"

I thought for a second. "We're on the northwest corner of town, or at least close to it."

"Stop!" a voice shouted in clipped Russian.

Strat turned around and answered in trained Russian, "Hello, comrade!"

I stayed perfectly still, hoping I was lost in the shadows.

The unfamiliar voice continued, "What are you doing here?"

"Freezing my ass off!" Strat bellowed his unaccented response.

The man laughed boisterously. I couldn't see anything, but the footsteps receded in the stillness of the night.

I watched Stratford turn in the other direction and walk away as if he'd gone about his business. Waiting about five minutes before finally peeking fully around the corner seemed like a good idea. It would have been hard to see much of anything in the gloom, but it looked clear enough, so I took off in Strat's direction.

I found him ducked into an intersection at the end of the block.

"Thought you might've been caught," he whispered.

"Good thing I wasn't. I don't know much Russian," I said.

"Neither do I. One more bloody sentence and I'd have run out." Strat motioned with his head and raised his sidearm. "I'll take point. Let's go."

Lights became far more sporadic as we made our way east into the city. We walked for close to an hour before we found what was obviously a main thoroughfare—it was both better lit and clearer of debris than the street we'd entered on. Following it far enough north would land us in Belarus, and what was left of Chernobyl was still southeast of town. When it was time to bug out, we'd follow the Pripyat River north.

It was easily the creepiest ten blocks I'd walked in my entire life. Strat's navigation was right on, though. Shining above the gloom were the lights of what the briefing packet indicated as Schweizer's apartment building.

Why hide the fact that the building was occupied? No one in their right mind would come here in the first place.

Of course, the people here hadn't had a choice—they were political refugees. I couldn't help but consider that when I thought about what they'd done and what we were doing. Some of them had undoubtedly been sent here without cause. Many of these people might have even done the right thing at the wrong time or in the wrong way.

"We need to get in without too much collateral damage," Strat said. "Ideas?"

"You keep the guns and go around back. I'll go in, open a door, and find you."

"Really?" Stratford's look made it obvious he didn't approve of me facing unknown dangers inside while he stood idle.

Frustrated, I tried the next permutation. "Okay . . . I'll hold the guns while you open a back door."

"Allison—"

Or perhaps I needed to stand somewhere without him to watch my back, evidently. Who said chivalry was dead? "Every time you call me by my full name, it's because you don't trust me. If we fight our way in, we'll have to fight all the way to the exfil."

He smiled his toothy Stratford smile. "Maybe the back door's open?"

"One way to find out." I straightened and stepped into the street separating us from the light of the apartment building.

Getting caught slinking through the shadows with an assortment of tactical gear was harder to explain than walking around a paramilitary encampment like we belonged there. We didn't raise our weapons, but we didn't hide them as we circled to the back of the building.

In the end, the back door was in fact locked, but Strat, even with his minuscule knowledge of Russian, meandered back around front and through the building entrance without issue. He was in charge, and I knew better than to roll my eyes even though it had been one of my two suggested approaches.

Nonetheless, the door finally opened in front of me onto a set of fire stairs, which was certainly appealing.

"It's only sixteen stories," Strat said. "Ladies first."

I fought the urge to lift my rifle or draw my sidearm. Anticipation and nerves were wrestling for control against my brain's admonition that we were a hit squad, not an invasion force. Our mission was over only when we'd cut the head off the snake—no more and no less.

The unmistakable clattering of gunfire erupted in the distance. Even through the crumbling concrete walls of the stairwell, it was impossible to mistake the rhythmic shots.

"One, we're engaged," Dakota snapped over my earpiece.

"You all right, Two?" Booming reports drowned out anything else Strat might have said. Seconds later, he added, "Two. Respond."

More heavy weapons fire filled the silence.

"Respond, Two," Strat said over the radio again.

The volleys came in threes.

"Respond, Two . . ."

"One hundred and twenty-five millimeters?" I asked.

"Probably T-72s pulled out of a pre-UPE junkyard. Bloody brutal."

"Up to us, then."

Strat grabbed my elbow. "Allie, they unmasked, and they got killed. We're here for Schweizer, and—"

"Hit, not strike," I whispered.

Strat nodded and pulled his suppressed HK45 from its holster. I secured my rifle on my pack and stashed it in a corner of the dismal stairwell. It was time to be stealthy, not necessarily well armed. We had bigger problems if I needed more than the fifty-two rounds I had between my weapon and spare clips on my belt.

Strat whispered, "Let's go."

Inside the apartment door, moonlight shone through the windows onto childhood pictures of me on the walls.

It was all me—not so much the baby, but I obviously recognized the little girl and the young woman in the pictures. Beautifully framed and enlarged, there was absolutely no way she'd brought them from our family home.

It was beyond creepy.

"Sorry," I whispered when Strat tapped me on the shoulder. They were just pictures—losing focus was going to get us killed.

He tapped his chest and pointed left down the hallway, presumably toward the bedrooms. I nodded, tapped my chest, and pointed right.

He nodded and stepped into the darkness.

I gave my sidearm's grip a squeeze, relishing the roughness against my hand. It anchored me to the here and now, assuring me of reality—not dream or nightmare.

Crouching low, I started down the hallway and into moonlight cast through the living room's wall of windows. For an apartment in a dilapidated 150-year-old building, the place bordered on luxurious.

I padded into the huge room, keeping my head swiveling, inspecting shadows and darkness for signs of—

Incredibly fluid hands caught the braid at the base of my neck and brought the steel of a kitchen knife to my throat. "Drop the gun."

"Hi, Mom." I let the HK fall to the floor.

"Hello, baby girl," she said. "What brings you here?"

"I've always wanted to see the exclusion zone."

Truth and lie in equal measure, it was enough to throw her off balance. I felt her hand loosen and the steel of the blade slide back from my skin. "Don't wiggle too much, dear. I don't want to hurt you."

"I suppose you didn't want to hurt Dad, either?"

"I didn't kill your father."

"Right. He just set his own house on fire."

She tightened her grip again. "You're not going to take me out of here, Allison."

"Abduction was never on the list."

"Victim or murderer? You're not leaving me a lot of choices, dear."

"You've already been one."

She released me cautiously, stepping back like one might from a cornered animal.

I knelt and picked up my pistol. The plastic grip was even more comforting as I raised it.

Her smile widened with the warmth of the mother that had fed me graham crackers and chased away monsters after bad dreams. "I won't make you live with the pain."

Slowly, as if wanting to evoke guilt in me, she turned the knife in her hand, deliberately took two deep breaths, and plunged it into her chest.

She might have become an animal, but the little girl in me still cried out when my mother collapsed. Kneeling by her side, I took her bloody hand in my own and squeezed it. She managed three words before she closed her eyes and fell into whatever abyss awaited her.

"I love you."

Watching the life drain from her eyes didn't bring me the satisfaction I'd predicted. Grief wasn't the right description either—it was pity. Sadness had gripped me when I watched other souls pass on. But the other people I'd lost had been good from the start, making sorrow easy.

I wished my mother would have followed that path.

I'd never get my questions answered about what had truly happened to my dad. That thought skittered through my mind but didn't stick. I'd probably regret that one day, but I couldn't help but feel relief that this book was closed.

CHAPTER 38

26 JULY 2126

"You still with me?" Strat asked.

It was a fair question. I hadn't said a thing since we'd left the apartment, collected our gear, descended the stairwell, and started down the road toward the communication facility. We were one street over from what looked to be the main road where only a few streetlights were working. Their glow only cast a deeper gloom over our efforts.

The night was as dark as my mood. "I'm here."

Strat turned and pushed me farther into the shadows covering an overgrown building. "This isn't the apartment, Allison. The soldiers down here are the guys that got Dakota and Claire. If you're not on, you need to bug out."

"I've got this, Strat!"

He looked deep into my eyes. His voice was still controlled. Still a whisper. "Do you?"

I wasn't about to have this conversation with him, much less here. My answer was to heft my weapon and start moving south.

We entered an area where the overgrowth was mostly accumulated into sporadic piles on the sidewalks. We were obviously nearing the highly populated and used portion of the city. More than a few buildings looked cleaned and opened. In this area of expansion, we were far more likely to run into someone. I decided to stow my rifle—blending in was still going to be simpler than fighting everyone in the end. Dropping the zipper at my collar and pulling my sleeves up was all I could think to do to make me look less out of place.

Claire had been the first to teach me that fitting in somewhere you didn't belong was hard only if you made it so. Acting casual could be a skill as much as anything else someone had to learn. "Why do you have a raised assault rifle?" was a second-level question, whereas "What are you doing here?" was only first level. Simpler.

The truth was that I wasn't with Stratford. My mind wandered through all I'd seen and done from my childhood up until the episode in the apartment. The memory of my mother, dead at my feet, had reformed again when the report of a single gunshot filled the air. Seconds passed, and then one shot had become two, and two had become hundreds.

✣

"Dakota or Claire!" I shouted, turning toward the echoing gunfire.

"Allison! Get back here!" Strat snapped, pulling me back like an errant child.

I fought against his cast iron grip. "We have to help them!"

"They're already dead," Strat said calmly. "We know where Schweizer is, and we can still follow our orders. We need to take advantage of this and finish the job while we have five hostiles to deal with instead of fifty or five hundred."

We locked eyes. Tears of frustration dripped hot on my cheeks.

"Move."

I hesitated.

"Move!"

I did as I was told more because I was afraid of the look in Stratford's eyes than I was supportive of his ideas. The predator stared at me with unblinking ferocity.

✣

"Covered advance. We stay together, understand?" Strat asked.

"Roger that." I nodded.

We unmasked from an alcove in the building facade and engaged a single guard at the door. His presence indicated that Schweizer's people thought they were relatively secure this far into town. We moved forward hard, taking down two more men and another woman before the alarm could be raised. There were no questions—just gunshots.

Outside of the main com hub, we slowed enough to be deliberate. At least nine people were visible through the glass doors, including Schweizer, backed by what appeared to be a couple of personal guards. The rest seemed to be com technicians going about their duties.

Strat's look was a question. *Are you going to do it, or am I?*

I tapped my chest and nodded once. Strat would only give me a few seconds to plan. I raised my HK with my right hand, taking careful aim as I worked the door open with my left. Ducking behind a console provided me cover until Strat made it in and did the same on the other side. Once he was settled, he held up three fingers, then two in a rapid countdown.

I went active when my mind clicked on zero, starting on the right side of the room and working left. My silenced pistol delivered five bullets, leaving behind nothing more than a muffled *fump* before each target fell.

I'd been trained to kill, and I did it well.

Schweizer was the only one I was sure deserved to die. Using my biometric scanner, I moved forward to confirm he was among those I'd shot. He was. I didn't recognize the others. They could have been the best or the worst people on the planet, but they were dead either way. I didn't worry about them. Right or wrong, they'd sided with the wrong guy.

Strat motioned toward the door. We egressed the building with weapons drawn and ready but, surprisingly, didn't meet any other resistance. It was less an escape than a disappearance into the trees. Pursuit was unlikely, and it would have been difficult outside of Pripyat. We had only the long walk alongside the Pripyat River to the exfil site left to complete the mission.

Gentle rain started falling soon after we stepped into the forest, and it intensified—with no sign of letting up—as we evacuated north from the city. The trek to the extraction point wasn't pleasant, but the rainfall gave us some advantage. It covered our tracks and made us that much harder to find in the forest.

We wouldn't be discovered.

Knowing the job was done was cold comfort. Going after any of our fallen comrades would have meant certain death, and that simple realization shook me to the core. Special operations would never become my forte. We'd lost three for sure, and maybe five if Mason and Winter hadn't made it home. Strat and I had taken eleven, counting my mother and Schweizer.

The mission would be considered a success if anyone ever asked.

I'd learned a different kind of math since the *Ticonderoga* incident, and it didn't work for me at all. There was no balance to it, and I was beginning to believe my UPE service had to end. I didn't feel like I was much good at anything anymore.

I understood why we were humping it out. Pripyat wasn't the height of civilization. Anyone could have killed Schweizer as long as we didn't get caught.

"And we operate like this now?" I didn't mean for the words to come out, but they must have, because Stratford answered.

"We always have. What is it with you? Did you think we were saving the world without sacrificing anything? We've always had enemies. Did you think they magically disappeared? Someone has always done the dirty work. You can't keep your hands clean forever if you're going to make a difference."

Whoa.

"Steady on, Commander." I took a few breaths to calm down before I snapped, but it didn't work. "There's more than one kind of sacrifice. We've all given plenty for the UPE. Just because I'm not comfortable with collateral damage or leaving men in the field doesn't make me any less supportive of the cause, you—" I clamped my tongue before I called him an arrogant prick.

Once my mouth was shut, I didn't have any trouble keeping it closed. Our extraction and flight back to headquarters was peaceful and quiet, and I was grateful.

Most of the flight was spent thinking.

I wish it hadn't been, but once I started, I couldn't stop myself. As far as I knew, *Ticonderoga* provided countless extractions for people in bad situations during my command. We got word someone was in trouble, and it became our job to get them out. Here I was on the other side, knowing this extraction had cost at least nine innocent lives to accomplish the mission. It was impossible not to try to calculate the number of extractions and, as a result, the number of lives that people had taken at my command in the name of keeping the peace.

I never managed to successfully carry the ten to get the total.

CHAPTER 31

27 JULY 2126

I stepped off the shuttle with the relative certainty that the scale was balanced. This particular bully was beaten and the UPE was safe.

Today.

Someone else could worry about tomorrow.

I detoured from my desired route only long enough to check my weapons back in at the armory. Considering my lack of insignia or ID, I was hesitant as I made my way to the gate. I should have guessed, but the corporal there couldn't have cared less. The fact that I looked like I'd returned from a battlefield was a nonissue. I wasn't a concern since I was heading out completely empty-handed.

Midday rain was getting started as I stepped through the gate. Philosophers had debated the meaning of rain throughout history. Some believed it was a harbinger of doom while others knew it was an avenue of renewal. At that moment, I could have gone either way.

Something had broken in me that no amount of superglue would ever put back together.

"Look who's back in town," I shouted when I saw Mindy about half a block in front of me. An embarrassing number of people turned to see who the voice belonged to, but only one of them was my friend.

Her eyes brightened instantly when she recognized me. "I'd just about picked out a new best friend, too."

I sped up, closing the distance between us at a pace slightly under a run. "You're not getting rid of me that easily."

She wrapped me in a zealous hug. "I'm glad you're back."

"Me too," I said. We parted. "How're you feeling?"

"We're good." Her smile was wide. It was the first time I'd seen her rub her belly. "You get what you needed taken care of?"

I nodded. "It's done."

"So . . . what happens now?"

"I'm not completely sure. More changes."

Mindy grinned. "Like fresh clothes?"

"Maybe even a shower," I said after faking an appraising look at myself. I gestured in the direction of home and walked alongside her. "Anything exciting going on around here?"

"I don't know if you can call it *exciting.* Yang's state funeral has been scheduled for 1000 hours tomorrow. All officers are required to attend."

"That works out for me," I said. "I'd like to pay my respects before I go."

Mindy's look was instantly fearful. "Go?"

I took a deep breath. "Maybe it was circumstances or maybe I let myself get pulled off the path, but what I am and what I want to be are too far apart. The UPE isn't going to fix that for me or let me do it myself, so I need to leave it behind."

Mindy's smile surprised me. "I'm not sorry to hear that."

"I made you guys promises, Mindy. I'm not walking away from that, but we have some decisions to make."

"What do you mean?"

"Just because I don't see another way doesn't mean there isn't one, but I have two options ready."

"Okay."

"None of us wants me sitting on the couch every day, but I can hang around here easily enough. There are tables to wait or I can join a consultancy. I'll find something to do, and I'm good with that."

"It sounded like there was an *or*?"

"Probably more than one," I admitted after a deep breath, realizing my two worlds might be about to collide, and that I wanted it to happen. "Before I left, I arranged to have a new house built back on my parents' . . . *my* farm. There's plenty of room for us all. It's quiet and out of the way—the kind of place where you can watch the world go by."

"You're ready for that? To watch history being made?"

"I've done enough participating for a while." I wasn't sure if she could see it in my face, but my heart warmed at the thought of the future I was imagining. "Besides, I think I'm going to be pretty busy with some other commitments."

Mindy wrapped her arm around mine, not saying anything.

"Thank you for sticking with me, Mindy. I know some of what I've done hasn't been comfortable for you."

"Allison, I love you like a sister. That makes us family, and the one thing I'm sure of is family should stand together through thick and thin. You knew that when you came back to *Ticonderoga* to save us from Kegar. I am purely following your lead."

CHAPTER 32

28 JULY 2126

My UPE-issued bra felt great. I looked in the mirror and smiled. But I didn't look professional. Looking cute was, of course, out of the question. I wasn't particularly comfortable, either.

But after twenty-one years of daily torment, I'd never wear this particular pinching, binding, slightly itchy nuisance again. And that was impossible not to appreciate.

"Would you hurry up? We're going to be late," Mindy huffed as she stormed into my room. "Yes, you have normal boobs. Want to cover them, or are you going to go to the funeral alfresco?"

Now definitively pregnant, Mindy still looked more put together than I'd ever manage. She grabbed my dress uniform top off my bed and held it up for me so I could get my arms into the sleeves. "Thanks."

She shifted to the front as soon as I had the fabric wiggled into place and started at the stifling clasp at the base of my neck while I worked from the bottom up. "This farm of yours, is it near town?"

"I don't know what you call *near*, but there's not much for about ten miles." Mindy wiggled in that way only a woman who had worn a UPE dress uniform would completely understand. My smile widened. "Yes. It's secluded enough that you can go without a bra if you want."

"Sold."

"What?"

"Sold." She stared at me in a way that said I should have known exactly what she was talking about.

I finally put the pieces together as I grabbed my cap. "Really?"

"Yup. Let's go be farmers," Mindy said as she led the way to the front door. "Now come on!"

~

The rain came out of nowhere, a challenge to our determination to honor Secretary General Yang. A lot of civilians failed—running for cover, snapping umbrellas into place, or holding programs over their heads. Military protocol dictated that you didn't flinch for a little rain while someone was being laid to rest.

I broke rank when the final hymn began to play. Admiral West placed a concerned hand on my shoulder as I passed by. Or perhaps it was a plea for me not to do what he knew was coming. Hopefully, my nonresponse conveyed a determination to finish what needed to be done.

Thinking about failure as I walked toward the ornately carved casket was unavoidable. Yang and I had both fought hard for her people, and in a way, we'd both died defending them. Water ran between my fingers and over the faux gold captain's rank insignia I pulled from my pocket. There was no reason to look at it—I knew every micrometer of the little piece of tin that had once represented everything I was.

Removing my cap and kneeling in front of the beautiful wood felt appropriate and brought the top of the casket within reach. With my insignia squarely in the center of the wood, I drove the pin in with a sharp blow from my fist, whispered a prayer for the dead, and stood, intending to leave without another word. Mindy read the cues correctly and fell in at my side as I passed her row.

I could have done without Admiral West right then, but grumpy old admirals tended to have their way and their say.

"I was hoping you wouldn't do that," he said once we'd left the service behind. Regardless of my personal intent, my actions seemed to have signaled the true end of the ceremony.

"Sir?" I asked, feigning ignorance.

"General regulation nineteen-alpha. Any officer that loses or abandons their insignia is, by de facto action, resigning their commission in the United Planet Earth organization."

"Well . . ."

"This isn't your fault, Allison," West said with a weak smile.

"It feels like it, sir. Entire countries are filled with dead and dying people. Every time I close my eyes or see them in my dreams, it certainly feels like I failed them."

"You're not being fair with yourself."

"Sir, if recent events have reminded me of one thing, it's that the world is seldom fair." We shared an extra deep breath before I asked, "What's ahead for you?"

"At the Senate's pleasure, temporary leadership of the UPE," he answered flatly. "They'll find someone better."

"No, they won't. I didn't think the UPE allowed military leadership."

"They don't. You just beat me to it by about an hour. Now I have to find a new Defensive Forces commander, too."

"You'll find someone better."

"No, we won't," he said as he came to a stop.

The rain wasn't letting up. It was good, though. I wasn't sure where the tears were coming from, but it hid them. It also widened the space between us, which, right then, felt far larger than three feet.

"I don't know why this has gotten so awkward."

"Endings usually are, Allison," he said as his smile warmed. "A salute is no longer appropriate."

I laughed through my tears. "I don't think a handshake is going to do it, sir. We've been through a lot."

"Well, then," he said as his arms parted.

His hug felt a lot like my dad's.

EPILOGUE

14 APRIL 2127

Being back on the farm taught me I wasn't as tough as Dad. I had to make a few changes in the name of comfort, the most notable of which was to install a cab on his classic tractor. It gave me a heater, a broadcast radio, and a spot to mount a two-way radio so I could communicate with units installed in other vehicles and at the house.

Dad had found the isolation favorable. I did too, but in small doses. Having the ability to hear from some other part of the world made me more comfortable. I kept the broadcast radio running virtually all the time to chase away both the boredom of monotony and the ghosts the isolation of the job cultivated.

Pauline Chase, the famous news host, had been narrating the morning's activities with her on-air partner, Harve Brady, in an unending stream of information I'd tried and failed to switch off. I smiled at a fleeting memory of Flight Technician Perry Chase onboard *Lexington* and wondered if there was a familial connection between them before Pauline continued over the radio. "Watching *Ticonderoga* leave the Garelki Dockyard after less than three months of fevered repair and refit work is incredible, Harve. Considered far too important to sit idle, UPE leaders understand her unprecedented importance to the future of humanity and therefore executed the most intricate space refit operation ever conceived to get the mighty ship ready for its new future."

A minor ballet, I pulled the left-hand steering clutch and pushed the foot brake, turning the tractor at the end of the row. My free hand pulled the handle that dropped the planter into the ground, and then I goosed the throttle, bringing the engine up to its usual roar as we started back across the field.

Harve's voice came over the radio. "What a shame Captain Mackenzie was unable to be here to see this moment. Largely considered her dream, seeing the ship set off on a true exploratory mission through the solar system would surely be a satisfying moment for her, Pauline."

"I can't believe she's not here, Harve," Pauline said. "Our Freedom of Information Act request filed with the UPE government confirmed she's still in retirement, but we were unable to track her down for comment."

I had said enough about *Ticonderoga* for one career.

Pangs of regret were there. I wasn't going to lie to myself about that. The future wasn't certain, though. Maybe Secretary General West would have had the sway to give me *Ticonderoga* back, but would I have gotten this one? Was it possible I'd set the ship on its course for change by what I'd done?

Including retiring?

It was my story. I could write it the way I wanted, and mine would be recorded to include that I'd been allowed to be part of something incredible by serving *Ticonderoga* and her crew. By knowing my time was done and I should move on, I'd helped usher in something even better than what had come before.

That was my story, and no one was ever going to take it away from me.

"Pauline, is it true *Ticonderoga*'s new captain, Pela Trulani, served under Captain Mackenzie?"

"She did, Harve. The press release packet says a lot of Captain Mackenzie's old crew returned to duty, including her chief engineer, Walter Brinn. I'm told former Captain Allison Mackenzie and Chief of Sciences Mindy Stykes are the only command-level crew members that didn't sign back on."

"Fascinating, Pauline. I'm told Edgar Stratford, who had a short tenure as Mackenzie's executive officer, also declined the opportunity to continue the post?"

Pauline laughed. "He said his feet needed to stay on the ground, Harve. We can't blame him for that. Space isn't for everyone."

"Isn't that the truth? I might have learned that on the way up here."

Harve laughed. "I know we all wish the folks a peaceful and happy retirement, Pauline. I'm sure they've earned it."

"Absolutely, Harve."

"Rebuilding the ship's scientific capacity was foremost among the priorities for this refit, Pauline. Half of the ship's Tomcat II fighters have been replaced with Mark I Einstein research platforms. Designed to operate in a variety of research mission tasks, the Einsteins are considered the real workhorses carrying *Ticonderoga* into her scientific research future as she embarks on this new mission of discovery. Thornton Experimental Industries has had their hands full outfitting the ship for the last several months."

"Harve, what else has happened to *Ticonderoga* during her refit? Is the replacement of the venerable Tomcat the only change to her scientific capability?" Pauline asked.

"The most extensive portion of *Ticonderoga*'s interior upgrades has been the replacement of the central computer in the science suite with a Newton Technologies—"

"Allison, I've got your lunch here." Mindy's voice broke over the two-way com hanging in the back corner of the cab.

I pulled the microphone from the hook and keyed it. "Awesome. The tummy is rumbling."

Old Blue sat at the edge of the field when I pulled over the last rise. I'd sat in that pickup a hundred times with Dad's lunch and looked at the same view out the window. Blue's finicky old doors opened when I was about a hundred feet away. Mindy was slow to get out of the driver's seat. She was likely working to release baby George from his car seat.

The dude in the suit that emerged from the passenger side was far more questionable.

I pulled the hand clutch, stopping the old tractor before the dust cloud enveloped Mindy and George. Just like my dad had taught me, I hopped down and surveyed my equipment, checking things over and stretching my legs a bit before I crossed to the pickup.

Mindy paid no attention to the light coating of dust on me and my clothes. She placed a sleepy baby George, wrapped in a blanket against the chill of the spring day, into my waiting arms.

Holding him made my whole world feel better.

"Who's your friend?" I asked.

Mindy's smile was hesitant. "Let him introduce himself. Please?"

I nodded and turned to the guy. He stepped forward and took my grimy free hand without hesitation. "Allison Mackenzie. And you?"

"I'm glad to meet you, Allison. Thank you for speaking with me. My name is Oliver Thornton."

"Oliver Thornton . . . of Thornton Experimental Industries?" I asked, shifting my weight from one foot to the other. "What can I do for you?"

"Ms. Stykes advised me to get straight to the point. I'd like to ask you to come to work with us. I believe you would add great value to our team."

I smiled as I watched George snuggle into his blue cotton blanket. "I appreciate that, Mr. Thornton, but I have wheat to plant, and I've made promises to take care of family."

Mr. Thornton took a single step forward and regarded George. "I understand the draw, and I'd never think to take you away from what you have here. The two goals are far from mutually exclusive. I've assured Ms. Stykes she'll be able to stay here for as long as she likes. We'd love to find a way to work with you in a way that works with you."

I raised an eyebrow. "You're with the UPE?"

"Indirectly."

"Not interested," I said as I turned back to hand George to Mindy.

"Please listen," Mindy whispered. Her eyes were imploring.

"Look, Mr. Thornton, I—"

"Call me Oliver, Allison."

The lights finally clicked on as I remembered the names I'd heard on the radio. "I'm surprised you're not watching *Ticonderoga* pull out."

He smiled. "I had an important business meeting. As you know, my company holds the primary contract with the UPE to operate *Ticonderoga*'s science division. You and Ms. Stykes are considered the most valuable consultants on the market. Your qualifications are obvious. We couldn't hire better analysts."

I leveled Mindy with a flat stare. "You've already signed up."

She nodded sheepishly. "Why wouldn't I? This is everything I loved about what I was doing with none of the baggage."

"We're not interested in forcing you into anything, Allison. Frankly, you have a unique skill set and experiential base we'd like to have access to, where and when you allow, of course. We're a small family, and a close one. We'd be thrilled to have you join us," Thornton said.

I had nothing left to consider, so I extended my hand. "I'd be thrilled not to be left behind."

He smiled, accepting my handshake heartily.

Mindy wrapped an arm around me, laughing with delight. Careful to help support George, I hugged her back. Her familiar embrace was . . .

Hopeful.

ABOUT THE AUTHOR

As a lifelong fan of sci-fi, Eric McMurtrey has always believed in the adventures of normal people overcoming extraordinary challenges. While certain the future will probably be a little bumpy, the one he envisions will always have hope.

Printed in the United States
by Baker & Taylor Publisher Services